2/03

W9-BKY-189

Over his dead body /

F G463o

OVER HIS
DEAD BODY

BY LESLIE GLASS

OVER HIS DEAD BODY

LESLIE GLASS

BALLANTINE BOOKS • NEW YORK

A Ballantine Book
Published by The Ballantine Publishing Group

Copyright © 2003 by Leslie Glass

All rights reserved under International and Pan-American Copyright Conventions.
Published in the United States by The Ballantine Publishing Group, a division of
Random House, Inc., New York, and simultaneously in Canada by Random House
of Canada Limited, Toronto.

Ballantine and colophon are registered trademarks of Random House, Inc.

www.ballantinebooks.com

Library of Congress Cataloging-in-Publication Data is available from the publisher
upon request.

ISBN 0-345-44796-4

Text design by Jaime Putorti

Manufactured in the United States of America

First Edition: March 2003

10 9 8 7 6 5 4 3 2 1

FOR DOROTHY HARRIS

Ah, nothing is too late
Till the tired heart shall cease to palpitate.
. . . .
For age is opportunity no less
Than youth itself.

— Henry Wadsworth Longfellow,
"Morituri Salutamus"

ACKNOWLEDGMENTS

A thousand thanks to all the people who keep me financially savvy and sound. Judy Zilm, my bookkeeper and friend, has kept track of every little financial detail of my life for going on a decade. I couldn't possibly do it without her. Thanks to Kenny Hicks, my accountant, who has advised and bullied and relentlessly overpaid the government but has finally been truly fun with something—research for this novel. Through ups and downs of all the markets in recent years, Donald Wolfson has always been there to carry the burden. Thanks for taking the graveyard shift so I don't have to. Thanks are also due to tax professor Jan Sweeney, who gave me the textbooks and the goods on the IRS, and estate planner Charles Baldwin, who helped with insurance and other questions. Thanks to Dr. Thomas Loeb for help with research on cosmetic surgery. Thanks to my agent, Deborah Schneider; my editor, Joe Blades; and all the good people at Ballantine, from bottom to top, who work behind the scenes to produce the books and send them out into the world. This one is for all of you. Cheers.

1

LIFE HOLDS OUT ITS LITTLE SURPRISES. Our stories unfold sideways, backwards, upside down. In a single second truth can be shuffled like cards and scattered in all directions, never to be arranged the same way again. So it was with Cassandra Sales. At the moment she had her epiphany, she was kneeling in her garden surrounded by the exploding beauty of spring. Years of devoted attention to this garden had yielded absolute perfection, a feast of nature's botanical wonders.

Daffodils, egg yolk yellow, frolicked in a light wind off Long Island Sound less than a mile away. Hyacinths, blue, were heavy with moisture and fragrant beyond belief. Narcissi, hundreds of them in all manner of the palest pink, heavy cream, bisque, with touches of apple green and orange, also had an aroma to dream and rhapsodize about all year long. They nodded, too.

Now the tulips, the parrot kind, with ruffled feathers in pink and green. So thick, no earth could be seen below them. The beds were fully planted. There was no room for more. Above, a number of dogwood trees were in bloom. Two weeping cherry trees wept copiously by the front door. The whole garden enchilada on just over a half-acre plot. The place was a tiny gem.

Cassie's lifestyle was nowhere near as grand as her husband's business success as a top wine importer suggested it should be, and her house was nothing special either. It was just a step or two above the ordinary clapboard colonial, surrounded by thousands of similar two- and three-bedroom suburban dwellings of brick or shingle with two-car garages in old and pleasant neighborhoods on the North Shore of Long Island. It was her landscaping and gardens that put the property in an altogether different league from anything else around it. Everyone who went through the gate into the backyard felt the magic Cassie had brought to the place. An arbor was covered with roses all summer long. A small greenhouse contained an orchid collection that seemed continuously in bloom. A flagstone patio around the twenty-by-thirty in-ground pool had teak outdoor furniture and was artistically arranged with potted plants in decorative planters that changed with the seasons.

That day the fifty-year-old woman, who could have been anybody's relative, was kneeling all alone in a fine April drizzle wearing rubber boots, damp khakis, a sweatshirt, and a baseball hat. The garden, the unpleasant weather, her acute attention to detail despite it, her outfit, her mud-caked hands, and complete lack of vanity told her whole story. Almost.

The piece that didn't show was that turning fifty had driven her crazy as turning forty to forty-nine had not. Now she was looking at her life through a different prism and not liking what she saw. Her children were grown. Her husband, only five years older than herself, had an obsession with his business so intense, it seemed like an illness that robbed him of his old sense of fun and desire. He was limp morning and night. When she asked him what they could do about it, his finger would jump to his lips, "shhh," as if merely voicing the problem might blow them both away.

Although she'd never counted the days and months since last they'd tumbled around, giggling and panting in the sheets, on that rainy April day soon after she turned fifty, Cassie allowed herself to acknowledge it had been *years*. Years since a thrill! And her own real achievements didn't seem enough to pick up the slack. Here she was, secretly longing for passion and purpose, and what she was doing was cooking, growing orchids, and watching the Discovery Channel. She also read the newspapers and *People* magazine, caught the evening news programs and magazine format news shows. She followed the biographies on the Biography Channel and was a secret devotee of the nascent lives in *The Real World* on MTV. And the *Survivors*.

Cassie Sales saw all these lives and wished she could start over, have a job that paid her money instead of endlessly donating her gifts to causes like world hunger, whales, rain forests, refugees, battered women, child abuse, and cures for illnesses no one in her family had. She'd been very useful to others, donating her special gifts, but she was fifty and she'd had it.

Now she wanted to be beautiful again, like her daughter, Marsha, like her garden. She wanted to sparkle and dazzle, be flocked to by the birds and the butterflies and the bees that just didn't seem to come to her anymore. The longing to be seen by her husband and have fun was so intense, so fierce and relentless, it felt like unrequited love.

Was fifty that old? Was it? She knew perfectly well that fifty *wasn't* old. It was her problem that dazzle was gone. Other people way older than they were had sex every day. You saw it all the time on TV. Mitch wasn't old, he'd just fizzled out. The sudden longing for the birds and bees, after a dry spell of—Cassie didn't want to count the years—was everywhere in her dreams. She loved Mitch she was sure, but she was dreaming plane crashes, car crashes, a spectacularly fiery end to him absolutely every night. And she was dreaming love from other sources every single day. It had to be around somewhere. Other people were getting it. She fantasized burgeoning cocks in every man she saw. Young men, old men, nasty-looking men. Bald men, fat men, small men.

Everywhere burgeoning cocks. In the supermarket, in the bank. At doctors' offices. On the playing fields when she drove past the high school. When she was with her daughter, Marsha, in the city. No male was immune to her imagination. She thought about everybody. Everywhere. Something upsetting and unnatural happened to her when she turned fifty. Something snapped. She had no idea what it was. Suddenly she was tired of being sensible, of saving money, of being endlessly understanding and good about Mitch's languished desire. On the outside she was middle-aged, as predictable and conventional as a boiled potato, but on the inside she was beautiful, reckless, independent, a hard-drinking playgirl of twenty-three. Younger than those *Sex and the City* girls. She dreamed of death and youth in tandem.

In the misty moment of her epiphany, Cassie believed that she and her husband loved and were loyal to each other in the way that husbands and wives were supposed to love and be loyal. But quite frankly, she also wished he were dead so she could be a widow with all the pleasures that accrued to the state. A silly thought, she knew. Death wouldn't help her.

Years ago, before she and Mitch were married and before her mother got cancer and died, she and her mother had foraged one day for treasure in an antiques store for the perfect Valentine's Day gift for her father. And they found it in a dusty frame with bars standing out in bas-relief across the sepia photo of a female lion lying in a cage with a male lion standing protectively by her side. Under the ancient photo was the title: LIFE SENTENCE. The idea of no way out but death had amused them then. Seventeen years after her mother died, Cassandra's father still had it on his bedside table. He never remarried. After he died, Cassandra kept it on her own desk for seven more years. And all the time, her own face slowly squared off to look like the face of her dead mother, frozen just at the beginning of middle age, only a year older than Cassie was now. Cassie's own life sentence had no end in sight, nor did she really want it to. For her, simple divorce was out of the question and widowhood wasn't at all likely; her husband came from the old school and resisted everything. No, death or divorce wouldn't do. A real change in herself was required.

That fateful day in April, soon after crossing the chasm of fifty, Cassie saw beauty waving at her from the other side. In a split second she decided on the surgical overhaul, and there was no turning back. In a few short days she'd read every magazine and book on the subject and obtained a consultation with an upcoming plastic surgeon who had delusions of grandeur.

The artist in flesh was certain he could make her over as she had been as a blushing bride. On the enormous TV screen in his office he projected her as she had been with round cheeks, smiling lips, and wide, hopeful eyes. She'd been a beauty. The surgeon was as totally inspired by the youthful Cassie as Cassie was depressed to have lost her. He liked her spirit and her little plot. She wanted to have the procedures done while her husband was away on a business trip, to heal while he was gone, and to surprise the passion right back into him upon his return. Would that it were so simple. The confident surgeon, however, saw no flaws in the plan and agreed to fit her in quickly. She charged the surgery to American Express for the True Rewards. It all happened in the blink of an eye. Cassie never considered the possibility of unanticipated consequences.

CHAPTER

2

A MONTH LATER, at the end of May, seven days after her surgery, however, Cassie knew she'd made a truly appalling mistake. Her dos and don'ts folder said she would feel "mild discomfort" in her first two postop days. And "minor" swelling. Excruciating pain was what she felt and major swelling. The Time Line of Recovery in her Instructions for Aftercare predicted that she would feel entirely better after the first week and looking forward to total recovery and miraculous results.

Cassie was feeling worse and worse as the days went on. It was almost as if the great upcoming surgeon she'd chosen to turn her lights back On had made a little mistake and switched her power button to Off. She looked really terrible. Her eyes were so black-and-blue and swollen, she could hardly see a thing. Everything hurt. She couldn't eat because she wasn't allowed to open her mouth wide enough to chew. Worst of all, she didn't care about any of the things she used to care about: the skirmishes between the Democrats and Republicans, the latest in the abortion wars. The Middle East. Beauty. She was way, way down, depressed, angry.

And her beautiful, smart daughter, Marsha, now twenty-five, was no help in the reassurance department. Marsha was on vacation from social work school that week and had returned home to take care of Cassie, to drive her back and forth from her postop visits to the doctor, and so forth. Marsha turned out to be less supportive of the event than Cassie might have predicted, so the visit had taken on a surreal quality.

In her youth, Marsha had been something of a chore to her mother. As a teenager, she'd had every color hair possible. She'd worn slut dresses up to her butt from the age of twelve on. She'd stuck pieces of metal in her tongue and nose and eyebrow and navel, then protested angrily when anyone said something. She'd smoked pot in the backyard, crashed the Volvo station wagon into Cassie's favorite dogwood while trying to prove she could turn the car around in the driveway without benefit of driving lessons (when she was not yet thirteen) on the very first day Cassie had brought it home. She'd been caught in a neighbor's hot tub naked with three boys. For a number of years she'd weighed 170. She'd taunted her mother, worn army boots and grunge. She'd failed Italian. Twice. The girl got 1400 on her SATs, but school counselors thought she'd never make it to college. When she got to college, she constantly threatened to not make it through.

That completely loved and accepted girl (no matter what she did) had metamorphosed into the Marsha of today. Somehow she'd lost about 150 pounds. She was down to nothing at all. Her hair was no longer pink. Or green or purple. It was tawny. She was cooking. She was bathing wounds. She was cleaning the house. Sort of. She was fielding the phone calls from her mother's benefit-giving buddies, lying to cover for her so no one would know what an asshole her mother had been.

Marsha didn't want anyone to know how bad things were. She was screaming at the doctor because her mother's face looked as if it were rejecting itself. She was demanding attention and care, and she was getting it. She was scolding and nursing her own mother. She was a fierce and ferocious disapproving protector. It was downright weird. Their roles were completely reversed.

On the Friday, seven days after Cassie's surgery, at twelve noon, Cassie had the final stitches removed from her eyes. On the trip home she felt utterly defeated because the doctor had refused to remove the stitches located around and in her ears, as well as a myriad of staples hidden in her scalp. He'd told her they weren't done yet. What was she, a roasting chicken? She was further upset because she didn't look like anybody she'd ever seen in her whole life (least of all herself), and her face felt like somebody else's, too. The numbness in her cheeks and chin that no one had told her would occur in the first place persisted, and she was beginning to suspect that feeling in those areas might never return.

As soon as she got home, she climbed the stairs to her room and sat on the closed toilet seat in her bathroom completely demoralized. Mitch, who traveled a lot more than he was at home, was in Italy at the moment, blissfully unaware of her distress. As he was blissfully unaware of most everything. He was no doubt checking out the Nebbiolo grapes in Piedmont or the Sangiovese grapes in Tuscany, the short- or long-vatting of producers, haggling for prices or position in the distribution chain, and making money they never spent. She longed for and resented him in equal proportions. Marsha, who'd been uncharacteristically nice for a whole week, was now taking her new and stunning self back to social work school. In her defeated situation, Cassie couldn't help thinking that sometimes her daughter was just as annoying as a do-gooder as she'd been as a teenage nightmare. Cassie loved and resented her in equal proportions, too.

After all she'd been through, it turned out that she was going to be all alone with herself once again. And she'd become someone she detested with no reservations whatsoever.

"Here, Mom. This should cheer you up." Suddenly, Marsha appeared in the doorway with a soft pink tissue–wrapped package. "Come on, life isn't so bad. We all love you no matter how rotten you look. So what if you look like a fright for a while? Think of poor people. Think of what it would be like to be in prison, or maimed . . ." Marsha's voice trailed off as she lifted her shoulders in a delicate shrug.

Cassie couldn't answer without weeping. She *was* maimed. Before her surgery, she'd been simply invisible. Now, she was impossible to miss, a plastic surgery victim guaranteed to elicit scorn, contempt, and pity wherever she went. Her friends would laugh at her, and she wouldn't even be able to react. Her face was so tight, all expression had been wiped away. She didn't want to be a good sport about it. Blankly, she took the gift her daughter offered and opened it.

Nestled in the tissue paper was a pair of exquisite aqua satin pajamas. The satin was thick and there was plenty of creamy lace around the wrists, neck, and ankles. The shade was lovely and strong. Even in her condition Cassie could see the quality and the cheering color of the thing. Mitch was a monochrome beige-loving kind of guy, but Cassie loved color. Her passion for it had always been confined to the outside, to the landscape, the flower beds. She couldn't believe her daughter's thoughtfulness and jumped up to give her a hug.

"Aw, Mom." Marsha was uncomfortable and moved away.

"Really. Thank you," Cassie gushed.

Marsha gave her a funny look and went into the bedroom. Cassie took off her gray cardigan and gray trousers and put the pajamas on. They felt silky and great and were only about four or five inches too long in the arms and legs. She wanted to show them off to Marsha and, trailing lace, she padded into the bedroom where Marsha was busily engaged punching the pillows on the bed.

"They're really gorgeous. You shouldn't have," Cassie murmured. The price tag tickled her wrist. She couldn't help herself. She picked up her glasses from the bedside table and brought them to her eyes backwards so they wouldn't touch the stitches around her ears. She peeked at the numbers on the bottom to see what Marsha had spent on her and almost tripped over the pants legs in surprise. One thousand eighty dollars? Could that be right? Maybe it was one hundred eighty dollars. She tried to get a better look. "Marsha, you *shouldn't* have!" she cried in alarm.

"I didn't." Marsha turned around, lifting those shoulders again.

"What?" Cassie took a step, tripped again, and fell on the bed. It was a king. "I thought these pajamas were a gift from *you.*"

"Well, Mom. They're very nice. I wish they were, but they aren't."

"Well, where did they come from?" Cassie was puzzled.

"Aren't they yours? The package was in a drawer in the dressing room," she said slyly.

"What? Uh-uh. Not one of my drawers!" Cassie protested heatedly. She was so careful with her spending. She would never be so irresponsible.

"Well, I don't know which drawer." Marsha made a little noise. Cassie didn't know why she should be impatient.

"It wasn't in *my* drawers," she insisted again, then collapsed against the pillows. A package in the dressing room that she didn't know about, impossible. She was furious because the doctor hadn't taken out the staples. Why hadn't he told her how *many* staples there would be? She would never have done this if she'd known what was involved: the procedures, the pain, the awful results! She'd rather be *dead* than look and feel like this.

"Well, maybe Dad bought them." Marsha sat down next to her. "Wouldn't it be a hoot if he knew what you were planning and—?"

Cassie raised her hand to stop the speculation from going any further. Her head throbbed. Her eyes throbbed. Her cheeks and neck and chin felt like those of someone who'd been firebombed in the Blitz. Mitch didn't believe in plastic surgery. That's the *reason* she'd planned to be completely healed before he found out. One thousand eighty dollars? For pajamas? Would he do that? She considered it. He used to spend on her. Back in the old days. She lifted a shoulder. Maybe . . .

Marsha rolled her eyes, then changed the subject. "Mom, remember what the doctor said. You need to be drinking something all the time. You're dehydrating."

"No, no. I'm fine." Cassie's eyes were dry and irritated. The nurse had told her she needed to hydrate them, too, with fake tears no less. She couldn't even cry anymore.

"You're not fine. You need to talk to someone."

"I'm talking to you," Cassie told her.

"Yes, but you're not saying anything. You're not talking about *this*, This thing. This—" she resorted to body language to describe the mess her competent mother had become.

"You're depressed. You're withdrawn. You're—I don't know—out of it. I think you need a professional. Maybe medicine would help." It was clear what she meant.

"I'm taking penicillin," Cassie told her.

"Not that kind of medicine, Mom."

"Oh, you mean *Prozac*. Thanks a lot! Now I'm crazy." Real tears finally arrived, filling Cassie's eyes. They spilled over. She felt so sorry for herself. Her formerly impossible daughter, who'd been so much trouble over the years and now was a wonderful dream-child-come-true, didn't approve of her. It really hurt.

"Well, one *wonders* about the self-esteem of someone who—you know—can't accept life's natural progression."

Oh, now they were on aging gracefully. Cassie *wondered* how this insensitive social worker wanna-be was going to do with prostitutes, drug addicts, and child abusers if she had no compassion for her very own mother's feelings of loss and loneliness at impending old age. She was too upset to reply.

"Let's face it, Mom. You're not taking this well." She was just like her father. Now that Marsha had gotten started, she wasn't going to stop.

Cassie stared up at her through the tears in her eyes. So what if she wasn't taking the ruin of her life well? Why should she take it well? She'd read all the self-help books. She was trying to better herself, not get left behind. She'd trusted a board certified doctor to give her a little lift. *She'd done exactly what the books told her to do:* Assert herself to look better and feel better. This wasn't the time to question her *self-esteem*. This wasn't the time to be a good sport or an obedient *soldier*. She was indignant at her daughter's unfeeling and cruel reaction. Now the truth was coming out. After all the love she'd gotten as a child, Marsha had the nerve to disapprove of her.

Well, so what about that? Cassie wasn't just some dying breed, some housewife gone to seed, some squaw who'd numbly grind the corn until she dropped *dead*! This was one squaw who wasn't grinding the corn anymore. She didn't want to be the sensible one, the prop and moral center for the whole *family*. She could have a breakdown, if she wanted to. Why not?

"Fine. Fine. Don't face it. Don't talk to me." Marsha clicked her tongue and left the room.

Cassie heard the stairs creak as the wonderful rehabilitated daughter she now thought of as the hurtful know-it-all went downstairs. Her finger stroked the satin of the aqua pajamas. In spite of herself, she perked up just a little. Maybe she was being unfair about her neglectful husband, who traveled all over Europe, Australia, Chile, and South Africa visiting wineries, tasting, tasting, tasting, eating, eating, eating, bidding, bidding, bidding at wine auctions and never never *never* taking her. Maybe Mitch *had* thought of her and bought the pajamas as a surprise. He had to be making tons of money. He had to be feeling older and older. Maybe secretly he felt as bad about the gaps in their marriage as she did. *Maybe* the pajamas were a very meaningful—indeed, symbolic—gesture and there would be love in the night again, after all. Oooh.

It occurred to Cassie that she should take the gorgeous pajamas off and rewrap them in the tissue so Mitch could make the presentation himself. A thousand dollars was a lot of money. She didn't want to spoil his surprise. She was stroking the satin and thinking about this when she heard Marsha's urgent voice downstairs. She must have hit the intercom button on the phone. Cassie sat up in shock at the sound of her voice.

"Dad, why don't you just sit down and relax a little. I'll give you some chicken soup."

What? Mitch, home? Naah. In all the years of their marriage, Mitch had never returned home from a business trip early.

"I don't want fucking chicken soup. I want to go to bed." His voice sounded peevish and angry. Cassie's stomach knotted at the familiar sound of her husband grumbling.

"Why do you have to go upstairs this minute?" Marsha was wheedling. "Sit down, have a drink with me. Let's talk for a moment, catch up."

"I don't want my daughter drinking. Since when are you drinking?" He was whining.

"Dad, I'm *twenty-five*."

"I don't give a shit. You know how I hate drunks." This from the man who made his fortune on drinkers.

Cassie heard Marsha click her tongue some more. Both parents crazy as loons. "Have some orange juice then, Dad."

"I don't want orange juice. What's going on here? I bet you're up to something."

"Okay, okay. To tell you the truth, Mom isn't feeling well." Cassie sat there paralyzed, listening to Marsha trying to help her out.

"What's the matter with her?" Mitch asked irritably.

"She has the flu."

"Well, Marshmallow, I don't feel well either, and I've been on an airplane for ten hours. I need to go to my room and get in bed."

"She has a *bad* flu, Dad. I don't think you want to see her right now."

"You know what? I know you're up to something. I bet your mother isn't even here. What are you doing, having some kind of pot party? Some kind of *cocaine* orgy?"

"Oh Jesus, Daddy. Don't even go there. You know I don't do that stuff."

"I don't know that. I bet you do. With you I wouldn't be at all surprised. I foot the bills for everything around here and this is how you repay me. It makes me sick." He went on muttering, inaudibly now.

"Oh, Daddy, be reasonable." Marsha laughed.

"This is my fucking house. What are you talking about, reasonable? I can go anywhere I want."

Cassie couldn't hear anymore. They must have left the room. She sat on the bed dazed, waiting for the ax to fall. It was Friday afternoon. Mitch must have flown in from Rome. He was in a bad mood. He wanted to go to bed. What was she supposed to do, jump out the window?

She was thinking about jumping to avoid his anger when he strode into the room. He took one look at her, his mouth fell open just like in the movies, and he stopped dead a few feet from where she sat paralyzed on the bed in the aqua pajamas. He was a tall man, beefy from a lifetime of the very best wine and food the world had to offer. He had a full florid face, plush pillow lips that were the envy of women, and tense brown eyes that captured rather than saw. He had an eye for detail, and a full head of hair. The hair had been black but was steely now. He was proud of his hair and his taste. The man was always impeccable. At the moment he was wearing his travel uniform of Gucci loafers with tassels, a navy Ferragamo cashmere jacket with brass buttons, black silk turtleneck. There was a maroon and navy silk square in his jacket pocket.

"What the fucking hell is going on here?" he shouted.

"I-I-I—" Cassie's heart thundered. She couldn't say anything else. But then she was nearly always mute when he was around.

"She was in a car accident," Marsha said quickly.

Mitch took a step forward to get a better look.

"I had my face lifted," Cassie corrected quickly. She'd never been able to lie.

"What? Are you *crazy*?" His face changed. His eyes narrowed with fury. "Where'd you get those pajamas?" He glared at her. Then his full face took on an odd expression. He looked surprised, puzzled. "I feel funny," he said.

His fine tan paled to putty. "Something's wrong." It was the last thing he said.

Before she was aware of moving, Cassie was up, jumping to his aid. She touched his forehead. His skin was wet and cold. His eyes pierced her for a moment, demanding one last thing of her that she couldn't fulfill. Then she saw his powerful personality leech out of his body. His eyes lost their focus. He staggered. He reached out his hand for the bedpost, missed it, and pitched forward. His loafered feet stayed on the floor, but the rest of him toppled like a tree. His forehead smacked the bedside table as he went down.

"Daddy!" Marsha ran to him.

"Mitch," Cassie cried.

The two women tried desperately to revive him, but he wouldn't wake up. Frantically, Cassie called 911.

3

"MOM, PUT ON YOUR CLOTHES. Mom! Come on, Mom. Get up." Marsha pulled on her mother's arm. "I'll stay with Daddy until they come."

"OhymyGod! OhmyGod!" Cassie whimpered, listening to her husband try to breathe. Her forehead was pressed against the carpet at a lower level than it should be. She could feel the blood pulsing in her face. Her surgeon's warning about blood clots and hematomas flashed into her mind. She pushed it away. None of that mattered now.

"Maybe you should get some ammonia to wake him up. He's okay. It's a cut, right? It's a just a cut. He hit his head." Cassie kept trying to reassure them both.

"Mom!" Marsha spoke sharply. "Get up! I'll stay with him."

"Marsha, do you think he's drunk? Did he seem drunk when he came in?" Cassie couldn't put this thing together in her mind. Could Mitch have been that shocked by seeing her like this? No, it couldn't be. He just fell over all of a sudden, so he had to be drunk. That had to be it. Mitch had toppled like a tree several times in the last few years. She'd never told this to the children, or anyone else, but he'd been a big drinker for at least five or six years. Maybe more. Big.

She blamed all those Syrahs he'd been slurping up. The finicky Pinots, the grapes that make the headache wines. Oh, and the zinfandels—so rich, they tasted like jam. The gamays, low in tannin with a grapey taste: the grenaches light colored, high in alcohol and not so great as reds went. But the best were like raspberries. All these he'd guzzled, and the whites, too. Chardonnays, the great universal white with the oaky flavor. They called the taste oaky because of the oak barrels in which the wine aged. The reislings were dry, light bodied, and fresh, *never* oaky. The Cabernet Sauvignons, fairly tannic, rich and firm, with great depth. Oaky, she'd always liked the word. Oaky, oaky.

She tried to remember all the grape names Mitch had taught her when she was young. Wine had seemed so innocent then, so promising. Not a drug at all. Wait a minute, there were so many names she'd banished over the years. Some wines were place-names, like Bordeaux, like Rhone. Like Haut Medoc. But some were grape names, like Chardonnay, Cabernet, Merlot. The Loire valley. One side of the river or the other? Quick, which side of the river was which? She used to know it all. And the blends, sometimes nine grapes to a label, the Graves, the Pomerols. Mouton something or other . . . Those wines had stolen him from her.

"Oh God. Mitch, you idiot. You're drunk! You're supposed to swish and spit. But you always have to swallow, don't you. Shit you always swallowed, swallowed a lot." She chafed his hands. "Come on, baby. Wake up. I forgive you."

"Mom! EMS is coming, put on your clothes." Marsha couldn't budge her. "Come on, help me out, here," she pleaded. "You have to go to the hospital with him."

"Medoc," she whispered. Place-name, not a grape. La Grande Dame Champagne, Le Grand Cru of Perrier-Jouet, right? Nine grapes or only three? The one he'd planned for their son, *Teddy's*, wedding.

"Come on, Mitch. Come on, baby." Cassie couldn't get off her knees. Mitch was her other half, the man to whom she'd been faithful all her life. Practically the only lover she'd ever had, except for Matthew Howard. And look at what Matthew had become: owner of a cruise ship line! Tears flooded her swollen eyes. What had she done? He looked so *pathetic*, lying there in his Gucci loafers and cashmere jacket, his ruddy face blue as skim milk. Had she done this, felled the captain of their ship with a face-lift?

"OhmyGod." She kept chafing the lifeless hand, terrified that she and Marsha had done the wrong thing when they thumped on his chest and breathed into his mouth. They had no idea if the CPR they'd seen on the TV show *ER* was the right procedure. It certainly didn't seem to make any difference. His heart had kept on beating throughout their ministrations, and he was breathing on his own. Porto, Portugal. Madeira, the longest-lived wine of all. It could keep practically forever. But it wasn't really a wine, more a *fortified* wine. That's right—right, Mitch?

"Oh God." Their failure to revive him made Cassie think he had to be drunk. His mouth against hers brought back all the memories, all the familiar smells. The dominant one right now was not wine at all. It was whiskey. Under that, the stale emanation of Havana cigar. Tobacco smoke, like the air in a musty old attic, was deep in the fabric of his jacket, in his hair, in his hot breath. Under that cigar smoke was sweat. Musk male and unusually strong this afternoon. And under all those masculine aromas, a peculiarly sweet cologne that didn't match any of the above, or indeed the man himself. None of the smells were reassuring to Cassie. All were dangerous in their ways. The cologne teased her nose. It was not his brand. But maybe he'd been trying a new one. The idea of a new cologne was too painful to linger long. Instead of getting up, Cassie collapsed further. She laid the ruin of her face on the carpet near Mitch's large, cauliflower ear that suddenly seemed not ugly and wrong on his handsome head, but dear, inexpressibly dear.

He lay on his back, conscious, but not conscious. It was odd. He didn't seem connected. He stared straight up, his eyes unfocused. The white fingertip towel with the gold embroidered sun on it that Marsha had used to swab the cut on his forehead was now soaked with his blood. So was the hand towel that replaced it. The cut where Mitch's head had hit the side table didn't seem so bad. Not bad at all, but it was still seeping red. Blood trickled down the side of his head into the thick pile of the carpet in a steady stream. It wouldn't stop. It was a beige carpet. He'd chosen it himself. A shocking thought paraded in and out of Cassie's head. If he died, she could get a brighter one.

"Where are they? Why are they taking so long?" she cried.

"It's been less than five minutes. Come on, Mom. Get up. You can't go to the hospital like this."

"Oh God," Cassie cried. "Maybe he's just dazed. Don't you think so? It's nothing more than that, is it?" She held on to his hand, trying to reassure herself like all the times recently when his plane had been delayed or he'd been late getting back from a tasting or a dinner in the city. She'd wish that plane had gone down or his car had crashed. So smallminded, she'd wished him dead for the petty reason that her kids didn't need her anymore and he, too, had left her behind. Then, full of remorse, she'd frantically reassured herself that he was fine, probably fine. And he always was. These sad and panicked feelings she had were such a cliché, she was afraid to tell a single soul.

"I don't know." Marsha was dressed in her new uniform, a little cashmere sweater twinset, this one baby blue to complement her lovely eyes. Her short black skirt ended just above her knees. Her sheer black panty hose set off her lovely legs, as long as her mother's and just as nicely formed. It occurred to Cassie that maybe Marsha had planned to go out. She'd always been something of a freak in high school, never had any fun. She really deserved a break. And now this, poor girl. Cassie's heart broke for her former loser of a daughter who so deserved a dashing suitor.

The heavy chimes of the doorbell resounded throughout the house. "They're here," Marsha screamed in relief, and ran out of the room. Cassie put her lips to Mitch's ear.

"Help is here," she whispered. "Champagne. You're going to be fine." She let go of his hand and pulled herself to her feet. Her head throbbed as she dragged herself to the bedroom door. Her face felt unbearably tight. No part of her body felt like it belonged to her. She went out of the room to the hallway and leaned over the banister. When she heard Marsha speak, she was overcome with dizziness and had to hang on for dear life. She wished she could just topple over it and break her neck.

"It's my dad. Up here." Marsha marched up the stairs with two oddlooking people behind her. They were dressed in gray pants and nylon zip jackets with the logo of their service on the front. The man was wearing Birkenstocks and orange socks. Cassie swooned as those socks moved up the stairs under a long graying ponytail. Oh God! She realized he had an earring in each ear. The woman with him was much bigger than he was; her hair was very short. It appeared that the two had switched genders. Cassie's vision blurred as she thought of a man in a ponytail touching her darling husband, the virulent homophobe.

"I don't know what it is. I don't think it's a heart attack," Marsha was saying.

"Did you check for the Babinski reflex?"

"What's that?" Marsha asked.

They rounded the top of the staircase. Cassie got a better look at them and swayed.

"Holy shit, it's a domestic case," the woman blurted.

"Take it easy, ma'am." The man rushed toward her.

"Mom!" Marsha said sharply as the two raced to the top of the stairs and wrestled her mother into a chair, examining her swollen black-and-blue eyes, her face, raw as hamburger, the blood on the aqua silk pajamas that were way too big for her.

In a second they had slapped the blood pressure cuff onto her arm and were pumping it up.

"Mom, are you all right?" Marsha's anguished cry revived her.

Cassie's vision cleared. "Mitch," she mumbled.

"What, Mom?"

"Take care of *Daddy*!" she said sharply. "They're here for Daddy."

The two EMS people talked to each other.

"Her blood pressure is—"

Cassie slapped their hands away. "Stop that. I'm not the patient."

"We understand, ma'am."

"I'm telling you I'm all right. It's *my husband*."

The two referred to Marsha. "My father collapsed," she told them.

"Must have been quite a fight. Where is the other vic?"

"Better call in for another ambulance," the man said to the woman. The woman pulled out her radio.

"No no, I'm fine," Cassie insisted.

"What about you, are you all right?" he asked, turning to Marsha.

"I'm perfectly well."

"Is there only one other victim? Is there anyone in the house with a weapon?" The questions came fast.

"There are *no victims*. Daddy collapsed and hit his head. It may just be fatigue, for all we know," Marsha cried.

"What about your mom, here?"

Marsha shook her head. "Car accident. Last week. She's on the mend."

"No kidding, looks fresh to me," the woman said, examining her critically.

"Hurry. Please," Cassie begged them.

"This way," Marsha said.

"Are you sure there's no one with a weapon in here?"

"Absolutely certain."

"Okay, then. Let's go."

They left Cassie sitting there and headed for the bedroom. Cassie remained in the hall just for a moment, trying to calm herself. She had to go in there and protect Mitch from these idiots. She didn't want to, but God help her, she had to. She only hoped they wouldn't stick anything into him. Or shock him with those paddles she'd seen on *ER*. Finally, when she felt able to stand, she followed them in.

CHAPTER

4

IT TOOK TWENTY PRECIOUS MINUTES for the EMS team to try to talk to Mitch, get no response from him, cursorily examine him, strap him onto a gurney, carry him down the stairs, and roll him out to the ambulance, where they firmly shut the doors on his women. The team would not allow Cassie to ride in the vehicle with them, given her own condition, so she was separated from her husband on the driveway, where a rising wind suddenly churned the air, shaking the limbs of the two cherry trees that flanked the front door. As the trees trembled, thousands of cherry blossoms way past their prime were seized by the current and jettisoned up into the air. The moribund blooms whirled around and showered down on the ambulance just like some deeply meaningful scene from a foreign film.

"Oh my God, look at that," Cassie cried as the flower-strewn ambulance sped away. "Look at it, Marsha, look."

"Get in the car, Mom, we have to hurry." Marsha already had her father's Mercedes out of the garage. She opened the car door for her mother, and Cassie gingerly edged herself in.

"You missed it," she said, thinking of the flower shower.

Marsha didn't care what she'd missed. As soon as the car door was shut, she peeled off, spewing gravel on the drive. She then broke every speed limit on the way to North Fork Hospital. There, she stopped at the E.R. entrance and let Cassie out to deal with the paperwork, because there was no parking space nearby. Four minutes later she found her battered-looking mother in deep conversation with a woman whose name tag read ESTELLE ROGERS.

"What's the problem?" Marsha asked.

"She won't listen to me. She thinks I'm the patient," Cassie said. She was nicely dressed now in gray slacks and a blue blazer like Mitch's.

"It's okay. Put on your scarf, Mother. And go sit down. I'll take care of this."

"What?" Surprised, Cassie saw the immense black chiffon scarf from her very best evening dress dangling over her arm. How had it gotten there? Had she grabbed it when she got dressed?

"Put the scarf on," Marsha urged her, making faces at the Frankenstein stitches around her ears.

"Oh." Cassie had forgotten how she looked. "Oh God." She struggled with the scarf, couldn't manage it.

"Here, I'll do it." Marsha wrapped the dressy scarf around Cassie's head, covering everything but her eyeballs. Now she had a crown of sequins. "There, isn't that better?"

With her newly dyed, aggressively blond hair, discolored forehead, and bruised lower face all suddenly hidden from view, Cassie found herself actually calming down.

"Good girl. Sit here, I'll be right back."

Oh God. Cassie had heard that before, a thousand years ago. Her mother took her out once for ice cream and the next thing she knew she was in the hospital having her tonsils out. "Don't leave me," she whimpered.

"Just for a second, you can do it." Marsha led her to a molded plastic chair, where Cassie watched helplessly when Mitch was rolled in on the gurney and rushed through so quickly, she didn't have a chance to offer him even one encouraging word before he disappeared through automatic doors, his face lifeless and gray. OhmyGod, he's going to die, she thought. I'm going to be a widow, after all.

"Hi, I'm Maureen. I'm your social worker. I'll be guiding you through the process."

Cassie's panicked thoughts were interrupted by a worn-looking woman with curly red hair and oversized purple glasses. She held out her hand as she introduced herself. "You're"—she checked her clipboard—"the Sales family."

Cassie blinked in surprise. Social worker? What did they need a social worker for? "How is my husband?" she asked timorously.

"Oh, that's not my department. I'm here for *you*. How are *you* doing?"

The woman regarded her with such deep meaning that Cassie gasped. "Is he—?"

"Oh no, no. Nothing like that. The doctors are working on him. We won't know anything for a while." Maureen pushed up her glasses, hesitating. Then she put her hand solicitously on Cassie's arm. "Estelle, the head nurse, tells me you don't want to be examined yourself. Can I talk to you a little about that?"

"Oh no, that's all right." Marsha suddenly reappeared. "My mother has already been to the doctor today. Thank you for asking, but we're *fine*."

Maureen shook her head. "Don't worry. There's nothing to be ashamed of. This kind of thing happens at all levels of society. We have many services to offer, and we're here to help you in every way we can."

"I'm not in the least ashamed. My husband hit his head. I think he tripped." Cassie spoke quietly from behind her sequined veil. "I'm sure he's going to be fine."

Maureen clicked her tongue. "Yes, well, I understand your reticence about addressing the matter. This is not uncommon. Reporting incidents of domestic violence is very difficult for everyone," she assured them. "But the reporting *must* be done. It's the law, and how else can we heal, hmmmm?"

She turned suddenly to Marsha. "Think of your daughter's future and the precedent you're setting for her." Maureen gave Marsha an encouraging look as she shoved some informational pamphlets into her hand, then charged right ahead without drawing breath. "We have a DV unit from the Sheriff's Department right here in the hospital. Someone's available 24/7. That's how seriously we take family violence."

Cassie bristled angrily. This was the *third* person to assume that she and Mitch had been in some kind of physical fight. "You're mistaken!" She was almost ready to issue a formal protest about this kind of offensive jumping to conclusions.

"My mother was in a car accident," Marsha chimed in quickly. "I told that to the EMS people. Her bruises are from a *car accident.*"

It was clear, however, that the EMS team with the gender identity issues hadn't bought the story. Maureen was looking pretty doubtful about it herself.

Marsha raised her voice. "Look, Daddy just returned from a business trip in Europe an hour ago. He had no idea how badly hurt Mommy was. Maybe he had a heart attack when he saw her. They're a very *devoted* couple." On a roll, the suddenly competent Marsha embroidered further.

Cassie stared at her in surprise. The girl was good enough to have been a lawyer. When did Marsha develop such a talent to lie?

"Oh my." Even Maureen was caught up in the story. Nervously, she shoved her glasses up the bridge of her nose, not sure what to believe. "Well . . ."

"Yes, well indeed," Marsha said pompously. "My father is a trustee of the hospital. Is there anywhere more private we could wait?"

Maureen tilted her frizzy head to the side, adjusted her glasses. Marsha's story wasn't really working for her, but she was impressed with the performance. "This is very embarrassing. But you know, so often people lie." She forced her lips into a smile. The patient was a trustee, after all. He must give the hospital a lot of money. Maybe she was wrong.

"Yes, I know it. I'm at NYU's Ehrenkranz School of Social Work." Marsha let her know they were *almost* colleagues.

"Really, I went there." Lifting her eyebrows as if that changed everything, Maureen scurried off.

About an hour later, without a word of apology, she came back and led them down a glass corridor to another wing of the hospital. There, she left them in a smallish turquoise lounge furnished with tables, sofas, and a TV set that was on. It was hardly private, and by late afternoon the garbage cans were overflowing with the remains of many take-out meals in soggy containers.

Cassie sat down on a sticky brown sofa, her nose twitching with indignation and hunger.

"You want me to get you something to eat, Mom?" Marsha asked.

Cassie's stomach churned. "No, no, sweetheart. I don't want anything. Maybe later."

Further conversation was prevented by the arrival of a young woman dressed in a lavender tennis outfit. "Get your hands off me, you fucking asshole!" she yelled at the deputy sheriff who was escorting her. "I told you to let me go." She launched herself at him, pummeling him hard.

The deputy was a big guy. He had a nightstick, a gun, and a pair of plastic cuffs dangling from his belt, but none of them were any help. He tried to ward off the woman's blows and talk her down. Almost immediately some hospital staff members arrived to help him.

Mesmerized, Cassie and Marsha watched the drama. Two male nurses calmed the woman. The deputy departed quickly. After he was gone, she became enraged again and tried to punch out the TV screen. More hospital staff arrived. They surrounded and eased her into one of the chairs. Their soothing voices hummed in the air. Now this was a domestic violence case. She put her hand over her eyes.

"Are you okay, Mom?" Marsha asked solicitously.

"Oh yes, fine. Don't think about me." She felt sick and frightened, but she had to be strong for the children.

"Mom, I hope you don't mind. I called Teddy," Marsha went on.

"Oh God," Cassie groaned. All she needed was to have the two of them together at a time like this. "Promise me you won't fight." Her body wouldn't stop shivering. Mitch would be upset about this. He was a private man, a gourmet. He'd hate the take-out food odors, the drama, the idea of his adoring son seeing him like this.

Suddenly the noise level increased. Cassie opened her eyes. The small room was filled with people screaming in Italian. The smell of garlic was strong. Oh, was it strong. Cassie swooned against her daughter's shoulder.

"I'll get you something to drink," Marsha said quickly. "You need to hydrate."

"Poor Mitch. This is such bad luck. I hope he doesn't die," Cassie murmured. And she meant it. She really did.

"I'll be right back." Marsha hurried away.

Cassie hid her eyes. There was screaming all around her. She couldn't help hearing the story. Oh God. The woman who'd tried to punch out the sheriff and the TV had good reason. Her husband had been driving their two kids to pick up a pizza for dinner. That's how late it had gotten. They'd been in an accident on the Long Island Expressway. He was dead on the scene; her son, too. The woman's nine-year-old daughter was alive, but her skull had been crushed. No one wanted to tell her how bad her daughter was. Protocol seemed to demand a certain order to things. A person could absorb just so much. An old man, talking to himself, was wondering what Tony had been doing, driving on the L.I.E. Apparently it wasn't his usual route to the pizzeria.

Marsha returned with two Diet Cokes. Cassie thought she was going to explode. Teddy was coming by way of the L.I.E.

"I called Edith," Marsha informed her.

"What?" Cassie cried. Oh, now her aunt was involved. Cassie couldn't bear it.

"She's your only relative. Except for Julie. Do you want me to call Julie?"

Edith, her mother's sister, was now seventy-three and the worst pain in the neck in the entire world. Except for Cassie's sister Julie. "No!" Cassie said. Julie lived in L.A. and hadn't spoken to Cassie in years. Cassie didn't want either of them here with her.

"You need support," Marsha told her.

What was that, some word she'd learned in social work school? "I didn't tell Edith about the face-lift," Cassie admitted softly.

"Car crash," Marsha said. "I've got that covered."

"Oh God," she whispered. It seemed so trivial now.

Another hour went by. The room emptied. The Italian family hurried away. Cassie realized she had been holding her breath.

"The poor little girl was never admitted here," Marsha said suddenly. "They let her go in the emergency room."

"They let her go?"

"She died."

"Oh no." Cassie's head throbbed. That poor woman had lost everything in a second. Cassie covered her eyes to stop her tears.

Dark descended outside, and the lounge filled up again. Old women came to see their old husbands, middle-aged women came to see their mothers, young parents came to see their kids, and every single patient was hanging on by a thread. Cassie was agonized by the wait. Why was it taking so long? Teddy finally arrived at eight P.M. Why had it taken him five hours to get there from Manhattan where he lived and worked?

"Oh shit, Mom! What happened to you? I thought it was Daddy!" He pretty much freaked out when he saw her.

"It is Daddy. *She's* going to be fine," Marsha told him superciliously, right away setting the tone for an unpleasant confrontation between them. "Where have you been?" she demanded.

"She doesn't look fine." Teddy was not as tall as his father and was much thinner. He had never grown into his nose. He didn't work out. His shirt and pants didn't go together. Two plaids. He had a golf hat on his head, but still he was a handsome boy. Very handsome, Cassie thought. And very good at numbers.

"Hi, Teddy," she said.

He paced back and forth in front of her as if she were an inanimate object. "She looks like shit," he announced. "Mom?" He raised his voice as if she'd gone deaf.

"She's fine!" Marsha insisted.

"She doesn't look fine, Marsha. What's that thing on her head? What's going on?"

"Shut up, you idiot, I told you she's *fine*!"

"What do you know about it?" Teddy stared angrily at his sister.

"I'm fine," Cassie said weakly. "Don't fight."

"I demand to know what's going on. What's wrong with her? She looks like an Arab," Teddy spoke to his sister.

"Mom was in a car accident," Marsha said quickly.

"No *shit*!" Teddy moved in for a closer look. "In Dad's Mercedes?" His voice was hushed.

"No."

"In the Volvo?"

"Yes, the Volvo."

"How is it? Is it totaled?"

Marsha rolled her eyes. She didn't, after all, think very much of her brother.

5

THE KIDS WERE STILL BICKERING twenty minutes later when three doctors hustled importantly into the lounge. The family internist was the one in charge. Dr. Cohen had taken care of both Cassie and Mitch for twenty years. They'd had dinners together many times. His cellar was stocked with their very good wines, nothing less than $140 to $200 a bottle. He had about a thousand-bottle cellar and could afford it. He was a short, wide, completely bald man with a round, usually smiling face like the happy stickers the kids used to get on their papers when they were small. He wasn't smiling now.

"Cassie!" Unprepared for the black eyes and bruised jawline, he stopped short. Truly shocked, he turned to Marsha for an explanation.

Marsha, however, missed his distress. She had caught sight of something she liked and had put three fingers to her forehead as if to keep her head on during a religious experience. The object of her attention was a thin, stern-looking, white-coated young man, about five feet nine, totally unremarkable, and a complete opposite of the long-haired, tattooed biker-types that usually caused her seizures.

"Uhhh, hhhhh." A third doctor, whose tag read NESSIM SALIM, coughed delicately. This one looked as exotic as his name sounded.

"Ah, Dr. Salim is a neurosurgeon. This is Mrs. Sales, Marsha, Teddy," Dr. Cohen introduced them, bowing slightly. He straightened up and smoothed his bald head as if he still missed his hair. "Cassie, what happened . . . ?" The question hung in the air.

"It's nothing at all." Cassie waved her hand at him impatiently.

"Ah. Unfortunate timing, then," he murmured with full understanding. "This is Dr. Wellfleet. He's our best young neurologist."

Dr. Wellfleet nodded solemnly. He must have thought so, too.

A fourth man, this one dressed in a black suit, hurried officiously in, his jacket flapping in his haste. "Sorry to keep you waiting, Mrs. Sales, I'm so sorry." He put his hand on Cassie's arm to comfort her and pulled her scarf off. Now everyone saw the black stitches around her ears and the change of hair color her surgeon had suggested to distract people from the changes in her face. Her hair was no longer the light silvery brown of the last decade. It was now a shocking daffodil yellow.

"Mom!" Teddy screamed.

Marsha gasped and dove for the scarf as it slipped to the floor.

"Uh uh uh." The man coughed to cover his dismay.

"Um, um. This is Reverend Ballister. He's the chaplain here at the hospital. We thought it would be a good idea to have him here with us." Dr. Cohen only choked a little on the awkwardness and the public revelation: Old Cassie had done some restoration work and dyed her hair an awful color.

"Mrs. Sales. I'm so sorry," the reverend intoned again.

Marsha rearranged the sparkling evening scarf over Cassie's head and blue blazer as if she were a mannequin in a store window, while Cassie wished she'd gone over the banister and broken her neck.

"My husband is not a believer," she said to the minister with as much dignity as she could muster. Never mind that the appalling man had humiliated her. Never mind her ridiculous blond hair and black eyes. This was something Mitch would not tolerate. This *God* thing she had to nip in the bud.

"Perhaps you'd prefer a priest or a rabbi." This from Dr. Salim. "We have both nearby, practically on the premises," he said, eager to please.

"My husband is not a believer in *any* God," Cassie replied firmly. "He's not a religious man. He's against organized religion of any kind. He specifically doesn't want special prayers . . ." Her voice failed her. Her hands flew to her face. It occurred to her that Mitch really was dead, and that that was the reason they had all come together. The last family members brought to this room had lost their little *girl*. Mitch was gone. She stared at the four of them, her hands fluttering helplessly. She'd been waiting for him all these years, and now he'd left her for good. The future flashed dangerously in front of her. What would she and the children do? Teddy couldn't run a sophisticated business. He might be able to add, but he could barely dress himself. Marsha didn't care about money. She was in the helping profession. And Cassie herself didn't know a thing about the finances. Mitch had taught her how to stock a cellar and what to serve with what, but yelled at her if she sampled the merchandise or wrote a check.

"It doesn't matter if your husband is not a religious man. I'm here for you, for the family, to help you through this," the chaplain went on as if he hadn't heard her.

Luckily, Cassie didn't have a gun handy. She would have shot him on the spot.

"Is Daddy dead?" Teddy, still in shock over the yellow hair and stitches, was the one to blurt out the question.

Marsha elbowed him. "Shut up, Teddy."

"What's wrong with that? He's being audited. I need to know." Teddy was offended.

"Shut *up*, you idiot. Don't you have any sensitivity at all?"

"Fuck you, I'm not an idiot." Teddy balled up his fists for a fight.

"Go ahead, hit me," Marsha invited him softly, rolling her eyes at Wellfleet as if she'd known the neurologist all her life. She had a crazy brother, right? Wellfleet raised an eyebrow, responding to her attractions.

"Oh my God," Cassie murmured. Marsha was making a conquest on her father's deathbed.

"Now, now. Let's calm down and take a break," Dr. Cohen suggested. "Come on, kids, I know you're upset, but have a little respect." His voice was soft and tolerant. After all, he'd known the family for a long time and had children of his own.

"I have respect. She's calling me an idiot," Teddy muttered.

"Well, but think of your father," he said. Mitchell Sales had pledged several million to the hospital.

"I am thinking of him. I'm closer to him than they are."

"Idiot," Marsha spat out again.

"Well, I am," Teddy said. "I'm closer to him—I know him better than any of you. I bet *you* didn't even know he was being audited."

"Teddy, now is not the time for sibling rivalry." Dr. Cohen put a hand on his shoulder and moved him and the rest of the group down the hall into a conference room with a mahogany table and ten chairs. Cassie shivered as they took their places.

At this moment Cassie couldn't help remembering the intense pride Mitch had taken in all the family funerals. He'd arranged everything for the funerals of both her parents and his mother. Three beautiful affairs. She remembered that they'd served only white wine (when she'd always preferred red), a Côte de Beaune, Puligny-Montrachet, Grand Cru Vineyard Chevalier-Montrachet. She'd forgotten the vintage, it was so long ago. She hadn't had to make a single decision, or even go to the hospital to identify their remains before the bodies were cremated. Mitch had insisted on cremation. He'd taken care of everything.

And now she wondered how she was going to manage the kind of affair he'd want. Ever since the news that red wine was better for the heart than white came out a decade or so ago, red wine sales had absolutely soared. Maybe a Petrus Pomerol would be acceptable to him now. Or maybe she should serve both red *and* white. But which ones? Mitch's father was ninety-two and hadn't had all his marbles since 1966. Cassie hiccuped on her panic, holding back a sob.

"The good news is we've got him stabilized," Dr. Wellfleet began.

Teddy let out his breath in a whoosh. "Well, thank God!"

"Amen," echoed Dr. Ballister.

Alive? Stable? Cassie was further confused by the good news.

"We couldn't get any more time on the audit even if the old man croaked," Teddy explained, all smiles in his relief.

"Teddy!" Marsha cried.

"Well, he's had it postponed twice. They won't take any more postponements now," he said. "Ira Mandel is resigned to going ahead with it no matter what."

"I never heard anything about this." Now Cassie was confused. Why was Teddy harping on this? What did an audit have to do with anything?

Mitch was alive. That meant no funeral. What else could possibly matter? Ira Mandel was Mitch's accountant. He also happened to be Teddy's boss. Nepotism was rampant everywhere.

"You never called me when you were in a damn car accident. It's obvious you don't love me as much as her." Teddy shook his head angrily. He was back on the car accident.

Cassie thought she was going nuts. Audit, stabilized. These words were not in her vocabulary.

Dr. Cohen glanced at Dr. Wellfleet. Wellfleet was lifting his eyebrows up and down at Marsha à la Groucho Marx. Cassie was shocked. They were connecting. Her daughter and the skinny neurologist. Dr. Cohen broke the silence.

"Let's stick with your father for a moment. He's in critical condition. It was touch and go for a while there, but we gave him TPA in the ER, and we've got him stabilized for the moment. Oh, and Dr. Salim is here on consultation. In case there's a need for emergency surgery."

"On what?" Cassie's head spun.

"TPA is the drug that halts brain damage after a stroke, Mom," Marsha translated softly for her mother. "Surgery would be for, like, bleeding, or a blood clot. It would be brain surgery, of course." Marsha put a protective hand on her mother's arm.

Dr. Wellfleet gave Marsha a melting smile for understanding the medical situation. "I'm afraid your husband had a stroke," he confirmed to Cassie.

"A *stroke*!" That was the one possibility that hadn't occurred to her. Life or death was all that had been on her mind. She swallowed hard. A stroke was a long-term kind of thing.

"Of *course* he's going to recover; he wouldn't want to miss his audit," Teddy quipped. He struck the pose of a madman with one eye closed and his right side drooping, hand crippled—his idea of his daddy as a stroke victim.

"Oh my God!" Marsha made a disgusted sound at the inappropriate, fifth-grade humor of her brother.

Teddy mouthed the word "bitch" at her.

Cassie was appalled. They seemed so heartless, without feeling of any kind. Suddenly it wasn't hard to understand why animals in the wild sometimes ate their young. "What's the prognosis?" she asked timorously. She had to focus on Mitch, poor Mitch struck down in his prime.

"Will he walk? Will he talk? Will he be able to write checks?" Marsha zoomed right in on the practical considerations. Daddy paid the bills, after all. Mommy was the idiot who didn't even know where the checkbook was.

Dr. Cohen tapped the table with his pen. "It's very early to predict. Some people do better than expected. Others—"

"What do you mean 'better than expected'?" Cassie cried.

"The CT scans show that your husband had a stroke. That means plaque on his arteries prevented the blood flow from getting to his brain. His brain shows quite a bit of damage from oxygen deprivation."

"How much damage?" Teddy broke in.

Dr. Cohen put his lips together. "We'll have to see. We're just going to have to take this one day at a time." He gave them his first bright encouraging smile.

"But you gave him PTA. Doesn't that arrest the damage?" Cassie asked hopefully.

"TPA," Marsha corrected gently.

"I know. I'm no dummy," she replied.

"Of course, you're not, *Mother*," Marsha said sweetly enough to indicate that she thought her mother was a great big dummy.

"Well, how long before we'll know something?" she asked slowly, trying not to take offense.

"We'll have a better idea in forty-eight hours." Wellfleet spoke slowly, too. It was pretty clear they didn't have much hope.

"The first few days are crucial. We'll know more in a day or two," Dr. Cohen added quickly.

"One day at a time. That has to be our credo." Dr. Ballister took this opportunity to say a few comforting words. Cassie didn't hear them. She was alarmed by the prospect of her husband in a wheelchair. Mitch had to recover, he had to. As an invalid, he'd be very difficult to manage.

"I'd like to see him. Is he awake?" she asked.

"He's in intensive care. You can go in for a few minutes, but don't expect much."

"Oh no." Panic overtook Teddy's face for the first time. Courage wasn't his middle name.

Marsha, on the other hand, had resolve written all over her. She squared her shoulders, the social worker kicking in. All three doctors gave her admiring glances. She glowed with the attention. The past week she'd been through hell with her mother. Now it was Daddy's turn. The girl was jumping into the parenting role with both feet. She draped her arm around her mother's shoulder. "Don't cry, Mom. Daddy's strong. He'll pull through this. I know he will."

Grateful for the comfort, Cassie reached across her chest and patted Marsha's hand. She didn't want to tell this finally empathizing daughter that the tears in her eyes were for the young mother who'd lost in a nanosecond her husband and both children when they went out for pizza on the L.I.E.

CASSIE FOUND MITCH IN A GLASS ROOM in the Neurological Intensive Care unit, where he and his many monitors were highly visible to the nurses and doctors responsible for keeping him alive. He was also mercilessly displayed in all his certain mortality to anyone else who happened to pass by. With breathing tubes in his nose, and hookups to any number of life-sustaining devices, he wasn't a pretty sight. Plastic tubing and drip bags were everywhere, several going in, and one tube that snaked out from under the covers led to a half-filled urine bag.

The head of their family, the captain of their little ship, lay on his back like a beached whale. His beautiful tan had turned to a putty gray. The hair that he had freshly blow-dried every single morning of his life was now a thin, oily mat on his scalp. The true extent of his receding hairline was now clearly revealed. He was motionless, yet there was motion all around him. A respirator breathed for him, making whooshing noises. Monitors clicked, showing his brain and heart activity. There didn't appear to be much. Mitchell Anderson Sales was alive, but only just.

Teddy hung back outside the window. "I can't take this. I'll wait for you outside."

Having ascertained no wedding ring on Wellfleet's finger, Marsha now took the opportunity to consult with the neurologist just down the hall. So Cassie pulled herself together and went into her husband's glass cocoon all alone. The first thing she saw was that his eyes were open, and her heart spiked with hope.

"Sweetheart, it's *Cassie*," she said brightly. "You're going to be just fine. I know it." The cheerleader in her went right to work. Go Mitch.

Mitch didn't seem interested. His eyes, directed elsewhere, did not register her optimism.

"Can you hear me, baby? It's Cassie. I'm with you." She leaned closer to catch his reply, but Mitch wasn't home. The breathing machine with its loud mechanical *whoosh* answered for him.

"Baby, I'm with you. Marsha is here. Teddy. We're all here, and we're going to stay with you until you come back from there. From wherever you are." She paused. Nothing. This emptiness where there used to be such power scared her.

"Listen, kiddo, remember that swami who came to see Mother in the hospital? Remember what he told her about going into the light? Mitch, listen. Whatever they tell you about heaven, don't go into the light, okay?" She paused again, thinking of her mother, who'd gone right into that damn light when Cassie was only twenty-four. Oh God, she still missed her mommy.

"Listen to me, Mitch, honey. I know what I'm talking about. That light thing, forget it. Look at me, sweetheart. I'll stay with you. I'll bring you back, I promise. I don't care what the doctors say. You can do it. I know you can. We'll travel together from now on. I'll keep you company. We'll have fun, live to be old, okay? An old couple, having fun."

She leaned down close to his ear. A big cauliflower ear. Five or six gray hairs were growing out of it. She swooned, dizzy from those hairs and the smell of intensive care. The tubes were everywhere. So many plastic tubes laced back and forth around him, they actually appeared to be mating. Cassie realized she was now in greater intimacy with her husband than she'd been in years. She closed her eyes and let the noise take over. She didn't realize that his unseeing eyes were empty. She felt a profound irritation, thinking he was resisting her attempt to be with and care for him.

This was not an unusual situation for them. She'd walk into a room, and he'd walk out. He only hung around long enough to have a fight with her. But this time she was here and he wasn't walking out. He wasn't fighting. He was stuck, and had to listen to her. And this time she wasn't taking no for an answer. He was hers and he had to survive. She wouldn't be able to live with herself if he didn't.

"Listen to me, Mitch. I won't let you go like this. It's my fault. I didn't tell you about the face-lift, and I know that was wrong. I'm sorry if it was a shock. Just wake up, and I'll never do it again. I promise. Okay? Okay? I'm sorry. I'll remember every single thing about wine. I'll drink white, or I won't drink it. Whatever you want. Okay? I won't complain about cigars. Honey, just come back." She finished her prayer and stood there, waiting for a sign from him. But there was no pressure back from his fingers. He wasn't going to forgive her for the plastic surgery, for not being whatever it was he'd wanted of her. The tears came again. She was sorry, oh was she sorry.

Finally she composed herself and went into the hall. Teddy was nowhere in sight. Marsha was in deep dialogue with Dr. Wellfleet. She could tell from their body language that the conversation would continue for some time. She found Dr. Cohen facing a window, talking to himself. When she approached, she realized he was on his cell phone. He finished the call when she touched his shoulder.

"Mark, I want to spend the night here," she told him.

"I know it looks bad, Cassie, dear. But I don't want you to do that. I want you to go home and get some rest. We'll call you if there's any change. I promise."

"I *have* to stay with him. I feel so responsible for this."

"What are you talking about? You're not responsible. He had a stroke."

"No, you don't understand. He saw me like this. He took one look at me and just . . . Mark, he keeled over!"

"Well, it is a surprise." Mark pulled back the scarf and turned her head this way and that. A doctor can never resist examining. "I'm surprised myself. We go back a long way, Cassie. You might have told me you were planning this. We could have consulted. I know the best people. But it's not bad," he admitted grudgingly. "Whose work is this?"

"Who cares, it caused a stroke."

"No, Cassie. Don't think like that. You know Mitch had dangerously high blood pressure. I told him months ago he needed medication. He was in denial. That's not your fault."

"High blood pressure?" Cassie tried to frown but couldn't.

Mark frowned for her. His forehead creased like an accordion. "Didn't he tell you?" he asked.

"Oh, you know Mitch and the privacy thing. He may have mentioned something a few years ago," Cassie said vaguely, trying to defend the indefensible. Her husband was sick and hadn't told her.

"No, no. This is not years ago. This is recent. I warned him a month ago. I gave him some medicine, but he wouldn't take it. He said it killed his libido." Mark smiled. That man thing.

Cassie stared at him. Mitch was worried about his *libido?* What libido? She blew air out of her mouth. Mitch had some ego. He didn't want his own doctor to know he hadn't been interested in sex in years.

"I'm sorry, Cassie. Mitch called me yesterday from Paris and told me he felt funny. Didn't he tell you he was coming back?"

"No, I guess he didn't want to worry me." Cassie didn't know he was in Paris. She defended him some more. It probably would never in a million years occur to Mitch that she might not be in any condition to care for him. Paris? She'd thought he was in Rome.

Mark gave her a funny look. "Is everything in order? You're going to have to take over now, you know."

"What?" The look on his face puzzled her. What else was she missing here?

"You know, the insurance—the paperwork, his will. . . . We don't want to be premature. But just to be on the safe side, you might check and see if he has a living will."

"Oh that," she said vaguely.

Mark took both her hands in his. "I'm sorry to have to tell you this. But you have to be prepared. In case his heart fails." He squeezed her hands.

She was puzzled by the warmth with which he was speaking and squeezing her. But he was an old friend, as well as their doctor. Why not? He was talking more, and she tried to listen.

"It could happen, you know. And you have a power of attorney, right? You need that."

"Is it that serious?" Cassie whispered.

"I don't want to alarm you. But yes, it's that serious. You know I'll always be there for you, Cassie. But you're going to have to make the decisions now. I'll be frank with you. Mitch may have a partial recovery, but not for a long time. You're a strong and beautiful woman. And you never know. This may all be for the best." He stared into her bruised face and squeezed her hands one last time. "Go home now. I'll see you back here in the morning."

It was ten-thirty on a Friday night. Cassie was reeling with the things Mark had told her. She didn't know what to think about it. Mitch was so stubborn. He'd come home because he was sick? He'd never breathed a word about it to her. He was being audited? He'd never breathed a word about that, either. She needed a painkiller badly. She was deeply hurt that he'd been hiding these things from her, but no matter what had been in his mind about it, she couldn't imagine why an old friend like Mark Cohen could think a disaster like this could possibly be for the best. She was still thinking about it when she found Marsha and pried her away from the neurologist. The two of them located Teddy in the lobby talking to a zaftig nurse with orange hair. For the first time in years, his face, too, was full of hope.

CHAPTER 7

FORTY-FIVE MINUTES LATER, when Teddy pulled into the driveway of the family house, he still had that happy grin on his face. Cassie went right inside through the garage. Teddy started to follow her, then saw the Volvo station wagon in its usual spot in the driveway. Marsha watched him stop and circle it curiously. "What's the matter, bro?" she asked.

He came into the garage where the Mercedes and Porche sat companionably side by side, then circled both of them with a dawning comprehension. "Mom wasn't in a car crash," he said.

"Of course she was. Don't make a big thing of it." Marsha draped an arm around his shoulder. "Look, idiot. We're going to have to stick together now. Dad isn't going to get better."

Teddy was a big boy, twenty-three and a half, but he looked about ten now, stricken by two felled parents in one day. "How do *you* know? Daddy's real tough. Maybe he'll get better."

"Tom said he's pretty much brain-dead. We're going to have to close ranks and help Mom," Marsha said.

Teddy shrugged off the diagnosis. "Well, Lorraine told me they do wonders with stroke victims these days. I'm not writing him off."

"You didn't *see* him, Teddy. He's nonresponsive. He's in a deep coma. Face it, he's not coming out of this."

"Well, you don't know him. He's a tough guy. He's not toppling."

"You didn't see him," Marsha repeated. "It was awful. . . ." She shook her head. "I almost felt sorry for him."

Teddy snorted derisively. "Well, I'm sure you'll get over it."

Marsha gave him a sharp look. "What is that supposed to mean? Who's Lorraine?"

Teddy's mood suddenly lifted. "Isn't she great? She's the nurse I was talking to. She gave me her number and everything. She told me to call anytime. She never sleeps."

"What is she, a hooker?"

"Bitch," Teddy spat at her.

"Teddy, you're disgusting. Your father had a stroke and you're flirting with nurses." Marsha turned her back on him.

"Well, who the fuck is *Tom*?" he mimicked her.

"*Tom is Daddy's doctor*. I was talking to *his* doctor! Don't you have any brains at all?"

"He looked like a little runt to me," Teddy muttered.

"You're such a jerk," Marsha replied loftily.

The door to the house opened. "What's the matter with you two? I could hear you arguing all the way in the living room," Cassie cried. The sequined scarf was gone, and her garish yellow hair stood out in the halo of light from the kitchen.

"Why hurt each other like that?"

Teddy stared at her, as if he hadn't seen her bad dye job before. "Mom, you dyed your hair."

"Yes, I did," she said quietly.

"I bet you had your face lifted, too. Oh God, it's gross!"

Marsha let her breath out explosively. "What a jerk! Teddy! How can you be so mean?"

"She had her face lifted. What did she do that for? It looks *terrible*."

"Teddy!" Marsha screamed loud enough to rouse the entire neighborhood. She was known for being something of a hysteric.

Cassie pushed the button to close the garage door and waved them inside. "Stop, Marsha. It doesn't matter. The only thing I care about is peace."

"What are you mad at *me* for? I'm the good one," Marsha complained.

"I'm not mad at anybody." Cassie threw up her hands and disappeared into the house.

"Watch out, the shit's hitting the fan," Teddy warned.

Marsha spun around and caught his arm. "What's going on, Teddy?"

"I don't want to go into it," he said.

"Give, asshole. What's going on?"

He shook his head. "Uh-uh. I'm sick of your calling me an asshole."

"Oh Jesus! You're something." Marsha followed her mother into the house and slammed the door. She found Cassie in the kitchen, sitting at the kitchen table, shredding a used paper napkin.

"Mom, are you okay?"

"No, I'm not. Why do you two have to fight like that? I heard every word you said. I'm demoralized with this."

"Oh we're just playing. Don't let it get to you, Mom." Marsha touched her mother's awful hair.

"It *is* getting to me. Everybody's fallen apart and it's all because of that face-lift. What was I thinking?"

"The face-lift had nothing to do with it. Daddy had high blood pressure. Tom told me he was a walking time bomb."

Teddy barged in. "What's for dinner? I'm starved."

The two women ignored him.

"No, no, Marsha. I know it was the shock. Daddy likes things natural," Cassie said.

Teddy laughed. "Natural, oh sure."

Marsha turned on him. "What do you know about anything?"

"Daddy couldn't stand women who had plastic surgery. He said you could always tell a mile away."

Cassie groaned. Why oh why had she done it?

Teddy snorted and opened the refrigerator.

"Teddy!" Marsha cried. "Stop that."

"What did I do? I'm hungry . . . Jesus, Jell-O! Soup! Cottage cheese! What happened to food?" he complained.

"Shh Teddy, we have to talk seriously about this. Mom, does Daddy have a living will?"

"I have no idea. He never tells me anything. I didn't even know he had high blood pressure." Cassie touched her cheek and didn't feel a thing.

"Well, where's his will? The document will be with that." Marsha spoke briskly. She was back in social work mode.

"Diet Coke, anyone?" Teddy offered.

Ignored again.

"I don't know where his will is. Call Parker, he'll know," Cassie said.

"Why don't I call out for a pizza, then," Teddy suggested.

"I'm trying to get something accomplished here," Marsha told him sharply. "Let's focus on the problem."

"Well, we have to eat," he replied reasonably enough.

"Can't you see Mom can't eat pizza? Where is your head, Teddy? Daddy had a stroke; Mom can't eat pizza. This doesn't take a rocket scientist to figure out. Order something else."

"Marsha, why can't he have pizza?" Cassie asked.

"You always indulge him," Marsha grumbled.

Cassie gave her daughter an angry look. "Let's not get caught up in this ridiculous bickering, okay?"

"Don't make me feel guilty. I'm just trying to—"

"Thanks, Mommy, you're a peach. What do you want on it, everything?" Teddy interrupted happily as he dove for the phone.

"I'd rather die on the spot than eat that poison. Mom, what about the health insurance policy?"

"And don't forget the life insurance," Teddy threw in when Domino's put him on hold.

"How can you talk about money when your father's in intensive care?" Cassie was shocked at the very mention of life insurance. She couldn't believe the way her children were behaving. And she had no idea where the documents were. Her ignorance made her feel like an absolute jerk, just as helpless and infantile in the situation as her children were.

"This isn't about money," Marsha said. "This is about caring for him. We have to know what he wanted . . ."

"I'm sure he'd want to linger," Teddy said.

"Teddy! Mom!" Marsha was boiling over.

"Honey, calm down. We'll sort it out."

"Fine, let's sort it out now. Where's the will?"

"Gee, I don't even know if he *has* a will. Your daddy never talked about things like that. Could I have a cup of tea, please, sweetheart?"

"What do you mean, you didn't talk about it? Didn't you plan for your future?" Marsha was shocked.

Cassie clicked her tongue. "Of course, he worked for the *future*. He wanted to be in the top ten, you know that. He just didn't want to burden me with the dust of life, sweetheart."

"What's the dust of life, everything?"

"Marsha, that's not nice!" Cassie put her head down on the table.

"He didn't talk about anything, and you put your head in the sand. Same old, same old."

"Amen," said Teddy.

Marsha sighed and put the kettle on. Crushed, Cassie watched her daughter move around the kitchen, putting together the cups, the teapot, the milk, amazed that she seemed to know how to do it. When the pizza arrived, Teddy paid for it himself, then sat at the kitchen table, eating it thoughtfully. Despite her contempt for it, Marsha also ate the pizza. Cassie, however, couldn't eat a thing.

"Poor Mitch." She kept thinking of his blank face and all those tubes going into him. Poor Mitch. How he had loved the good things of life. He would absolutely hate seeing his children resort to the humble pizza. He'd hate being a vegetable.

Marsha finished her pizza. "Come on, Mom. I'll clean this up. You need to lie down."

"I am tired," she admitted, and let Marsha take her upstairs and help her get ready for bed. It wasn't so easy. Cassie had to sleep sitting up, bolstered against the pillows so her head would be above her chest and the blood wouldn't collect in her face. All week she'd kept waking herself up to be sure she didn't relax too much and fall over. Plastic surgery was like giving birth the first time. No one had told you beforehand any of the things you needed to know. In this case the doctor had promised that she would look gorgeous and completely natural. He didn't tell her that to achieve this she'd have to be practically immobile for weeks to prevent scarring. Cassie was certainly scarred for life now. She'd been so humiliated by everyone looking at her in that ridiculous scarf. She lay back against the pillows, groaning, wishing she could put a bullet in her head.

"Just close your eyes and get some sleep, Mom." Marsha covered her sore eyes with a plastic bag filled with crushed ice even though the time for cold packs was long gone.

"Thank you, Marsha. You're a nice girl." The cold was comforting, but it didn't stop Cassie's seeing the same thing over and over. All the devastating moments: Mitch's unexpected return home. His angry conversation with Marsha in the kitchen. The way he'd looked when he walked through the bedroom door and his handsome face went purple at the sight of her in bed, a mess, wearing his beautiful aqua lace pajamas. The sweat that beaded his forehead. The color leeching out of his face. Just like in a movie, frame by frame, she watched it all again and again. She saw him teeter and fall. She saw his head crack against the corner of the bedside table. She saw his blood spilling out of the cut onto the boring beige carpet she'd never liked. Marsha left the room and returned a few moments later to give her a pill. Gratefully, she took it. In a little while she wasn't seeing anything anymore.

Many hours later when it was still deep night outside, Cassie was startled back into consciousness. Sounds of people in the house alarmed her. She wasn't used to hearing anything but the wind and rain. Squirrels running on the roof. At first she thought Mitch had come home and was down in his den, doing his paperwork. Then with a start she remembered he was in the hospital. She realized the sounds were her kids. Teddy and Marsha were quartered in their old rooms that had never been remodeled from the days they'd lived there as children and teenagers. But they were not asleep. She could hear their voices drift up from downstairs. What were they doing down there?

Cassie dragged herself out of bed, grabbed her old bathrobe, and padded downstairs to see what they were up to. When she came to the door of Mitch's office, she was horrified to see that they had invaded their father's territory. Mitch's computer was on. The locked filing cabinet was open, and her two children were deep in conversation surrounded by his sacred private papers.

8

CASSIE STOOD IN THE HALL FOR SEVERAL MOMENTS trying to figure out what her children were doing in their father's office and why they were talking so loudly. She tried to yawn herself awake, but the yawn wouldn't come because she couldn't open her mouth wide enough to pop her ears. Once again she had the feeling that more than a few inches were missing from her neck and chin area, and a completely separate heart throbbed in her cheeks. Why did they have to wake her up with all their noise? Marsha's and Teddy's voices were so loud, they had disturbed her drugged sleep. Not only that, they had gone into their father's private space without his permission.

As she struggled for a clear thought, Cassie realized that she'd never seen the room from this perspective. Even when Mitch had been home, the door was always closed. He'd kept it locked so not even the cleaning lady who came once a week could get in. The desk where he'd worked was deep and wide. The filing cabinets spread across one wall. Mitch had stored his personal papers here since the early days of their marriage. He'd felt it was safe here. Safe from his secretary, from his managers, his sales force, from whomever it was he didn't trust at the warehouse. He'd been consolidating with other small distributors for years, taking them over, buying them out, trying to get a bigger piece of developing wineries abroad and also the growing American producers' pie.

This was an important point that he'd impressed upon her. American family-owned wineries in forty-three states had grown from 377 to over 1,770, a 430 percent increase since Mitch had started his business in the late 1960s. This was a fact he liked to tell her to let her know how important he'd become in the scheme of things. In the same time frame, while the number of producers had grown, the number of distributors had decreased from 10,900 to just over 2,800. He was very proud of that. His piece of the action was getting bigger. Since laws in the United States prevented direct sales from vintners to consumers and, in many states, the sale of wine in grocery and convenience stores, the distributor's role of choosing which wines to represent, and how to sell them to the consumers through liquor stores and restaurants, was a key one. Distributors like Mitch were desperate to preserve those antibootlegging laws and keep their lock on the market. Cassie was sure much sensitive material was in those filing cabinets.

Now seeing her children eagerly engaged in studying what she herself had never dared to open filled her with a mixture of horror and awe. She hugged her old bathrobe around her excitedly, the hearts in her cheeks and chest beating like mad. Here, finally, was a good reason to find out how much money Mitch had amassed in the bank accounts from which he alone paid the bills, how much life insurance he had, how much there was in the pension fund.

From the way Mitch had talked about his operations, she suspected millions, more than $10 million, maybe as much as twenty, because he was very tight with money. Everyone else they knew had traded up their houses and lives at least once in their twenty-five-year-plus marriages. Mitch was much richer than any of them, but they alone hadn't moved up. He was always telling her he was putting all his earnings into the company, to grow it bigger and bigger. He'd gotten into trading Bordeaux futures. The future was what he was banking on. In the future, they'd be very rich. He'd promised.

Cassie's robe was medium-weight cotton with a raised pattern like turn-of-the-century bedspreads in summer cottages. She'd had it so long, the hem and cuffs were frayed. The bathrobe was comfortable, a little like the ignorance of not knowing how rich they were. She'd always suspected Mitch was hoarding. There was no reason to be so cheap, and now her heart raced with the thrill of acing the control freak and finding out they could afford anything in the world they wanted, after all.

"Hi," she said after a minute. "I must have nodded off for a few minutes. Any word from the hospital?"

"No. Go back to bed, Mom. It's only five o'clock." Marsha spoke sharply.

"I don't want to go back to bed. I'm wide awake. What are you doing?" Cassie was quite pleased that it was they and not she who'd betrayed Mitch's trust and started the digging.

"We wanted to check on the health insurance," Teddy said, avoiding her eyes.

"We have plenty of health insurance, right?" Suddenly she got a chilly feeling. Neither of her children would look at her. "What's the matter? Is something wrong?" she asked.

"Yes, plenty is wrong. Mom, since when did you become a compulsive shopper?" Marsha demanded.

"What? You know I'm not a compulsive shopper." Cassie laughed out loud.

Marsha gave her a scathing look. "Uh-huh. Right. So where's all the stuff you bought?"

"What stuff?" Cassie stared at her.

"Tiffany, $65,000 in March, nearly three months ago? What's *that*? East Hills Jaguar. You leased a $53,000 car back in January? ABC Carpet and Home, $154,000 for curtains and bedding, are you crazy? Where's the Jaguar, Mom? Where are the curtains? What did you think you were *doing*?"

"Marsha, don't be silly. You know I don't have a Jaguar."

"Here's your name on the car insurance. Here's your name on the MasterCard. You have an $89,596 balance due at Bergdorf Goodman, for clothes and shoes and accessories, for God's sake. What about *that*?" Marsha shook a sheaf of receipts at her.

Bergdorf Goodman? Cassie put a hand to her head. She was dreaming. She was having a bad dream. She knew that pill Marsha had given her was a bad thing. Better to wrestle around sitting up all night than to have dreams like this. She shook her head and turned around to go back upstairs, get out of this dream.

"Don't walk away. You have some big explaining to do." Now Marsha was talking to her mother as if Cassie were a teenager arrested on drug charges. "How could you do this to Daddy? To all of us?"

Cassie was agog. "I don't know what you're talking about. I haven't been in Bergdorf Goodman in years. You know I shop in Daffy's. Bergdorf's must be your *father's* bills. You know how he is about his clothes."

"No, Mom. This is not men's department stuff."

Marsha was the one sitting at the computer. Teddy had pulled up a chair. He had a pile of files on his lap. They had a lot of nerve.

"Teddy, you know your father. What is all this about?"

Teddy was still busy avoiding her eyes.

Marsha went on. "And how about *this*? Taxes! You paid the taxes with a *Visa* card at a twenty-one percent annual rate? Are you crazy?"

"I don't pay the taxes at all," Cassie said. "I don't earn the money. I've never paid the taxes. I'm not crazy."

"Four hundred and fifty thousand dollars to the IRS on a *credit card*? It's in your name. This debt. All this debt is in your name. What were you *thinking*?" Marsha lost it altogether and was now shrieking.

Cassie's brain whirled. "We paid that much in taxes?" she said in a hushed tone. "I had no idea he made that much." She did the math quickly. He must make close to a million dollars a year. Wow, she had new respect for her husband. Then she wondered, where was it?

"Mom! You're some kind of psychopath. You're . . . you're . . ." Marsha had no words for what her mother was. She'd jumped to a conclusion just like the EMS people.

But things were not as they seemed. Right between the rib cage, above the belly button and below the heart, Cassie was stabbed with a vicious truth. It hadn't come to her slowly over hours or months or years. It hit her all of a sudden, like a sword striking home. She got it in one, then she wanted to cover it up. "Shhh. Let's not talk about this now," she said. A person could only take so much in one day.

"Mom!" Marsha screamed. "We're talking *now*. What did you do with the *stuff*? You have to send it back."

Okay. Maybe he gave it to the poor, but probably not. Cassie glanced at her darling son. Teddy was wiggling uncomfortably in his chair. "Maybe Teddy knows where the stuff is," she said softly.

"Mom's right. We don't have to talk about this now," Teddy murmured.

"What's the matter with you? Of course we do. The debts are huge. Almost a million dollars."

"Well, Daddy must have it saved somewhere. He's very careful. I'm sure he's got it covered," Cassie said with a quavering voice. They didn't have to do it now.

"Why are you glossing this over?" Marsha was beside herself.

"Sweetheart, when Daddy wakes up, I'm sure he'll explain all of this to us. He always has reasons for everything he does."

"Mom, these are *your* signatures."

Cassie tilted her head to one side. For a second, her vision failed her. Her signatures? How could that be? Red spots appeared before her eyes. They turned to green ones, white ones. Marsha handed over a Tiffany receipt. Cassie took it. She squinted at the slip through puffy eyes and the fireworks of spots, and she saw, clear as mud, her very own signature, Cassandra Sales. All those s's skipping along just the way she always wrote them. Proud and perky as can be. She scratched the side of her face and didn't feel a thing, nothing except the sword between her ribs, ripping her guts out. "Shh," was the only sound she could make. "Shh."

CASSIE PACED BACK AND FORTH IN THE KITCHEN, brooding about her children. It was as if she and they had become instant enemies, standing, armed and dangerous, on opposite sides of the great unbridgeable divide that was the family fortune. Even when Marsha and Teddy finally stopped yelling at her and marched off to their rooms in a huff, it was clear that they were dying to prosecute her for unspeakable crimes that could deprive them of their inheritance. If she'd allowed them to continue, they might well have subjected her to harsh lights and hectoring interrogations all morning until she broke and confessed to spending sprees from which they had been excluded.

But she hadn't allowed them to question her, so they'd been forced to succumb to fitful sleep instead. The truth was, Cassie didn't want to dignify their accusations with a denial. Further, she didn't want to adjust their skewed perceptions just yet. Her heart throbbed in her face, distracting her from the hunger that had been gnawing at her belly for over a week. She was starved, but she wasn't able to eat a thing. She looked worse than ever. Since yesterday, her bruises had started to yellow, giving her both a beaten and jaundiced appearance. Yesterday her face had been a plastic surgery postop horror. Now it was a Noh mask of acrimony and psychic pain.

How could the children she'd loved and cared for, cherished all their lives, believe she'd done something so wrong when they both knew it was their father who was the finagler in the family. It was no secret that he liked to cheat the IRS. He called his ways with money the entrepreneurial spirit. It was an actual philosophy. For every honest and straightforward way of doing something, he came up with three corners to turn and two tangents to follow to get the job done in a much more convoluted manner to hide something. What had never occurred to Cassie was that he might cheat not just the government but real people. He might cheat *her*. It was horrifying.

Mitch had always told her he was saving, saving, saving, but he was also something of a kidder, kidder, kidder. And now she could easily see that, for all she knew, he'd been spending all along. He might already have purchased their retirement home in Boca Raton and furnished it from ABC just for her. And he'd used her signature for tax reasons, just like he'd lived way below his means for tax reasons. This explanation of house buying in secret was not entirely beyond the realm of possibility, but she knew that's not what he'd done.

Outside, the sun rose on Cassie's perfect garden. Inside, her secure home shifted under her feet. A sudden flash of red betrayed the flight of a cardinal across the lawn. Unaware of her standing motionless for a moment at the kitchen window, the bird aimed for the feeder near the back door. It landed and began to pick at the seeds, and Cassie trembled in awe at the spectacular beauty and ordinariness of the new day. As the light fused the sky and filtered through the leaves of the oaks dappling the grass, she struggled for balance. She didn't want her husband to die, but she didn't want him to be a cheat and a liar, either. And she didn't want to be another one of those people who jumped to a conclusion without real facts in front of her.

She knew he was reckless, but it was a leap to think he would actually *hurt* her. Still, someone was driving around a new Jaguar charged in her name when she'd had her Volvo for so long, it was old enough to go to college. That hurt. She made a sudden angry movement, and the cardinal darted away. Disappointed, she turned to the clock and was disappointed again. She wanted it to be nine, but it was still only six-thirty, too early to call anyone, to take any action, to do anything at all.

Time was passing so slowly, she thought she'd go crazy. She longed to drink a quart of vodka, or at least to smoke a cigarette to punctuate her frustration and pass the time. The last cigarette she'd smoked was in 1970. Same with the vodka. Mitch sold fine wines but didn't like seeing her drink in his presence. He had a philosophy about that, too. He didn't want her pilfering, wasting the product, and becoming a drunk. He despised all drunks except himself. He had a very high opinion of himself.

She paced back and forth. What to do? What to do? Her surgeon had decreed that she must not put her glasses on while the stitches remained around her ears. She must not worry or think angry thoughts. She was not supposed to drive the car. She was supposed to gobble down tranquilizers and painkillers to dream happy dreams for a lovely, unscarred beautiful young face. But how could she do that now? She wanted to put on her glasses and get into those files of Mitch's to discover the truth about the house in Boca Raton that he had not bought just for her. She wanted to drive to the hospital on her own. She didn't care if Mitch was in a coma. She had to talk to him.

But old habits die hard. She couldn't help following orders. Afraid of infection, she didn't put on her glasses. Afraid of driving into a wall, she didn't take out the car. While she waited for Marsha to wake up and chauffeur her, she foraged in the refrigerator, in the freezer. Now she was ready to eat, but that girl had not provided any food for her. There was not a damn thing in the house to eat. No coffee cake, no sticky buns, no bagels, no croissants. Nothing gooey, nothing sweet. Nothing! Marsha had gone off food and wouldn't let anybody else eat. Cassie sipped a little orange juice, but not through a straw. She was starving.

Around seven, after waiting around for hours, she wandered into Mitch's den, where Teddy and Marsha had left things a big mess. So thoughtless of them. The computer screen had colorful fish on it that swam back and forth as the sound of water gurgled out of the speakers. She punched a button and a menu came up. She couldn't exactly see it, but she knew what was on it. Office something. Windows something. AOL something. Quicken something. She bet their whole life was in that computer, and she'd never dared to look in it. Never. Even the simplest bills had waited until Mitch had gotten around to printing them out.

She'd always been a little phobic about the computer, and she'd always accepted the deal. She had a husband who was fussy about privacy.

The house had been her territory. Finance had been Mitch's territory. Now she was angry that Teddy and Marsha had been the first invaders of it, had thought they had discovered some terrible secret about her and were eager to believe it. She had no idea how many hours they'd been looking into his files, or how much they thought they'd learned. She shut off the computer and went upstairs to take a bath and brood some more. She did this for quite a while.

At nine A.M. she dressed in a pair of pants that were now too loose and a blazer she'd grown out of years ago that fit her again. She was eager to get to the hospital. She had a thousand things to do, a sick husband to visit, doctors and lawyers to consult. Enough brooding, she now had to take charge of her life. It occurred to her that she didn't want Marsha and Teddy in the files again, so she went back downstairs and locked the den, then slipped the key into her pocket. She was fully alert now. She took the stairs two at a time and marched into Marsha's room without knocking.

Marsha's room was the timeless fantasy of sweet femininity. The wallpaper was pink with white stripes. The printed chintz on the bedspread and chairs was cheerful sprigs of pink rosebuds. The curtains were frilly dotted swiss. The single bed had a canopy that dated from Marsha's childhood, when her daddy had been hopeful that with the right incentives she'd snap out of her prepubescent doldrums and turn into an Ivy League preppy. This room, too, was a total mess. The navy skirt and baby blue twinset (that Cassie now saw was cashmere) were twisted up on the floor as if Marsha had wrestled out of them. The pile of clothes she'd worn all week was heaped on the ruffled chair. More cashmere. Partially flung over it were two towels that still looked wet. The room smelled intensely floral, as if a bottle of expensive perfume had been spilled in there.

Marsha was sleeping with the bedspread over her head. Only a very little of her hair showed at the top. Cassie approached the bed cautiously. Then, feeling like the wicked witch of the West, she suddenly pulled the covers all the way down to the foot of the bed. She was startled to see that Marsha was sleeping in one of her father's undershirts and a pair of his boxer shorts. The twenty-five-year-old was hugging a small Curious George that her daddy had given her when she was about four. Marsha's identification with her father was clear. This hurt Cassie even more.

"Time to go see Daddy," she said.

"Huh?" Marsha didn't move.

"It's time to get up, Marsha, honey. We have to go visit Daddy."

"What time is it?" Marsha mumbled into the monkey's head.

"It's late. It's nine-thirty."

"Nine-thirty!" Marsha patted the area around her, searching for the covers. When she couldn't find them, she gave up and curled around her pillow.

"Marsha, get up." Cassie stamped her foot.

"I just went to sleep," she grumbled.

"It's not my fault you stayed up all night."

"What's the rush? Has there been a change?"

"I want to be with him. I want to see him," Cassie said. Did she ever.

"Fine, just ten minutes." Marsha turned over and stuck her thumb in her mouth.

Cassie circled the bed to talk to her on the other side and saw that Marsha was refusing to open her eyes. "Marsha, sweetheart. I want to go *now*."

"It's too early. They won't let you in."

"How do you know?"

"Tom told me. We're meeting him at eleven-thirty."

"Really. When was that arrangement made? I don't know anything about that," she said.

Marsha rolled over on her back and spoke with her eyes closed. "Mom, go take a nap. Everything is being taken care of. You don't have to do a thing."

"What?" Cassie was very alert now.

"Teddy and I have talked about it. I've talked with Tom, daddy's neurologist. We're on top of everything. You just concentrate on *healing* that new face of yours." Still with her eyes glued shut against the day, Marsha spoke in a tone guaranteed to insult a retard. It hit Cassie like a jolt from the electric chair. Her yellow hair practically stood on end with shock. Her children were excluding her from her own tragedy.

"How dare you talk to me like that! Get up right now," she cried.

"Mom, don't overreact. We know what we're doing." Marsha turned over again.

"You think I don't know what I'm doing! Get up!" Cassie marched around the bed and grabbed the pillow from Marsha's arms. This violent action opened Marsha's eyes.

"What's the matter with you?" she said irritably.

"*I'm* the mother here. *I'm* the wife. You don't make any decisions for your daddy or me, you understand that?" Cassie hopped up and down on one foot. Her energy had returned with betrayal. This was her and Mitch's life, not their children's.

"Look at you." Marsha sat up and rubbed her eyes as if she couldn't believe it. "You look bad and you're acting crazy, Mom. You're not up to this."

"Don't you dare talk to me like this." Cassie couldn't stop hopping.

"Well, look at you. You're out of control. You're not qualified."

"I'll show you out of control, Marsha Sales. Don't think you can social work me." Cassie turned her head and caught sight of herself in Marsha's full-length mirror. The Noh mask of wrath with the bloodshot eyes and porcupine stitches around her ears animated by the frenzied dance stopped her mid-sentence. She did look crazy. What was happening to her? What was happening to all of them? The heat left her. She sat down abruptly on the bed. Her face looked the same, but when she spoke, her voice was calm. "Your father and I love you very much, Marsha," she began.

"But . . . ," Marsha said bitterly, clearly expecting the usual reservations from her mother.

"*But* even though Daddy is in intensive care, I am still The Mother. We can talk about certain things as a family, but I am in charge here. From now on, I will be the one to look after the financial situation. Let's face it. This is my problem, not yours."

"*Mom*, with your record, I don't think that's a good idea," Marsha muttered sarcastically.

"I wouldn't jump to that conclusion so fast, young lady," Cassie retorted through her teeth.

"Okay, what am I missing?" Marsha raked her fingers through her hair. "Crazy Mom, or what?"

Cassie inhaled sharply, stung by her daughter's bitterness. She'd been nothing but the most loving mother, had thought of nothing but her daughter's welfare every single day of her life. She'd had almost no pleasures of her own—none, in fact, that were not connected with doing good for the family. What did Marsha have to be so bitter about?

"What are you missing? You're missing everything. What do you know about me? What do you know about anything but yourself and your own selfish feelings."

"You're obviously projecting," Marsha said haughtily. "Just tell the truth, I can take it."

"You're very hurtful, Marsha." Cassie shook her head. Where had she gone wrong with this girl?

"Look who's talking."

"You're talking about money, is that it? Money? That's ridiculous. What if I did spend money on myself—I'm not saying I did, but if I had, would it be so *terrible*?" The words were out of her mouth before she could stop herself.

"Yes," Marsha said. "Yes, Mom, it would."

"I've given my whole life for you, for all of you. You got your camps and your trips to Europe and your college and your graduate school . . ." Outraged, Cassie ticked the items off on her fingers. She'd never even been to a day spa. Why were they arguing about money?

"What are you two yelling about?" Teddy stumbled into the room, rubbing his eyes.

"Mom's gone psycho," Marsha told him.

"And you, Teddy. *Every* advantage. Special schools, special tutors. College enrichment programs." Cassie pointed an angry finger at him. "Vineyards in Italy. Vineyards in France . . ."

"Teddy did get everything. He was Daddy's boy," Marsha confirmed, nodding at him.

"No, I didn't. *You* got everything," Teddy jumped in, his rage topping everyone's.

Marsha made a disgusted noise. "What?"

"You got the nervous breakdowns. You got the attention," Teddy spit out.

"And what did I get?" Cassie demanded. "Tell me, what did I get!"

They both looked at her, then turned to each other and cracked up.

"You got a face-lift," they said in unison.

I hate them, Cassie thought. She was amazed at herself. I hate my own children.

10

CASSIE WAS SO INCENSED by the behavior of her children that she went back to her bathroom and put some concealer on her face. Then she tied a scarf around her head à la Jackie Kennedy. She was furious that her children thought she was vain and a spendthrift. She wasn't vain. How could they think she was vain just because she'd gotten a face-lift? She was going to show them. And she was going to show Mitch. How dare he make her look like the bad guy? She was the good guy. She'd always been the good guy, staying home and taking care of them all. She marched downstairs and got into the car. She sat there for a few minutes muttering to herself. When the children didn't show up, she honked the horn.

After what felt like an hour and a half Marsha came into the garage looking like a movie star in her size zero slacks, high heels, and (now) pink cashmere twinset with little embroidered flowers traveling up and down the cardigan's placket. She pushed the button on the garage door, swinging it open and blinding Cassie with the morning light. Where did all that cashmere come from? Saks, Bergdorf's, Neiman's? The girl's hair appeared to have been carefully styled by Frederic Fekkai in the last five minutes, and huge sunglasses covered half her face, enhancing rather than disguising her very good looks.

"What's the big hurry?" Marsha complained, taking the glasses off and frowning at her mother as she rattled the car keys.

"Where's Teddy?" Cassie demanded, feeling hurt for so many reasons, she thought her heart would explode just like Mitch's brain.

"He's having breakfast. He'll meet us there."

Cassie shook her head. "I don't want him in Daddy's den."

"Well, you locked the door. How's he going to get in?"

So they'd checked. It was war. Cassie jumped out of the car and marched back into the house. Teddy was sitting at the kitchen table wearing khakis and one of his father's expensive Italian knit shirts. He was reading the sports section of the newspaper, eating a bowl of his father's favorite cereal, the one holdout from his childhood—Frosted Flakes, with the tiger on the box. "Hi, Mom," he said without looking up.

"Teddy, what are you up to?" Cassie demanded.

"I'm eating breakfast."

"I don't want you in Daddy's files."

"No problem. I don't want to know."

"What do you mean you don't want to know?"

"Whatever," he said, taking a huge bite, crunching loudly, swallowing, taking another, as if actually trying to infuriate her further.

Cassie hesitated in the doorway. Her tone softened, though her heart remained stone. "What does 'whatever' mean?"

"Marsha's the one who wants to know. I told *her* whatever, too."

"Teddy, what are you talking about?"

Teddy didn't look up from the page. "Nothing."

Something about the way he said "nothing" alarmed her. Teddy had been the one with the sweetest disposition in the family. Everybody else walked all over him. It occurred to her that with the good business sense inherited from his father, maybe *Teddy* was the finagler. It had to be one of the three of them. Would Mitch protect his children if they went crazy with the spending? Marsha? Never. But his boy Teddy . . . ? She considered it. Teddy was his father's favorite. Cassie couldn't see Teddy at Bergdorf's, though. He probably didn't know where it was. Not Teddy. "Well, are you coming?" she asked finally.

"If I have to," he muttered.

From the garage, Marsha called out, "For God's sake, what are you *doing* in there?"

"Yes, you have to, Teddy. Daddy wants to see you," Cassie told him.

"Sure he does," Teddy mumbled, lifting the bowl to drink the milk.

Cassie closed the kitchen door quietly, headed back into the garage, got into the Mercedes, and closed that door quietly, too. Something was up between those kids.

Marsha was busy powdering her nose in the mirror. "I don't know what you're so worried about. Teddy got all of three hundred on his math SATs. You don't actually think he could read a bank statement, do you?"

"Marsha, what's going on?" Cassie asked.

"Nothing." Marsha started the engine and pulled out.

Again that "nothing."

"Teddy is no dummy," Cassie defended her son.

"Yes, he is," Marsha said.

Agitated by the sibling rivalry and all the things that she didn't know about the doings of her own family, Cassie grabbed Marsha's sunglasses off the dashboard. Carefully, she put them over the scarf tied around her head so they wouldn't come in contact with those awful stitches that were pulling her face so tight, she couldn't breathe at all. She felt as if she were choking to death from those stitches, and they itched like hell. If she could rip them right out of her head and go back to her old life, she would do it.

How cruel it was for Marsha to wave those Tiffany receipts with her signature on them at her and to look so young and great when her father was in the hospital and her mother was falling apart. Cassie was so hurt, she didn't say a single word all the way to the hospital. In the parking lot, she switched her attention to Mitch so sick in intensive care and composed herself for him. She went into the hospital lobby, determined to become the family hero. She'd bring Mitch back from the dead. He'd be so grateful for her help and support that his character would change completely. He'd give her his money to manage, and they'd all live happily ever after. With this strategy all planned out, she marched down the glass corridor into the wing that housed the Neurological Intensive Care unit.

"How is Mitchell Sales?" she asked the tough-looking nurse guarding the nine glass rooms reserved for head traumas.

"He's doing just fine," Nurse Helen Gurnsey said smoothly without looking at her. "His doctor has been on rounds already. Don't stay too long, honey. We have a five-minute rule here."

Five minutes! Cassie's breath caught. What could she accomplish in five minutes?

"You okay, honey?" Now the nurse looked up at her with just a hint of concern.

"Yes, fine," Cassie said. She didn't want any more sympathy for the car crash she hadn't had.

Two picture-windowed rooms down, she slipped into Mitch's cubicle, which was packed with expensive computerized monitoring devices and the spiderweb of plastic tubes that kept those oh-so-important fluids moving from plastic bags to Mitch's inert body and out of his body into more plastic bags. They still looked obscene. The respirator pumped air into his lungs, and the sound was enough to unnerve anyone. "Doing just fine" seemed to mean unchanged. The space was still too cramped to accommodate a visitor's chair, so Cassie stood by the bed and looked at the pathetic creature her husband had become.

"Mitch?" she whispered. "Can you hear me?" She saw him lying there and was actually, truly touched by his vulnerability. It was the first she'd ever seen in him. In recent years, with his great success, he had developed a slightly sarcastic, even sneering way about him that always made her nervous in his presence. Whenever he came in the door, she could feel her body begin its dance of anticipatory agitation. It was as if he came home looking for something wrong, which made him find something wrong. It was always some omission on her part that she could never guess in advance. Right now there was nothing critical about him except his condition.

Like yesterday, his eyes were half open. The young Dr. Wellfleet had told her that if the pupils were enlarged, maybe a blood vessel had exploded. Or something. Now that Mitch was stabilized, though, Mark Cohen, whom Cassie trusted, seemed to be afraid that more clots would form and move around—to his brain, his heart, his lungs. Maybe a whole freight train of them. Cassie thought of those blood clots traveling through Mitch's arteries that had to be badly clogged with foie gras and hollandaise. Maybe they wouldn't make it through.

As she studied him, immobilized and helpless, a quartet of thoughts played in counterpoint in her mind: IhatethismanIlovethismanIhopehelivesIhopehedies. And then the fugue played more slowly. What will I do without him? Where will I go? Who will I be with? How can I manage my children, who think I'm the enemy? Oh God, help me please!

Yesterday she'd been so stunned by Mitch's great fall that she hadn't been able to listen to all the things Mark had to say about those pupils and clots and vessels. But now she leaned over to see for herself what state Mitch's pupils were in. His eyes were not open wide enough for her to get a good look. She didn't want to pry them open with that picture window exposing them so clearly to view from anyone passing in the hall, so she gave him a tight little smile.

"Honey, it's Cassie. The nurse says you're doing just fine," she said brightly, figuring that she'd just used up about four of her five minutes. Those fake signatures of hers burned in her gut and hampered her breathing. The I-hate-this-man theme came up loudly, drowning out the others.

"Mitch, honey. I don't have a charge account at Tiffany's, or Bergdorf Goodman. I don't have a Chase MasterCard. In fact, I don't have a single account with only my name on it. There's been some kind of mixup." She said this very sweetly. He was in intensive care, after all.

His eyes remained at half-mast.

"You're doing fine," she said stoically. "Can you hear me? We have a few things to talk about."

Fugue: Why would he talk now if he never has before?

"Sweetheart, if you can hear me, squeeze my hand. We're going to get you out of this. Is it Marsha? She's certainly had her behaviors over the years. But steal in my name? Mitch, tell me who it is. Marsha, or Teddy? Teddy wouldn't . . . would he?"

She stroked his left hand with two fingers, trying to feel some tenderness for a man who'd kept a big secret like this. Maybe this was the reason he'd been so hard on Marsha. Cassie's heart beat like a jungle drum. But why would he cover up for her to her own mother? Mitch's nails were manicured. Hers were not. She'd never been that interested. But his hand was bloated. His face was empty, slack. His color was scary. The machine breathed noisily. Tentatively, she curled his fingers around hers. "Squeeze my fingers if you can hear me," she said. "Come on, honey. Help me out."

Nothing.

"Mitch, you're going to be okay. I know you are. We have to establish some kind of communication here. I want you to know I'm here for you all the way. I can't stay with you. They won't let me. But I'm with you. Show me you know I'm with you."

Nothing.

Tears filled her eyes because he was so out of it. She told herself that people sicker than this survived every day. They had total recoveries all the time. The miracle of modern medicine. Total.

Cassie blundered on. "Honey, can you wink? How about this. Wink once if you can hear me, and twice if you can't."

He didn't wink. He didn't move. Nothing. Maybe a little gurgle. But then again maybe not. His torso was thick. His stomach protruded even when he was lying down. He'd gotten so fat. He had a forest of black hair on his bare arms. A tube in one nostril drew out his stomach's gastric fluids. A tube in his other nostril suctioned mucus from his respiratory system. This was disgusting to observe. Cassie tried to assign some tenderness to the lump that was her husband. She searched her memory for loving moments when they'd been happy together, when he'd held her hand or kissed her or told her she was a good woman, after all. But those memories were curiously absent in recent history. She scoured her mind for them frantically the way she scoured for her wallet throughout the house when she knew it was mislaid but present there somewhere. She was sure the absence of recent happy memories was due to her present frame of mind and that down the road when she returned to look for them, they would be there in plenty.

Instead, the memories to which she had easy access were old scars, the two occasions she returned home from the hospital after giving birth to their two children when Mitch had looked at her with a perfectly straight face and asked her what she planned to serve him for lunch. She remembered his looks of disdain at gifts she gave him that weren't good enough, and the way he abruptly changed the subject when she asked where he'd been and what he'd done when they were apart. Recent inflicted injuries that had seemed like thoughtless slights, but not intentional hurts. She thought he'd become insensitive with success, not mean.

"Mitch, I know you're not in a coma. This is what you always do," she said, getting impatient now. The least he could do was wink. Other stroke victims could wink.

Whoosh, whoosh. Click, click. Not Mitch. He wasn't even going to try. He was holding out as usual. She tried another tack.

"Mitch, the kids were going through your files. Teddy says you're going to be audited. If you don't wake up, I'm going to have to deal with this myself." There, it was out. Guiltily, she sneaked a look out the window to see if anyone was watching. She was talking to him harshly, raising forbidden subjects. He was supposed to take it easy. He was supposed to feel it was safe to come back into the world.

A voice came up, loud and urgent. "Code, room six." Doctors and nurses rushed out. Lots of noise and urgency. Everyone converged on the room across the hall. After several intense minutes, the curtain was drawn and it was over. The second one in two days. Cassie was shocked. This was how they died.

"Oh God. Mitch, don't leave me." The words came out a cry from the heart if ever there was one. She dropped her chin to her chest and prayed. Save this man. Oh God, save him.

11

THE CODE YESTERDAY IN THE HOSPITAL had been for a toddler who'd fallen off his swing five days ago. Compared with the tragedy of three dead children in two days, Cassie's problems with her own children seemed like nothing, a pseudo problem. What were they really doing that so annoyed her? Teddy had come home and appropriated his father's best sports shirts, his most colorful socks and boxer shorts from his father's closet as if he were already gone. And he was eating all his father's favorite foods from the kitchen shelves.

Teddy also couldn't stop humming George Michael's song "Freedom." On Saturday at the hospital he had spent all his time trying to locate and hang out with his surprising choice, Lorraine, a big-boned, overweight operating room nurse who wore polyester and had a Long Island accent. The Sales family did not have strong New York accents.

On the positive side, Teddy's having to locate this girl in the very large hospital required some social skills. He was too shy to call her on the phone, so his strategy had been to hang around in hopes of running into her. On Saturday night, after Lorraine finished up assisting the emergency repair of a ruptured spleen, Teddy ran into her and asked her out for pizza.

Cassie heard him return home just after midnight. On Sunday morning, he ducked out at ten-thirty, earlier than he'd ever gotten up in his life. He didn't arrive at the hospital to visit his father until three in the afternoon. By then she was steaming.

"Teddy, where were you?" she asked when he found her with all the other visitors in the head trauma lounge.

"I took Lorraine out to brunch," he said, grinning happily despite the family tragedy.

"Where?" Marsha asked curiously.

"International House of Pancakes."

She snorted with contempt at his sudden sinking to the lowest possible food denominator.

"Shut up. How's Daddy?"

"The same," Cassie told him, thinking that her son looked happy. After all the praying she'd done for her wonderful, terribly shy boy to meet a lovely girl, Lorraine was the thanks she got.

And Marsha! Well, Marsha was under some kind of constant advisory alert with Dr. Thomas *Wellfleet*—thirty-two, unmarried, and definitely on the prowl. They had called each other on the phone. They had met for a consultation in the hospital. Afterward, they had sipped a not very good Merlot and talked on Saturday evening about the case in a very pleasant restaurant on the Miracle Mile, the posh shopping mall near their house. While their father was in intensive care, her two children were having *fun*. They were going out, were dating. At home, they were talking together, whispering. They became instantly quiet whenever she walked into the room. In just one weekend they had become allies. Clearly, they were hatching some plot to take over her life. Cassie dreamed that they were four again and swept away in a giant flood that covered the whole North Shore of Long Island, sparing absolutely no one but her.

During the many hours that Cassie waited in the visitors' lounge expecting Mitch to come out of his coma and return to normal any second, dozens of other patients' relatives schooled in and out, eating, drinking, telling one another their stories, and visiting their stricken family members who were usually too sick to recognize them.

Dr. Mark Cohen came to see Mitch several times, and each time he stayed for a few minutes to comfort Cassie. He'd sit down next to her on one of the leatherette sofas for two and talk about the past, about the changes in their lives since they'd known each other. Having children, raising them, getting busier and busier. Mitch's phenomenal success, and his own lesser one. Each time Mark settled on the sofa, he leaned close to her and examined her face carefully with caressing fingers. It never seemed to bother him that other visitors were around or the TV set was on. He must be used to them, Cassie thought.

After the first time he saw her on Friday, he arranged for a nurse to bring gel packs for her face every few hours. After that he had an investment in her convalescence and came to check on the results. He must have wanted a good result with at least one person in the family. On Sunday morning Mark took her for a short walk. On Sunday afternoon he took her for coffee in the hospital cafeteria. She had hers with hazelnut creamer and toyed with the spoon. She wondered how much he knew about her husband and family that she didn't know. Mitch had been a *phenomenal* success?

"Thanks for the gel packs," she began.

"Oh, forget it. It's nothing. You're looking much better today. Are you using those creams I suggested?"

"Yes, Marsha got them for me." She got the feeling that Mark, like Mitch, was avoiding all the meaningful subjects.

"Your doctor probably didn't tell you to, but just between you and me, it doesn't hurt at this point to start softening up the stitches. When are they coming out?" he asked, sticking to her face.

"I'm not sure. Maybe Thursday."

"You're looking very good, really." Then he gave her a frankly admiring nod that made her think he'd lost his mind.

"Thanks, Mark, tell me about Mitch."

"Honey, he's holding his own. That's all I can say for now. Have you checked into his arrangements for a catastrophic event?"

Cassie stirred her coffee. "I don't want to go into the files just yet."

Mark gave her an incredulous look. "That's not like you, Cassie. You've always been a practical girl. Don't you want to know what his wishes are should his body fail him?"

"I don't know what you mean."

"He's on a respirator," he said gently.

Cassie blinked. Of course she knew that.

"Does Mitch have a living will? I'm not sure he would want extraordinary measures to keep him alive in this condition forever."

"Forever?" Cassie blinked again.

"Look, maybe I'm speaking out of turn. But we're old friends, Cassie. I don't want to hide anything from you."

"Forever? He could live like this forever?"

"Well, not forever, but for a long time. People can hang on for years."

"Years? Like this?" Cassie knew Mark intended to be kind, but his raising such a possibility felt somehow like an assault. She started shredding her paper napkin. Just two days seemed an eternity.

"I told you, he made it through the first forty-eight hours, but that's about it." He shrugged. "We'll have a better picture in the next few days, and we have to be hopeful, of course. But . . ."

"I'm very hopeful," Cassie said. Today was only Sunday. Hard to believe.

"But Cassie, you have to be your practical self, too. You need to look into the arrangements he's made for a major event like this. I'm assuming you've checked and made sure Mitch has provisions in his health insurance for all the long-term care he's going to need when he comes out of intensive care."

Cassie didn't want to tell her doctor and old friend that her kids were plotting against her, and she wanted them to leave the house before she started investigating those arrangements.

"What are the odds he'll recover?" she asked again. He'd told her already, but she couldn't take it in. She just couldn't absorb the alternatives: death or a partial recovery.

"Oh, I don't want to go there, Cassie. A lot of people do very well." Mark was distracted by a dapper man in a sports jacket at the coffee machines far away. He waved.

"But you don't think Mitch will do very well, do you?" she pressed. "You told me that yesterday."

"They can surprise you," he said, vague again.

"I'll say," she murmured. She'd had about as many surprises as she could take. As far as she was concerned, Mitch should just make up his mind: Walk into that heavenly light, or return to the chaos of life. Right now, if she were in his situation, she wasn't sure which she would choose herself.

She sighed, and Mark refocused on her. His round face was pink and healthy. He was overweight, but had a nice smile. He smelled of soap and fruity cologne. He was a man who liked women. She could feel it in his touch as he patted her hand. Mark, who'd always been so brisk and professional, was acting like a real friend. It made her feel important for a moment, and she realized that she'd forgotten what a man's comfort felt like. She enjoyed the warmth of his hand as it rested on top of hers. Her heart beat a little faster. A real friend.

Mark shifted a little in his chair, giving her a knowing smile that she felt all the way down to the tips of her toes. What was this? She withdrew her hand, ostensibly to adjust the scarf on her head. "How's Sondra?" she asked suddenly.

"Still very short. She's concerned about Mitch, of course, and sends her best," he replied, wry for a second, then casual again with the doctor voice she knew so well.

"It was nice of her to call." Cassie kept adjusting her scarf.

"Well, she's a very nice woman," he said without conviction. "Cassie, has anyone else called, been to visit? Any of your friends? You need a lot of support right now. Family and friends help."

"Oh, I totally agree." Cassie nodded. If there was one thing she didn't want, it was support. Mitch would hate having people know, having people see him like this, gossip about and pity him. She couldn't talk to anyone until things were more settled. It was a family thing. She had to handle it herself. And there was the little thing of her face-lift.

"Mark, what is this long-term health care you're asking me about? Why is it so important?" she asked. She just didn't get it.

"Oh, you know. When Mitch comes out of this, he may need to go to another facility for aftercare. We don't keep patients here long-term."

"Another hospital?" she said faintly.

"For rehabilitation, therapy. It can take a long time. But let's not talk about that now." He reached out and squeezed her hand one last time, then ended the conversation. "Well, I'll see you tomorrow, okay? Just before noon is when I make my rounds during the week. But I'm in constant touch with the staff here. And you can call me on my cell anytime, night or day. You keep that pretty chin of yours up, okay?" He chucked her under the chin.

"Okay," Cassie replied gamely. "Absolutely." She tried to smile bravely as he left the cafeteria. She was still trying to figure out what had happened. Had he been coming on to her? Had she turned him off? The fleeting electricity in his smile and the delicate touch of his fingers lingered for a while in her mind after he was gone. She was unnerved by the heat she'd felt and the undercurrents, the innuendo of the conversation. She was concerned, but after a while she concluded that nothing bad had happened. Mark was a friend. She'd been starving for the personal touch and had gotten it, that was all. Still, she couldn't drink her coffee, even with its pleasant hazelnut-flavored creamer.

Sunday evening, ten days after Cassie's surgery and two days after Mitch's stroke, Marsha and Teddy further trashed their rooms in preparation for their return to their studio apartments in Manhattan. Just before they left, Marsha came into the kitchen, where Cassie was still on her feet, dazedly trying to find things to do.

"Mom, you okay?"

"Sure, I am," Cassie told her. "Fine."

"I've washed my sheets and towels. The towels are in the dryer now. Teddy was only here for two nights. I figure his sheets are good for a few more days. When is Rosa coming back?"

Rosa was the cleaning lady they'd had for the last fifteen years. She'd been on vacation in Peru for three weeks.

"Soon. I don't know."

"You should get someone else. And you don't have to sit at the hospital all day tomorrow. Why don't you rest for a few days. It wouldn't hurt."

"I want to be there when he wakes up," Cassie said.

"I hate to leave you like this, Mom." Marsha drew Cassie over to the kitchen table and sat her down. She looked sad as she patted her mother's hand. "Are you okay?"

It reminded Cassie of Mark's pats. She thought she must look pretty pathetic to engender this kind of reaction from both of them.

"You're a nice girl, Marsha," she murmured, her eyes puddling as she realized for the second time that day how unused to touch she'd become. "Marsha, about those receipts—"

"Oh, Mom, let's not talk about that now," Marsha cut her off quickly.

"I didn't sign them," Cassie told her. "I want you to know that."

"I know that, Mom." Marsha gave her another sympathetic pat.

"You do?"

"Yes. I'm really sorry." Marsha hung her head. "I shouldn't have jumped on you like that."

"Marsha, why did you do it? We would have taken care of you, gotten you therapy. Why—?"

"Mom!" Marsha's tone changed into a whine. "You don't think it was me? Are you crazy? I wouldn't do anything like that. How could you think it was me?" she cried.

"Teddy?" Cassie was astounded. "Was it Teddy?"

"No, Mom. Not Teddy, either."

Cassie tried to frown with her new forehead. "Daddy? Daddy? Your father did this on purpose, didn't he?"

"We'll talk about it tomorrow."

This was hard to swallow. Cassie swallowed it. "Your father opened credit card accounts in my name? Signed my name? Bought a Jaguar?" She was really annoyed about that Jaguar. "Who has it?"

Marsha shook her head, didn't want to say.

Teddy came in. "What are you two talking about?" he asked suspiciously.

"Teddy, Daddy took out credit cards in my name? Bought all that stuff? A car? Where is it all?"

Teddy put his arm around her shoulders. Another one. Gave her a pat.

"Why?" She looked from one to the other.

"Must be some kind of a tax thing," Teddy said vaguely. Suddenly he found his shoes very interesting. Very interesting indeed.

"What kind of tax thing, Teddy?"

"Mom, Teddy and I will talk to you about these money things some other time. We'll get a tax lawyer and, I don't know, we'll work it out." Marsha gave Teddy an angry look.

"I'll get a lawyer," Cassie said. It was her life. She felt forlorn. "When are you coming back?"

"Maybe tomorrow night. Maybe Tuesday. Mom, Edith is coming over to be with you tomorrow. Are you okay for tonight?"

Cassie knew it was useless to question them further. She told them she was just fine. But where was that Jaguar? She kept focusing on the car because hers was such an old one.

12

BEFORE CASSIE WENT INTO HER HUSBAND'S OFFICE for the first time, she called the hospital to see if there had been any change in his condition. It was half past ten on Sunday night, and she wanted to give him one more chance at returning to his life before she entered his world and took command of it. She was frightened by the responsibility of having to do it, terrified of what she might find. Money had never been her thing. She didn't know what to do about it, how to handle it. She'd never had any of her own. She'd been told to trust, and so she'd trusted.

Her stomach felt like a volcano, erupting intermittently in hot, dizzying waves of anxiety. It bubbled up again after the kids left. Her life had become a mystery she had to crack. How could she have let the big questions slide? She and Mitch used to be happy. They used to have fun. Why hadn't she confronted him more directly when the fun stopped? Even now she still couldn't help feeling that it wasn't right for her to search for the health insurance, the will, the simplest things about their lives with which she should already be thoroughly familiar.

On the phone, the night nurse told her Mitch was still holding his own. Those words pretty much summed up their marriage. After Cassie hung up, she put Mark's special cream on her stitches, wound sterile gauze around her glasses, and carefully eased them on. Then she went into Mitch's office and opened his file drawers one by one.

What she found in them hit her like an atom bomb. First thing:

Mitch had a bank account at the Bank of the Cayman Islands with a May balance that topped a million and a half dollars. The statement reassured her that he'd told her the truth when he'd said she never had to worry about money. On the other hand, there was a balance of less than two thousand in their joint Chase bank account. She didn't know what day he deposited money for household expenses, or how much it was, but she didn't worry about it. She could get money easily; he owned the company.

He had a balance of $523,000 in his pension fund. It didn't seem like much after a quarter century of harping on her to save for it. A little note of alarm buzzed in the back of her head about the money he'd stashed outside the country. What was that about? On the other hand, the life insurance policy she found seemed adequate. The various pieces of it added up to a cool $3 million. If he died, she'd be a wealthy woman, better off than she was now. However, the date on the policy was old and the premium bills were not in the house, which led her to believe he might have a newer and bigger one whose premiums he paid from the office. At the moment everything they had was in his name, and she couldn't put her hands on a nickel. Their affairs were as clear as mud. She was sure somewhere there was more than this.

She opened the filing cabinet and plunged into the accounts in Mitch's name for which she had her own card. There was nothing surprising there. The picture of their joint life jibed pretty well with her knowledge of it. She herself used the family resources sparingly, almost ascetically, always mindful of Mitch's constant admonitions about sensible spending. And Mitch in turn faithfully, and fully, paid off all the expenses of the house and all the bills that she incurred every month. Virtually none of his personal expenses appeared on these charges. The house had a small mortgage, but their life, considering Mitch's income, was modest indeed.

The first discrepancy came out with the spending habits of the fictitious Cassandra Sales. Cassie discovered that her fictitious self had two of her own American Express cards, as well as accounts at Tiffany's, ABC Carpet and Home, Bergdorf Goodman, Saks Fifth Avenue, Bloomingdale's, Neiman Marcus, Fancy Cleaners, a Chase Platinum MasterCard, several gold airline MasterCards, and two Visa Platinum Card accounts.

Mitch kept a separate file for each one right here under her very nose. This was both gross stupidity and colossal nerve on his part. Clearly he'd understood her character well, and she'd had not the slightest inkling of his.

A whole life was documented in the receipts: Prada dress, aubergine, $1,500. Armani suit, gray, $3,400. Lavender silk tank, $850. Armani dress and coat, mauve wool, $4,500. Chanel silk scarf, $350. Bergdorf Shoe Department: mauve suede sling backs, gray leather pumps, $575; black crocodile loafers, $1,250. Escada red leather coat, $3,900. Escada red leather bag, $850. Escada red leather shoes, $495. Bliss Spa: La Mer face products, $890. Microbrasion treatments, $150 times ten. Salon de Daniel: peach satin robe and gown, $1,200. La Perla uplift bra, $125. Matching panties, $65. Hermès handbag, $8,600. Louis Vuitton luggage, $10,000. It went on and on.

Cassie was stunned, could hardly absorb what it all meant. It took her until past one A.M. to look through the purchases of just the first five months of this year. She couldn't believe it. *Couldn't believe it!* Eighteen thousand dollars for a string of pearls at Cellini. Where was that? Boiling lava filled her stomach and throat, and still she could not process this appalling picture of a life in her name that she didn't have. It was beyond her powers of imagination. It was like a horror story, a made-up nightmare for shock TV. Not only that someone else had been enjoying the fruits of her husband's labors, but worse than that the woman had taken Cassie's very own identity, the financial credit she was due. And the woman had used it with absolutely no restraint. Cassie didn't know that people like this existed.

The real Cassie was frugal. She did not buy ten thousand dollars' worth of clothes every month at Escada and Prada and Armani. She did not get her nails and hair done every three days at Fred's on the Miracle Mile, did not buy expensive lingerie at Danielle in the chic and costly Americana Mall in Manhasset, so close to home. She did not have her clothes cleaned at Fancy in Locust Valley. She did not use the expensive Martin Viette Nurseries in Old Brookville for her plants. The real Cassie had not bought new carpets or furniture for their house in twenty years, much less in the last few months at ABC Carpet and Home. She had not bought silver or dishes at Tiffany's, nor would she even dream of spending three thousand dollars at Williams-Sonoma for *nothing*, nothing at all. The extent of the spending of the fictitious, but nonetheless very real, Cassandra Sales exposed the habits of a pathological shopper, a thief with staggering ambition. Moreover, her debts were steadily building up, for Mitch had paid nothing beyond the interest on all those charge accounts. That interest had to be very considerable. And to this already stupefying debt only a few weeks ago, Mitch had added even more when he used the Cassandra Sales MasterCard to pay the Sales family tax bill.

In all the years of her marriage Cassie never considered that her husband might be unfaithful to her. Why not, she didn't know. After seeing the fake Cassandra Sales bills, Cassie checked Mitch's American Express business file. Here, she found that he was in the habit of spending from twenty-five to fifty thousand dollars a month on hotels and luxury items in places where she hadn't known he'd gone. Even about this he'd lied. In January he'd been in the Caribbean; in February he'd been in Australia, Hong Kong, and Thailand; in March at Grand Cayman Island (probably depositing more money), and all this time she'd been a jerk, alone at home.

This new knowledge about her husband triggered a long-forgotten memory. After a few years of marriage, Mitch's lovemaking dramatically improved after a business trip to Paris. Overnight he'd acquired a sudden interest in things he'd never done with Cassie before. She was thrilled and wanted more. She'd teased him in what she'd thought was a friendly kind of way that he must have been inspired by another woman. She was interested, intrigued, fantasized competition, and was excited by the possibility. Mitch's response, however, had been denial all the way. He had been so vehement that he could never even look at another woman that Cassie had been lulled into letting the intriguing suspicion drop out of her mind.

Mitch had piled on the scam of their marriage so heavily that he'd destroyed her ability to see. He'd been a fog machine. He'd lied to her about everything, every single thing. He'd never given her an opportunity to compete for him, to share any of the fun. Instead of just divorcing her—letting her be jilted and go on with her life—he and his girlfriend had made her an object of contempt. They'd stolen her. It was a stunning feat. No wonder Marsha had looked at her that way. No wonder Mark looked at her that way. They all knew. Everybody in the world knew.

For hours, Cassie ransacked her husband's files and still couldn't find anything like a will, or a living will. Maybe there was no will. Maybe it was in Parker Higgins's office. When Cassie could no longer see straight, she sat at Mitch's desk with her heart pounding out a new fear. What else could the fake Cassandra Sales steal?

It was two in the morning when it occurred to her to start calling to cancel the cards. It was then that the nightmare started to spiral. Not one of them would allow her to cancel her own cards. They were in her name, but she was not the cardholder. Mitch was the cardholder. Only he could cancel the cards. And he was in a coma. She went to bed and tossed around all night, wondering what to do. At around four, she closed her eyes and began to dream.

Selma the faith healer was massaging Charlotte Trotter's bare scalp, exhorting the dying woman to give up her beautiful pearls in exchange for a cure. "This is why your hair is falling out. Pearls rob you of your energy," she scolded, holding out her hands to get those pearls. "Let me keep them for you until you feel better."

Cassie's heart beat frantically in her sleep as her dream showed her mother being fleeced on her deathbed. The poor woman had collected only a few treasures in a life that was ending far too soon at only fifty-one. Charlotte had two daughters, her husband, Albert, a diamond from Amsterdam that became the center stone for her engagement ring, a heavy gold bracelet that had been *her* mother's, and the pièce de résistance: a string of dazzling white pearls the size of quail eggs. In her final days, when her looks, her personality, and—most important to the family— her love for them and God had been corrupted by the illness, the pearls disappeared, too. Cassie never knew if it was her sister, Julie, who'd lifted them, or Selma, the healer. The last blow to the three of them was that after all the months of staying with her night and day, Charlotte had died alone while they were across the street having lunch. Then, before they got back, some nurse or orderly at the hospital took the diamond from her finger, too. At the very end, Charlotte left Cassie nothing but a curse.

Instead of saying goodbye and good luck, Cassie's mother's very last words to her had been "trust no one." She'd been angry at Cassie for being pregnant with a baby she would never live to see. And she was angry at her husband, who'd promised he would die first. She could not bear the fact that the good soldier who'd so carefully planned her widowhood would be the one to be freed from the lion's cage. Widowhood was getting to be a big theme, even in Cassie's dreams.

Suddenly Selma disappeared, and her mother rose from her hospital bed, looking like a mummy. All her hair was gone and so was the water that had bloated her body beyond recognition at the end. She was very thin now, a model with a mummy's head. She was wearing the lost pearls. They were at a hotel in Italy. Somewhere on the Amalfi coast. Graham Greene was there, writing The End of the Affair. *Cassie's father, Albert, was wearing a dinner jacket and a bad toupee. Must have been his wife's hair he was wearing. He was smiling, trying to take a photo of them all where they sat at a table on a hill overlooking the blue, blue Mediterranean. Marsha, Teddy, Mitch. Baby octopuses with red sauce were piled on a platter in front of them. The octopuses were still alive, wiggling and multiplying like crazy. Many wine bottles cluttered the table, too. It looked as if they were having a tasting, a good time, while the octopuses spilled onto the table and then the ground. Nobody seemed to care about the lunch being alive and multiplying.*

"Cassie, honey, are you there? Pick up, pick up if you can hear me." On the answering machine it was her aunt Edith, who'd never held a place of honor at the party of life.

"Pick up, I mean it." Edith's voice was full of worry and resentment.

Cassie reached for the phone without opening her eyes. "Hello, Aunt Edith," she mumbled miserably.

"Cassie, Cassie. How are you doing? I heard about poor Mitch. Why didn't you call me? Oh, my dear, my poor darling. Marsha told me he's *very* bad." Her voice sounded peevish that this could be happening without her knowledge.

"Yes, he's very bad," Cassie told her.

"Honey, I've been so upset what with the accident and all. I'm furious that you didn't call me. I'm your aunt. I should have been there for you. I could have driven you."

Edith's driver's license had been revoked years ago for moving violations that were so creative, no one else in the entire world had ever thought of them before, even in emerging third world countries. But that little detail never stopped her from taking the car out.

"There was no accident. Mitch had a stroke," Cassie told her.

"*Your* accident, honey. I'm talking about your accident. You had a head-on collision with a Mack truck. It's lucky you're alive. Oh Cassie, I'm so glad to hear your voice. Marsha told me you've been out of it for weeks."

Fighting the dream of her mother, the mummy, Cassie sat up and saw the light of the digital clock. Even without her glasses she could tell that it was eight A.M. How could she have slept a single minute when this was the day she was going to kill her cheating husband? Her heart started hammering away in her chest at the thought of turning off that respirator, watching him struggle for breath. Then canceling the credit of his mistress who drove the Jaguar that should have been hers. That bitch! Wherever she was. The billing address on the credit cards was Mitch's at the warehouse. She wondered how she was going to find out where that woman lived and shoot her in the face.

"What, honey? Speak up. I can't hear you."

"Nothing, I'm just all broken up," Cassie murmured. "This is so hard. I had a dream about Mother. I still miss her so much."

"I do, too, honey. Marsha told me you're lucky to be alive. I'm coming right over. I want to make sure you're all right."

"I had a face-lift," Cassie said quickly.

"What? I think we have a bad connection."

"We have a fine connection, Edith. Marsha lied. I had a face-lift."

There was a moment of silence. "You didn't have an accident?"

"Well, I had an accident, but it was planned. I know I never should have done it. I'm sorry now," Cassie admitted to the aunt who drove her crazy.

"How do you look, dear?" Edith asked at last.

"Terrible. I look just terrible." And my husband has a mistress, she didn't say.

Silence again as Edith tried to digest the news. "What about Mitch, honey, did he have a face-lift, too?"

"No, Mitch had a stroke."

"What bad timing. I'm so sorry. Is he . . . a-a . . . vegetable?" Edith asked bluntly.

"He's a piece of shit," Cassie told her.

"Oh honey, don't talk like that. I'm sure he didn't do it on purpose."

"Oh yes, he did it on purpose." Truth was truth. Cassie wasn't hiding from it now. She was up. The breathtaking spring sunlight had drawn her out of bed to the window, where she surveyed the mess of her yard after its first glorious spring bloom.

The tulips and daffodils and hyacinths were finished. The drying husks, listing to the ground, looked forlorn in the beds. Growing up between them, however, the peonies were blooming and the poppies were getting ready to burst open. A few days, maybe a week and those poppies would pop. Cassie had no time to clean up the beds. This upset her, too. She was a tidy person.

There she was yearning for the simple pleasure of cleaning out the old to make way for the new in her flower beds when she caught a movement by the edge of the garage. She was startled when a man walked boldly through the pretty white gate into her yard. Without her glasses she couldn't see him that well, but he had a black thing in his hand. He pointed it around, at the patio, at the pool. He pointed it at the garage. She was puzzled, but unafraid until he disappeared into the garage that she locked only from time to time. Then she became frightened. What was going on? What was the man doing in there? He didn't look like a thief. He was wearing a suit and some kind of hat. She couldn't see his face, but his movements didn't fit the furtive profile of a burglar.

Suddenly he emerged from the garage again and moved slowly toward the house, pointing the black thing up at the windows. Cassie stepped back behind the curtains. "I've got to go, Edith. I'll call you back," she whispered into the phone.

"What do you mean, you've got to go? You and Marsha have been avoiding me for two weeks. I'm not hanging up now," Edith retorted angrily. "Family has to stick together in troubled times. If you hang up this time, I'm coming over."

"Edith, there's a man with a gun in my backyard. I'll have to call you later. And don't come over. You don't have a driver's license."

Cassie hung up and peered into the yard from behind the curtain. The man was definitely pointing the gun her way. She gasped and ducked below the windowsill, half crawling to the chair where she'd left the sweater and khaki pants she'd worn the night before. Shaking all over like a teenager caught in a sex act, she fumbled with her clothes.

She knew right away that the man with the gun was a hit man Mitch had hired to kill her so his girlfriend could step in and be his wife without benefit of divorce. It was perfectly clear. He'd bought another house. His girlfriend was furnishing it. The house had to be someplace where no one knew what the real Cassie looked like. Now he was going to have her assassinated. He'd probably planned to move into his new house right after she was dead. Lucky for her he'd had a stroke instead. Life threw its little curves. She was trembling all over.

The phone started ringing again. "Shhh." She didn't have time to answer it. She got to the door of her room and looked down the hall. No one. She crawled below the window line to the stairs. There she froze. It occurred to her that one of the kids might have left a door unlocked, the door to the kitchen from the garage. Or maybe the basement or patio door. She almost never used the burglar alarm. The hit man could come in without a sound and shoot her with that gun. The phone kept ringing, but she was afraid to answer it. It rang and rang.

Cassie thought she was having a heart attack. What should she do? What could she do? The phone finally stopped ringing, and she breathed a sigh of relief at the sudden quiet. She had to think. Mitch had his stroke on Friday. Now it was Monday. What if the hit man had taken the weekend off and didn't know Mitch was in the hospital, didn't know there would be no one to pay him if he shot her and left her dead on the floor? She had to tell him that. But how could she talk to a hit man? They didn't give a shit. She was so scared, she could hardly breathe. All these years she'd believed Mitch was a dull and faithful husband, and now she had to face the fact that he was a crook and a killer, too. The phone started ringing again.

For the second time it rang and rang as she tried to figure out what to do. Finally it stopped ringing. Talking was useless. She knew she had to conquer her terror and get downstairs to lock all the doors and activate the alarm so the hit man couldn't get in and shoot her. She inched down the first stair. The phone didn't ring again. Cassie knew if it had been Edith, she wouldn't have given up. She wondered if it had been Mark or the hospital calling to say that Mitch had died. She wished she'd told Edith to call the police. Why hadn't she done that? Stupid.

She moved down the stairs one by one. It took her many minutes to get to the first floor. Now it was deadly quiet, like a horror movie without the scary music. Opposite her was the front door. The windows in the rooms on either side were so bright with glare, she couldn't see outside. From where she was curled in terror on the bottom step, it almost looked like that light she'd heard about from heaven. She was quaking with fear. She didn't want to die. She could tell that the top lock on the front door, that unpickable Medeco, was locked; but still she knew she couldn't stop the freight train about to run over her. She was going to die, but not of natural causes like her mother. And Mitch was going to live on for another twenty years, in a wheelchair with his whore pushing him around. It was more than she could bear.

She got up and caught sight of herself in the hall mirror, let out a little scream. Mitch's mistress might be beautiful, but she was a horror, a freak. She didn't recognize the woman in the mirror with the blond hair, the black stitches, and puffy eyes. She wanted to obliterate that face. Her scarf and Marsha's huge sunglasses were on the hall table. She put them on to hide the damage she'd done to herself. Then she remembered the hit man didn't care what she looked like—he was going to kill her anyway. She fell to her knees and crawled down the hall to the kitchen.

She made it to the basement door. That door was locked, too. The garage door had a chain. The chain was still in place. With a sigh of relief she turned around and saw the man peering in through the windowed kitchen door. She screamed. Startled, the man on the other side of the window jumped back. As he turned to flee, his foot caught on one of the many decorative pots she'd left out on the patio before Mitch's incident in preparation for the ritual potting of red geraniums. He stumbled backwards, falling hard on a garden tool with many spikes for breaking up the ground. As he went down, the black thing dropped out of his hand. Now Cassie got a good look at it. It was a camera. Further shocked, she started screaming at him. "What the hell do you think you're doing?" she yelled at the window.

The man was down. He didn't move. Cassie thought she detected some blood on the flagstone. Uh-oh, maybe he was hurt. Maybe he'd sue. She stepped closer to the door. She saw the scuffed suede shoes. The baggy pants of a glen plaid suit. The camera on a flagstone. Looked like a good one, an Elph. The hat. A ridiculous hat, a crushed fedora. She couldn't see the man's face.

"Hey you," she said tentatively. Now the phone was ringing again. Cassie ignored it. She opened the door and stepped outside.

"Hey you," she said louder. In the distance she could hear sirens. She always dreaded the sound. It meant bad things, someone's house on fire. Somebody in an accident. She kept her eye on the downed man. "Hey, you all right?"

Suddenly, he held up a bleeding hand and gave her a jaunty little wave. After a second or two, he picked up his head, then his shoulders. He turned over and gingerly got to his feet. On his feet he adjusted the nonexistent creases in his unpressed trousers. He looked around the patio and collected the camera, the hat. His movements were all matter of fact, as if he felt perfectly at ease in the situation and nothing untoward had happened. Finally he turned toward Cassie and slowly looked her over. He did it with frank curiosity, up and down, the way men look at things that interest them. He tilted his head quizzically at the scarf and sunglasses. Finally he cracked a little not-bad smile. It was the smile Cassie had seen yesterday from Mark, but hadn't seen for such a long time before that she didn't recognize it yet as admiration. Her face was so tight, she couldn't adjust her expression. Terror, rage, sorrow, uncertainty—her face couldn't seem to register. Luckily, her voice still knew what to do. "What do you think you're doing here?" she demanded, hands on hips.

"Nothing at all, ma'am, just looking around." The man put the squashed hat back on and saluted with his bleeding hand.

"Looking around?" she said indignantly. "What are you, some kind of Peeping Tom?"

"Oh no, nothing like that." He laughed easily. Not a bad-looking kind of guy. "Are you Mrs. Sales?"

"Yes. Who's asking? Mafia hit man, FBI, CIA?" The sirens got louder and louder, until they were almost deafening. Cassie shifted uneasily from one foot to another. Somebody's house was going up in a puff of smoke.

"No, ma'am. Nothing that sinister. I'm with the IRS," he said with a modest smile. "Do you mind if I come inside for a minute?"

"Ahhh." She hesitated. IRS? What did he want?

He held up his hand to show the cut. "I could use some water."

"Ahhh, we're in a bit of turmoil right now." All those files in the house. All those purchases by the girlfriend. The account in the Bank of the Cayman Islands. Her husband was a crook. Dizziness hit her. She didn't like to lie.

"Oh, don't worry about it. Mess doesn't bother me."

The wailing sirens stopped abruptly. It seemed as if they'd stopped in front of her house. Cassie turned around. A loud voice issued a command from a speaker.

"Police. Please drop your weapon and move slowly to the front of the house. I repeat, police, you are surrounded. Put your hands over your head. There are fifty officers here. You are surrounded."

That's when Cassie realized Aunt Edith must have called the cops, after all. She did the only thing she could think of: She closed the door on the IRS agent and ran inside the house to hide in her closet.

ONLY A FEW MINUTES LATER, Cassie emerged from her closet to see what was going on. From her new perch in a second-floor window seat she counted four squad cars in the street in front of her house. The doors of the cars were open, and seven uniformed officers crouched behind them, pointing guns at the house. An eighth officer was speaking over the P.A. system in his car, his voice reverberating like thunder in the morning quiet. There was no sign of the IRS agent.

"You are surrounded. Come out with your hands up."

Cassie couldn't understand why the IRS man didn't come out and show himself, talk to them, do something to end this nightmare situation. Then it occurred to her that he wasn't really with the IRS. That was just a lie. He was really a hit man or a robber out to get her, after all. The phone started ringing again. She crawled away from the upstairs hall window where she'd been hiding behind the curtain to answer it in the bedroom.

"Yes, hello," she said impatiently. If it was those Sprint people still trying to get her business after a hundred perfectly polite nos, this time she wouldn't be able to resist screaming at them.

"Oh my God, sweetheart, are you all right?" It wasn't the Sprint people. It was Aunt Edith.

"Aunt Edith, we're in the middle of a shoot-out here. I'll have to call you back," Cassie informed her importantly.

"Did the police come? They gave me such a lot of trouble when I called. They wanted to know what kind of gun the perpetrator had. How would I know something like that?" Edith complained.

"You must have said the right thing. They came," Cassie told her.

"I told them it was a machine gun," Edith said.

"Good job. It was a camera. I hope they don't shoot up the house."

"A camera?"

"Yes, I have to go."

"Don't worry, honey. I'll be over as soon as the cops are gone. I don't want them to run a warrant check on me."

"For God's sake, Edith, don't drive that car! I have so many—oh no—" The line went dead. Cassie groaned. Now she had to worry about Edith driving on top of everything else.

When she got back to the window in the hall, all the cops were getting back in their cars except the one with the microphone. The small thing that looked like a computer mouse dangled against his thigh from the wire attached to his car as he conversed easily with the suddenly reappeared, so-called IRS agent. They were now having such a comfortable conversation, it looked as if they knew each other, had beers together at the Landmark after work.

Then the conversation between the two ended. The last cop, an older, gray-haired, heavyset man, got back into his unit and slammed the door. Then, probably the entire fleet of the sheriff's office turned on their engines simultaneously, backed up, drove around the circle and out of the development without even trying to speak to the homeowner under siege. Amazed, Cassie watched them leave. Eight deputy sheriffs had come over to save her from a man with a gun, then left the scene without even ringing her bell to see if she was all right. For all they knew she could be bleeding on the floor, knifed to death. Or raped and strangled.

"Hey, wait a minute, what about me?" She wanted to run after and yell at them. She wanted to yell at somebody. They hadn't even taken her statement. She returned to the phone in her bedroom to call them and complain. She was full of resolve about the matter until she was distracted by the sight of herself in the mirror with the sunglasses and the scarf on her head. "Oh God, I'm being punished," she whispered.

Moaning, she started slowly down the stairs. Her life had spun out of control, but the coffeepot had come on hours earlier at the usual time and now drew her into the kitchen with its delicious aroma. She put one foot down after the other on the beige carpet treads on the stairs. Suddenly she saw it the way the IRS agent would have seen it if she'd let him in. Shabby. The carpet had worn thin with twenty years of constant wear. The color was blah. At the bottom of the stairs the furniture in the living room and dining room was early American, a period that never matched Cassie's flare for the baroque. Blah, too. Mitch had come from Long Island, from Huntington Station. Cassie had grown up in Westchester in a better family. They'd met in college, at Cornell. Cassie had been very pretty then, quite a catch. Shape up, you're a regular person, not a victim, she told herself.

But she'd made some bad choices. Instead of going to law school, she'd married a handsome, ambitious man who'd turned her into a caterer. Mitch was a fanatic about food, so she'd cooked with the great restaurant chefs in Manhattan, always trying to please him. When he'd gotten too busy to eat at home, she'd stayed home with the kids and catered to them. Then she'd begun designing events for not-for-profit causes in the area. She'd planned the menus, done the flower arrangements. Sometimes she'd made the desserts, too. She had a talent for it. Everybody said she could have been a Martha Stewart.

Cassie moved through the dining room into the kitchen, her territory, where she had a Viking stove, a Sub-Zero refrigerator, two sets of dishes, six different kinds of wineglasses, and enough utensils to equip a small restaurant. The tiles on the floor were Mexican terra-cotta. The tiles between the cabinets and the countertops were yellow sunflowers in a deep blue sky. A pots-and-pans rack suspended from beams in the ceiling had bunches of her own dried flowers and herbs hanging on its hooks. Cassie loved her kitchen. She reached for a cup to pour herself some coffee, heard water running, and spun around. Outside, the IRS man was hosing his hand off into her swimming pool.

"Hey." She opened the back door.

"Oh, hi." He turned around and smiled his nice smile, as if nothing unusual had happened. "I wondered where you went."

"I hid in the closet," she said.

"I see. What's with the sunglasses, the scarf?"

"What's with the camera?"

"Cassie! Oh, Cassie, is everything all right?" Carol Carnahan marched through the gate, an entire invading army in one person. A tall, slender woman with long, tapered legs and a big chest, Carol was wearing pedal pushers, and a yellow T-shirt with a plunging neckline. She was fifty-three but looked twenty-five, and took up all the space wherever she went. Now she took up Cassie's whole yard, eyeing with a good deal of interest the attractive stranger on Cassie's patio.

Then Carol saw Cassie's face. "Oh, shit, Cassie! What's with the—?"

"Carol, I'm fine. Just a misunderstanding." Here was one of the thousands of people Cassie didn't want to know she'd had work done. The mortification kept right on coming.

"And who's this?" Carol asked.

The agent turned off the hose at the hose bib. He looked very much at home at her house, but Cassie didn't know who he was.

"Ah, ah . . ."

He was not as tall as Carol, who was over six feet tall in her five-inch sling backs. He was closer to five ten and had a medium to sturdy build, looked as if he did regular exercise. He certainly had a relaxed manner in the face of any drama. At the moment the drama was Carol, and his intense blue eyes evaluated her slowly, curiously, the way he had Cassie a little while ago.

"How do you do, ma'am," he said, swiping the hat from his head to reveal sandy hair going gray, cut in a crew cut. "Charles Schwab, at your service."

"Charles Schwab of the brokerage house?" Carol yelped. Cassie had a boyfriend, and he was a big cheese—all this was in the yelp. "Is Mitch at home?" Her eyes swept the upper windows. The cops, a boyfriend, a disguise. Very big!

"Thanks for dropping by, Carol. I'm fine. And Mr. *Schwab* was just leaving." Cassie gave him an ironic snicker. Schwab, indeed.

He waved at Carol. "Nice meeting you," he murmured.

"I can take a hint. Do you have any stock tips for me before I go? God knows I could use a few."

"Oh, no. Sorry, I don't give tips."

"I bet you do," was Carol's parting shot.

Cassie went into the house and carefully closed the door. Oh God. Her head was pounding. Agents and cops and Carol Carnahan all in one day. She glanced at the clock. It was now nine-thirty. Mark was meeting her at noon. She had things to do. She couldn't remember at the moment what they were. She poured herself a cup of coffee, her first of the morning. A noise at the door made her turn around. The man who called himself Charles Schwab was tapping on the glass, still there.

Cassie shook her head. "I'm not entertaining."

"Just one question," he mouthed as if she couldn't hear him perfectly through the glass doors.

"I have to go out soon." She opened the back door. The storm door was still in place. She didn't open the storm door. He opened the storm door.

"What a gorgeous kitchen!" he said, sticking his head in.

"Thank you." Cassie blocked further progress.

"Wow, copper pots and everything."

"Uh-huh." She wasn't going to budge.

"Do you use all those things?"

"Yes, I do."

He shook his head. "That's very impressive. Have you noticed how few women do food these days?"

"It's good for the restaurants. Charles Schwab?" she said sarcastically.

"That's my name." He smiled engagingly. The man was a big smiler. "I love your kitchen; your garden, too. You must be very creative," he said admiringly. "I bet you're good with roses."

She shook her head. Uh-uh, she wasn't buying.

"Do you mind if I take a closer look at your kitchen? I've been considering copper pots."

"It's a bad time." Cassie was trying so hard to be civil. He said he was a civil servant, after all.

"Let me give you a little advice. This is not the way to treat your auditor. First, I break my ankle on your damn potting stuff." He backed away from the door to illustrate a little limp. "Then you cut my hand with your gardening implement. I could call that assault. And *then* you call the police to try to have me arrested."

Cassie snorted. "Auditor? I don't know what you're talking about."

"I'm the one who's doing your audit," he said officiously.

"Well, I don't know anything about an audit. I'm just the wife here," Cassie told him.

"Wives are equal partners," Schwab said.

"Not in this house," she muttered.

Schwab laughed suddenly, and it was a genuinely pleasant sound.

"I don't think that was so funny," she retorted.

"Look, just let me in for a minute. I won't touch anything, I promise, and then I'll get out of your hair." He held up his hands. "I like your style, that's all."

"That is some kind of joke, right?"

"No, ma'am."

"The IRS doesn't go into people's homes for a tax audit." What did he take her for, a dummy?

"Of course we do. We look at property, possessions, cars, and jewelry. We do whatever it takes. Here." He handed her his card.

The card went into Cassie's hand without her actually taking it. Alarmed, she thought of the files. Mitch's million plus in that Grand Caymans bank. The expenses of the girlfriend who bought so much in Cassie's name. Whatever current practices were, she didn't think a home visit right now would be a good idea. "My husband had a stroke," she said quickly.

"Oh, I'm sorry to hear it. They usually recover during the course of investigations." Schwab had sunglasses of his own. They were the mirrored kind, like the state troopers wore so you couldn't see their eyes when they stopped you for speeding. He gave her a funny look, then put them on.

"No, no, you don't understand. My husband really did have a stroke. He's in intensive care," Cassie told him.

"Oh, that's terrible. Would you mind if I come in for a cup of coffee?" he asked, chilly now.

"Coffee?" Didn't he hear what she just said?

"Just a quick cup. It smells so good. I bet you make a terrific cup of coffee. What kind of beans do you use?"

Cassie licked her lips. What was with this guy? She'd just told him her husband was in intensive care.

Before she could open her mouth to tell him he couldn't have coffee right now, a loud metal crunch announced the arrival of Aunt Edith. As on many other occasions, she misjudged where the road ended and drove her 1963 monster Cadillac into the mailbox. "Cassie! Cassie," she started screaming, "I can't get out."

"Oh my, what's that?" Schwab asked.

"My aunt has come to drive me insane," Cassie told him.

CHAPTER 15

AN HOUR LATER the Cadillac was separated from the mailbox and was parked in the driveway. The lovely conversation azalea that had been blooming in its myriad colors was a mangled mess. Above it, the post that secured the mailbox was bent to the ground, and the mailbox itself was crushed like a cookie in a toddler's hand. The bloodred clematis that had started winding its way up the post on its way to becoming a glorious flower bower that would camouflage the mail by July was in leaf but hadn't yet produced a single fist-sized crimson bloom. The vine lay on the grass, twisted forlornly around the wreckage.

Charles Schwab, the IRS one, had taken off, but Edith was still there, unrepentant about the damage to her niece's house and eager to be of help. Her idea of help was telling Cassie how awful she looked, how thin she'd gotten; requesting a breakfast of goat cheese and pancetta omelette with raisin toast, none of which Cassie happened to have in the house; and scolding her about wanting to improve herself (the surgery). She also encouraged Cassie to think of the pleasant future they would have together when Mitch was gone.

"Sweetheart, I'm going to take you on a cruise the minute this thing is over." She said as they left the house to drive to the hospital to visit the vegetable who was not likely to be with them long.

Edith wanted to drive, but Cassie wouldn't hear of it. So now the old woman was sitting regally in the passenger seat of Mitch's brand-new

Mercedes that Cassie wasn't supposed to drive herself for another four days, doctor's orders, or forever, if Mitch had anything to say about it. Edith was wearing a white jogging suit with red chevrons on her thighs that matched the white Cadillac and made her look almost as large. Her moon of a face was round and rouged. Her lips were drawn on big and red. Her chins were multiple. Her hair was done like Debbie Reynolds's in 1952. And she was in a jolly mood, for there's nothing in the world a widow enjoys more than the impending widowhood of a close friend or relative.

"I don't know, it's almost summer, so we could go to the Greek Isles, how does that sound? Or maybe the Mediterranean. Heaven knows you'll be able to afford it. Mitch did very well for himself, didn't he? And you! You need to get away, get some rest, recover from your ordeal. Poor Mitch," she rambled on. And on.

"But, you know, it won't be so bad without him. He wasn't around much anyway, was he poor thing?"

"No, he wasn't," Cassie affirmed stonily.

"Well, men aren't all they're cracked up to be, if you want my opinion," she said. "Keeping up your curiosity. That's what keeps a person young. Look at me. I done all right for myself, haven't I?"

Cassie didn't want to look at her aunt. After the weekend she'd had, her nerves were completely shot. And now the thing that was beginning to gall her was that she couldn't even talk to Mitch, couldn't confront him with all her years of loyalty and the heartless way he'd repaid her for it. She was driving very slowly in the Mercedes, reminding herself that she mustn't hit anything and have an encounter with the police on the day she was going to murder her husband. If she couldn't yell at Mitch, at least there was the plug to pull.

"Who was that Charlie you were with?" her aunt demanded abruptly.

"I told you, Edith. He's assessing all the houses in the area for the IRS," Cassie told her.

"I never heard of such a thing," Edith clicked her tongue. "Casing the place in the morning before anybody is even up. My land! What is this world coming to?"

"My land," as far as Cassie knew, was an expression that dated back two centuries from the Midwest, where Edith's grandmother was said to have fought the Indians. Or maybe it was the far West. "My land," indeed.

"I never heard of it either," she said grimly about the sneak IRS attack. She couldn't get Charlie Schwab out of her mind. Hadn't she read somewhere that the IRS was trying to improve its image and wasn't auditing people anymore? *The New York Times*? *People* magazine? How could this be happening to her? Why now? What were the procedures? Could the agency really make home visits without warning, check out people's cars in their garages? Do anything they wanted? Maybe this was one of those "random audits," like the pat-downs at the airports.

"You two seemed very cozy. Did you know him before?"

"No, of course not," Cassie snapped.

She stopped at a red light on Northern Boulevard, only a few blocks from the hospital. She hadn't heard from anyone there this morning, and she hadn't called the nurses' station to check in. She didn't know what she was going to find when she went into that intensive care unit. Maybe Mitch had had another "event" in the night. He could be gone already. She forgot about the IRS incident, was filled with trepidation about the medical situation. Code, code. Where was a code when one needed one?

The light changed. Cassie reminded herself that she had to tell Mitch's employees what had happened to him, take charge at the warehouse. She had to call his lawyer. All kinds of arrangements had to be made. She pulled into the hospital, her head spinning again. She didn't know who Mitch's girlfriend was, what that woman was doing right now, or how she and Mitch communicated. One thing she did know was that the two of them were not talking again. She was going to pop that woman's balloon.

Cassie parked the car and got out. She adjusted her scarf and sunglasses. The tide was rising in her. Mitch had underestimated her. She wanted revenge.

"Come on, Aunt Edith, come say goodbye to Mitch."

"Oh dear, oh my, your poor children, losing their daddy so young," Edith said. Then, "You know, dear, I never liked that man."

"What?" Cassie turned to look at her. Edith was heavy. It wasn't easy for her to get out of that Mercedes, roomy as it was. She moved one enormous chevroned leg out the door, then another. Cassie had to haul her to a standing position. Upright, she examined her niece again.

"Cassie, are you sure you're all right? You look so thin."

"You never told me you didn't like Mitch."

"Oh well, you know. People don't say these things. They don't want to hurt your feelings. But he was a difficult man," Edith said vaguely.

Cassie blew air through her nose. Edith's opinion of her husband came as a surprise to her. She thought everybody liked Mitch. This was getting to be the longest day of her life. Slowly they made their way through the lot and into the hospital. There was the same bustle in the lobby on Monday at midday as there had been all weekend. They moved down the glass hallway into the head trauma wing. Cassie tried not to look at the people around her, all suffering losses.

When they got to the intensive care unit, everything seemed the same. The nurses at the station. Other staff with their blue pajamalike uniforms. In Mitch's cubicle of a room, his body was in the same position on the bed. His eyes were still at half-mast. Today, however, there was a little tremor in his hand. Cassie watched it with horror. The hand seemed to have taken on a life of its own.

Edith moved her great bulk toward the bed. Her chubby face held an expression of astonishment, as if she'd been ambushed by an unexpected feeling of sorrow over the mortality of a man she claimed she'd never liked.

"Mitch, honey. It's Edith," she said in her loudest, bossiest voice. "You remember Edith, don't you? Charlotte's sister. Cassandra's aunt. I've come to see you in the hospital. You look good, Mitch. Really good. How are you feeling, honey? A little better?"

Stupid question.

She gave him a big bright smile. "We're all praying for you, honey."

That would get him. Mitch hated God. Didn't believe in the power of prayer. The big woman's smile faded just a little as she stood there eyeing all those tubes going in and out of him. Her face was one big pucker of wonderment until she noticed Mitch's twitching hand that seemed to be trying so hard to say something. This got her going again.

"You'll be on your feet in no time," she said softly and with real conviction.

This wasn't the goodbye that Cassie had envisioned on the way over. On the other side of the bed, she held her breath, for Mitch seemed to be coming out of it. He looked drained, but definitely alive. Maybe that noisy machine pumping air into his lungs was actually charging him up again like a car battery, and soon he would roar into life again. A disheartening thought.

Cassie tried to muster some sympathy for him, to remember the bright moments, the good times of their twenty-six years together. As before, she was stuck in the later years, after he'd left her for another woman without her even knowing it. All the joy she could remember was being the mommy of Teddy and Marsha when they'd been babies, bathing them and changing them and cooking their favorite foods, teaching them those ABCs and making life fun. She remembered their hugging on the big bed, cuddling like puppies. Those long-gone days brought tears to her eyes.

She watched in horror as Aunt Edith picked up Mitch's puffy hand. "Give me a little squeeze," Edith instructed him. "We're all rooting for you, Buddy."

Not Cassie. She was imagining the lights flashing. Code, code.

"Look, honey, he's coming back," Edith said.

No, that was not possible. Cassie didn't want him back. She planned to turn off that respirator and make him history. Don't squeeze, she prayed. No swimming back to the surface now, you bastard.

Long, suspenseful moments passed as Edith experimented with Mitch's hand, curling his fingers around one of hers just like Cassie had done only yesterday.

"Can you hear me, Buddy? Give me a squeeze," Edith coaxed.

Suddenly the finger that had been moving around on the sheet stopped. The hand in her grasp lay there limp as a fish fillet. Aunt Edith extricated herself, and Cassie exhaled with a little hiccup of thanks.

"He was always a stubborn man," Edith remarked. "Can he hear us or not, honey?"

"We don't know," Cassie said.

"I had a friend once. Rosalind Witte, remember her? She lives in Florida now. Roz's husband, Paul, had a stroke. She pushed him around in a wheelchair for ten years before he finally passed on. Couldn't say a word." Edith clicked her tongue.

"She kept a pencil tied to his wrist. Every little while, she'd put that pencil in his hand and he'd make some squiggles. She told everybody he was writing his memoirs." Edith pointed to Mitch's finger suddenly making circles on the sheet again. "I don't envy you," she whispered.

16

SHAKEN BY EDITH'S OMINOUS REACTION to Mitch's condition, Cassie paced the hall outside the lounge, where she had spent so many hours over the weekend. In the cluttered room, the TV was playing loudly to an audience of some ten people, who all seemed to belong to a distraught family Cassie hadn't seen before. Every minute something else reminded Cassie of her mother's death. She didn't want to sit in the lounge, in case a code was called and another family lost someone they loved. She waited impatiently for Mark in the hall, and he arrived, as promised, only minutes after noon. Time had slowed to a crawl.

"Mark." She felt safe as soon as she saw him.

"Hi, sweetheart." He kissed her cheek and peered at her intently right in front of everybody, thumb and index finger turning her chin from side to side as if he hadn't examined her face just this way only yesterday.

"Not a bad job at all," he confirmed again, shaking his bald head, since they were old friends and she hadn't trusted him enough to make the referral.

"Let's go somewhere. I can't talk in there," she said about the lounge.

"No, no, of course not. I thought we'd have a quick lunch somewhere close by." Today he was wearing a different sports jacket and different aftershave. His cheeks were smooth and moisturized. His color was excellent.

"Lunch?" A warning bell went off.

"Yes, looks like you need some sustenance." Mark Cohen was a study in contrasts. There was nothing handsome about him. In middle age, his flesh was filling in all around him. His face was round. He was shorter than she was. His nose was a blob on his face.

But to Cassie, the well-dressed teddy bear also had the suave and comforting air of a professional. His gentle and sympathetic hand on her arm, his expression of short-term deep concern for her pain combined with absolute acceptance of the inevitability of death. His wry expression, indeed his whole demeanor, seemed to say: "I've seen it all a hundred times. This, too, shall pass." This message of competence and empathy felt like the very last thing left over from the age of Cary Grant and Jimmy Stewart.

"How are you holding up?" asked the only man Cassie knew who could understand and help her.

"Oh God. You wouldn't believe what's happening. Mark, I don't even know how to tell you this." She wished she could lower her head onto his chubby chest and rest it there for a year or two and let him take care of everything. His navy blazer was the very best, just like the kind Mitch wore, with gold buttons and a pink shirt under it. The shirt had a dazzling white collar, and cuffs that were held together with gold golf ball cuff links. Mitch happened to have the same ones.

Cassie couldn't help being impressed by the close attention to sartorial detail and personal care that some men took of themselves. In Mark, it reminded her of the kidney infection he'd cured twelve years ago, and the way he'd handled her breast lump scare several years later. Mitch had left town the day of her biopsy, but Mark had remained staunchly by her side.

"Where do you want to go?" Mark patted her hand.

"Oh, that's sweet of you, but I can't go out. My aunt Edith is here with Mitch."

His face registered a moment's disappointment. "Tomorrow, then."

Cassie still had her very dark sunglasses on over the scarf tied around her head. "Oh definitely," she murmured, shaking her head no. They'd never had lunch alone together. She absolutely adored him, but how could she think about going out? She steered the subject to Mitch. "Have you seen Mitch?"

"Yes, of course, early this morning." He sniffed the air around her. "Nice perfume, what is it?"

"Really, Mark, I don't know."

"Sublime, I think. You've been wearing it for a long time, haven't you? I've always liked it."

"Well, I just saw Mitch. Have you seen what his finger is doing?" Cassie didn't want to think about her perfume.

"Of course. I saw all of him. What about it?"

"It was moving around on the sheet. It looked like he was trying to say something. Write something."

"Oh, yes. They do that sometimes. It doesn't mean anything." Mark was studying her intently.

"What's the matter?" She touched her cheek and didn't feel a thing.

He shook his head. "Nothing. Just the change in you. You really look different. I'm not sure I would have recognized you."

"I know I look terrible. Let's not dwell."

"Quite the contrary. You look very good. Really good."

"For God's sake, Mark, I don't care how I look. I want to talk about Mitch. I think he's coming back," Cassie said wildly. "He has motion in his hand. I saw it."

Mark raised a shoulder. "Well, random movements. That doesn't mean anything." He raised the shoulder again. "I don't want to be pessimistic, Cassie. But he's still in a very deep coma—"

"I think he's coming back. I really do," she insisted.

"Does he respond to the things you say? Does he seem to know you?" Mark asked gently.

"No, but—"

"Sweetheart, he's not responding to any outside stimuli. We're not seeing any brain activity on the EEG," he said solemnly. "I have to be straight with you."

"No brain activity?" Cassie asked hopefully.

Mark pressed his lips together and shook his head. "Mitch is a tough nut. He's hanging on, but we'd hoped for more of a rally, some return of awareness." He massaged Cassie's hand and put his other arm around her shoulder and squeezed that, too. "You okay?"

"No brain activity. That's—" she shook her head. Great!

"Look, on the other hand, I've seen patients who've been in a vegetative state for six, seven, eight months, even years, who just wake up one day."

"No!" Cassie didn't want to hear that.

"I know, it's rough. Are you sure you don't want something to eat? Starving yourself won't help him."

"No, no. Thank you, but I couldn't think about food right now."

"This isn't good for you. You look like you've lost about fifteen pounds. You've had a trauma. You're depressed."

More than he guessed. "Mark, I haven't lost an ounce."

"I'm your doctor. I would know." He said this with his wry little doctor smile. Then he patted her bottom, lightly. Just a touch, then he pressed those lips together appreciatively, and nodded. "Ten pounds, at least."

"Mark!" Cassie was shocked by the inappropriate gesture.

"How are you sleeping?"

"Oh, I don't know. All right, I guess." She was irritated by the tone, distracted.

"We don't want you getting depressed."

"Oh, for heaven's sake, let's not beat around the bush about depression."

"Oh?" Mark raised his eyebrows.

"It's not as if Mitch and I were that close. I bet you know the whole story," she said angrily. "Why don't you just come clean."

He changed the subject. "Cassie, I checked some things out with Parker. He knows pretty much everything where Mitch is concerned. Here's the insurance story. You're fine with North Fork, for a while. But there might be a problem down the road." All of a sudden Mark looked uncomfortable.

"Fine, you don't want to be straight with me about his personal life," Cassie said. Parker Higgins was Mitch's lawyer. She'd get the truth out of him.

"Of course I do. We'll have some things to talk about later, but you don't have to worry about them right this minute," he said evenly.

"Well, I *want* to worry about them right this minute. I have some decisions to make, and I need your help."

"You know you can count on me," he said staunchly.

"Can I, Mark?" She stared at him hard through those dark glasses but couldn't read him.

"Of course. We'll go through it all right now if you want to."

She nodded. "Thank you."

He steered her to a stone bench in a little alcove on one side of the glass hallway that she'd never noticed before. It looked out on a Japanese garden with three large rocks, a collection of dwarf conifers, and a pebble path surrounded by buildings that no one could get to. Cassie sat down on the bench. Mark sat next to her, still in possession of her hand.

"Go ahead, shoot."

"I think I mentioned over the weekend some of the issues surrounding the practical side of health care. I'm sure you know that the hospital and the insurance companies look at patients in a different way from patients' families. Insurance companies want to resolve the cases. The families want only the best care for their loved ones. The hospital's challenge is to find reasonable ways to work out the conflicts between the two."

"Mark, what are you talking about?" She wanted to talk about the girlfriend.

"Patients in crisis are treated one way, Cassie. Like Mitch when he came in. Every treatment possible is performed without question. Terminal patients, who've had every treatment we can give them, who are alert and aware at the end, are treated another way. They have some control over the final days of their lives. And, finally, patients in a persistent vegetative state are in an altogether different category."

"I don't understand. Cut to the chase." This got her attention.

"Just listen for a moment. I want to give you some background on this. Our job as physicians is to sustain life whatever the cost. But we can't do that in defiance of the patient's wishes . . ." Mark paused in midsentence.

Cassie gazed out at the neat little dwarf conifers. The Japanese didn't like messy gardens the way she did—with flowers that waxed and waned, so slow to bud, quick to bloom, showy beyond reason for only a few short days, then the long fade-out of wither and drying while the season progressed and the next crop developed. Flower gardens took so much care to look well in every season. In cultivated spaces, the Japanese preferred their gardens spare and predictable. They stuck with evergreens, pruning them down to a tidy shape, stunting nature for pretty much the same view in all seasons. She knew that Mitch was no tidy Japanese. Like her love of excess in the flower beds, he was more the messy type. He'd opt for the long fade-out, never giving up or letting go, as he'd never let go of her.

She felt as cold as that hospital garden that had no visible access. What Mark was telling her was that in her husband's time of crisis she had a spousal right to give up for him. He couldn't choose now, so it was up to her?

"You can't do it in defiance of the patient's wishes. Go on, I'm listening," she murmured.

"We're not there yet, Cassie."

"Where is 'there,' Mark?"

"In a terminal case, we get together, the patient and the family, and together we discuss how the patient wants the end to be. And they can choose, machines or no machines, hospital or home. Patients have some control over the situation, and you'd be surprised the kind of choices they make. A lot of people don't ever want to be hooked up the way Mitch is. But acute care patients are another story. In the absence of the patient, it's the insurance company and the family—and, of course, the hospital, too—that make the decisions."

"I understand," Cassie said.

"You think so, but it can be very difficult. There are many feelings involved—and not least, guilt. Sometimes you think something is best, and later have regrets. . . . I don't want to frighten you. This is down the road."

"Oh, it's okay, scare me to death."

"Come on, I'm being serious."

"So am I."

"You wanted the bottom line. The bottom line is we can't keep him on the respirator forever."

"I thought you said people can stay in a vegetative state for months, even years."

"Yes, I said patients in a vegetative state."

"Isn't Mitch in a vegetative state?"

"Yes. But Mitch is not in a vegetative state on his own. He's got considerable brain damage and he's being sustained. This is the issue."

"Oh, of course." The brain damage helped. And the respirator. How could she forget? "How is the decision made to . . . um . . . ?"

"Oh, I said that was down the road."

"How far down the road, Mark? Are we talking days, weeks, months. How long?" Cassie coughed to cover her impatience.

"Well, there's nothing written in stone about it. But once the patient is stabilized, and there's been no improvement for a period of time. Well . . ." Mark looked away, then back. "You won't be alone with this, Cassie."

"His father is gaga. He only has me and the children. What would that period of time be?"

"I meant you have me and the hospital. The hospital is not cold. We like to keep them as long as possible. The insurance companies, as I said, like to move the cases along. Once the patient is stable, they will want him to move to another hospital. Here's the problem. You don't have that kind of coverage. I know Mitch's business is doing very well. There's no doubt you can handle the costs privately for some time, even indefinitely, if you choose that route."

Cassie swallowed. "What would happen if the respirator were turned off right now?" she asked softly.

Mark didn't answer.

"So what do we have—a week, two weeks?"

"Why don't you call Parker? I'm sure you have a power of attorney. You can explore the options with him."

"Yes, I'll call him." Given the situation, Cassie was pretty sure she didn't have a power of attorney. Mitch would not want his life in her hands now or ever.

Then something new and awful occurred to her. Maybe the

girlfriend had the power of attorney. She closed her eyes against rage rising in her chest. Whenever Cassie thought about this girlfriend, she could hardly breathe. She told herself she had to snap out of it. Jealousy was a waste of emotion. She had to go find Aunt Edith, get rid of her, call Parker. She needed to get to the warehouse and circle the wagons. She wished her son, Teddy, were a little older and wiser, because she had no idea how to circle those wagons.

Behind her sunglasses, Cassie's eyes closed against the chilly Japanese garden out the window and the pain that roiled like lava in her stomach and her throat. Funny how her heart and lungs worked well, drawing in oxygen, circulating it around her body. Everywhere she was alive with feeling except in her numbed face. Suddenly her stomach did a little flip, heralding another feeling that had been dormant, long dormant. Mark had moved his hand. He'd dropped it to her leg and was rubbing the outside of her thigh in a lazy, but persistent circular motion. Startled, she stood up, her eyes blazing with indignation. He couldn't see them, though. She was wearing those sunglasses. "Mark, I've got to go."

He hauled himself to a standing position. He was smiling. He couldn't read her either. He thought things were going well. "How about lunch tomorrow? We'll talk about it some more then, hmmm?"

"Mitch had a girlfriend. Who is it?"

"Ah, I wouldn't know that." Mark was caught off guard. "He didn't share his private life with me."

"His private life? Come off it." Cassie laughed. "I thought I was his private life."

"You know what I mean." Uncomfortable again.

"No, I don't. He was being audited, did you know that?" Cassie went down the list of things she hadn't known.

"Yes. He talked about that. I suspect that may have contributed to this little event. The stress of having to account for one's life, well . . ." He spread his arms out. "No one likes having to explain. I'm sorry, Cassie."

"Thanks." She walked quickly through the glass corridor. Mark followed her, trying to catch up without skipping.

"A horrible man came over to assess the house this morning. He was sneaking around, so Edith called the police."

"Really? Who was it?"

"The IRS. It was very humiliating. Why are they doing this?"

"It's rough. Anything I can do to help?" He skipped even with her and tried to take her hand again.

"We have to stop this," she muttered, meaning his attentions.

"You can ask your accountant. Tax audits are not my department."

He didn't get it. "You don't know this woman's name?" she tried again. "I won't be mad if you tell me. It's not your fault."

"Ah, well, I don't know it." He pursed his lips, looking solid and doctorly.

"Why don't I believe you?" She heaved some oxygen into those lungs. Okay, she had the lawyer to talk to, the accountant. She'd find the girlfriend, and maybe murder her for the simple pleasure of it. She had the IRS audit to deal with. Who could she trust? No one. She found Aunt Edith with Mitch, still cajoling him to squeeze her fingers.

17

CASSIE DROVE HOME SLOWLY, worrying in equal amounts about long-term care, how much it cost, and whether she should come right out and tell Mark not to put his hands all over her. When they were just a few blocks from home, Edith started screaming at her.

"Honey, turn here."

She always turned here. "Here" was the gorgeous Americana, where the North Shore rich went to buy their haute labels. Armani, Prada, Ralph Lauren, Chanel. Hermès. It was just like Beverly Hills or Palm Beach, a mall where shops had awnings, and security guards watched the cars. The Americana was practically her home. The community where Cassie lived was right behind it, hidden by trees. Just driving past it now made her queasy. This was where Mitch's girlfriend did her damage.

"No, don't go straight. Turn left," Edith demanded.

"No, I'm not going shopping now, Aunt Edith. I have to call Mitch's lawyer," Cassie told her.

"I said *stop*! Can't you hear me?" Aunt Edith didn't like being thwarted.

Her screech was so insistent that Cassie jammed on the brakes when ordinarily she would have kept right on going through the yellow light. The car halted with a jerk, throwing both women forward into their seat belts. There went Cassie's new face.

"What's the matter with you?" Cassie cried, terrified that the staples in the back of her scalp had popped open and blood would soon start pouring out into her hair, down her neck.

"I want to get you a hat," Edith said, all sweetness now. "What's wrong with that?"

"You scared me to death, Edith."

"Well, you need a *hat*, Cassie, and I'm going to get you one. Come on, turn in. Something soft, you know, with a big brim and maybe a veil. You can't go out looking like that, Cassie, it's upsetting."

"Edith, I don't want a hat."

"You're no Jackie Kennedy, honey. You look dumpy in that scarf."

Cassie glanced at her very heavy aunt bulging in the white jogging suit. Look who was talking about dumpy. "I don't need criticism right now." Cassie tried to ease the hysteria out of her voice. Next to her two children and her sister, Julie, who may or may not have stolen a number of her mother's most valuable possessions, Aunt Edith was about her only living relative.

"Don't get testy with me, young lady. It's not my fault you lost weight and look dumpy in those clothes. You should get a few new things. And a hat. Anybody with a brain would do that."

"I don't need a single thing." Cassie thought her aunt had gone right around the bend talking about shopping while Mitch was in the hospital.

"You always say that. Now, come on, consider your own needs for a change. He isn't getting out of that bed any quicker if you let yourself go."

This was the second time in an hour that someone had made that comment. What made them think she wanted him out of bed? The light turned green. Cassie accelerated, and the Americana swept by them. "Do you think I let myself go?" She couldn't help asking. It was the last thing she'd meant to do. She hadn't meant to let herself go.

"Let's not get too introspective. Let's just say, you have some problems in this area."

"Edith, did you ever suspect that Mitch was fooling around?" Cassie broached the subject quickly before she had a chance to change her mind. Naturally, she regretted it immediately.

"Oh, honey. I didn't suspect. I knew he was. Didn't you?"

"You knew?" Cassie coughed on her surprise. Was she the only one who didn't know?

"Well, sure, honey. Why do you ask?"

"A terrible thing happened on Friday. Uhuh-uhuh." Cassie tried to clear her throat. "After my eye stitches were removed, Marsha brought me this package all wrapped up in pink tissue paper. I thought it was from her to me, so I opened it. Silk pajamas," she said grimly.

"Nice," Edith said approvingly.

"They weren't just nice, they were gorgeous and very expensive. The price tag was still on them. They cost over a thousand dollars."

"My, my. That Marsha is a nice girl."

"I put them on, and that's when Mitch came home. You know his temper. When he saw those pajamas on me, he had his stroke."

"Honey, are you telling me those pj's caused Mitch's stroke?"

Cassie took a deep breath. "Not the pj's, Aunt Edith, me wearing them. They weren't for me, see?" There, the words were out. Those pajamas had not been for her. She'd known it from the minute she'd seen that price tag.

"How do you know?"

"He had a stroke, didn't he? The whole thing was going to come out. There was no way he could explain it. The man had a stroke to avoid me. Just like him." Another block east and Cassie made her right turn into the forty-year-old development, where she and Mitch had lived their whole married life. In front of her neat colonial the mangled post and mailbox were still on the ground. They seemed to symbolize her ruined life.

"That's *speculation*, not evidence," Edith dismissed her.

"What are you, a lawyer all of a sudden? You said the man was a womanizer. What's *your* evidence?"

"Oh, you get an instinct about people," Edith said, suddenly as vague as the garden under fog. "You should get someone over to fix that post. It's too close to the street. I've told you that a thousand times."

"It's the regulation distance," Cassie told her reflexively. They had this conversation regularly.

"No, it's way too close. No one can park there without knocking it right over. It's the post's fault. Are you hungry, Cassie? You need to eat something."

"I moved the post back once, don't you remember? The mailman refused to deliver." Cassie shook her head. It was way past the time for Edith to give up driving. "Aunt Edith, you don't have a license, you can't see that well. You should get someone to drive you." She'd said it a thousand times.

Edith ignored her as usual. "Cassie, I'll just fix you a little lunch and we'll talk about that girl. Do you know who she is?"

"What girl?" Cassie asked. Like a bird in a tree, Edith jumped from topic to topic, never sticking with anything long enough to make sense.

"Mitch's girl, of course. You need to make sure she keeps away from him."

"Oh, yes," Cassie agreed grimly.

"You never know with these things. These sick old goats give the farm away to whoever changes their diapers. You'd better be the one to change his diapers. Cassie, are you listening to me?"

"I heard every word." Cassie parked in front of the house because the garage was full. She got out, looked around for signs of IRS snooping, saw no strange vehicles on the street. Satisfied for the moment, she went around to the passenger side to pull Edith out.

Getting Edith into a car was easy. She just turned around and backed in, letting herself drop to the seat with a thud that sometimes resulted in a loud fart. Getting her out, however, took more stages. A hand, an arm, a foot extended tentatively out the car door that was open as far as it would go. A heavy leg. Then Edith shifted that butt and inched out by degrees, with a few experimental heaves of her upper body that expelled those internal gases with the authority of a motorcycle thundering down a country road. At the same time, Cassie hauled on her aunt's flabby arms as hard as she could. She had no idea how her aunt accomplished this hydraulic maneuver when she was alone. Edith kept talking as she worked her way out.

"You haven't heard from her yourself, have you?"

"No." Cassie waited for the first sneaker to appear. This new idea startled her; Mitch's girlfriend in actual contact with her.

"You want me to find out about her? I'm pretty good at this kind of thing. There are things we can do, you know."

"No, that's okay." Cassie didn't want to think about what kind of things her aunt meant.

"We could get something on her," Edith mused.

Cassie snorted. The sneaker appeared, the leg, the thigh, the shift. The haul. Miraculously, Edith came out without a gastric fanfare. Proud of this, she waddled regally up the walk to the front door. Cassie didn't want to say she already had something on the girlfriend. Credit card fraud was a felony.

"Listen, Aunt Edith. Why don't I settle you in front of the TV for a few minutes while I make a call. Then I'll drive you home."

"Oh no, I can take my car. You're not grounding me, Cassie. That post was right in the middle of the street. You damaged my car. You'll have to have it fixed for me."

"We'll talk about it later."

"I have to take my own car, Cassie," Edith wailed. "I have to have my independence."

"We'll see," Cassie told her.

But no, they wouldn't. The little stunt this morning had been Edith's last chance at independence. Cassie would not have on her conscience some fatal car crash like the ones she'd seen in the hospital. She got the front door open and led her aunt into the kitchen.

"I'll just make you a little lunch," Edith promised. But right away she found the clicker to the TV and turned on *The Young and the Restless*. She sat down at the kitchen table and forgot about cooking lunch for anybody.

Cassie moved quickly down the hall to Mitch's office. As she turned the corner, she moved like the cops in the TV shows, jumping to stay out of doorways just in case that IRS man was in there looking for the wine Mitch had in his cellar and other stuff he must have stashed away.

The IRS man, however, was not at Mitch's desk going through his papers, so Cassie sat down there. She picked up the phone and called Parker Higgins, the family lawyer. As she waited for the receptionist to get through to Parky's secretary, she hit the AOL button on Mitch's computer, then the automatic Sign On. Clearly, he hadn't been afraid of her gaining access. Ah, Mitch had mail. A lot of it. Cassie scanned down the ridiculous names people gave themselves: Abscul. MAD. Hopup. Winebuff. Kringeetc. She didn't know any of these people. Kringeetc. Who the hell could that be? Hopup? Didn't that sound like a prostitute? Maybe Mitch didn't have just one girl. What if there was a whole army of them and they all used a card with her name on it? Cassie was nauseated by the thought of having to change Mitch's diapers to stop his girlfriends from getting the farm. She wished it wouldn't ruin her face to heave up her guts.

"Yes, this is Diana, can I help you?" queried a woman with a thick Long Island accent.

"This is Cassandra Sales. Is Mr. Higgins there?"

"I'll check for you, Cassie."

"Thank you, Diana. Will you tell him it's urgent? Mitch is in the hospital." Cassie scanned down the list of e-mail names and didn't recognize any of them.

Five seconds later the friend they called Parky was on the line talking fast in his hearty lawyer voice. "Hey, Cassie, how *are* you? Long time no see, babe."

Even when she'd been young, Cassie had never been the babe type. "Yes, long time. I'm not so good, Parker. Mitch had a stroke on Friday. He's in intensive care." And I had my face lifted.

"Yes, Mark called me. It's a real shocker."

"Yes." It certainly was.

"How is he doing?"

"He's not doing well. That's the reason I called."

"Oh gosh, I'm sorry. What can I do to help?"

Gosh, indeed. "I need the papers, Parky."

"To what papers are you referring?" Parky's voice took on that furry-edged garden fog Cassie was beginning to recognize as the cover for all requests for information about her husband.

"Oh, I don't know. The doctors say I need a power of attorney, things like that."

"What for, Cassie?" Parker sounded sincerely puzzled.

"He's on life support."

"Oh, that's a shocker," he said more slowly this time as if Mark hadn't already discussed it with him. "It's hard to believe. We had lunch together only a few weeks ago. He looked in the pink then."

Uh-huh. "What did you talk about?"

"Oh the usual things, business . . . why do you ask, Cassie?"

"He's left a few things to be taken care of. The business, his personal affairs, an audit I didn't know anything about. Let's face it, there's a whole lot I didn't know a single thing about. I need to go through it with you. Just to get the finances all sorted out in my mind. And, of course, I have some decisions to make concerning his care."

"Uh-huh. I know what you're talking about, Cassie. But I don't know if I can help you there."

"Can't help me where, Parker? With the care or the decisions or the finances?" Cassie's own voice took on an edge.

"With any of it. I hope you won't take this personally."

"What are you talking about? Of course I take it personally. You're our lawyer. I need you to act in that capacity."

"Well, I'm sorry to have to be the one to tell you this, Cassie, but there's a little problem with that. I represent Mitchell, as you know. That means there's a confidentiality issue here. And there are ethical issues as well."

"I thought you represented *both* of us, Parky. I don't understand."

Parker Higgins, a smoothie from way back, inhaled with such ferocity, Cassie could hear the rasping breath all the way from Garden City. "I've always represented Mitch, Cassie. Both for business and personal. We went to school together, you know that. Our relationship goes way back."

"So?"

"Let me stress that this is not personal. My responsibilities are with him and his wishes." He said this as if any reasonable person would understand this.

But Cassie didn't understand it. She exploded. "You're being a dickhead, Parker. This is a life-and-death situation. You have a responsibility to tell me, his wife, the things I need to know to determine what kind of care he gets. It's not a hard one."

"Well, of course, if he wants me to," Parker stonewalled.

"I'm not sure I understand what you're saying. You can't tell me if there's a power of attorney, a living will, simple things like that?"

"Well, there might be a conflict of interest here."

"Conflict of interest? What kind of conflict of interest?"

"The usual kind, between one person and another."

The man was being more than a dickhead. Cassie boiled right over. "Between who and who?" she screamed.

"Between you and him, Cassie. Don't get crazy on me."

Cassie's surgeon had told her to watch happy movies and think lovely thoughts during her weeks of recuperation to promote healing and lessen the chance of scarring. She opened and closed her mouth, then her puffy eyes. Both were as dry as the desert. She was going to be scarred for life because of this, she just knew it. Getting crazy? Getting crazy? Was he *crazy*? What was this about conflict of interest, and why hadn't she heard about it before today? And by the way, where was *her* loyal, personal lawyer?

"What are you trying to tell me, Parky? We've known each other for a long time." Her voice meek now.

"I know we have, and I have very positive feelings for you personally, Cassie. I think you're a wonderful woman. Just wonderful. And I really, truly wish I could help you."

"And I really, truly think you're a callous prick, Parker. Your friend and client had a stroke. Don't you want to help him?"

"I'm very sad about that. What hospital is he in? I'll go see him. I have an hour at five. How's that? If he gives me the okay, I'll tell you whatever you want to know. Is that fair?"

"He's in a coma. He can't give you an okay," Cassie told him coldly.

"Really?"

"What do you think I'm calling you for? Mitch is brain-dead. He can't talk, he can't even breathe on his own. He's not giving out okays right now. So where does that leave us? You and me?"

"Well, that's—a shocker."

I'm not crazy, Cassie told herself. I'm *not* crazy. The man in the coma had been preparing to divorce her. The deep silence that followed confirmed her suspicion that Mitch Sales had been about to divorce her, and he'd set her up to cheat her out of half his assets. It was another one of those things she got in a second. It wasn't a hard one, and it took her breath away. The two of them, Mitch and his old college friend, Parky Higgins, and maybe this woman, too—all of them had been cooking up a plan. She'd seen enough TV to know the story. Mitch had traveled to Grand Cayman Island, where he'd deposited a large sum of money in a bank out of U.S. jurisdiction and her sight. Right here at home, he'd had taken out accounts in her name and racked up huge bills that he would claim were hers and demand that she take responsibility for in the divorce settlement.

Without any warning that anything of this kind was in the wind, he'd probably believed that she would be so stunned and frightened and hurt and ashamed by the accusations of all those excesses that she would have to accept his terms just to be free of public humiliation.

And if he hadn't had his stroke, she might have gotten caught up in the scam, might well have ended up poor, poor, poor, just like Mary Ann Kaufman, who couldn't even get enough money from her deadbeat husband to pay for computer school. Or Sue Whistle, who'd gotten a brain tumor after she was dumped by Willie and had died of a broken heart.

Cassie knew just how this kind of thing worked. Mary Ann Kaufman's ex-husband was a heart surgeon worth millions who'd suddenly gone into a downward spiral. He claimed his hands hurt so badly, he couldn't operate. This caused him to become depressed and impotent. He couldn't bear to be with anyone. He had to be alone. No medication but divorce would work for him. Mary Ann loved him *so much* and felt so sorry for him that she agreed to let him keep the five-bedroom house and the cars in the divorce settlement. She moved into a studio apartment too small for an overnight with her college-age kids and took a job selling perfume at Lord and Taylor so he wouldn't be burdened with her care.

And guess what happened then? Harry immediately had a miraculous recovery. It was a complete miracle. His hand stopped hurting. He got over his depression and his impotence. He resumed his booming practice, and the nurse he'd been screwing for years moved in and redecorated Mary Ann's house. Within a year they married, and Mary

Ann's two kids went to the wedding. And Harry never had to give her a dime.

"Cassie, are you there?"

"Yes, I'm here, Parky. And I may be wrong, but I think the law regards me as Mitch's wife and next of kin no matter what he was planning down the road. But you can research that."

"Yes, of course you are, Cassie, of course. Don't even think about that."

"What's the woman's name?"

"Woman? I don't know what you mean."

"The woman Mitch was divorcing me for, Parky."

"Cassie, I don't know what you're talking about. Mitch adores you. What are his chances for recovery?"

"Very slim, I'm afraid."

"Gee, I'm so sorry, Cassie. I'm shocked and I'm sorry. Are you sure?"

"You can ask Mark Cohen again. I'm sure you did already. Is he in on this, too? You guys together, all of you?"

"I'm sorry to cut you off, Cassie, but I'm going into a meeting right now. I'm going to get back to you later on this, okay?"

"Cassie. Cassie, Cassie," Edith was screaming from the kitchen. "I'm starving, honey. What had you planned to serve for lunch?"

18

MILD-MANNERED CASSIE, who'd always been so careful to feed the birds in winter, who couldn't even think of killing the moles that tunneled through her garden and ate her bulbs, who'd bought one of those beeper boxes to keep the mice out of her basement so she wouldn't have to catch them on sticky tape or trap them or poison them, was wondering how to stop this unconscionable girlfriend from doing what Cassie couldn't do: get her husband's attention from wherever he'd gone and bring him back to life so he could leave her in ruin. She didn't want her anywhere near Mitch or the hospital, or anything. Who was this woman with the power to destroy her?

Cassie went through Mitch's e-mails, and it wasn't too hard to find the one she was looking for. Her rival signed her messages M. The first one was dated Friday night. It read, "Still in Paris. Call me when you get home. M knocks your socks off."

Huh? Cassie's stitches were itching terribly. Knocks his socks off? M's Saturday morning e-mail said, "No answer at your house or mine. Honey, where are you? I'm worried. M knocks your socks off."

Saturday afternoon, M wrote again. "Precious pumpkin, no answer anywhere. What's going on? Are you all right? M knocks your socks off."

Sunday's crop included one about Teddy. M said, "I called Teddy at home. He wasn't there, either. Where is everybody? PLEASE, you know

what a WORRIER I am. Ira hasn't heard from you. Parky hasn't heard
from you. Stephen and Bill haven't heard a thing. I'm frantic. The
weather in P is just gorgeous. I saw a little apartment I liked in the 16th
near the park, but we'll talk about that later. I'm on my way home. Probably ovulating on Tuesday. Hint. Hint. Can't wait to see you. M knocks
your socks off."

Apartment in the 16th? Ovulating Tuesday? It was a funny thing
about anger. Every time Cassie thought her rage was as hot as it could
get, more reality took her deeper into it. She felt her body would ignite
with it. And Mitch must have been just as excited in his own way, too.
He must have been like that Dutch boy with his finger in the dike. All
around him the waters of his other life had been rising around him, en-
snaring him, drawing him ever deeper into the currents that would eventually kill him. He'd gotten bolder and bolder in his scam. The only
thing that got in his way was that little thing called the IRS.

She, his wife of twenty-six years, was nothing. She was a nonentity
he thought he could fool as long as he wanted, then just end at will. He
must have relished the idea of keeping that flood of knowledge back
from her just by closing a door in the house. But now the door was open,
the real story was out. The IRS man, Charlie Schwab, was searching for
his millions. She was boiling with rage, and he wasn't getting away with
anything.

Parky was their lawyer. Ira Mandel was their accountant. Stephen
and Bill were both salesmen in the company. And Teddy. Teddy was
her own son. No wonder the boy sometimes had the look of a half-wit,
a dolt who didn't know his ass from his elbow. He'd been hiding
out. What if even Teddy had been in on the conspiracy? Hurt enlarged
her and spun her out of her natural orbit. She was a volcano, a hurri-
cane, a tornado—one of those really big natural disasters about to
occur.

As she processed the extent of her husband's betrayal, it became
clear to Cassie that she had no choice but to kill him. Tomorrow morning she had to go into his ICU room and pull the plug on that respirator.
Put the man out of his misery. It would be an act of love, a mercy killing.
No one in the world could fault her, and if not she, then Mark or a nurse

would do it for her. They did it all the time; Mark himself had told her this was one of the choices she could make. It was a viable and legal option. No wonder Parky Higgins had acted as he had. She got it. She finally got it. She had the motive and the power to snuff her own husband, and snuff him she would.

AT TWO ON MONDAY AFTERNOON, Mona Whitman was having that sad, hurt, and lonely feeling she got whenever Mitch gave her a hard time. She was on the phone at her desk, trying to be enthusiastic for a buyer from Montana, but it wasn't easy. Eustace Arcs was a rancher with a large handlebar mustache who was using Sales Importers, Inc., to stock his new lodge in Montana, and Mitch just loved him. Mitch had a special attraction for very rich people.

To custom-design Stace's wine cellar for his clientele and menu around his $200,000 budget, they'd traveled to New Zealand to fly fish with him for three horrible days last year, and Mona herself had actually been up to her thighs in freezing water for at least an hour. Mitch, however, who fancied himself something of a sportsman, had reveled in every miserable minute. The promise of a bigger account on the come, and more rich people to cultivate as new friends with ambitions to develop their own prestigious cellars kept him interested. Mitch was at the $890,000,000 mark in gross sales a year. He wanted to hit the billion-dollar benchmark by 2003. It was not out of his reach. But she herself didn't care a fig about money.

As she listened to "Stace" describe his seven-figure restaurant renovation, she was also rehearsing her present situation with the man she'd thought of as her fiancé for the last two years since she'd hit her thirty-sixth birthday and started freaking out over tiny wrinkles and her aging eggs.

Mona was a very practical girl whose bible was *The Art of War*, written by Sun Tzu at the dawn of history to codify the successful techniques of warring Chinese chieftains seeking to establish sole rule over a vast realm of bellicose clans. Its credo was, *"Warfare is the basis of life and death, the Way to survival or extinction. It must be thoroughly analyzed."*

Mona used the book as her horoscope, her guide, her confidant, and best friend. She analyzed it daily and applied the strategy of the Seven Military Classics to human relations, romantic liaisons, and company infighting. This was how she analyzed the present situation in the hundred-year war of the worlds between her and her intended. They had been separated for three whole days, ever since he'd left Paris early Friday morning. The night before he'd taken off they'd had a truly wonderful and unexpected sexual adventure. It made Mona so confident of her success on the battlefield of marriage that she hadn't packed up and flown back with him from Paris on a moment's notice as he'd wanted her to.

The evening had started as the usual sort of thing. They had gone to a new restaurant called Nouvelle Etoile, where the tab had been nearly seven hundred dollars. She hadn't eaten the main course or the dessert (calories). The wine was sensational, however, and she'd had a lot of that. After chatting with the new star's owner and chef, they'd returned to their room at the Georges V, where the movie stars and moguls stay, although sometimes they did prefer the Ritz. Just as Mitch was pouring his brandy nightcap, they heard the entrance of a hooker through the connecting door to the next room. This was an occurrence unheard of before at the V, where they'd always thought the walls were a whole lot thicker. Lucky for them the whole thing went on in English.

The "gentleman" next door clearly asked what the girl's name was and if she'd eaten yet. She told him her name was Claire, and no, she hadn't. He ordered her some smoked salmon and champagne. Very considerate.

Mitch drank his brandy as the couple had casual conversation and waited for the food. Mona was particularly excited by the idea of the hooker performing next door and wondered what she looked like and how good her technique was. Mitch was pretty aroused himself, although he wouldn't admit it. Mitch was a large, powerful man who dressed impeccably and had pretty simple tastes in sex. Mona didn't like to brag, but he was in no way a management problem. He liked to look at her in pretty underwear and pretty outfits. He liked to watch her taking some of the items off, but not all of them. He didn't think perfectly naked was fun either for her or for himself. The sight of her lovely body partially clothed or fully clothed, but with no underpants, excited him most of all.

As soon as he got an erection, which was as soon and often as she wanted him to, he had to get into her right away. He was in such a big hurry, he rarely took the time to take his pants off. He unzipped and jumped her like a cowboy wrestling down a steer, banging her enthusiastically, either from the front or back, depending on how confident he felt. He preferred her pussy tight, which was easy enough to provide since they never did much in the way of foreplay. Mona was totally crazy about him and rarely had to do a thing. Her fantasies during the four minutes it took her lover to come alternated between Leda's rape by the swan, penetration by the huge dick of the bull that sired the Minotaur, and being a favorite sex slave in a steamy, sultry, torrid harem of a sheik of Araby.

On blow job nights, it was another story altogether. Blow jobs were specialty items she doled out carefully because they took for*ever*. Mitch liked thinking she loved him so much that she could joyfully suck and lick him all night and he never had to feel the slightest bit rushed. He did not like feeling rushed. Even the tiniest threat of pressure to get it *over* with could keep him on the brink for another hour. If the deal was for orgasm, she had to go for completion no matter how tired she got of sucking and yanking. She only sucked him to orgasm and swallowed when a deal was on the table. Thursday night a deal had been on the table. They were getting married so she could be a mother before her eggs got too old.

Then a surprising thing happened in the sex next door. It turned out not to be a meat-and-potatoes job. The john liked to spank noisily, and pretty soon the smacks and accompanying moans traveled through the walls like shots across the water. (He must have done some practicing.) In any case, this idea of punishment as an accompaniment to sex had never occurred to Mitch before, and he was captivated by it.

He told Mona to strip to her bra, garter belt, and stockings, which of course she did. He sat on the chair by the desk, by the door to the room next door. He emptied the brandy glass and pressed it against the door, the better to hear what was going on. Mona *loved* her costume—gold stockings, gold bra, and a gold garter belt. Gold was one of her best colors. Her bottom was bare. Still in her fuck-me shoes, she knelt on the carpet without even wondering when last it had been shampooed. In a second she was between his knees, unzipping his Sulka Cavalry twills. Mitch was not a badly hung man. Maybe seven inches. Maybe as much as eight. His endowment was certainly nothing to scoff at, and she was totally crazy about him. She always got excited just thinking about his cock. Tonight the thing was absolutely huge with the added thrill of hearing Claire cry, "*Oui, oui, oui!*" each time a slap resounded on her French fanny and thighs.

Thinking about living happily ever after with him, Mona settled into her job with a fervor unknown to her before. Her tongue traveled round and round the head of Mitch's cock, darting in and out of the hole the way he liked it, while her hands moved energetically up and down the shaft. She got it really wet but didn't slurp. Her energy and skill got the thing throbbing almost immediately. Mitch was huffing and puffing and gasping and moaning like a man in absolute paradise. He made a few experimental squeezes and claplike pats at her bottom and came like a rocket in no time flat. This time she knew she'd be a bride before September for sure.

But then the next morning he went home to Long Island without any warning at all. First of all, any separation between them was extremely unusual. But even more unusual was the fact that he hadn't spoken to her once since.

> One who knows the enemy and knows himself will not be endangered in a hundred engagements. One who does not know the enemy but knows himself will sometimes be victorious, sometimes

meet with defeat. One who knows neither the enemy nor himself will invariably be defeated in every engagement.

Know your enemy. Mitch was a very dependent man parading as an independent one, so it wasn't like him to sulk for long about anything.

Know yourself. Mona would be the first to admit that Thursday night she *might* have pushed him just a little too hard about telling Cassie she was history, but the end of the evening had turned out so well, she was certain the two of them were chapel bound. She certainly had not anticipated that he would overreact on the way home. They'd been planning to stay abroad for three weeks. In France they would do the heart of Burgundy, the Côte d'Or, the golden slope, where some of the most pricey wines in the world were made. Then they'd hop down to Italy, where they'd been wooing two important producers for several years. The two stuck together, even though they were in different regions and were just on the verge of changing distributors and signing with them. If Mitch pulled it off, the well-known Tuscan Chiantis and Piedmont Barolos would give them a 3 percent increase in sales.

As for the audit, Mitch always left the audits to Ira and never had any trouble. They had sales figures for a company of $600,000,000. Every year there was a little audit. Every year they paid a little extra, and it was no problem. But this year, for some reason, Mitch was worried and had changed his mind about going to Italy. He was a big baby. All she'd wanted was for him to set a *tentative* September date for their wedding. Tentative was not *absolute*. And she hoped to be pregnant by then anyway. He had to get used to the idea. She'd waited for twelve years. She wasn't waiting anymore.

It did not take a brilliant strategist to know that this was the time for action. He hated his wife, was rarely in the same room with her. They had no interests in common. They hadn't been together sexually for years. She ticked the items off on her fingers. It made no sense for him to drag his feet anymore. Every single day of Mona's life he insulted her and her ovaries and their child-to-be with this delay. Was there something she was missing?

He had insulted her further by calling her selfish (after their wonderful night) when she didn't go right home with him. Anybody would agree it was *much* more selfish of him to go home early than it was for her to stay two measly days more in Paris. They were supposed to be having fun! Now he wouldn't even let her back down and tell him she was very sensitive to his dilemma. Very sensitive.

"One who knows when he can fight, and when he cannot fight, will be victorious."

The last thing Mona wanted to do was hurt Cassie. She loved Cassie. She was totally sincere when she said, "Mitch, Cassie is the greatest, honey. You underestimate her. Believe me she's strong enough to face reality."

She studied her nail polish as Stace's voice drifted back into her consciousness. He was talking about chopping down entire redwood forests for his stupid lodge and illegally shooting the wolves that had been reproducing like crazy, killing dozens of cows and chickens and dogs. Stace had told her it was a felony to shoot a wolf, but what was a rancher to do when the government was run by a bunch of tree huggers who couldn't see a natural disaster when it hit them in the face? Mona saw Cassie the same way and totally agreed with him.

Mona's last manicure had been three days ago in Paris, but it wasn't a very good job. Specks of burgundy polish flecked her cuticles. She hated that. She tuned out, then in to the conversation again when Stace started agitating for her and Mitch to come see his magnificent building in Brilling or wherever it was, as if they didn't see a bazillion million-dollar restaurants right here in the tristate area every day. Stace was such a small-town boy.

Mona sighed. She wished Mitch would just grow up and stop going psycho on her every few months. Every time he did his psycho thing, she felt so alone and unprotected that he had to pay big-time to make her feel safe and secure again. And then, of course, she never really did. *"Which ruler has the Tao?"* She or Mitch?

"By next week the snow should all be melted, and we can get you up on a horse," Stace was saying.

Horses. Snow in June? Nothing could be less appealing. Mona didn't care if Robert Redford or anybody else lived there, she wasn't going to Montana.

"Know your Terrain." Mona had strict rules about traveling in America. She would go to New Orleans, yes. Chicago, yes. Anywhere in California, yes. Tucson, yes. Kansas City, yes. Miami and Boca, definitely. But Montana, hill country, and mountains, no! She fluffed her burgundy curls, thinking for a moment about silver Indian jewelry and leather skirts with fringes as shown in *Vogue* and *Elle* recently in stories about "the new West." Still a definite no!

"We're planning to come out to the ranch in August," she lied, gazing out the internal picture window of the office she'd been sharing with Mitch for all of eight months. His moving her into his office was supposed to signal his readiness to leave Cassie and marry her. Had it happened? No, it had not. Did she have a right to be annoyed? Yes, she most certainly did. Age was terrifying her. Thirty-eight and unmarried was Not Acceptable.

"Know victory and defeat." But still the office was something. Her old office had been airless, tiny, and lacking a view of the cavernous insides of the temperature-controlled warehouse that was the second love of her life. Seeing all that *primo* vino gave her the same surge of pride she felt whenever she neared Manhattan and saw the skyline of her and Mitch's playground rise right out of boring old Queens.

The vino was housed in a building in Syosset that was as large as an airline hangar. When Mona had first encountered the aisles of wine racks in the much smaller warehouse that Mitch had owned back then, she'd been a young bookkeeper, not beautiful, but so determined to be somebody that she'd already left her car dealership first husband with goals of knowing people of greater taste than those who shopped for Saturns. When she'd seen all that wine, she was reminded of the stacks in her childhood library where books were lined up like hundreds of soldiers waiting for their chance to march off into readers' little hearts. Just like a certain book had marched permanently into hers, so had Mitch.

Now, twelve years later, she no longer did the books or read very many of them. Sales Importers, Inc., was a big company with a big inventory in several great big warehouses. She and Mitch dispensed taste and memories by the hundreds of thousands of cases, in small liquor stores and large ones, to Internet suppliers and restaurants. Some of it was cash business, strictly secret. The money was rolling in. They traveled extensively, studying vineyards and soils and production all over the world, tasting wine after wine. They chose their stock carefully, and didn't bother with wines that sold under ten dollars. Mitch liked to focus on clients who were used to good wine and drank several bottles of it every single night. Thousands of cases from Italy, Germany, France, Chile, Australia, South Africa, and dozens of wineries in the United States rested on metal racks that towered fifteen feet, twenty feet, thirty-five feet into the steel beams that held up the roof. Security guards watched their stock at night, and two forklifts were kept busy chugging around all day long on the cement floor, moving orders in and out. And this was only here.

The company was doing so well that they had nearly a hundred sales reps traveling around the country, servicing the thousands of accounts that were solidly on the books. Mona herself did a huge business, and Mitch was the Bordeaux futures expert, the gambler. And they had their lobby in Washington to keep things status quo. Mona was proud of all that she had accomplished, but all that mattered to her really was love. She was frequently tortured by doubts that Mitch would really keep his promise and marry her.

She made an irritated noise. Down on the floor was that IRS guy. This was another thing that had been carefully orchestrated. Ira had particularly advised them to be out of the country during all their audits. He'd told them it was crucial never to have a personal involvement with any governmental agent, especially not an IRS agent. Ira warned them that those small-minded people were terrorists, armed by the Feds and dangerous. You had to insulate yourself from them, and he was the insulator. Now she could see that he was absolutely right. This man was someone they didn't know, who was not supposed to be here until tomorrow, and his presence made her nervous as hell. He was walking around the precious racks as if it were a great big gold field just waiting for him to plunder. Somehow he looked familiar, a little like the rat Bruce, who'd dumped her in junior high.

Where Ira was, where Teddy was, where Mitch himself was, Mona had no idea. But here she was, all alone, holding the fort against a threat too terrifying even to imagine. It was the story of her life. A nuclear attack, a holocaust could not be worse persecution than this tax thing. Here was an enemy she did not know and could not prepare for. The whole thing was out of her hands. She tried not to let the fact that she was not the true and actual Mrs. Mitchell Sales, of Sales Importers, Inc., arouse what Mitch called "her paranoid side."

"We'll take the horses and go on a pack trip," Stace was saying.

"That sounds *wonderful*," Mona murmured, allowing herself a moment's amusement at Stace's thinking he was important enough to lure her out to the middle of the country—where she was not sure planes even *landed*—with the promise of a large dumb animal to sit on. She already had one of those right here.

"What about those auctions in Italy you were telling me about? We still doing that?" he demanded.

"Oh, yes, the auctions in Verona. We have it all planned." Mona said this in her sweetest voice, even though she and Mitch had already been and done their buying at the auctions in Verona. The auctions were at the end of March.

The IRS agent disappeared in the racks. A minute later he rounded a corner, and a forklift about to make a pickup at waist level almost pronged him in the groin. His wild scramble to get away caused her to giggle.

"What's funny? Is Mitch there? I want to say hey."

Mona tuned back into Stace for the last time. Well, he wasn't the only one who wanted to say hey to Mitch. The man was not picking up his e-mails, not picking up his cell phone. If she didn't know for a fact that Cassie was a dodo, she might think something was up.

"Well, honey, I wish I could put you on with Mitch, but you know I'm handling all the details of the Italy trip myself. You can certainly tell me all your special requests." She tapped her fingers on the desk. Time to hang up.

"I just want to say hey."

"Well, of course, you want to say hey. And Mitch wants to say hey, too, but you know, Mitch. Always on the run. How about I have him call you as soon as he comes in?"

Finally Stace was ready to hang up, and Mona's jet lag dizziness hit. She checked her watch. Mitch was really making her sweat. She hadn't planned to come in today. She'd planned to touch base with him and make up last night, then sleep late, and have a beauty afternoon with a salt rub, a massage, a manicure, and her hair colored in the afternoon. But he hadn't come in. She checked her e-mails again, then dialed his cell.

"Hello?"

"Ah—" Mona hesitated. It was Cassie.

It is essential for a general to be tranquil and obscure, upright and self-disciplined, and able to stupefy the eyes and ears of the officers and troops, keeping them ignorant.

"Hello, Mona. Mitch isn't here right now."

"Cassie, sweetheart. How are you? I was just going to call you."

"Really, why?" That bland, blank voice always set Mona's teeth on edge.

"Why? What kind of question is that? I miss you, of course, silly. Haven't seen you in months and months. And Mitch is off the radar screen, too. He didn't come in this morning. Know where he is? I've got clients looking for him."

Cassie didn't answer, and Mona went on super alert. She had special powers and respected them. Every reader she'd ever consulted had said the same thing. She was acutely sensitive to auras. She could tell a stranger's future. She especially knew who were the winners and losers by their smallest gestures. She could also tell what people were thinking about her.

Mona was so sensitive, in fact, that sometimes her body felt like one giant vibrating nerve. She'd read that rocks and stones and beer cans and bottles that looked solid were really filled with cells that were moving all the time. She was like those cells in matter. She might look like a fragile flower with trembling petals, but really she was the cells in stone. The puppet master of everything; nothing could break or outlast her. She was never lost, whatever challenge she took on. Never. She never lost.

"Are you okay, Cassie? You sound kind of stressed," she said warily.

"Well, I am stressed," Cassie replied tartly.

"Where are you? Why are you talking on Mitch's cell phone?"

"I'll tell you in a few minutes, Mona. Just stay where you are." Cassie broke the connection.

20

MONA GOT UP AND MARCHED straight to the bathroom. She surveyed herself in the mirror. She looked pretty good for someone who felt old and ugly no matter what she did. She gave herself a happy little smile and touched up her makeup. Then she galloped down the metal stairway to the floor, where one of her four-inch spike fuck-me shoes suddenly caught on a tiny invisible crack in the cement. Her chronically weak right ankle gave way under her.

"Ow!"

The IRS agent, lurking in the stacks, reached out and caught her deftly, preventing her from falling on the hard floor just as she'd hoped he would. No man or boy had ever been able to resist her except the one from junior high and the ones who were gay.

"Oh my," she cried.

"You okay?" The man's very nice blue eyes lit up only for a second at the sight of her pretty legs, then switched right to concern.

She gazed at him, sizing him up. The eyes were deep blue, like the Mediterranean. Gentle, she could tell. He was attractive, nice build. Nice mouth. His suit was not expensive, though, and she figured him for one of life's losers. From her contact with many men, Mona knew that the jerk who'd let her down in seventh grade could definitely be hers now.

This assessment of the IRS agent made her feel a lot better about life in general. She did not touch his IRS agent biceps to test for muscle. She was nothing if not subtle. She forgot that she was supposed to be out of town for governmental agents and thought this not-bad-looking man might do her some good. She could turn him. You could never have too many IRS agents on your side. *"Internal spies—employ people who hold government positions."*

"Thank you. I'm so embarrassed. That was so clumsy." She tried to stand on her terrible turned ankle. She did not touch him with such subtlety, only an expert would know she had. The whole thing about men was that you had to know how to go about winning them. Nothing overt, ever.

"Did I hurt you?" She detected a little excitement on his side and let her ankle flop over again, but once again did not cave enough to encourage him.

"Oh no." He created more space between them. "Ha-ha, there you go."

"Oh, thank you." Mona gave him a worshipful glance. "What's your name? I'm supposed to know you, right? I know I know you."

"Charles Schwab," he said, keeping his gaze at eye level. He had as much confidence in the effect of his name as Mona did of her looks.

Mona gave out a great whoop of joy and grabbed her chest. She'd made a mistake and underestimated him. "Oh, I've seen you on TV. Really, I had no idea you were a client. Are you buying for your firm? How exciting. Who's your account executive? I can't believe we've never met."

"Sort of." He showed her his I.D., then passed her an Internal Revenue Service card with his name on it. A pretty blush warmed her tan. She hadn't underestimated him. She always knew everything.

"Oh my, I'm really getting off on the wrong foot with you, aren't I? Revenue agent, what a joke on me," she murmured.

"No, ma'am. It's no joke."

"I mean, I thought you guys were all toads. Oops. I didn't mean that." Mona noticed that the man's eyes went as cold as a hit man's.

But Schwab laughed pleasantly. "A lot of people think we're a lot worse than toads."

"Well, I'm Mona Whitman. Are we getting audited again?"

"Yes, indeed."

She gave him a teasing frown. "Well, I'm a little hurt about this, if you'd like to know the truth. Every year it's something and every year we come out clean. There are so many compliances in our business. It's, like, the most regulated business on *earth*. But you know that." She heaved a great sigh. "Frankly I thought by now we'd be getting a medal from you people."

She paused for breath.

"And then, after doing everything right, to have to face such scrutiny. What went wrong this time? Ira, our accountant, answered every single question you asked. It took him months to get all that paper together. No one thinks about all those trees we have to cut down. The whole thing just upsets me so much." She gave Schwab a tremulous, searching smile. "Why us?"

He smiled back, almost knocking her out with his white teeth.

"Frankly, I'm just the concept person. I consult for the restaurants. I bet you didn't know they need designers to plan their cellars and menus. I love the company so much. That's why this hurts, you know?" She massaged her foot with one hand, then slid her shoe back on. "That's a lot better."

Schwab was silent, so Mona took this as a sign to keep talking.

"I thought the IRS was getting nicer these days. Didn't I read that in the *Times*? Are you persecuting Mitch just because he's successful? Or what?"

"How's that ankle?"

"It's terrible. I'll probably never walk straight again. But what can you do, right? Listen, is there something I can help you with? Mitch isn't here right now, and neither is Ira. They were expecting you *tomorrow*."

"Yeah, it's too bad about his stroke."

"Ira had a stroke?" Mona grabbed her chest a second time.

"No, Mr. Sales did."

"Oh no, you're mistaken," she said confidently.

"I was with his wife this morning. She told me."

"*She* told you?" Mona's face froze.

"Yes, when we were over at the house."

Mona snorted. "Oh dear, I'm so sorry you had to meet her. Was it terrible for you?"

"It was unusual."

"I'll bet." Mona knew that silly Cassie must have been terrorized by a visit from the IRS and unable to deal with the stress, so she'd blurted out this ridiculous, transparent lie because she couldn't think of an effective strategy like Mona.

Schwab let out a laugh. "She called the police on me. Four squad cars, guns, and everything."

Mona erupted into tinkling laughter herself. "That's priceless. Cassie's a dear in her own way, but she's been a real financial drain. It's like a sickness, a big burden on him. Poor man. Mitch has been a real saint to put up with her." Mona raised her eyebrows. "A wife like that, Mr. Schwab, can ruin a man. But very sweet as a person."

"Are you telling me that Mr. Sales didn't have a stroke?"

Mona laughed again. "No, no. Of course not. This is the first I've heard of it. I just spoke to Cassie a few minutes ago, and she didn't mention a thing about it to me."

Mona took special note that there were brown spots on Charles Schwab's shirt cuffs. His hat looked as if it had fleas. The blue eyes that she'd thought were sweet only moments ago were marbles now. He was not thinking of making time with her.

"That's good news," he murmured.

"Poor Cassie, you really can't believe anything she says. If someone's not with her every minute, she forgets to take her medicine. It's very sad. Can I have Ira call you tomorrow?"

"No need. We have a meeting scheduled."

Mona thought she might just lead Schwab out to his car. "It's just that nobody who knows anything is here right now, and I have to—"

"That's no problem. I don't need anyone. I was just looking around, getting the lay of the land."

"I'm concerned that you're being ignored."

"No, no, not at all. I like to get the feel for a place and the people. Some people think it's absolutely all in the paper, but you'd be surprised how helpful impressions can be. You, for example, have been very helpful."

"I have? I'll walk you to your car," Mona said happily.

"Not with that ankle, you won't."

"No, it's fine, really. You know, you remind me of my first boyfriend. It's just amazing." Actually, the handsome Bruce had never given Mona the time of day, but she had loved him with all her heart. Probably still did. She gazed at Schwab. "He was the best-looking boy I ever met."

"No kidding." Charlie tipped his hat without losing his crooked grin.

"When you come back will you teach me about audits? I don't know a thing about the business side."

"I know. You're the concept person." He smiled. Clearly the man was very attracted to her.

Mona thought this encounter was going extremely well. What a break that Cassie had called the cops. Giving herself the benefit of the doubt here, even she couldn't have thought of a better stunt than that. Schwab grinned as they walked out into the parking lot, where he remarked, "You look like you're doing okay with that ankle."

"Oh, it hurts like mad, but what can you do? Hey, maybe I'll see you tomorrow. Does your wife also work for the IRS?"

Charlie IRS Schwab actually stopped short and looked at her as if no one in the world had ever asked him that question. Mona put her hand to her mouth in surprise. She couldn't believe she'd said such a thing. She never made mistakes like that.

Schwab didn't reply. He gave her a little wave, got into a beaten-up black Buick, and drove off. Trembling, Mona drew her own cell phone out of her pocket and dialed Mitch's number. This time Cassie didn't pick up.

21

MONA KNEW SHE WAS ABOUT to have an asthma attack. Asthma attacks were terrifying. First the wheezing, then the throat closing up. Choking and gasping for air. Water filling her lungs and static filling her brain. Panic that she might have a heart attack, too. She could just see herself collapsing in the parking lot with no one there to save her. Well, maybe someone would save her. There were no windows in the warehouse, but surely someone would save her.

As a child, Mona had barely survived many asthma attacks. In fact, it was her first bad attack when she was only three that had caused her mother—who disappeared for long stretches of time—to take her to the hospital, leave her there, and not come back for her for nine whole years. During all those years, each time she had an attack her bitch of a grandmother (who was so rich) and her aunts (who didn't like her one bit and always hinted she was illegitimate) would scold her and tell her to get a grip until she was almost at death's door. They always let her get really sick before they'd finally bundle her up and take her to the emergency room. Death's door every time. No wonder she was insecure.

She felt so sad and lonely and panicked right now, she could hardly breathe. Mitch always knew what to do when she felt an attack coming on. He'd calm her right down, then he'd yell at someone to get her a warm drink and tell her a joke to distract her while they waited for it. Usually the joke was something about balls and chains, how he had two.

Mitch was a big kidder, and she loved him so much that she hadn't had a single full-blown attack in all the years she'd known him. Only little mini ones that all had to do with Cassie.

As she stood in the gap in the parking lot made by Mitch's missing Mercedes, she scratched the first mosquito bite of the season. It was in the middle of her knee and starting to swell like a huge hive. Maybe it was a hive. She was an allergic person. She panted a little, experimenting with her wheeze and heartbeat. Her brain was as clear as Evian, however. Of course it made total sense. For Mitch not to call her, he had to be really sick. And since the first day they'd met, he'd never been too sick to call her.

She took control of her panic, found her car key, and unlocked the door of her little red Jaguar. She slid in, grimacing a little at the blistering heat of the tan leather seat and the sunbaked stale air. She fanned herself with the take-out menu of a Chinese restaurant she used when Mitch was at home with Cassie, and dialed Ira Mandel's number on the car phone.

"Local spies. Employ people from the local district."

Cissy, the receptionist, answered on the first ring. "Mandel and Blathar."

"Cissy, it's Mona. How are you doing, honey?"

"I'm doing just fine, Miss Whitman. He's not here right now."

"Who isn't there?"

"Ira isn't here, and Teddy isn't, either."

"Do you know where they are, Cissy? This is very important."

"No, I don't."

"This is so urgent, it's really life and death."

"I still don't know, Miss Whitman."

"Cissy, honey, how could you not know where they are? You know everything."

"I don't know everything, Miss Whitman."

"Of course, you do. You sit right there by the door and they always tell you what to say before they go out."

"Well, they didn't this time."

"Now, Cissy. Who's on your side, huh? Who buys you perfume in

Paris? And I got you some more of that kind you like. I have it right here in my bag. And you know what else? I brought you a Pashmina scarf and a Prada bag."

"Miss Whitman, you shouldn't do that." Cissy's voice quavered. She was a pushover.

"Well, friends are friends. How about you don't tell me and I just suggest possibilities."

No answer.

"Did they go out to lunch?"

"Nope."

"Are they in the conference room?"

"Nope."

"Are they in a meeting somewhere?"

"Uh-uh."

"How about the hospital? Are they at the hospital?"

"Well, now that you mention that, Miss Whitman, I think maybe they did go to the hospital. Mr. Mandel was very upset."

"How is Mr. Sales doing?"

"I'm so sorry, Miss Whitman. I don't think he's so good."

"Thank you, honey. You're just the greatest. I'm going to get those little gifts to you right away."

"No, no, don't even think about it," Cissy said quickly. "I don't want to lose my job."

"Oh, you won't lose your job. And I won't forget you, okay? Friends are friends, right?"

Mona's blood thundered in her ears as she hung up. Now she could feel her breath rattle. Asthma, for sure, the one time Mitch wasn't there to calm her down and save her. Tears came and ruined her mascara. Mitch, the one true love of her life, really was in the hospital, and no one had told her. So cruel. So cold of the family to ignore her like this. Teddy was her friend. She couldn't bear it. Mitch must be so upset without her beside him. The hurt feeling, the terrible burden for her terrible young life that she carried like a heavy boulder, grew and grew. The betrayal was terrible. No one had told her. They were trying to keep things from her. Mona's mind began to race.

If large numbers of trees move, they are approaching. If there are many visible obstacles in the heavy grass, it is to make us suspicious. If the birds take flight, there is an ambush. If the animals are afraid, enemy forces are mounting an attack.

It was perfectly clear to her that Cassie, the enemy, must have fed her husband rat poison because she found out Mitch was leaving her. Mona clutched her chest. She and Mitch were getting married. They had a new house all ready. She'd stopped taking the pill. Any day she'd be pregnant. Only the date, only telling Cassie—that one last dreadful little detail—had been holding them up. Once he told Cassie, there would be no more pretending.

Now Mona knew that Mitch had not been so angry with her, after all. He must have gone home to tell Cassie the marriage was over, and the spoiled, selfish, infantile woman had put rat poison in his coffee. Another wheeze tickled her throat at the thought of Cassie murdering her husband. Tearful and sweaty in her jaunty red sports car, she dialed Mark Cohen's number.

"It is subtle, subtle! There are no areas in which one does not employ spies."

"Doctor's office."

"Marta, it's Mona. I just got back from Paris and heard about Mitch. This is terrible. I didn't know anything about it. When did it happen?" She could barely control her voice. This was no act. She was distraught.

"Friday."

"Friday! Friday!"

"Yes, sometime in the afternoon."

"Oh my God, where is he? I have to see him."

"He's at North Fork. But he's in intensive care. He can't have visitors."

"Oh my God!" Mona shook her head. Her burgundy curls bounced on her shoulders. "Intensive care. I had no idea. Is Mark there?"

"He's with a patient."

"What happened? Tell me everything."

"He had a stroke, Mona."

"Oh Jesus, a stroke." Mona was silent for a moment. Could a person get a stroke from rat poison?

"Mona, are you there?"

"I'm just so upset. Would you tell Mark to call me right away? On my cell." Mona hung up. She felt horrible, more than horrible. But she couldn't go back into the warehouse with the news. Everybody would panic, and she had to keep her mind on Mitch.

She decided to go see him and keep mum to everyone else. She dialed her assistant, Carol. "Honey, I'm taking off. I'll see you tomorrow. Anything comes up, call me on my cell." She tried to keep good cheer in her voice.

She turned and caught her reflection in the rearview mirror. Her weeping had really messed her up. Mascara was all over the place, and little rivulets snaked through her foundation. She definitely couldn't go to the hospital looking like this. She had to be strong for Mitch. She had to look really good, like an angel from heaven, to bring him back to her. To look that good she had to go home. She grabbed her sunglasses and put them on, hit the ignition. The car growled to life. As she started to back out, she saw the black Mercedes in the rearview mirror. Oh shit. It was on the service road, heading this way. For a tiny second her heart spiked. Mitch had done it again: The whole thing was a big joke. He was fine, after all. No stroke. Then she saw that Mitch wasn't the driver, and she kept going.

She agonized all the way home. How could this be happening to her? It was like cancer, the atom bomb striking. The Nazis. Something out of a spy movie or a thriller. Her lifelong enemy had done something to him. He'd been fine, perfectly *fine*, on Friday. First the audit, now the stroke. It was too much. Now in the mirror, she saw the Mercedes behind her. It looked as if Cassie was following her home. Too fucking much.

The major configurations of terrain are accessible, suspended, stalemated, constricted, precipitous, and expansive.

Mona lived in a town house complex in Roslyn. She'd lived there for ten years with the profound belief that any minute she was going to marry.

She'd been frugal to a fault. She had two completely inadequate floors. Downstairs, a tiny kitchen and small living room/dining area. Upstairs, a bedroom and den. Full bath and powder room. There were hardly any closets at all. The only way to make the place work for her was to give away her clothes after three or four wearings. She did not like her neighbors, who were either old, very young with children, or middle-aged, divorced, and desperate. The old people wanted to talk. The young couples had noisy children who left toys on the sidewalks for people to trip over. And the divorced women wanted to go on trips with her. Mitch didn't like them, either, and never came there. Not only that, the garage was not attached. It was cut into the hill behind the house. She didn't like to use it.

Today only one thing went right. She found a parking spot out front and hurried into the house. She hadn't seen the Mercedes for the last two blocks but slammed the door and double locked it anyway. She didn't want to see Cassie no matter what.

As soon as Mona was inside her second-rate house, her whole history did a number on her impossible situation. She felt even more terrible that she hadn't been informed immediately of Mitch's illness. She was his partner, as important to the company as he was. Didn't anybody realize that? She was so careful and meticulous about everything. Everything was arranged just so. It wasn't right for Teddy not to tell her this, her friend Mark, their accountant Ira. This had to be some kind of conspiracy to keep her isolated and in the dark.

Once inside the house, she focused on an old complaint, her lack of help and closets. With the millions in business she brought in, she should have a full-time staff to take care of her house and clothes. When she'd arrived home yesterday afternoon, no one was there to carry the heavy suitcases upstairs, so she'd been forced to unpack downstairs in the living room. As usual, she'd laid everything out on the sofa, on the floor, in a very precise way. Her stuff was all over the place. The suits and coats and dresses and tops and shoes and purses from her trip were in piles, carefully sorted for the cleaners and the laundry whether she'd worn them or not. She was too upset to appreciate the profusion of pale colors and expensive fabrics strewn all over the white, top-of-the-line wool, mile-high shag carpet and white silk sofa and different patterned white silk throw pillows with gold bullion fringe.

A wheeze clutched at her throat. She felt sick. She felt hurt. She felt like a tiger with a sick cub she had to save. She felt the hot breath of the crazy, unloved wife and the IRS Nazis coming to take away everything she cared about in life. All those feelings were roiling around in a single wounded bird. It was just too much.

The cheap doorbell of her second-rate house sounded its half-assed dingdong. At the same time the doorknocker clanged against its fake brass plate. Mona's heart almost stopped. Shit. The enemy had actually dared to follow her right into her private home. *"As for constricted configurations, if we occupy them first we must fully deploy throughout them in order to await the enemy."*

She raced up the stairs. Peeled off her skirt, threw on a pair of baggy black pants and a blue work shirt. Grabbed her hair and pulled it back into a ponytail. In the bathroom she scrubbed at the dissolving makeup with a washrag until only her healthy tan showed.

The doorbell and knocker continued to sound as she flew in bare feet down the stairs. In the living room, wheezing and coughing, she grabbed clothes, flung what she could back into the cases, jammed the cases into the closet. She was throwing the rest of the stuff into the powder room when Cassie started shouting through the door.

"For heaven's sake, Mona, open the damn door. I know you're in there."

"Cassie, honey, is it you?"

"Of course, it's me. Who else?"

Simulated chaos is given birth from control. The illusion of fear is given from strength. Order and disorder are a question of numbers.

Mona closed the powder room door. Without her shoes she looked a whole lot shorter. Without her makeup, hardly dazzling at all. She was wheezing steadily. She held a handkerchief to her mouth. She was coughing, trying to clear the phlegm beginning to clog her bronchi. She flung the door open and faced the helpless, nonworking weakling who all these years had been the only obstacle to her happiness.

22

MONA'S EYES POPPED at the change in Cassie. She stood outside only a few seconds, wearing a scarf and sunglasses à la Audrey Hepburn. The disguise was pretty good for someone who didn't know what to look for. Mona knew right away what major event had occurred in Cassie's life, however, and from all appearances it was extremely recently. She took a moment to study her. The big, dark shades hid Cassie's eyes, but not the telltale red cheeks and yellowing jawline. Gone was the soft chin, the folds by the sides of Cassie's mouth, and the pale, trusting manner that had distinguished her rival. Mona was prepared for everything in life, but she was unprepared for this. Self-improvement was the very last thing she would have expected from Cassie.

Cassie had been at least four inches shorter and many pounds plumper than Mona the last time she'd seen her. She looked thinner and taller now. In fact, she looked like a completely different person as she pushed her way into the house.

> *Whenever possible victory should be achieved by diplomatic co-ercion, thwarting the enemy's plans and alliances, and frustrating his strategy.*

Mute but for her wheezing, Mona let her in. Luckily, she had been careful almost to a fault about making changes in her life every step of the way. Therefore at this moment, in this place, she had the moral advantage of having absolutely nothing to hide, and Cassie had the moral disadvantage of being out of her mind with fury.

"You fucking bitch. You will not get away with this."

Cassie stopped in the middle of the living room. As cold as an ice statue at an Italian wedding, she assessed Mona's white sofa, white rug. White silk throw pillows with the gold bullion fringe. White curtains with the gold braid and balls. Glass coffee table with expensive brass base. Everything white and gold. Cassie's survey halted at each of three silk flower arrangements: roses, lilies, orchids. Each arrangement was white and each one was in a gold filigree vase. There was not a live plant, not a silver candlestick, not an extra embellishment anywhere. Also, the house was as neat as if no one really lived there, which 90 percent of the time was true. Mona had pretty much moved to her new address. Still, the place looked exactly the same as it always had. And the new owner would take possession in three weeks' time. The young couple had bought it "as is."

"Cassie, Cassie. What is it? What's wrong?" Mona was shocked to see Cassie so aggressively angry, so she decided to counter hostility with love and understanding. She went right over to her lifelong enemy to give her a warm embrace.

Cassie jumped back, stiffening like a cobra.

No wonder Mitch found Cassie to be a cold bitch. "Tell me, what is it? What's wrong?" Mona said, not letting it bother her.

"I told you to stay where you were, Mona. Why did you drive away?" Cassie spat at her just like an alley cat.

"What?" Mona coughed.

"I told you on the phone to stay where you were. I wanted to talk to you. You are despicable. You are a—"

"Stop, Cassie. Don't upset yourself." Mona wheezed and hacked, just like Mimi in the last scene of *La Bohème*, Mitch's favorite opera.

Cassie's witchlike expression didn't change. "I hope you choke to death," she said coldly.

"Cassie, please." Mona coughed uncontrollably some more, sounding bad and feeling very hurt. Any sign of weakness historically had generated sympathy from Cassie. This response was spiteful and totally

unlike her. She put the handkerchief to her mouth and tried to spit a little blood. As she inspected the blob of sputum that came out, Cassie
came alive with a shriek.

"Oh my God, you've had your face lifted! Jesus Christ, I don't believe it." Cassie flapped her arms like a whooping crane trying to fly. "I
don't believe this. Jesus Christ. I don't believe this. When did this
happen?"

This was an incendiary attack, just unforgivable. "What are you talking about, Cassie, you're flipping your lid," Mona retorted.

"Everything that comes out of your mouth is total shit, you damn
freak. You've had your face done!" Cassie spit out. She took a moment to
examine and absorb it, then gasped. "*And your boobs!*"

"I don't know what you're talking about." Mona chose to effect sad-
ness at such a misunderstanding. She took a step back, shrinking into
her work shirt, the only piece of clothing she owned from Old Navy. She
did the turn well, acting as if Cassie were the hurtful aggressor and that
every harsh word unsettled and grieved her. "Cassie stop this, please."

"What did you do, *everything?* Nose, eyes, chin, neck? Oh my *God.*
Every goddamn thing. Who paid for this, my *husband,* who doesn't believe in plastic *surgery!*" Cassie was shrieking and stamping her feet now,
completely out of control. "You *fucking,* fucking bitch. And you're only,
what, not even fucking forty?"

"Somebody must be telling you stories, Cassie."

"Don't you dare walk away from me. You *fucking* bitch. So this is
why you haven't shown your face in my house for three whole years."

"I need my inhaler, Cassie." Mona actually hoped she would choke
nearly to death and show Cassie what an unreasonable bitch she was
being.

Cassie blocked the way, screaming some more. "I would not have
believed that you of all people—ugly, fawning *bitch*—would try to take
everything I have. Not in a million years. Look at that face. You have a
new nose. New lips!"

"I don't know what you're talking about. I was at your house only last
month."

"Not when *I* was there," Cassie screamed.

Mona inched past her. She knew that people were frequently truly nuts, they really were. She dealt every day with wine nuts who weren't careful about temperature, drank six bottles of a case, then claimed the whole lot was "off" and wanted a full refund. Clearly, she had underestimated Cassie. Mitch was right: The woman was disturbed, a mental case. This was her second incident today. Maybe she was having a psychotic break.

Mona wanted to call the police and document the event. She reached her purse that was hanging by its expensive strap on the kitchen door. But neither her inhaler nor cell phone were in it.

"You and my husband. You and my company. You and my *credit* cards. And just look at *this*"—Cassie pointed her finger at Mona like a loaded gun—"the dowdy frump with the receding chin, the bad skin, and the big nose, a fucking *swan*." Cassie was positively frothing at the mouth. "How dare you? How dare you? You little fuck! Goddamn it, Mona. That's my husband's handkerchief, too."

"Oh please, take it." Mona held out the sodden handkerchief.

"I will not touch anything you've touched," Cassie screamed.

Where were the cops when you needed one? Mona was beginning to think Cassie's craziness was an intentional malicious act to drown her. Literally. Because fluid was just filling up her bronchial tubes and throat. She knew that people died this way. Once you started coughing, you could not stop. The hacking went on and on. The pain was terrible. You could crack your ribs coughing. She sucked some air. "Cassie, you're"—she gasped for oxygen—"you're upsetting yourself for nothing."

"I'm upset for *everything*, you bitch. Don't you understand yet? Mitch had a stroke. Everything's come out. You will be punished. You will go to *jail!*"

Mona's response was an artistic gurgle.

"He's in the hospital, and he's not going to make it. You don't get my husband, or anything else, understand? It's *over*."

Sure, sure, it was over, but not the way Cassie thought. Mona pointed at the kitchen. "Okay if I get some water?"

"No, it is not. I'm on to you. Don't even think about trying anything."

"Trying *what*? Stop this, Cassie, I can't breathe. Do you want to kill me?"

"Did you really think you would get away with leaving me *broke!*" Cassie just wouldn't stop.

"I don't know what you're talking about. You're hurt. You're imagining things. You're recovering from surgery. You need a doctor."

Cassie sucked air. "I'll kill you. I will kill you."

Mona shook her head sadly. "Oh Cassie, Cassie, it's not smart to threaten me. It's not smart. Stop and think for a moment. I know you're lonely and sad right now. I know how you feel. For years I've been urging Mitch to spend more time with you. I begged him. Every day I told him. All work and no play makes a dull husband. Would he listen? No, but he was working for you all the time. And now he's had a stroke."

Mona's tone changed to curiosity. She couldn't help herself. "Let me see your face. You've had a *lot* of work done, Cassie."

"I was in a car accident," Cassie spat back.

"Well, good for you. I'm proud of you. Gee Cassie, all that liposuction under your chin. How much did they take, a quart?"

Cassie's eyes were hidden behind the shades, but Mona knew she'd made a hit. She shook her ponytail, holding on to her lead. "Don't think I'm not hurt by the way you're acting. After all I've done for your family. You know I've loved you like a sister. I wouldn't hurt you or Mitch for anything in the whole world. Or the kids." Mona said all this between gagging and coughing.

"Since when is stealing not hurting?" Cassie screamed.

"I need my inhaler, Cassie." Mona broke the inhaler impasse. "Fine. I'll die on the spot. And you will have *two* deaths on your conscience." She threw herself on the sofa, panted and gurgled. She gasped for air and choked.

"Two? Two?" Cassie screamed. "I've never hurt a single soul in all my life. I never shoplifted a Chiclet, stole somebody's man, never had any *fun*." She stamped her foot. "I should have. God knows I should have."

"What did you do to Mitch?" Mona cried.

"Nothing, he keeled over. All I did was watch."

"So you watched, how awful. Poor Mitch, all alone," Mona wailed.

"He's not alone. He's with me, and guess what? Every goddamned thing you bought is going back."

That was it. Mona had had it up to *here*. The maniac had to be stopped right now. Her lovely body was racked with great heaving, hawking coughs. She hacked up some more globs into Mitch's handkerchief. It was gross, but finally she hit pay dirt. A streak of blood.

"Cassie, listen please. I know you're upset, but listen carefully. I need to go to the emergency room. I need Adrenalin. Do you understand?"

"Pooh, everybody knows you're a big faker. Where's the stuff you bought?"

"I don't know what's happened to you, but you're going to find out you have made a very big mistake. You're wrong about everything. Don't have another death on your conscience. I need a hospital now. Are you going to be a murderer?"

Cassie paused, but only for a second. "Get in the car," she said angrily.

MONA SUFFERED TERRIBLY in the car. She was flooded with fluid. It came out of her nose and her eyes and clogged her lungs. Her lungs actually itched. Whoever heard of itching lungs? She knew she could die before she got to the emergency room. And right in the middle of this catastrophe, selfish Cassie would not give up her rage. Mona had never seen anything like Cassie on a rampage. She was really pissed off. It seemed to Mona that she was driving two miles an hour on purpose just so Mona would expire before they got to the hospital. Then she drove right by.

"You're crazy. What are you doing? You passed the hospital," Mona cried.

"I did?" Cassie said.

"Where are you going?"

"To the walk-in."

"The walk-in?" Mona was horrified. She didn't want a walk-in clinic. She wanted to go to North Fork, where Mitch was. "Why?"

"It's faster," Cassie replied, driving the Mercedes one mile an hour. She'd actually slowed down.

Mona made a few death rattles. "Please, Cassie. Take me to North Fork," she pleaded.

"It takes too long. All those people waiting with their headaches and broken arms. This will be faster." Cassie drove to the walk-in on Forest Avenue. When they got there, Cassie speeded up.

"Cassie, *there's* the walk-in."

"Okay, okay." Cassie slowed down and pulled into the parking lot. "You're here. You're not going to die, you faker. You never do. Get out."

Uh-oh. Mona realized she had a problem. She had only Cassandra Sales credit cards in her wallet. She could not use one of those in front of Cassie. She'd wanted to make a scene to document the danger to which Cassie in her evil jealousy had subjected her. But if she collapsed in the waiting room, Cassie might take over the situation, get her credit cards out of her purse and see them. For a second Mona was stymied. She always anticipated everything, but she hadn't anticipated this. She hadn't changed the cards when she came back from Paris.

Never mind. She stayed in the car, trying to catch her breath. "Leave me here," she said. "I'll go in alone."

"No, no, I want to go with you." Cassie got out of the car and came around to the passenger side.

"Please Cassie, you're scaring me."

"Oh yeah? Well, keep away from my husband. He deserves to die in peace." She opened the door.

"I don't know what's happened to you," Mona sputtered.

"Figure it out, Mona. I found out what you did to me." For a second Mona thought Cassie was actually going to hit her. She cringed in the car seat.

"Get out." Mona's show of fear caused Cassie to stand aside.

Mona crawled out of the car.

"Go get your Adrenalin," Cassie told her. "I'd be very surprised if you really need it."

Mona dragged herself into the horrid walk-in. She felt triumphant. Cassie drove away, but she was still the weakling. Cassie had responded to the cues and spared her rival. Therefore, Cassie was the one defeated. Mona hated her. As soon as she was inside the building, she found her inhaler. She took it out of her purse and used it. Inhalers were magic. They really were. Her inhaler cleared her bronchial tubes in seconds. She coughed up the dangerous phlegm and spit it out. Her lungs cleared. By the time the nurse called her name, she was feeling a lot better. She didn't think she needed to see the doctor after all. But she was careful to have the visit documented by the receptionist just for the record anyway.

A nice old gentleman who'd recently been widowed drove her home. All the way he told her about his high blood pressure. Then, just before he let her off where she directed, several doors down from where she lived, he asked her out for a date.

CHARLIE SCHWAB DROVE HOME to his regular Monday night tennis date with Taj Rau, the proud owner of five blue Lincoln Town Cars in the APlus Car Service. Only ten years in America and already a total success in his world, Taj had taken up tennis—the better to nag his nine-year-old daughter, Sonia, whom he fully expected to be the next Venus Williams as soon as she could serve into the right box. Charlie was bolstering Taj's own lessons with a weekly hitting session that included vicious volley, lob to the moon, quadrant splitting, slice and spin. Working on the finer points of the game, however, was a waste of time since Rau lacked any hand-eye coordination whatsoever.

Mostly Charlie was supporting his neighbor's dream to be a real American in possession of a sport, sports equipment, clothes, and a club of his own, with all the outrageous monthly expenses the endeavor necessitated. Every bill was a joy to him. Every weakness on the part of his U.S. government agent neighbor thrilled him even more. He nagged Charlie about his beat-up car almost as much as he nagged Sonia about her tennis and Taj Jr. about the awful music he played so loud, it made him want to cry, and the oversized pants that were falling off his skinny rear end.

Charlie's old Buick was coughing again. For the last week the muffler had been attached to the underside of the car in a complicated way that involved a piece of laundry rope provided by his father, Ogden. But now the laundry rope had come loose, and the muffler was sparking along on the highway to a chorus of honking from other drivers to let him know about it. As if he didn't know about it. His car was a sore point with everyone. Disgruntled taxpayers were always doing things to it, and he couldn't get the Service to compensate him for the damages. Still, as long as the car got bashed and he didn't, he was cool. A car was just the means to get around.

But it was not the car or the ridiculous tennis game that was on Charlie's mind right now. He was in a state of obsessional seething over the events of the day. In almost equal measures, Charlie loved his job, prided himself on his work as a top snooper, and was dogged by the profound humiliation of knowing that his private life was a flop. On the occupation front, all the news was good. He was productive and, as long as he didn't step on anyone's toes, he had job security.

He was such a fine detective, in fact, that the Brooklyn District Director, Mel Arrighi, was always telling him he should transfer to the special agent branch and top the ranks there. As a special agent, he'd have a lot more power in the field. He'd have bigger cases, mob related, drug related. He'd get more juice. He'd be on the road all the time. That was a plus. And life would be exciting. That was another plus. Special agents who worked for the Treasury and the Justice Departments had almost unlimited power stalking their prey, much more power than FBI agents.

But Charlie couldn't do it. He had to stay close to home for Ogden. He hopped around the tristate area with no problem, but treks to God-knew-where every single week would be too stressful for his father. Charles Schwab was one of 120,000 employees of the IRS. As a revenue agent, he was part of the main snooping body in the federal tax force. Revenue agents carried out routine audits and tax examinations. When they suspected tax evasion or fraud, they worked with special agents and the CID to build the cases that the Justice Department would prosecute. His was a safe path for a careful person who had sustained a couple of losses so great that even an accountant such as he could not calculate the damage.

Charlie's special skills involved the alchemy of turning disappeared assets into found ones. Over the years he'd learned the ten thousand ways that people shaded the truth, used their stories like sleds in the snow, slid all over the place, hid their assets, schemed, played with the numbers. He knew how honest people shielded their money from taxes in relatively innocent ways, and how dishonest people schemed to cheat the old U.S.A. any way they could. At work, digging through mountains of paper, he felt like a detective. When he was out in the field he wore a hat and thought of himself as a Columbo. He took pride in his juice "finds." He was a doggedly persistent man, untrusting, unyielding, obsessional about the details.

He loved playing tennis, but only two times a week. He cooked imaginative meals four times a week for his father, went out two times, and one night a week he hung out at the bars in Bay View. His car had gone completely to hell. He was bored, he was lonely, but his world was safe. He worked mostly with accountants, usually men. A few were women, but they were not good-looking. Likewise, the large force of female revenue agents were not generally hired for their looks or personality. His supervisor, Gayle Katz, had never married and cared only about her cat. Charlie rarely had the opportunity to see, much less get to know, any of the high-profile women whose lives he examined through their documents. Even when he evaluated women's houses or yachts, their assets of all kinds, they themselves were in the background, shadowy and inaccessible. When they came on to him, it was always to cover something up.

Although Charlie fantasized about excitement every day of his life, longing for something more that he couldn't really name, he actually counted on the status quo. He didn't want to fall in love and risk his life like last time. Years ago he'd married young to an unremarkable girl of ordinary attractions he'd thought he loved well enough to last a lifetime. Her name was Ingrid, and he'd never in a million years thought she would leave him. They'd had a baby. The baby died when it was two weeks old. Soon after that, Ingrid left him for a podiatrist she'd consulted a year earlier about her bunions. Ingrid's sudden departure raised a doubt in Charlie's mind that the baby he'd anticipated with such excitement and loved with all his heart had really been his. After both mother and child were gone, it was too late to investigate. Charlie went on to investigate other puzzles.

His personal tragedy occurred so long ago that torment had long since been replaced with cynicism about the opposite sex. Just as really bad dental experiences leave behind perpetual anxiety about all practitioners in the field, Charlie's experience with Ingrid left him skittish about women. His name and occupation were an added catastrophe. It was always the same thing: When women thought he was the financial giant, they threw themselves at him. Literally. The bodies flew at him the way Mona's had when she'd tripped on nothing and tried to fall into his arms, breathing hard with mint-freshened breath.

Then everything changed the second they found out he was not the "real" Charles Schwab. As soon as he told them he was a revenue agent with the IRS, he suddenly became the "fake" Charles Schwab, less than a nothing, a poisonous toad. A dangerous enemy. But this had not always been the case. Once the "real" Charles Schwab had been an unknown and the "fake" Charles Schwab had been young and handsome. And it was not completely true that Charlie was a total loser now. He just felt like one. The Beech Avenue strip of bars in Long Beach was near Kennedy Airport and the place where the stewardesses came for R and R. He dabbled with them easily enough, especially since the next flight out was only a few hours, or a day, away. He didn't like to stick with anybody longer than that, couldn't really stand prolonged encounters. He liked the getting-to-know-you part. But he became nervous when anyone tried to stake a claim on him. He didn't think he'd ever meet someone he really liked.

Charlie was still smoldering and obsessing about his humiliating experiences with the strange duo of Cassie Sales and Mona Whitman. He drove east toward his house in Long Beach. He didn't know what was up with the two women, but something definitely was. Cassie had looked crazy to him even before Mona had tipped him off. With the sunglasses and the scarf on her head at eight in the morning? Come on. And the story about the stroke? Please. Cassie was a borderline personality like Livia in *The Sopranos*.

As for the latter, he could still see her soft, tanned inner thighs, almost feel her breasts close to his chest. And smell her perfume. She must have managed to touch him somewhere. The perfume was clinging to his jacket. It made him want to laugh. She was sexy like an Italian, bringing out the big guns for him as if he could be swayed by anything she had to offer. Her little patter about compliances didn't fool him one bit. Something was up at that place. He had an insider's eye view, and his own. The warehouse was too big even for the volume of sales on their returns. Any lamebrain auditor who had a chance to see the place would pick up the fact that they were moving more product than they reported. Obviously, Mitchell Sales hadn't been expecting visitors. But why should he? Only about 1 percent of tax returns got audited, and of those usually the audit was limited to a single transaction, and the query on behalf of the service was done, mercifully, by mail.

Charlie kept thinking about the curvaceous Mona Whitman and the way she'd said, "IRS agents are toads." It annoyed him, it really did.

If she'd done anything wrong, he'd hang her out to dry; crazy Cassie, too. He was distracted by the sight of young Taj out in front of the only yellow house on the street on an all-white-house street. He was washing one of the three robin's egg blue limos parked along the curb. The music pounding out of his boom box sounded like Spanish rap again. He'd done something new to his hair. One side was gone. The other was green. Along this portion of Lake Avenue the air was filled with the pungent aromas of Indian cooking. And Ogden was on the lawn, jumping up and down.

"You okay, you okay. Taking it easy. Taking it easy." Taj Sr., wearing a white warm-up suit with red and blue chevrons on the legs, was chattering excitedly and banging the old man on the back, desperate to get down just a little lower whatever he'd given Ogden to eat that had caught in his faulty esophagus.

"Ah, Charlie home," Taj screamed.

Ogden's face cleared and he stopped jumping. "Hi, son," he called. He loped into the street between two limos to meet Charlie at the car. Just then, Taj Jr., engrossed in the joy of the moment and the beat of the music, let out a whoop. He twirled around with the spurting hose as his microphone and dance partner and sprayed the old man in the chest. Revenue Agent Charlie Schwab was home.

25

THE ART OF WAR was on Mona's mind when she got home from the walk-in. She was not afraid for herself. She was terrified for Mitch. Anyone who reacted to rejection in such an insane fashion as Cassie did was more dangerous than she'd ever imagined. Mona was breathing freely, but she was scared enough of Cassie to decamp. Mitch had been right when he'd told her Cassie was a toxic person. Even before Mona had opened her front door, she'd known she had to get out of there. Cassie turned out to be more than just a toxic, passive-aggressive, secret ball breaker. Cassie was a genuine killer. No wonder Mitch had been apprehensive about leaving her.

Cassie's driving Mona around for all of fifteen minutes while Mona faked an asthma attack was a nonevent compared with her murdering her vulnerable husband on life support in the hospital just because he wanted to leave her. Mona would not let Cassie hurt either one of them. She unlocked her front door, glanced quickly around in case Cassie had returned, then raced upstairs for her makeup case. She found it in the bathroom still packed for the trip to Paris. She stowed it in the car. Then Mona raced upstairs again and foraged around in the closet long enough to locate two pairs of Hermès alligator pumps and two alligator purses in red and purple. Mona believed she didn't care about things. She was a frugal person. Even as she stowed away the expensive accessories, she told herself she'd give up everything she had with the snap of her fingers to save her honey. She grabbed the few bills that had accumulated since Friday and left the junk mail on the table. That was it. She was traveling light, hurrying to save her man.

Three minutes from start to finish, she double-locked the front door, checked the street for Cassie and the Mercedes, dove into her car, and took off. She was still wearing the work shirt and black pants she had donned for Cassie, but she had another outfit for the hospital at her new house. She headed down the hill to Roslyn Harbor, then turned onto Northern Boulevard, heading east toward Matinecock. At Wheatley Plaza, Mona turned north again on Glen Cove Road and drove past all the new stores that proved Glen Cove was coming up in the world.

Sometimes she liked to travel on Hegeman's Lane, then take Chicken Valley Road through the horse farms and grand estates, backtracking to Duck Pond Road. But today she went the shorter way, down Glen Cove and across Duck Pond.

Mona was in a hurry. She skimmed along Duck Pond, which was visually and fragrantly at its best in spring, but she didn't respond to any of its attractions. All she could think of was Mitch in peril. The stone house he'd named Le Refuge, with its natural stone swimming pool, tennis court, guest house, pond, waterfall, and five-car garage, was halfway across Duck Pond, sited on ten delightfully landscaped acres that Cassie had always particularly admired on garden tours of the area.

Mona caught a glimpse of her roof and chimneys from the road. The old-timers in the area called the house Chimneys because there were so many of them. Ten in all. She turned in at the brand-new wrought-iron gates with the crossed swords, shields, grapes, wine barrels, and Sales logo in gold. The graceful S of the driveway and towering oaks that lined it were over ninety years old. Seeing it now almost broke Mona's heart. The house had been built just before World War I, and getting it before it ever appeared on the market had been a major coup. She had especially admired the lawns—acres of green garnished in spring by huge clumps of daffodils.

The daffodils were finished now. The flowers were withered and dry. The spindly leaves, too, had a limp, bedraggled look. Later in the season, variegated hosta would wreathe each tree with white and green that would spike with purple flowers in the summer. Mona knew all about how gardens should look, because she'd been listening to Cassie talk about plants and fucking trees ad nauseam for many years. Mona had a gift for listening and picking things up. She rounded the circle, pulled up by the front door, and turned off the engine.

In the last six months she'd almost always come here with Mitch—to discuss decorating plans, to supervise the painting and wallpapering, the hanging of the drapes, positioning the furniture, and to make wonderful love. The first night they'd stayed there, back in March, Mitch had made a fire in the bedroom. They'd sat in front of it wrapped in new silk dressing gowns, eating beluga caviar off a spoon and sipping '90 Grande Dame Champagne from Baccarat flutes. When the caviar was gone, she'd taken out the Kama Sutra massage oil and rubbed Mitch's hands and feet, trying to envision and articulate every bone. Then she'd moved on, to his neck and shoulders. She'd rubbed and pulled his arms straight out of their sockets as hard as she could. He'd lain on his back moaning happily, attended to like the prince he was meant to be.

She'd drizzled the sweet oil down the hair on his chest and massaged it into his thickening waist, between his strong legs, up behind his balls. His eyes had been half closed as he'd watched her work on him, twitching her robe open from time to time for a better view of her breasts. She remembered it as if it were yesterday. He'd built the fire high. It had crackled and roared up the fireplace, drawing the smoke up and out of the room like a real champion. Candles had flickered all around them. On her knees, Mona had poured oil into her hands, warmed it between her palms, and gone to work on his towering cock.

"Ohhhhh, Mama," he'd moaned.

A glass had toppled over on her new satin quilt, spilling champagne as he'd shifted his big body, but neither of them had minded. He'd risen up from the floor, flipped her over, and plunged that slick sucker home in one muscular thrust that had hurt like hell. Mona had treasured the fierce burn in her furnace that had lasted for hours. She clicked her tongue.

The baptism of the bedroom was on her mind as she got out of the car. There were no workers or decorators to greet her today, not even a housekeeper to open the door. Grand and lifeless, the house was frightening. She'd never imagined having to stay there alone. She opened the heavy wooden door and deactivated the alarm system. Then she switched on the huge hall chandelier and sconces that glittered with enough crystal to dazzle a Las Vegas hotel owner. "Oh Mama," she muttered.

The hall galley had a pink marble floor and pink marble columns; the staircase was deeply carved mahogany, dark as bittersweet chocolate and shiny with new polish. Struggling through her misery for a breath of good air, Mona trudged up to the master suite at the top of the stairs. It consisted of a honey-colored, wood-paneled study, dressing room, and bathroom for Mitch, and a large, lovely bedroom overlooking the pond with a four-poster bed, dressing room, and a large bathroom for her. She headed straight for the bath.

An hour and a half later, Mona infiltrated the Head Trauma ICU at North Fork Hospital without incident. She was wearing a dashing turquoise Dior suit with a short jacket that nipped in at the waist and plunged low in the neckline. A touch of crisp white eyelet showed at her cleavage. The fact that it wasn't clear whether she was wearing a blouse or bra invited second glances. The suit skirt was pegged so tightly, she could hardly get in and out of the Jag much less hobble down the long hospital corridor from one wing to another. Every single thing was a misery to her, but her burnished shoulder-length curls and Nicole Kidman-esque finely sculpted features drew many admiring glances and not a single difficult question. She was thirty-eight but looked every bit as fresh as Mitch's twenty-five-year-old daughter, Marsha.

With very little effort, she located Mitch's room. There, all alone, she faced her lifeless intended and the bank of noisy machines for the first time. "Holy shit," she murmured.

One of Mitch's eyes was closed, the other was open just a slit. Frowning at the tubes and plastic bags collecting his revolting bodily fluids, Mona suddenly had the thought that she had overdressed for the occasion.

"Baby? I'm here." She moved with trepidation closer to the bed, tilting her head one way and then the other.

"Who knocks your socks off?" she queried softly. Like Grace Kelly trying to get Cary Grant's attention in *To Catch a Thief*, she struck a seductive pose in the lovely Dior suit, then answered the question.

"Mona does." Mona tried to keep her feet moving. But she was afraid to get any closer than the sick man's feet in case what Mitch had was catching. Mona was an asthmatic, a very allergic person. She couldn't afford to take any chances. From the foot of the bed, she leaned over to display her famous cleavage.

"Mona's here for you. Honey, wake up. I've come to take you home." She held her breath.

Mitch didn't move a muscle. Not a hair. Nothing. Maybe his hand twitched a little. Mona's lips twitched; her eyelid, too. This was more than scary. It occurred to her that the machine making all the noise was actually breathing for him or making his heart beat, one or the other, maybe both. She didn't know anything about these things.

She straightened up and looked around for a little support here. A doctor, a nurse. A chair. It was disgusting. There wasn't a chair to sit on. Not even a stool! The place was a hellhole. Her heart started beating faster. That wasn't good for her asthma. She wasn't supposed to get upset, and having Mitch in a place like this was a complete disgrace. He'd hate it. The room had a fucking picture window in it. How much could she do to cheer him up with the whole world watching? She looked closer at the machinery. Was that big white one breathing for him, or what? She looked around for an answer, but none was forthcoming. She was very afraid.

"Honey, can you hear me?" she whispered.

No answer.

"Oh Mitch, do you have any idea what's going on?" She took a step closer. His face was bloodless. His eyes were pretty much closed. She had to get those eyes open.

"Cassie's on the rampage. You have to get out of here. Listen, wake up. I'm not kidding here. Oh baby, I love you so much. Don't leave me."

It seemed pretty hopeless. No part of Mitch moved except the lid of one of his eyes. For a second it looked as if he winked at her. She turned to the window, seeking help. When she turned back to him she was certain that he winked at her again. Fat lot of good that was going to do.

"Wake up, honey," she urged. "You have to get out of here. Did Cassie hurt you, baby? Tell Mona."

Nothing but the winking. It was terrible to watch.

"Honey, I mean it. This is serious. Wake UP!" Mona tried and tried, but no matter what she did, Mitch refused to get up and walk out.

26

"YOU HAVE TO MAKE A DECISION about the car," Ogden announced at breakfast the next day.

Ogden Schwab had been a handsome man in his youth, tall and slender with sharp blue eyes and wavy brown hair. But now he was very thin, almost emaciated, because of his swallowing problem caused by a disease called acalasia, which interrupts the usual smooth undulations of the esophagus, so the food just stalls midway to the stomach. Every swallow is touch and go. No one but the Rau family had bothered to nag him about anything since his wife Trudy had died thirteen years ago, so his clothes didn't always match either the season or each other. Likewise, the bath issue. Back in the 1950s a doctor had told him that he shouldn't bathe every day because of his dry skin. None of the thousands of advances in skin care products since then had been the slightest bit effective in persuading him that it was now safe to go into the water.

He was spry at seventy-six, though, and never let his little peculiarities stop him from making himself useful in every way he could. He kept up with politics and the stock market on CNN, and took a keen interest in the affairs of his son, Charlie.

"What do you say, son?"

"About what?" Charlie poured himself some of the nasty coffee that was one of his father's many morning rituals. This important one he couldn't seem to get right no matter what he tried. Every day there was a major complication with the coffee process. Ogden would set up the machine wrong, so that the little drip hole that should be closed was open. Whenever the carafe was not in place—which was often—hot water flooded the filter and kept right on going. The coffee poured out on the hot plate and hissed like an angry cat. Alternatively, if the hole was stuck in the closed position, the grounds became a tidal wave of sludge that poured over the top, flooding the counter. Whenever coffee actually made it into the carafe, it tasted like a mouthful of dirt. Today the coffee was the color of tea. Maybe it was tea.

"About getting a new car from Taj."

"What's wrong with my old one?" Charlie asked. He wasn't in the mood for car talk after last night. During their game, he'd encouraged Taj to brush up, *brush up*, with his racket in hopes that it would eventually connect with enough spin to get the ball over the net. Taj was always leaping around the court energetically chasing down the balls, but he had no force behind his swing at all. Who would have guessed that yesterday he'd acquired a new power racket that could make any hopeless child a Safin? Taj had brushed up on the ball just when Charlie wasn't looking and hit him in the eye. Then he wanted to sell him a car because his old one was such a piece of shit.

Charlie looked so ridiculous with today's bruise that he'd made a huge sartorial effort with a brown tweed suit, a yellow and blue tie over a blue shirt, and rust-colored suede shoes. All from his happiest days, before he'd ever thought of marrying Ingrid: the seventies.

"You've got to get that muffler fixed. You're gonna get a violation for that. Then jail, mark my words."

"Oh, I don't think so."

"Oh yes, mark my words," Ogden insisted.

Charlie had been marking his words for a long time. Ogden always predicted the worst. Now he spooned a bite of oatmeal and grated apple into his mouth, then forgot to work on it for a while. His face took on the odd, comic expression of surprise he always got when a swallow wasn't going well.

"Drink," Charlie commanded.

Odgen pounded some water. When that didn't do the trick, he got up and jumped up and down a few times. He was wearing Charlie's

Yankees sweatshirt and a winter parka with the hood up over pajama bottoms. He looked weird and needed a bath, but Charlie didn't like to bother him about things like that when every bite was a life-threatening peril. Still, the outfit was pretty funny and reminded him of the Sales lady who'd called the cops on him. He smiled at the thought of the crazy woman who was as bad as his dad.

"What's so funny? You laughing at me?" Ogden's face cleared, and he sat down.

"No, of course not. I was thinking about a girl I met yesterday."

"You met a girl?" Ogden's eyes lit up.

"Not a girl, really. I'm working on a case of a wine importer. Perfectly run-of-the-mill tax returns. Nothing out of the ordinary. It's a big operation, but not one of the giants. The guy reports good profit, doesn't take huge deductions, and pays pretty much what it looks like he should. But . . . you okay, Dad?"

Ogden nodded. "So you think this is an ATF case," he said, nodding sagely. He was so proud when his son worked the big cases that made it to the newspapers.

Charlie laughed. "Well, not ATF, yet, Dad." But he wouldn't be a bit surprised if it came to that.

The Bureau of Alcohol, Tobacco, and Firearms did rigorously control the many regulations that had to be met when distributors moved alcohol in and out of the country, and even from state to state and buyer to buyer. Regulations were so strict in New York that a private collector could not sell to another private collector unless the buyer happened to have a retailer's license. It was a whole big thing. Every case of wine and liquor had to be tagged and checked and reported and rechecked. Still, it was just amazing how much stuff disappeared one way or another, off trucks and out of warehouses. These cases were never reported either stolen or sold, just disappeared.

"So, how did you meet the girl?" Ogden asked.

Charlie was still thinking agency protocol. "This case may have some connection to OC."

"Organized Crime, wow," Ogden said.

"So both Justice and local would be involved. The whole enchilada." Charlie's heart soared just thinking about it. His supervisor, Gayle, had given him the case, advising him not to tell anyone at Sales what the IRS was actually investigating. And it was perfectly legal to keep mum. The IRS didn't have any obligation to tell anyone what they were up to.

Gayle also told him definitely not to inform D.C. or the district special agents branch, or even ATF, what he might be on to. Her feeling, and he agreed, was that the CID would be all over it, taking over the case from the get-go. That way, Revenue wouldn't get the credit for bringing it in. Neither of them wanted that. He'd open the doors as soon as he had something solid. That was the deal.

"Are they mob girls?" Ogden asked, back on the girls. The possibility of his son's meeting hot girls impressed him hugely. "Got to watch out for those mob girls, Charlie. Those guys will kill you for sure if you touch one of their girls."

"Could be." One of them could be. The Mona one. Could be a mob girl, no doubt about it. Charlie had already been thinking about turning her. "Do you want to hear about the tip?" he asked to distract his father.

"Yeah, yeah, tell me about the hit." Ogden took a bite of cereal.

"Tip, Dad. Not hit. You okay?" Charlie gave him a sharp look.

Ogden's eyes watered. He got up and hopped hard on one foot. "Go on," he ordered, waving away his distress as soon as the crisis was over.

"We get a *tip* that this Sales guy has been moving out cases of his best wine. Some of it disappears into his own secret cellar. Really good stuff. This he reports stolen and takes a tax loss. Sometimes his insurance will reimburse him for the loss, so he's getting it both ways. The story is, the guy also gets paid in cash for at least part of many of his restaurant accounts, and totally in cash for some of his restaurant accounts that aren't on the books at all. That would definitely be 'way in' for local."

"A way into the mob?" Ogden said delightedly. "Oh, that's great, Charlie. Tell me about the girls."

"One of them was about your age." The one who crashed into the mailbox, but Charlie didn't want to go into that now.

"A mob girl, my age? What does she look like?" Excitedly, Ogden took a large bite of cereal and Charlie braced himself for disaster.

"Got to go," he said quickly. Sometimes he could take his father's eating travails and sometimes he couldn't. Today, no.

But surprisingly, Ogden swallowed just fine this time. "Already? You didn't eat your breakfast," he complained.

This was Ogden's favorite time of the day. The morning news, the newspaper, browbeating Charlie about getting out and enjoying life more, meeting girls, maybe getting married again. He wanted to debate Taj's offer to sell Charlie one of his gently used, four-year-old light blue Lincoln Town Cars for an overpriced twenty-five thousand. Or at least borrow one for a few weeks while he got the Buick repaired by one of Taj's mechanic relatives. Preferably the one who put the car in this condition in the first place. Charlie was too excited by his new case to linger.

"You take it easy, Dad," he said. He patted the old guy on the shoulder, then worried about the parka. "You okay? You want me to turn up the heat?"

"No, the place is boiling. I don't know how you stand it this hot."

"It wouldn't be so hot if you took your coat off," Charlie told him.

"And freeze to death?" Ogden took an indignant bite of apple and oatmeal. Charlie went out the back door before its fate was decided.

The spring sunshine was intense and the air was fresh as he went to inspect the Buick. This time, Ogden had tied the muffler up with something that looked like piano wire, so now the trunk couldn't be opened without a wire clipper. Charlie shook his head. At that moment a robin yanked a worm out of the lawn and took flight with it. He turned to watch it and quickly surveyed his yard in the process. He had an acre in this pleasant old neighborhood close to the beach, a lot of space. Along his fence were rosebushes, inside it a lawn with a gazebo in the center. He noticed that the hydrangeas around the house and gazebo were showing signs of life. The rosebushes were filling in and budding nicely. He was proud of his yard, but it was nothing compared with the much smaller Sales place. Charlie had been particularly impressed by the orchid house in the middle of the backyard. He wondered if it might be hiding something in plain view, and wanted to see it again.

MONA WAS IN MARK COHEN'S OFFICE at eight Tuesday morning. She was wearing a very conservative lightweight black gabardine pantsuit, a purple turtleneck cashmere sweater that matched her purple alligator bag, and very high-heeled purple alligator shoes. She had not slept well in Le Refuge. Anxiety about Mitch's condition had roiled the acid in her stomach and the suspicions in her head. He had been perfectly well when he'd left her in Paris, and now all he could do was wink.

During the night she went over every single one of her discussions with Mitch on the subject of marriage, divorce, and beneficiaries. Since he'd been so ardent about protecting the future of his precious children, the talks had always centered around protecting them, not her. Over a period of years, however, she'd managed to persuade him that she was more likely to take good care of Marsha and Teddy (both of whom she truly did adore) than Cassie, who had no idea about money. She'd assured him that even after they married, the children would still get everything in the end. She had no parents, no sibling, no family but his; after all, who else could it go to? What Mitch had done was throw in a condition that put her in jeopardy now. The condition was that if Mona had already passed on at the time of his death, the assets would go directly to his children. Mona knew that Teddy would never in a million years harm her, but Marsha was another story. Would Marsha and

Cassie kill her? Would they kill her to cut her out of Mitch's will? she asked herself. Yes, they would.

During the long night Mona had kept her expensive new drapes open. She couldn't bear being shut in at the best of times, but now she was afraid of being murdered in her sleep. The house was equipped with two sets of lights. Some came on at dusk and went off at eleven, like the runway lights along the driveway and the spotlights in the trees. Others were strategically placed in the eaves of the vast roof and were equipped with motion detectors that flashed on a battery of powerful sodium lamps every time a cat or squirrel ran across their field of vision. The lights were activated four times.

Each time darkest night had become day in her bedroom, Mona sat up in a panic, thinking that Cassie's hit man had come to kill her. She was sorry she'd misplaced the pistol Mitch had bought her in Florida a few years ago. She was sorry that she'd left the telltale Jaguar out in the driveway. The property's five-car garage was about an acre away, down a hill. Same damn thing as Roslyn. She'd moved up in the world and still didn't have an attached garage.

Dr. Cohen's office in Manhasset was near the hospital in the kind of modern four-story medical building with an elevator that spoke for the blind. "You have pressed two. Elevator doors close," it told Mona when she got in and pushed the button.

"You have arrived on the second floor. On this floor are the suites of Drs. Cohen, Garfeld, Saperstein, and Gelfman. Have a good visit," it recited.

Mona's blood pressure was way up. She entered the doctor's office wheezing badly. "Marta, I have to see him right away," she cried.

Marta was the sort of invisible woman well past middle age that Mona and Cassie alike had a total horror of becoming. She was plump and had pale, crepey skin that she overblushed and overpowdered. Her boyish haircut was steely gray. She was all business; and no matter how nice Mona was to her, Mona knew this difficult, jealous old woman was going to refuse to like her.

"Mona, you should have called first. He's fully booked all day. I know you're upset about Mr. Sales, but—" she started in on her now.

"I'm not just upset, Marta, I'm ill. I had a very bad night. I have crushing chest pains, and my left arm is numb. I guess I'm having a heart attack."

"Oh, for heaven's sake, why didn't you call?"

"Some people believe consideration comes first, even with doctors. I didn't want to worry him. Or you." Mona checked the waiting room. Two half-blind old people (clearly the ones for whom the elevator had been given that wonderful upbeat voice) sat next to their walkers. Other than that, the place looked pretty empty to her. She coughed up a mouthful of phlegm. "And my asthma is kicking up, I need a shot of Adrenalin."

"Oh, for heaven's sake. Come in here right away." Marta took Mona into an examining room and left her there.

Mona weighed herself just for the hell of it. In spite of Paris, she'd lost a pound. Gratified, she quickly climbed up on the table and crossed her legs. In less than a minute Mark raced in with her chart under his arm, looking appropriately concerned.

"Mona. What's this about chest pains?"

Mona was wheezing terribly. "This is so terrible about Mitch." She took his hand for support.

"Take your time." He went to the sink and filled a tiny cup with water.

"I'm just so sorry to bother you, Mark. I know how busy you are and how much you have on your mind."

"This is what I'm here for, Mona. I called you last night, but you didn't pick up." He handed her the cup.

She took a moment to sip from it. "Well, I couldn't. Cassie followed me home! Mark, I was so *terrified*. She threatened my life. I had to leave and check into a *hotel*."

"What?"

Mona burst into tears. "What happened to Mitch?"

"He had a stroke." Mark gave her a handful of tissues and took her pulse. Then, with a flick of his wrist, he indicated that she take off her black jacket so he could listen to her heart.

"How could he have a stroke? He was *fine* Friday." She took off her jacket, hopeful that this would lead to a hug. He must have pushed his little button, because just at the moment he flicked his fingers at the eyelet blouse, the nurse came in. Off came the blouse. He didn't even look at the bra or cleavage as he used his stethoscope to listen to her chest and back.

"Have you been using your inhaler?"

"Of course."

"How often?"

"Four or five times a day. It isn't working."

"Have you been taking the Aminophyllin?"

"It makes me nauseated. Mark, how could he have a stroke? Everything was going so well."

"Sometimes the stress of a divorce can do it." He let the stethoscope drop on his chest. "Your asthma needs attention, Mona. That's probably why you're having chest pains. But we'll do an EKG and Crow enzymes. And of course you need new pulmonary tests. I want to do it while you're in crisis."

Mona grabbed his hand again. "Did he tell you we are getting married?" The nurse, Irene, looked on from the door, placid as a cow.

Mark went on unfazed. "And he was ignoring his high blood pressure."

"What high blood pressure?" Mona cried.

"He called me from Paris a week ago. He had headaches, felt dizzy. I warned him that he was playing with fire and told him to come right home. He waited until *Friday*. That's not good."

Mona gasped. Her fiancé was sick? This was news to her.

He turned to Irene and ticked off the procedures Mona was getting, including a shot of Adrenalin. As soon as she was gone, he turned to leave. Mona was crushed. After all the gifts she'd given his silly wife, the dinners they'd had together. The patients she'd referred him! Getting this kind of short shrift was unconscionable.

"Mark, wait! I'm very concerned about Mitch. I need to discuss this with you."

He stood with his hand on the doorknob, his face as neutral as a blancmange.

"What's his prognosis?" she asked softly, softening toward him immediately, her breathing now deep and even. She was falling apart. She needed a hug, any idiot could see that.

He shook his head. "Wait and see," he murmured.

"Mark, I'd like you to consider moving him."

His expression didn't change. "He's on life support, Mona. He can't be moved."

"But I'm afraid for his life." Mona was so upset at the cold reception she was getting, she almost forgot to cough.

"We're all afraid for his life," he said, cool as could be.

"Mitch and I were getting married, Mark. I may even be pregnant. I missed my period this week. Just think about it. Cassie doesn't exactly have his best interests at heart here. I'm worried that she wants him to kick off."

He shook his head, opening the door just a little to indicate his wish to leave.

"I'm dying here, Mark. Whose side are you on?" Mona cried.

"I'm not getting between you two on this, Mona. I'm his doctor. I'm doing the best I can for him."

"What if the best for him is not the best for her?"

"This is too much for me, Mona. I'm just a doctor. Please call me later for the results on your tests, I think you're going to be okay."

"Mark, could we have lunch and talk about it then?"

"I won't have results by lunchtime, Mona."

"And I bought a little something for—honey, we've always been so close. . . ." What was his damn wife's name, Candy, Sandy?

"Mark, I'm all alone with this. There's only you."

Mark peered out the crack in the door, poised to bolt. Mona jumped off the table and went to him.

"Please don't get distant with me because of this Cassie thing. You know I love her with all my heart, and no one could be more sorry than I am about the way she's behaving. But we have to face this together. She's hurt him. She wants to kill him. And you know I don't want anything to happen to him because of me, Mark, and I don't want you dragged into a big legal thing."

She lowered her head to his shoulder. It wasn't that easy a trick since he was much shorter than she was. His white coat was starched and fresh. His closely shaved cheeks smelled delicious. Quickly he closed the door against spies from the outside.

"You're amazing," she breathed. "The greatest."

When she went downstairs a few minutes later, there was a little smile on her face. She was certain Mark was on her side.

CHARLIE SCHWAB HAD CHOSEN the Sales warehouse in Syosset as the site for his audit. It was an unusual move, since audits were typically held in the accountant's office or in the IRS branch office. He'd chosen the Long Island location because the juice he was looking for would not be in Ira Mandel's Manhattan office, and he didn't want to travel into the city every day for an indefinite period in any case. He was also strapped for time. Gayle was ruthless about keeping their cases quick and productive. Move fast and move on, was her motto.

A limited audit to clear up a teeny question about one detail of a transaction that had been recorded some years ago might require a stack of paper several feet deep and take a full day. To examine the books of a business like Sales Importers with a lot of product moving in from many countries and moving out to thousands of highly active monthly accounts in numerous states for even one year could take weeks. Full audits of big holding companies and conglomerates typically took months. It all depended on how much time was being covered, how much paperwork had to be examined, and how compulsive an investigator was. Charlie was very compulsive indeed, but he could also move as fast as the wind.

In the middle of traffic he mused that the Bureau of Alcohol, Tobacco, and Firearms would definitely want in on this case. It was a big one, and ATF got involved at the drop of a hat. Charlie worried about the risk he personally was taking. He hoped that he wouldn't be making too many enemies by following his boss's instructions to do the grunt work alone. He didn't want to upset himself thinking about office politics, so he contemplated the question of spies instead.

Because the possibility of finding uncollected revenues was ever present for the IRS, no one cared who informers were. The tax force relied on spies for tips. They also relied on newspaper articles about all sorts of events, both criminal and civil. Charlie himself had a large collection of obits of prominent and wealthy people who had died in the region. These obits helped them decide which estates to target with an audit. On the spy front, suffice it to say there were a lot them. Spurned spouses. Fired employees. The discriminated against, for one reason or another. The IRS was an equal opportunity tip taker.

In the Sales organization someone was holding a grudge, a big one, and stood to win a nice bonus if the assertions proved correct. Sooner or later he'd find out who it was, or maybe he wouldn't. Didn't matter to him. Charlie concluded his thoughts and pulled up in the Sales parking lot. The red Jaguar was there, and he felt a little glow with the intuitive feeling that Mona would be useful.

Inside, past the reception area, several banquet tables had been set up in an empty space near the bathrooms. Documents were stacked on the tables along with bottled water, sodas, a coffee urn, and bakery goods. Boxes filled with supporting documents were piled around and under the tables. One table had four folding chairs set up. The first thing Charlie noticed about the setup, aside from its lack of comfort, was that no one could possibly read there. It was dark as a cave.

Ira Mandel was sitting at the food table eating a bagel with cream cheese. Never one of Charlie's favorites, Ira was a short man with an easy smile and forgettable features. He looked a little sleazy this morning in his shiny blue Italian suit and silver tie. As soon as he saw Charlie, he put the bagel down and stood up, licking his fingertips one by one. When he finished licking the hand, he held it out to Charlie, who pretended not to see it.

"Ira," Charlie said neutrally.

Ira did not appear in the least put off by the snub. "Nice to see you, Charles. This is my associate, Ted Sales."

A young lug stepped out of the shadows.

"How do," Charles said pleasantly. The youngster looked like an overly large twelve-year-old, very nervous in a tan suit and red tie. Small eyes and mouth.

"Sir," he said formally, then bit down on his lower lip, losing it altogether.

"Any relationship?" Charlie asked him.

Ted seemed terrified by the question. "Sir?"

"Your name. Sales."

"Oh." Ted glanced at Ira before answering.

"Yes, yes, he's Mitchell Sales's son. Very bright young man, wants to be an accountant."

"Good for him," Charlie applauded. "Let's get going."

"Please. Be my guest. Have some breakfast, will you? I have something I want to go over with you before we start."

Just up the steel staircase a picture window showed where the main offices were. From where he stood, Charlie had a clear view of Mona Whitman leaning over the desk with her backside to him. Ira followed his gaze.

"What can I get you?" he asked.

"What?" Charlie blinked.

"Breakfast," Ira prompted.

"Oh yes. Thank you, I've already eaten." Charlie sat down at the table and took out his equipment. Calculator, laptop, pens. Pads. Altoids.

Over his head, Ira glanced at Ted. "Pull up a chair, Teddy."

Oh, now he was Teddy. Charlie ignored the scraping sound as Teddy pulled up his chair. He was minding his own business, paying no attention to anything but his own notes when quick steps on the cement floor let him know that the decorative Mona had arrived.

"Teddy! I didn't know you were here yet. Isn't this terrible? I tried and tried to call you. How are you holding up, darling?" She rushed over to him and threw herself into his arms.

Since Teddy didn't have the manners to rise for her, she ended up almost in his lap.

"Hi, Mona." Teddy's reaction was a mixture of confusion and alarm.

Ira lifted his eyes heavenward. Charlie wondered what the story there was. Mona regained her balance and stepped back to examine the young man's face.

"I feel so bad for you. How are you doing, honey?"

"I have a girlfriend," Teddy said with a shy grin.

"No kidding, that's wonderful. Who's the lucky girl?"

"She's a nurse," Teddy said proudly.

"A nurse, she's a nurse?" Mona cried. "What kind of a nurse?"

"Operating room. Isn't that cool?"

Mona's attention wandered over to the accountant.

"Ira, sweetheart. Hello." She clicked her tongue. "Terrible thing, isn't this?" Instead of embracing him, she made a little face. "Oh, don't be mad. I have no intention of butting in, I promise. I was just going to the ladies'. How do you like the little spread I put out? That's whitefish salad, right there. Your favorite, Teddy. Ira, could I have just a word with you?"

"Of course, Mona."

Then she registered Charles Schwab sitting at the table very busily tapping on his laptop, totally ignoring her. "Oh my goodness, Mr. Schwab. I didn't know you were here."

He glanced up at the sound of his name. She gave him a big smile as if they were old friends. No one could say *he* didn't have manners. Charlie jumped to his feet, wondering what it would take to turn her. "Miss Whitman, how's that ankle of yours?" he said cheerfully.

"Still aching something terrible. What happened to you?" She raised her hand and came closer to touch the bruise on his forehead.

"A little tennis mishap. It's nothing."

"You play tennis, too? You're amazing. Did Ira tell you about our problem?"

Ira frowned furiously at her. "Thank you for the food, Mona. No, we haven't gotten that far yet."

Charlie divided his attention between them. And what was the story there?

"Oh, well, sorry to interrupt. Is there anything else I can do for you?" She smiled brightly.

Charlie held up his hand. "Light," he said.

"What?"

"We need some light."

"Oh." She put a hand to her mouth like a little girl who'd made a big mistake. "Oops. Of course you do. I'll take care of it right away."

But she didn't. Charlie returned to his laptop, and Teddy squirmed in his chair during the short hiatus while Mona had a private conversation with Ira. Finally Ira returned to the banquet table, and Mona went into the ladies'.

"Are you sure you won't have some coffee?" he offered a second time.

In such situations, Charlie was always reminded of a colleague of his who'd gotten very sick from rat poison served in a cappuccino during an audit. "Yes, but thanks anyway," he said.

"Well, then, we can get right to it. Here's our situation. I want to alert you to a personal tragedy. Mitchell Sales had a stroke over the weekend. He's in extremely serious condition in intensive care, and we're concerned that he won't make it."

Charlie was digesting this information when the distracting sound of a flushing toilet came from behind the door marked LADIES. "That's a real shame," he replied. They were back on the stroke. He lifted one shoulder in what he thought was a sympathetic shrug.

Ira took it the wrong way. "Now don't get me wrong," he said belligerently. "We're perfectly prepared to go through with the audit right now. This is for your convenience only."

"I don't see how it changes the situation," Charlie replied blandly.

"Of course, you know perfectly well in a private company it would make all the difference," Ira argued.

Charlie shrugged with both shoulders. "I don't see how. Any adjustment that we might ask for would have to be complied with in any case."

"Oh for God's sake, Charlie, my man, the company CEO is dangerously ill."

"You weren't expecting him to participate at this point, were you?" Charlie stuck to his guns. He wasn't anybody's man.

"Well, no, but his illness—"

"You told me Mr. Sales had no intention of being present."

"True, but—"

Mona emerged from the bathroom and made a cute little face of contrition for interrupting again. "I'll just see about those lights for you." Now her jacket was unbuttoned. The little white thing underneath revealed her tiny waist. Charlie's eyes followed her as she walked away. He knew designer dresses when he saw them and wondered what the story was here.

"Look," Ira said. "I'd like a postponement for a few weeks. Is that an unreasonable request?"

Charlie sat back in his metal folding chair and pulled on his ear. From the moment the stroke had returned to the table, he had decided that an official delay was an excellent idea. It would give him time to do some background checking on the wine distribution business in general, and Sales's operations in particular. He wanted to check out the Sales house, talk some more with the wife, find out what the story was there. But he let Ira pompously argue his position. He always enjoyed hearing the arguments of the clearly guilty before giving them something that might lead them to think they had him in their pocket; they'd won the first battle.

CHARLIE SCHWAB CAME OUT INTO THE SUNSHINE and plopped his hat
on his head. The warehouse was climate controlled to the temperature
of an estate cave, Teddy had told him when he was leaving. That was the
reason it was so cold. Outside, he paused while his skin warmed up and
his eyes adjusted to the light.

"I don't know what's wrong with this thing," Mona complained. She
was click, click, clicking that fancy key door opener and not getting the
response she wanted from the Jaguar.

Schwab saw her in the parking lot and waved. She stepped away
from the car feigning surprise to see him. "Mr. Schwab, are you finished
already?"

"Not even begun," he said.

"Oh?"

"There's been a postponement." He smiled.

"Wow, you're amazing!" She took the two steps to where he'd paused
by the row of short fir trees with dwarf conifers between them that separated the building space from the parking lot, grabbed his hand, and
shook it warmly. "That's *very* handsome of you."

Then she blushed for using the word "handsome." She'd meant that
he himself, not just the gesture, was handsome, and wanted to make
sure that that was how he'd understood it.

"No, not at all," he said smoothly.

"I know this will mean a lot to Mitch. The stroke has really knocked him for a loop."

"I can imagine." Schwab was neutral.

"You know, I'm glad you're here, because I wanted to clarify things with you. When we talked yesterday, I had no idea Mitch was really—that he really—" Mona stopped and lifted a crumpled handkerchief to her eyes. "I just wanted to set the record straight," she said, dabbing her eyes.

"What do you mean?" Schwab tilted his head to one side.

"I'm sorry." She flapped her hands delicately as if to rid herself of these embarrassing rushes of feeling. "I'm just all alone with all this. Isn't it funny I had no idea about the stroke when we met yesterday? I didn't find out about it until last night. I was—flabbergasted—to say the least." She shook her head. When he made no remark, she explained further.

"What I mean is, Cassie is like that boy who cries wolf, you know? She lies so much that no one believes her. Yesterday morning she told you Mitch had had a stroke, but she didn't tell the *rest* of us. Here at the warehouse we didn't know a thing about it. Isn't that awful?"

Schwab did not comment.

"She just has no idea how to manage anything."

"I understand."

"And she doesn't want you to know about her, of course." Mona tossed her head. "And then I kept thinking and thinking about you. It was so strange. It was like destiny when we met like that. . . . What were you *doing* at Cassie's house, anyway?"

"Just looking around." Schwab shrugged.

"That's so thorough. Do all IRS agents do that?" Mona gave him an interested look, but he didn't help her out.

"Do what?" He tilted his head to one side again, his attitude watchful.

"You said you were looking around. What are you looking for?" Her wide, lovely eyes were frankly curious. She was giving him her full range of expression, but he wasn't responding. She found him heavy going.

"Whatever there is" was his answer to this question.

Mona persevered. "That sounds *so* mysterious. I mean, I'm into the wine and the customers. I don't get the business end at all. All of this is way beyond me."

"It's pretty simple, really," he said. "I bet you know all about it."

She *almost* brushed his tennis arm. "I bet I don't."

He smiled.

"You don't say much, do you?" she murmured.

He moved his chin a little, but didn't answer.

She inhaled, started to say something, then stopped. "Well, I know I'm supposed to keep out of it . . ."

"I understand," he murmured.

"I just, I thought, well, is there any way I could be of help to you?"

Finally his smile broadened a little. "Maybe."

"What with Mitch out like this, I guess I'm going to have to learn what's what. Maybe I could facilitate in some way." She said this as if it were a surprise even to herself.

"Well, that might be very helpful," Schwab said.

"Of course, Mitch is the complete business genius. He pretty much runs the show," she said quickly. "But I'm the spirit of the enterprise. I love the wines, you know. They have such a life of their own, like characters. Do you like wine?"

Schwab became sheepish at the question. "Oh, I don't know much about it."

Mona clapped her hands. "A beer man, I bet. I could teach you, and you could teach me about taxes. Wouldn't that be the greatest? You know, I could make you the envy of all your friends. Wine is very in, you know, and we deal only in the best."

"No kidding." Schwab seemed to ponder this question.

Mona had the oddest sensation. Here was this attractive (but not well-dressed) man who seemed intelligent and should be attracted to her. But his eyes were cold, and he was a lot of work. She didn't get it. Most men were not so much work. She was doing everything exactly right. She let the silence hang there for a few moments while she examined him further, trying to size him up. Maybe he was a gay IRS agent. Maybe he spent all his time watching sports and didn't have any conversation. Or he was married. That would account for the blush and awkwardness. Some men were faithful. A few.

She smiled. On the other hand, a lot of people were getting divorced these days. Maybe this Schwab's total lack of finesse was his newness to the dating game.

"Would you like to have lunch sometime?" she ventured.

"Well, that would be nice," he murmured.

"Are you allowed to fraternize with the enemy?" she joked, taking it a little further.

"I have no enemies," he replied quickly, his blue eyes wary, wary.

"Oh, yes. You work for the government. Your job is to make people's lives *miserable*." Mona shook her finger at him, enjoying this. "I hope you're one of the reasonable ones. You'll be reasonable with poor Mitch, won't you?"

He laughed at the word "reasonable." "I'm always reasonable."

"That's good, because I *know* Mitchell Sales wouldn't do anything wrong. I've worked for him all my adult life."

"It doesn't look like that's been very long," Schwab said.

"Thank you, but I'm older than I look."

He lifted a shoulder, noncommittal.

"So, we'll have lunch. That's great," she murmured. She was going to go a tiny bit further, but didn't have time.

Suddenly he was on the move, a little nervous, a little excited. Hurrying on to the next part of his day. It was a male reaction Mona was very used to. They always got nervous when they liked a girl.

AN HOUR LATER Mona was having lunch with Mitch's lawyer, Parker Higgins, at the American Grill, in Garden City. Parker had been one of those tall, good-looking boys who was just so cool, everyone had always known he'd get ahead in life. He and Mitch had gone to Hofstra together. Even before that they'd known each other in high school. His offices were on the boardroom floor of a ten-story building that used to be a bank. He owned it and the one just like it directly across the street.

Parker was as tall as Mitch, quite a bit heavier now, with a deep tan from weekly visits to a tanning parlor where he also got intimate massages. Mona knew this as she knew almost everything. Mitch talked. Parker had less hair than Mitch, but wore a lot of gold to compensate. He wore thick gold chains around his neck and wrist, a gold Panther

watch, and the same large eighteen-karat gold golf ball cuff links that
Mitch and Mark wore, though only Mark played golf. And he was very
shaken by Mitch's stroke. He was wearing a black tie.

Mona was doing everything she could to engage Parker in a useful
conversation, but all he wanted to do was talk about old times. They'd
been served their two grilled chicken Caesar salads and two glasses of
iced tea. While he waited for the salads to arrive, Parker had wolfed
down the entire bread basket. When his salad arrived, he wolfed that
down. Mona hadn't touched the mound of limp, overdressed lettuce
loaded with thick croutons from a box and whole anchovies that were so
salty and prickly with tiny bones, her mouth rebelled just at the thought
of them. Parker loved this place with the fake palm trees and trellises on
the wall with fake ivy all over them.

"That six months we backpacked around in Europe after college was
the best time of my life," Parker was saying for about the tenth time.
Next would come the stories of drinking and Mitch's falling for the wine
and how he'd borrowed ten thousand dollars from Cassie's *father* to start
his business. Mona hated that story.

"I know, must have been the greatest." It was getting really hot in
there, so she unbuttoned her jacket. "Parker, I know how busy you are,
and I really need to go over some things with you."

"Of course you do," he said, still mooning over hostels he wouldn't
dream of even entering, much less staying in now.

"You've been to see Mitch, yes?" She knew he had.

"Yes. This is really a shocker. One day in the pink of health, and the
next day—grim reaper. It doesn't look good. Mark told me he's brain-
dead." Parker shook his head and glanced around for a waiter.

Mona guessed that he figured he'd been "good" for all of thirty minutes and now could no longer resist having a drink.

"We'll have a Bloody Mary over here," Parker called across the room
to a girl who wasn't paying attention. "You?" he asked Mona.

Did she know people, or what? "Not right now," she murmured
about the drink. "Look, Parker. Mitch is *not* brain-dead. He spoke to me
clearly. Very clearly. He's on the mend. I swear it. Please don't write him
off," she begged.

"That'll be two Marys!" he yelled.

When he turned back to her, her famous pout was on her face, and her famous wheeze was beginning in the back of her throat.

"You *know* I'm all alone with this, Parker." Her voice caught. This was no act. She was dying here. What kind of asshole was he? They'd traveled to Italy together. They'd chartered that sailing boat in the Greek Isles. She'd been completely nauseated the whole time. They'd swum with fucking dolphins in Mexico. Wasn't all *that* the best time of his life?

His eyes were on the bar, yearning for those Marys.

"Come on, have a heart, Parker. Don't back out on me now. There's no one but you," Mona said.

Parker heaved a deep sigh. "This is a shocker, Mona, no question about it."

Mona talked to her invisible audience. See what she had to put up with! A complete narcissist. All he could think about was himself. A genuine tear filled her eye. "What about the will, Parker? Not that I want you to reveal confidences. But you know what Mitch's intentions were. Did he sign his new will, or what?"

Now he gave her a frank stare. "Look, Mona. I'm going to do the same with you that I did with Cassie, and Teddy, and Marsha." He made the motion of a zipper being closed across his mouth.

"What the dickens is that?" She maintained her sweetness. She was not going to fall apart.

"My lips are sealed."

"How can your fucking lips be sealed, Parker? You know what your friend wanted. Did he get it done? That's all I'm asking."

"You're not eating your salad," Parker said.

"It's a yes-or-no question. You could even nod or shake your head. What's the big deal?" The tears welled into puddles, and Parker looked away. He was not one who responded well to emotion. "Parker, please."

"I know how upset you are, Mona," he said softly, squirming for that drink.

"We were getting married. We were having a family together. You *know* this, Parker. I may be pregnant already. I *need* you on my side. Don't let this wonderful man go," she cried. "I love him so much. He's my whole life. What do I care about anything else? Puh, I spit on everything else."

"Mona, please, it's not in my hands."

"Don't give me that shit, Parker. A man's life is in your hands."

"Mona!"

"Sorry, sorry. You know I think the world of you." She controlled herself. She brought the sweetness back, leaned over the table so he could see her lovely breasts. "Parker?"

He was too busy thinking about death to look at them.

"Parker, speak to me."

"I think the world of you, too, Mona. You know that." But where were those drinks? "Ah, thank you."

The two Bloody Marys *finally* arrived. One was placed in front of Mona. Parker raised his glass to her, clinked the ice, and downed the drink in a few greedy swallows.

Mona pushed hers across the table toward him.

"Thanks, I'll just have a sip," he said. This one he drank more slowly.

"Parker, you know I'll keep you as my attorney. You stand to keep Sales as a client—you *know* what I mean. Help me out, and I'll help you out." She watched him chew on celery, this man who all his life had despised vegetables.

"What about the power of attorney? Surely you can tell me that," she wheedled.

Parker finished the second Bloody. "Okay, Mona, he didn't sign it."

Mona gasped. "He didn't sign it?"

Parker shook his head.

"There's no power of attorney?"

"Nope."

"Well, who's in charge, then?"

"He is."

"He's in a coma, Parker."

"Yes."

Mona gasped again. For sure she was going to die with her beloved. "Why didn't he sign the fucking power?" she wailed.

"You know Mitch. Superstitious. He'd planned to when he got back." Parker shrugged.

"Oh shit. So he didn't sign the will, either, did he?"

Parker shook his head "no" to the will.

Mona's blood pounded in her ears. The love of her life just couldn't let go. The story of her fucking life. She had to get a handle on this, couldn't let Mitch die. How could she save him? She watched Parker point at the empty glass for another drink. The waiter nodded. Alcohol might help. Mona knew about the girl in the massage parlor, and there were a few other things Parker wouldn't want his wife to know. He was a weak man, putty in her hands. She thought of Mitch hooked up to life support. What had his last will provided? They'd been together twelve years, but she had no idea.

Parker shook his head, waiting for his third Mary.

"What about a living will? What about a health care proxy?" Mona demanded.

He shook his head again.

Mona perked up. "Well, that's good. If he has no living will, doesn't that mean Cassie can't kill him? You *are* aware Cassie intends to kill him, aren't you, Parker?"

"No, Mona. She's not like that."

"Yes, Parker, she is. She's been stalking me. She tried to kill me just yesterday. You know my loyalty to the family. I love the woman to pieces, but let's face it, she's over the edge. And quite frankly, if she hurts Mitch, I'll have your *ass*."

"Oh, Mona, don't talk like that. You know you're no toughy."

"Of course not, but I love him *so* much. He's my whole life. Except for you, he's all I've got. Is the power prepared?"

"Huh?" The lawyer blinked in confusion.

"The document giving the power of attorney to *me*, Parker. Remember?"

"No." Now Parker shook his head firmly. He wasn't going there.

"You remember, Parker. I was here when we discussed it. We can sign it now."

Parker rolled his eyes and called for the check. "I have a meeting at two." Typical male fade away. It made her want to puke. This kind of thing might work with other people, but it wouldn't work with her.

"Of course, no problem," she said graciously, and reached for her purse. She'd let it go now, but it wasn't over, not by a long shot. As soon as Parker was reminded that Cassie could cause him a good deal of trouble if Mitch died, he'd fall into line, she was sure he would.

EVERY DAY, wearing a scarf and her daughter's huge sunglasses, Cassie went to the hospital during the visiting hours of eleven to four to visit her husband in intensive care. On days five, six, and seven after his event he was no better and no worse than he had been on days one through four. He was stable and as uncommunicative as ever. As she stood by his side watching the machine breathe for him, she chewed on the inside of her mouth until it was raw. She wished she could make contact and have it out with him just once.

Then on Friday, a full week after Mitch had his stroke, Cassie received a letter from Carl Flauber, a lawyer whose name she had never seen before. Carl Flauber wrote to inform her that he was representing Ms. Mona Whitman in the case of Whitman versus Sales. He had obtained an Order of Protection from a judge in Nassau County against Mrs. Cassandra Sales to keep her more than five hundred yards away from Ms. Whitman. In addition, he was preparing a civil suit against Mrs. Sales for harassing Ms. Whitman in her home Monday, June 3rd, and for kidnapping and driving Ms. Whitman around for two hours while she was having an acute asthma attack, thus recklessly endangering her life. Ms. Whitman was seeking ten million dollars in damages for injuries incurred during the incident. In addition, Carl Flauber advised Cassie that if the life support for Mitchell Sales was terminated prematurely, Ms. Whitman would sue the hospital and doctors for malpractice and Cassie for wrongful death.

Cassie read and reread this letter and chewed some more on the inside of her lips. She folded and unfolded the single sheet so many times in the next few hours that the creases wore thin. It was both absurd and masterful and felt a little like being checkmated in the game of life. The situation reminded her of Nino Palucci's case. A year ago, Rosa Palucci's son, Nino, hired a limo to take him and some friends into the city for an evening of safe drinking. The driver followed them into a friend's apartment where a party was in progress and attacked Nino, knocking him down. While attempting to get the man out of the apartment, Nino punched him in the nose. The limo driver called 911. When the cops arrived, they arrested Nino for assault. The limo driver pressed charges, and when Nino refused to plead guilty to a misdemeanor, the judge and jury convicted him. At his sentencing the judge changed his mind about sending Nino to jail for a year. He got a suspended sentence, but had to pay a fine of five thousand dollars to the complainant. Defending the case cost the Paluccis twenty-five thousand dollars, and the limo driver, flushed with success, filed a civil suit for an additional hundred thousand dollars in damages for post-traumatic stress disorder. Nino was twenty-three, white, and had never been in trouble before.

Cassie Sales was fifty and had never been in trouble before, except unknowingly as a wronged wife. Now she was in the wrong in every respect. She had been wrong to drive to Mona's house and scream at her. She had been wrong to let Mona get in her car. She had been wrong to engage with the enemy in any way. She had learned a lot since then. She did not answer the letter.

That day she had the very last stitches removed from her scalp. When the last one was out, she felt if not entirely whole, at least human. For the first time she looked at herself in the mirror in the surgeon's office and actually saw that the sagging skin and complacent chubbiness of the constantly nibbling caterer were gone. She now resembled an earlier version of herself, an attractive person of indeterminate age with an oval face (just a little on the full side because her cheeks and jaw were still swollen), nice strong chin, bee-stung lips. No wrinkles at all. While her skin was still quite pink in places, the area around her eyes had passed the telltale blue-and-yellow stage. At the two-week mark, the period of pain was over. The tightness and numbness that remained made Cassie feel as if she had the armor of a gladiator. From the doctor's office she went to the hairdresser, where everyone said she looked amazing. There she had her hair color adjusted from the horrendous daffodil to a tasteful golden honey, and then she was in condition to drive to Garden City to confront Mitch's lawyer and best friend, Parker Higgins.

At quarter to two, without first calling ahead, Cassie arrived at the mirrored building Parker owned and where he had his office. She announced herself to the receptionist, and he had the good sense not to make a fuss about seeing her on no notice at all. He fit her in at two. As soon as she walked into his glass-and-chrome office and sat in one of his leather-and-chrome chairs, she could see that he'd imbibed a martini or two at lunch. He lurched across the room to kiss her fondly on the cheek. She tried not to wince in pain.

"Cassie, what a nice surprise. You look wonderful. Have you lost weight?" He gave her a puzzled look as if to make sure it was really her.

"Thank you for seeing me without an appointment," she replied.

"No need to thank me. I'm delighted." Parker's attitude seemed to have changed since his visit to Mitch. He threw his bulk into the chair next to Cassie's and raised an eyebrow that was so thick, it extended from one side of his forehead right over to the other without a break. He was black Irish, and generally a delightful kind of guy.

"I thought it would be a good idea to sit down and go over a few things with you," Cassie murmured, thinking with some satisfaction that he'd lost a lot of hair and had run to fat since they'd last met.

"Of course, no problem. I hope I didn't leave you with the wrong impression when we talked the other day. I was caught by surprise."

"I understand," Cassie murmured, her voice smooth as the color of her hair. She couldn't help noticing that he wasn't offering her coffee, or even a glass of water.

"You look different, Cassie." Parker frowned, trying to figure out what was so different about her.

She was wearing an old navy and white designer knockoff that had been in her closet since the eighties. The skirt was short, and the blouse was a tiny shell of pink silk. The size six was almost loose in the butt. It fit her perfectly, which was a nice feeling.

"Parker, I'm in an interesting situation in which you have the better of me," she said with a self-deprecatory smile.

"Oh, please, don't demean yourself. You're a fine, wonderful woman," he protested. He opened his manicured hands. "You'll get over this. You'll find someone else and get married."

"I'm already married. I'm married to Mitch. And whatever he intended for the future, he can't cut me out of his will without a divorce. New York State Law."

"Oh ho ho, Cassie! There's no question of that. Whatever happens, you're going to be all right, I promise you."

"That's nice to hear. But with everything that's happened, how can you give me assurances like that? How am I protected?"

Parker shifted uncomfortably in his chair. "Well, I understand what you're saying. Men can be little more than monkeys sometimes. They age, they make fools of themselves—"

"They die," Cassie finished the sentence for him. "What I want to discuss with you is your involvement with Mona and the deals that were made with her."

"I have no involvement with Mona." Parker's tongue suddenly failed him. He slurred over the sentence, hardly able to get the word "Mona" out at all.

"Well, good for you, because Mona is suing me for ten million dollars," Cassie told him, still very smooth. She plucked a thread off her skirt.

"What?" Parker's mouth turned into a little O of surprise.

"She has an order of protection against me."

Parker was either dumbfounded, or a good actor. "Cassie, this is very serious. Why?"

"I'm just wondering, did you give her the name of a lawyer to use against me?" Cassie had no sunglasses on now. She looked him in the eye and could see he was shocked.

"Good God no! Do you think I'm crazy?" he cried.

"We'll leave that for another time." She crossed her legs the other way.

He watched her anxiously, trying to figure out what was going on. "You appear to be misinformed," he said after a beat.

"Oh well, that's true. No one informed me that Mona opened charge accounts in my name and charged up a storm, nearly a million dollars. I gather the idea was to leave me with the debt at the time of the divorce settlement."

Parker's wet lips that had been pursed in shock now dropped open altogether. "What?"

"Mitch and his girlfriend bought a house and furnished it on credit acquired in my name. I don't know the law in this area, but I would say either it's my house and my furnishings or else a fraud has been perpetrated against me."

Parker heaved in some air. "Ah, Cassie. All this is news to me."

"You didn't know about the house?" she demanded.

"Well, Mitch didn't share his private life with me."

"Yes, he did," she countered. "He consulted you about everything."

"I may have heard something about a house," Parker admitted. "Mona bought a house; Mitch could have helped her with credit."

"Parker, I'm not going to ask you about details at this time. I just want to make it clear that I have documentation on purchases of silver, china, jewelry, furnishings, and a bunch of other stuff that Mona made in my name."

"Wow, are you sure, Cassie? This doesn't sound like the Mona I know."

Cassie made an impatient, who-are-you-kidding? noise. "Who's in on this? Mitch, Mona, you, Ira, and who else—everybody?"

"Cassie, there's no conspiracy here, I promise you. You're overreacting." He opened his nice big hands with black hair all over the backs. Women get so worked up, he seemed to be saying.

"You *know* Mitch was divorcing me. That was the reason you wouldn't talk to me on Monday," Cassie said softly.

"Just take it easy, you're going to get through this just fine. Are you going to trust me, or not?" Parker asked.

"You must really think I'm an idiot. A forgery of my signature is on every receipt. Whose idea was this? Yours, hers?"

"Look, slow down and consider your accusation. Just consider it.

Proof is the issue here. I'm not taking sides, I'm just saying that you can make things very difficult for yourself taking on an enemy as litigious as Mona."

"Parker, she's already sued me. I have nothing to lose." Cassie wondered how much he had to lose.

His hands did a little dance, soothing the air around her. "She's *threatened* to sue, Cassie. It's not the same thing. She's a negotiator. She's negotiating, that's all. Don't take it personally. There's a lot at stake here."

"Well, I'd like her to sue me. We could have discovery and then everything would come out in court."

"Cassie, Cassie, think of the cost. Think of what's at stake here. We're in the middle of an IRS investigation. You don't want things to get muddled, do you?" Parker was very alarmed.

"Muddled?"

"She'll claim he gave her everything, then when you lose, there will be gift tax to pay." Parker clenched and unclenched his fingers, drunk no more. "You see. Culpability can get mixed up, and other things could come out."

The ground was shifting under Cassie again. She knew he meant Mitch's moving cash out of the country, but what was this gift tax thing?

"I'm your friend. I've always been your friend. I'll help you find a way out of this. Trust me, will you?" Parker urged.

Suddenly queasy, Cassie rose to go. "I'll think about it." As she put her sunglasses back on, she wondered how many ways his actions were unethical and whether he could be disbarred for conflict of interest.

CASSIE DID NOT DRIVE to the hospital to see how Mitch was doing as she had planned. It was clear that she and Mona were in a deadly game of chess, and she had a disturbing premonition about the files and the credit card receipts with her signature on them in Mitch's office, as well as all those folders in the computer dating back years that she hadn't had time to go through. If Mona felt strong enough to threaten to sue her, then she wasn't afraid of prosecution. And if she wasn't afraid of prosecution, then she must have some plan for acquiring the evidence.

The sun was high in mid afternoon as Cassie raced home. Even with the air conditioner on in the Mercedes, she was uncomfortably hot, sweating in the straw hat and sunglasses she wore to protect her new face against dangerous ultraviolet rays. She was sweating in the pseudo fancy nubbly suit and pink silk blouse she hadn't fit into in years. She was sweating buckets. When she got home, she was alarmed by the battered black Buick that was parked in front.

31

CASSIE DROVE PAST THE BUICK, puzzled by the trunk wired closed. Maybe there was a body in it, maybe her files. Chewing on her lip, she crunched onto the only drive in the neighborhood whose asphalt was covered with gravel, a landscape feature that she'd always thought gave her home a nice little rural touch. She pushed the automatic garage door opener in the Mercedes, and the garage door rumbled up. Inside, the Porche was resting comfortably all alone, but something didn't feel right. A strange car was parked outside, and even her garage was giving her the willies. She didn't want to risk getting caught in a dark space by a burglar, so she backed slowly out again. It seemed that every action she took now was a reaction to a threat. She had to plan every move like a strategist in a war. It was all new and frightening. After twenty-six years of playing everything in her life so safe, she was now teetering on a tightrope over a chasm.

Shivering, she stopped the car just outside the garage, turned off the engine, and got out. The Mercedes door was heavy. Solid steel. She had to push hard for it to close with a solid thunk. More creepy feelings prevented her from entering the house through the front door. Everything was a potential threat. Everything. Heart beating, she went around to the gate. There she let out her breath. The owner of the shabby black Buick was Charles Schwab, back in her yard again. More precisely, he was in her greenhouse. She recognized his shape and crew cut through the glass.

Shaking her head, a little angry now, she entered her Eden. She strode across the patch of lawn that was surrounded by borders planted thickly with dwarf lilies, half of which were ambrosially in bloom. She moved quickly past the patio, where the pool sparkled and the geraniums had yet to be potted. She walked under the arbor, heavily weighted with leaf and rosebudded vines that any day would burst open in a riot of color.

Mr. Schwab was turned away from her, leaning on the bench, apparently in deep contemplation of a particularly showy double spray of monarch butterfly–sized, yellow phalaenopsis. She turned the handle of the greenhouse and startled him.

"Wow, what a specimen!" he exclaimed without missing a beat as he turned his head and saw her in the doorway in her nubbly tweed suit with the short skirt and pink blouse, her sun hat and glasses.

"Hello Mr. J. P. Morgan," she said, "fancy meeting you here."

"Very funny," he replied. "It's Charles Schwab."

"Oh yeah, Schwab. I knew the name had something to do with money. What can I do for you, Mr. Schwab?" All of Cassie's own code buttons were flashing. She was scared of this guy Schwab, and at the same time she was not scared of him at all. It was funny. She was aware he could do her a lot of harm, and somehow he still managed to remind her of a cute guy in high school. No one in particular, he was just the type she used to like. The one with the shy smile who wasn't really shy once you got to know him.

"Nice outfit. You can call me Charlie if you want." He turned around all the way to get a better view.

Click. High school. Cassie blinked. The feeling of the past in the present was strong. She shivered in the heat. "Thank you. What are you doing in my greenhouse, Charlie? Interested in gardening?"

"Girls are supposed to like it when you compliment them on their outfits." There was the smile.

Click. Cassie was back there, eighteen, attracted to a guy, hoping he would ask her to dance. Click. She was fifty, married to a comatose man who hadn't loved her in years.

Puzzled, she ducked her face into the shade of her hat. "Checking out my orchids?"

"Yes, I hope you don't mind. Very impressive. They really are."

"Sublimation," Cassie quipped.

"No kidding, which one is that?"

"All of them. Orchids are amazing. I don't even think of them as flowers. They're more like exotic creatures." She smiled.

Just their names alone set Cassie dreaming: phalaenopis, dendrobium, cattleya, paphiopedlium. She dreamed of them at night—their colors, their shapes, delicate and extravagant, like butterflies and moths and bees and tigers, firebirds, fish, with beauty unmatched by any other species on earth. Each orchid small or large, in bunches like vandas or sprays like dancing oncidium, felt to Cassie like stirrings of the senses she'd lost, teasingly sensual yet entirely accessible. Her substitute for sex. The globes of the paphs were like full, round testicles of athletes, the cats like richly dressed court ladies in heat.

"They're very splendid," Schwab said, neutral on the subject of sublimation.

"So, what are you really doing in my greenhouse?" She knew his job was to catch her husband at tax evasion, embezzlement, everything Mitch enjoyed doing.

"I love these orchids. I didn't know orchids smelled like this. What do you call this one?"

"That's a cattleya. It's called Hawaiian sunset."

Charlie tilted his head at it, sniffed, stuck out his bottom lip to examine it more comprehensively. The two large flowers were elaborately frilled purple and orange, outrageously scented.

"Hmm, of course, tropical sunset," he murmured. "Very nice. This one smells, too." He pointed at a large oncidium with two dancing sprays of mothlike blooms in brown, pink, and lavender.

"That one smells like chocolate. Isn't it amazing? It's an oncidium." Cassie couldn't help being proud of her babies. Not everybody could do even easy orchids like these.

"Amazing. You have quite a talent for this." He looked her over some more. "How are things going?"

Click. The question felt personal. Click. She shook her head.

"That's a not good?"

"That's a not good." She lifted a shoulder, feeling like eighteen. Feeling like a hundred, both at the same time.

He rubbed at an ink stain on one of his fingers. "I'm sorry to hear it. Your husband's still in intensive care?"

"Oh yes, still out of it." She scratched an eyebrow, chewed on the inside of her tortured lip. She was still reeling over the events of the week, the doctors and lawyers. And she was shaken that she could also feel like a teenager in spite of it all. She was hanging back in the doorway because the greenhouse was too small a space for two people who weren't close friends. Nervous. She was very nervous because of the dangerous stranger in her space.

Charlie bent his knees a little to peek under the brim of her hat. "Does that mean you're still not serving coffee?"

She laughed.

"I noticed that you have one of those fancy cappuccino makers in there." He pointed at the house and her wonderful kitchen. "Does it work?"

"Were you peering through the windows again, or have you been inside?" Cassie asked anxiously.

"Just peeping. I saw the car was gone. The alarm button is on. I didn't want to mess with it." He smiled his disingenuous smile that made it clear he knew how to disengage burglar alarms when he wanted to. "I thought I'd hang out for a few minutes and see if you came back."

"Thanks, I appreciate the courtesy."

It was his turn to laugh.

"Actually, I came back because I had a feeling someone was here," Cassie told him. It just wasn't who she'd expected. "Sure, it works. It works very well." She backed out of the door to let him out. "Come on in the house, I'd like some coffee myself."

All the dancing moths on Cassie's oncidium jumped into her stomach as she led the IRS agent into the minefield of her house. She had no clear idea what Mitch had hidden there or what the agent was looking for. But she had a strange, upsetting feeling that he wasn't here only about taxes. He was here about her.

She opened the door and turned off the burglar alarm that she'd used only rarely up to now. Then she went about grinding beans, setting up the machine, getting out the milk for frothing while Schwab looked around.

"Nice Viking, Sub-Zero. What a pot collection!" He took it all in.

"Don't get too excited. It's all fifteen years old," Cassie informed him.

"Age doesn't matter with quality items," he replied, touching another nerve.

"Some maybe. Do you like to cook?"

"I fool around a little. I cook for my dad."

"That's nice."

"Not really. He has special needs. He has a problem swallowing." Charlie checked out the cupboards of dishes, good ones.

"Really? That sounds unusual." The coffee machine started chunking and spitting, getting its job done. It was a big and fancy one, but it took a while.

"It's a rare condition," Charlie said.

"That's a shame," Cassie thought of the soft food groups. Purees, soups, ice cream. Puddings, soufflés. She didn't want to ask if Charlie lived with his dad or vice versa. Or if his wife lived there, too. He was the one who was investigating her.

"He's been living with me for thirteen years, since my mother died." He answered her unasked question easily, pulling out a chair and plopping down at her table as if he'd been drinking coffee there for years. "I don't like to talk about it. Must be your kitchen that got me going." That smile again.

Click. "I know what it's like. My mother died first, too. Widowers can have a lot of trouble if they don't remarry." Cassie kept it conversational.

"Everybody has a lot of trouble if they don't remarry. But I agree with you about geezers. My dad is a handful."

Cassie thought of Edith and nodded. Then a big thing happened in a tiny beat without her deliberating about it at all. She'd met a man she might have liked if she'd known him in high school. His investigation of her felt like a date, so she led with a strength. She'd skipped breakfast and missed lunch, and wanted something to eat with her coffee. There was nothing in the house, so she preheated the oven to four hundred and began to assemble scones. She filled a measuring cup with flour, added salt, sugar, baking powder, then cut butter into it, sprinkling in enough milk to create a small lump of soft dough. She patted the lump out on her granite countertop and kneaded in a handful of currents and some candied orange peel. Then she cut out eight tiny biscuits with a shot glass and frothed the rest of the milk while they were baking.

By the time perfect scones came out of the oven, Cassie had set the table with her own strawberry jam and cappuccino in big cups, and her visitor was speechless with wonder.

"Tell me about gift tax," she said matter-of-factly, as if this kind of hat trick was an everyday occurrence, which it was.

"This is just the most amazing thing I've ever seen," Charlie said, lifting a tiny browned scone to his nose to sniff, as he had the orchid. "You just did that?" He snapped his fingers.

"Well, we needed a grain food group," she explained.

"Wow, a competent woman."

She sipped the coffee. That was not bad, either. "Well, thanks. It's not as great as it looks."

"Yes, it is. It's better than it looks," he murmured.

She snorted. "The picture of perfect domesticity, I mean."

"Oh?" He tilted his head in that way he had.

"My comatose husband has a girlfriend." Cassie took a scone and broke off a tiny piece. "I didn't know he was planning to divorce me until the stroke. When I found out he and this girl had been together for years, I got upset, drove over to her house, and yelled at her, so she's suing me for ten million dollars. You came as a surprise on the same day." She sucked her lip into her mouth. "Actually, I'm a nervous wreck."

"Well, you could have fooled me." Charlie drank some coffee and put the cup down. "This is the best coffee I've ever tasted. The best scones. About you, this says it all. It really does. You have a lot of style."

Her lip trembled. "Thank you."

"And I've seen it all. This is the oldest story in the world. I've lived it myself. What do you want to know about gift tax?"

32

ON SATURDAYS CHARLIE SCHWAB HAD A SCHEDULE. In the morning he spent three hours working at his office. It was quiet there, and he liked to get out of the house, where Ogden always wanted to do father-son stuff together, like play Scrabble or poker and gamble with spare change. After work he had an hour and a half of real tennis at the indoor courts on Ocean Road with his friend Harvey—also a revenue agent—who was once ranked 143 on the tennis circuit and never got over it.

After tennis, in which the score was always 6–4, 4–6, 6–5, with the two men taking turns at winning, they made the short hop across the street for lunch at Steven's Fish House. The one who lost did the grumbling, and they both had the same lunch year-round. Clam roll, fully loaded. Couple of beers. If the kitchen didn't have clams, they'd have an oyster roll fully loaded. After that, goodbye to Harvey. Charlie did the weekly food shopping for Ogden to reduce the risk of the Rau family giving him things he shouldn't eat. Chickpea fritters, onion *kulcha*, deep-fried pastries, vegetable tandoori. Everything big enough to choke a horse, not to mention a man who had trouble with applesauce. Then he'd go home with the groceries and play around in the kitchen whipping up some really yummy soft foods.

This Saturday he expected the usual. He'd spent his workweek sniffing around the Sales situation, giving some thought to Mona Whitman and Cassie Sales. At first, he'd thought that since Cassie was the man's wife, she had to be in on it. He figured he could get her to open up easily enough. His plan had been to get down into the cellar and inventory the valuable wines their informant claimed was hidden there. The private cellar was only a small piece of the puzzle. What could Sales have down there, a few hundred cases? But it could serve as the "way in," the discrepancy in documenting that would justify a wider investigation.

Their informant, via a number of anonymous letters on Sales stationery, had revealed that Mitchell Sales personally was taking in a lot of cash off the books. If that was the case, he had to be laundering the money somehow, or else getting it out of the country—maybe into a numbered account in Switzerland or offshore. Maybe both. The wife would certainly know about that.

On Thursday when he was in Newark auditing a dry-cleaning chain—ironically enough, also a company that took in a lot of cash— Charlie had checked out a second Sales warehouse in New Jersey. It had been described in various documents as a depot, just a staging area of about 1,500 square feet. The warehouse at the address listed, however, turned out to be more on the order of 165,000 square feet, almost as large as the Long Island warehouse. Pay dirt indeed. He had been considering the ways to go with it. They could track the truckers, go through the garbage for the paperwork on the deliveries. Check the files in the computers inside there. Lot of things they could do.

But yesterday the picture had changed for him. He'd searched the greenhouse at the Sales home, looking for a safe or a false floor in which Sales could be hiding gems or cash. He'd found only magical orchids— gorgeous, but probably not worth more than a hundred dollars each. During his three-hour talk with Cassie Sales over the coffee and the biscuits she'd made, then over fruit and a tiny glass of very good sherry, she'd filled him in on the wine distribution business as she understood it, and he'd explained gift tax.

Maybe he'd been smitten over the coffee and homemade baked goods, maybe it was the sherry and grapes. But he believed her story about the girlfriend. If Cassie had only just learned about the girlfriend, as she claimed, it didn't seem likely that she was the informant. In any case, he hadn't had the heart to question her about the wine cellar in the basement or the offshore accounts. It seemed pretty clear that whatever he did, this beautiful, classy, and very nice lady stood to lose a great deal from his uncovering her husband's business dealings. So he'd done something unusual, he'd backed off.

Charlie was in a deep brooding state when he stepped out of the district office building in Brooklyn after finishing up his work for the morning. Coming outside he was momentarily blinded by the dazzling mid-June sunlight. Then, just as earlier in the week in similar circumstances, he saw Mona Whitman leaning against her car. It was seventy-eight degrees warm. The sky was robin's egg blue, and there were no clouds floating around up there where heaven was supposed to be. Mona was wearing sunglasses, tight pants, high heels, and a little sweater that didn't hide her magnificent chest.

"Charles Schwab. Hi." She waved and called out to him. "I think I found something that might help you."

"No kidding." He walked over to see what it was.

"Wow, you look different on the weekend," she said admiringly.

He was dressed in the cut-offs and white T-shirt he always wore for tennis. None of that fancy stuff for him. The T-shirt he was wearing had a few holes in the ribbing around the neckline. Mona pointed at the bulging Bloomingdale's shopping bag sitting on the car beside her.

"What's in the bag, money?" Charlie joked.

"I wish. How are you?" She said this as if they were best friends who'd been apart for too long.

"Okay. How's Mr. Sales doing?"

"Oh, he's coming along just fine." Mona glanced down at her feet. "Have you been working on our case on a fabulous day like this?"

Charlie's smile broadened.

"What's funny?"

"Everybody thinks theirs is the only case we ever work on. I have others, you know." He was thinking, bingo the girlfriend, no wonder Cassie lost it.

"Everybody says *you* work too hard." Mona was flirting.

"Who'd say that?" Charlie scratched his head.

"Oh, you think you're the only one who finds out things about people." She laughed. She had a very pleasant laugh that Charlie found chilling.

She could be an informer. She could be a spy for the other side. The first person who'd ever smashed his windshield had been a woman. Charlie never forgot he had to watch himself. He glanced at his watch. By now Harvey would be on his way to Indoor Tennis. He had to go.

"Harvey, right?" Mona said coyly.

Charlie raised his eyebrows. This woman actually knew where he was on Saturday morning, where he was going. Not good.

"You'd be surprised how much I know about you." So she read minds, too. Very cute.

"I know, you've got to go." She pushed herself off the car and reached for the shopping bag, offered it over. "Here."

"What's this?" He looked inside. It was full of paper.

She waved her hand at it. "Sales records." Her giggle was like a bird-song. "Sales records for Sales's sales. I thought you might find them useful."

Great. This was the kind of thing his mother used to do. Bring him the tax stuff in a shopping bag. Of course, he'd loved his mother. He nodded at Mona, tilted his head to one side. Mona certainly wasn't anything like her. His tongue poked at the side of his cheek. He got the feeling she was like the car bomb Rau had found attached to his poor muffler last month. He didn't know who'd planted that.

"Are you always this hard work?" She shifted hips.

He clicked the tongue. Tsk, tsk, tsk. She was good.

"Well, I'll be getting along then." The door was locked. She fumbled with her car key. After a short struggle, in which he watched her shake with the huge effort of pressing the remote, she twirled around like a dancer.

"I mean, I'm all alone with this. Poor Mitch is in the hospital, and his wife wants to pull the plug on him. It's so upsetting. I never thought she'd go so far. First the terrible financial drain. Now this. The truth is, I don't know what to do." She blurted all this with a great spurt of emotion.

Charlie didn't respond. He knew a good act when he saw one.

"I thought we could talk about it over that lunch. After your tennis game, I mean," she amended quickly.

"Fine." Charlie nodded. Maybe she was asking him out for a date. Maybe she was coming on to him. Maybe she was a spy or the informer or the girlfriend or all of the above. He held on to the shopping bag filled with papers. Could be something, could be nothing. Whatever Mona had for him, though, she activated Charlie's alarm system.

"That's a yes, right?" Mona said, clapping her hands, triumphant in a win.

TWO HOURS LATER, after Harvey had beaten Charlie 6–4 in the first set and 6–2 in the second and was out of the picture, Charlie and Mona were sitting at one of the picnic tables ordering clam rolls at Steven's.

"Thank you for meeting me," Mona said, triumph still written all over her. "This is really a cute place. Do you come here with your father?"

"I'd guess this isn't the sort of place you come to," Charlie said. He was pretty sweaty even though he'd let Harvey beat him. He hadn't showered because there was no shower at Indoor. It was just a bubble. He was sure he stank, but didn't care. He was working now.

Mona laughed and held up the menu. She pointed at the page of beer choices and only two wines, house red and house white. "I'd say you're right. But I love it," she added quickly. "I just love working-class places."

"No kidding." Charlie hid his grimace. It was clear she thought he was a blue-collar worker.

"No kidding," she returned quickly. "My grandmother was a Rockefeller, but my mother was a hippie before stoned and cults were fashionable. But enough of that. Tell me about your life." She propped her elbow on the table and nestled her chin in her hand as if suddenly he'd metamorphosed into the kind of fascinating high WASP captain of industry she liked.

He talked for quite a while about absolutely nothing that could help her, watching to see if her eyes glazed over. They didn't. She gazed at him with rapture throughout his long, complicated, and excruciatingly dull monologue about the tax structure.

"How about a woman? Is there a lucky woman in your life?" she asked when he'd finished.

"Oh, sure." He was working on the clam roll.

Her little face fell. "I bet you have a girlfriend."

"Ummm." Chew, chew, chew. Swallow. Great clam roll with lots of sauce oozing out all over him.

"What's she like?"

"What about you? Are you attached?" he asked with his mouth full.

"Attached? Oh no, there's no one, just Mitch. I mean, I've really devoted my entire life to the business. I was married for a while, but it didn't work out. Soooo, I just took my name back and Mitch's family as my own. Cassie and the children are like my own flesh and blood. That's why her behavior is so . . . painful." She pressed her lips together to keep the tears back.

Charlie wiped his mouth with the paper napkin and pushed his plate away. So she'd devoted her life to Mitch. She was the girlfriend who was suing Cassie for a cool ten mil.

"Maybe you should think about having a family of your own," he said, gazing back at her with interest. "I bet it would be pretty easy to get a husband if you wanted to."

"Do you really think so?" She seemed to doubt it.

Charlie nodded, amused that this wily woman of self-proclaimed excellent pedigree was trying to get him to believe she was insecure. She worked on it a little more.

After lunch, she offered him a ride in her car. She gave him the keys, and he actually got a huge kick out of driving a car he could never own himself. He followed the road out to Long Beach, where they got out of the car to look at the water. So far she hadn't told him a single useful thing, but neither had he. They were playing it very cagey.

On Long Beach itself, there was a five-mile boardwalk. Mona said she loved hiking, but couldn't exactly walk in the shoes she had on. So, they stood in the breeze for a while and contemplated the beach and the ocean. Beautiful. People were out there in their bathing suits, sitting on the sand, walking, playing volleyball. For a moment Charlie thought that it would be nice to be part of a couple, to have a classy, competent woman in his life who wasn't a transient he couldn't wait to get rid of at the end of an evening or early the next morning. Someone he could cook and eat with, talk to, relax with.

As he was thinking this, Mona took his hand and held it tight. "You're amazing," she told him with eyes as big and deep as the ocean in front of them.

CHAPTER
33

AT FIVE O'CLOCK CHARLIE DROVE HOME to change his clothes for a drink at Mona Whitman's house. He felt he'd hit pay dirt with the invitation to come to her home. Usually their residences were the last places taxpayers wanted agents to go. Whatever Mona wanted him to see there, however, Charlie knew he would learn a lot. In the last few days he was working overtime for the service, being more popular and having more dates than he'd had in months. He was doing fieldwork, and the field was coming to him. The only question was how much sowing he would have to do, and what kind of harvest he would get for his efforts.

The Sales case wasn't numbered for criminal investigation yet. As far as the district director and the regional commissioner were concerned, he was still doing background for a routine audit. But he could smell fear emanating from every corner of the case. There was so much quaking going on, he'd begun to think conspiracy. He had his eye on a bigger target now, Ira Mandel, accountant, adviser, and third-party record keeper to many high-profile taxpayers. If he was a rotten apple at Sales, he was a rotten apple elsewhere, too.

Mitchell Sales might be in the hospital, but the case of Sales Importers was spiraling on its own. Inside the company there was an informer, teasing, teasing, and not yet out of the closet. Whoever it was could get immunity if he or she came forward voluntarily with information leading to a conviction. Often, however, informants did not come forward and identify themselves, not for anything, even high fink fees.

Most people didn't know that the government paid up to 10 percent on recovered revenues in evasion cases. If the numbers were up there in the hundreds of thousands—or the millions—the fees could add up. But of the 1,200 plus informants who came forward every year, only a small minority attempted to get their money. Charlie had six cases right now with fink fees no one wanted to claim. It turned out that a lot of people ratted to get even but feared disclosure because getting even could go both ways.

The IRS picked different professions to target with audits every year. A few years ago when it was dentists, a nurse had tipped the service off to an oral surgeon she worked for who had several offices. He'd been cooking his books for fifteen years. She got her ten-thousand-dollar fink fee, but was blackballed and never got another job in a doctor's office again.

Charlie pondered Mona Whitman. He had his eye on her. Mona was a third party, and all third parties counted. According to Mona's own testimony, she was not a third-party professional record keeper, like Ira Mandel, or Mitch's various lawyers, banks, customers, and creditors. But as a partner in his business, as a friend, and maybe girlfriend, Mona was a non-record-keeping third party. She had intimate knowledge of his and the company's dealings and as such could quite possibly be a coconspirator in his activities. A conviction as a coconspirator in an evasion case would garner her a prison sentence up to five years and a $250,000 fine in addition to any unrecorded, unpaid additional income she had. Prosecution was a discretionary action that the Treasury requested and the Justice Department carried out.

All the way home to Lynbrook, in addition to feeling regret at being back in his own noisy, undistinguished car, Charlie pondered the question of how to protect Cassie Sales. From Long Beach it was not a long way. He drove down Lake Avenue, checking the rearview mirror every few minutes to make sure the Jaguar was not behind him. He didn't trust Mona Whitman and her own investigative techniques. His house came into view and he sighed with relief. No Jag behind him. No Jag was out front, either.

Lynbrook had a number of great old houses like his with its wrap-around porch ringed with late-blooming peach azalea (showing now) and blue hydrangea that would flower later in the summer. The property border picket fence was covered with climbing roses, one or two flowers of which were already in bloom. He and his father tended the property with loving care, and though it was nothing compared with Cassie's, Charlie thought the property wasn't too bad at all. His real estate friend, Carol, who was heavier than she should be and whom he didn't find as attractive as she found him, was always telling him he could sell it in a heartbeat. On an early summer day like today, he thought it was probably true. But after owning the place for twenty-five years, even with the first $250,000 tax free, the capital gains tax would still take a big chunk. He didn't see how he could ever sell.

Upstairs, Charlie showered quickly, then hesitated in the closet for a long time, considering his wardrobe. Nothing he had was up to the tight pants and sweater Mona Whitman had been wearing. Finally he decided on a houndstooth jacket, a yellow shirt, and khaki trousers. Then he drove northeast to the other side of Long Island, where his possible informant, the girlfriend who probably had not a drop of blue blood in her veins and who was suing the wife he liked, said she lived.

ROSLYN WAS A WHOLE OTHER STORY from Long Beach and Lynbrook. Roslyn had a nice town park with a duck pond, real ducks, and many gracious old white houses with porches and peaked roofs and green shutters that were larger and finer versions of Charlie's. In this neighborhood, they'd be triple the price, too. Charlie drove down the hill into Roslyn Harbor, an even cuter little town without a grocery store that looked like it belonged on Cape Cod, or out in the Hamptons. Then he swung back up the hill taking a little tour of the neighborhood.

Halfway up the hill, before he reached Roslyn Heights, he saw the red Jag parked on the street. In light of the flashy car, Mona's place was nothing special, just a tiny brick attached town house, one of dozens in a complex called Beech Tree Hill that lined both sides of the street. From the outside, there appeared to be no special features. The long squat row of brick structures had small windows, nonexistent landscaping, no balconies or sun porches, and rows of ugly garages behind them. Compared with Cassie Sales's pretty house and superb gardens, it was a tenement. Charlie parked the Buick behind the Jag and got out.

As he started to approach the house, he had his second flash of the day to the car bomb on his muffler that hadn't detonated as planned. He didn't enjoy having feelings of paranoia, but frankly this didn't look like the kind of place where a girl like Mona Whitman would live. He had a sudden fear of being set up. The alarm bell clanged so loudly, he almost turned around to get back in the car. But Mona had seen him from the window and had come out her front door to welcome him before he could get away.

"That was fast. I didn't even have time to wash my face. Come on in," she said.

Too late. Charlie gave her a lame smile and hoped for the best. Inside, he was reassured by the furnishings. This was her taste all right. Everything was white, white, white. Neat. He'd seen enough places to know there wasn't a speck of dust anywhere. He could tell without even running his fingers along the moldings. Immediately he was struck by the fact that there were no photos, no souvenir-like things. No books, no stereo. And then he knew she didn't really live here. Girls were messy. Even neat girls were messy. They had stuff from high school, from college. They had Valentine-shaped chocolate boxes from ten years ago in which they kept little odds and ends. They had stuffed animals. They had knicks and knacks. Mona had nothing.

"It's not much. Not a beautiful place like yours," she said, looking around at it critically.

"Mine?"

"You have a lovely home," Mona chirped, "but I wasn't so lucky. I had no inheritance. I started with nothing."

So she had followed him to his lovely home. "Well, this is just great!" he said, approving the house. "Very nice."

"Come on in, don't be shy."

Charlie wasn't shy. He just didn't like being manipulated.

She held out her arms to the place. "Come on, tell me the truth. What do you think of it, really?"

"Very nice." But Charlie knew she didn't live there.

"Well, let's just say I worked hard for it, and I did it on my own. Face it, it's not very impressive, considering the lifetime of work I put in. There are no closets at all, and real entertaining is out of the question."

"Well, it's small, but elegant. You've done a nice job with it." Well, maybe there was another story. Maybe Sales had been cheating on her, too. Planned to dump her, buy her out, return to his wife. And she was getting even by informing on him.

"No, it's tiny," Mona insisted angrily, one hand tapping furiously at her hip.

Then suddenly her mood changed. She dropped the annoyance about the house and sat on the sofa. "Seeing somebody so ill makes you want to celebrate life," she said, perky again. "Know what I mean?"

"Oh yes, definitely." Charlie took a seat himself. Right about now he was thinking about a drink. Someplace safe, far from here.

"Mitch was such a strong, vital man. Now he's on life support. It just makes you reconsider everything."

He nodded. He was thinking, give me the juice, babe, so I can bail out of here.

"You know, seize the day," she murmured. She was getting emotional, and he was yearning to be somewhere else with a different kind of woman altogether. He wanted her to squeal, not throw herself at him.

"I loved them so much, and now I'm totally out of the loop. I'm so afraid." Tears puddled in her eyes.

"What are you afraid of?" he asked. He knew what he was afraid of.

"Oh, murder is such a terrible thing," she moaned.

"Murder?" Oh, now they were on murder. He hoped she didn't mean his.

"I'm not going to burden you with it, Charles."

"Go ahead, burden me," he said magnanimously.

"No, no. I promised you a drink, and a drink is what you'll get. I have something I know you'll like." Mona jumped up and ran into the kitchen, which was only a few feet away. She returned with some delicate crystal champagne glasses and a bottle of pink champagne on a silver tray. "You know, Charles, there's no one else. I feel like you're all I have now." She popped the cork and poured expertly, handed him a glass, then raised hers.

"Oh, I'm sure that's not the case," he demurred.

"Yes, that woman is going to murder Mitch. She's going to take everything I have in the world. Would you let someone get away with murder, Charles?"

"Of course not," Charlie said.

"Good. Have some more. This is a very good vintage." Mona finished her glass of champagne and poured herself another.

"So give me what you've got," Charlie said.

"Uh-oh. I'm having an asthma attack. I need my inhaler." Mona was suddenly coughing uncontrollably, her chest heaving with the effort of breathing.

What now? Charlie thought he'd seen everything in his years of service, but he'd never seen this.

"Would you run upstairs and get it for me? It's in the drawer in the bedside table," she pleaded.

Good God. He was being tested today. Charlie charged up the stairs into her bedroom, then stopped short at the sight of the frilly white bed. He opened the bedside drawer. Inside was something called Kama Sutra massage oil, a number of smelly candles, and an asthma inhaler. Ventolin. That was it. He grabbed it. Then, before going downstairs, he stopped to examine the bathroom. In the medicine cabinet he found several bottles of NyQuil, aspirin, Motrin, Tampax, toothpaste, toothbrush, a hair dryer. Not a lot else. No birth control pills, no condoms, nothing of an intimate nature. She may have stayed here from time to time, but this woman didn't live here. He took a leak and washed his hands, checked himself in the mirror. He looked pretty good, if he did say so himself. He went back downstairs, ready to go. The woman wasn't spilling, and he wasn't hanging around to find out what the game was.

"Do you know how to give a back rub, Charles?" she asked, wheezing on the sofa when he trotted down the stairs.

"No, not really." He was out of there for sure.

"Could you just give me a little back rub, just so I can relax? I know I'll feel better in a minute. Then we can talk."

"Here's your inhaler."

"Charles, you're the greatest. The *absolute greatest*."

"Thanks for the champagne. Feel better now." He wouldn't sit down.

Mona's face went into a pout. "Are you going already? We haven't had a chance to talk," she complained.

"Yeah, well, my dad isn't feeling well. But thanks, I had a really nice day. I'll go through those papers you gave me. And if you have anything else you want to share with me, don't hesitate to call." Then he fled.

34

MONA CALLED IRA FROM HER OFFICE in the warehouse several times the following week. He was still having a fit over her behavior at the audit meeting. He didn't seem to understand that she knew what she was doing. All the men in her life were being difficult. He simply wouldn't concentrate on what she was telling him.

"Mona, let me try to explain something very basic to you. The IRS doesn't have to tell you they're investigating you, got that? They can investigate you *in secret*," he told her heatedly.

"Ira, I don't know what you're referring to," she said, irritated that he couldn't stick to the subject. "I'm talking about *Cassie*. I'm trying to get through to you. There are going to be consequences if she doesn't leave me alone."

"Look, I understand the situation, but you have to sit tight here. You can't *do* anything. You can't make friends with *IRS* agents. Do you read me?"

"I would do no such thing. It's not my fault if he's coming on to me. The guy calls me every day."

"This is very upsetting to hear," Ira said angrily. "You have to be careful. You don't want to get him angry at you."

"I told him I can't have a relationship right now, but men just like me. I don't know what it is."

"Mona, he doesn't *like* you. He's working a case."

"I know. Sexual harassment is a terrible thing. If it goes any further, I'll just have to make a complaint."

"Don't you do that!" Ira screamed.

He was losing it, a very small-minded man. Mona changed the subject. "Look, Ira. You don't know what's happening here. Cassie is coming in and having checks cut. I can't have that. Do you understand me. I *cannot have* that."

"Look, she's not getting what's due her. Her regular checks aren't coming in. She can't pay the doctor bills."

"She's a very extravagant person, Ira. She should economize, not try to take advantage of the situation."

"I'm not arguing with you about this again, Mona. You can't cut the owner's wife off when her husband has doctor bills. You don't have that kind of power."

"I don't know what you're talking about, Ira. This woman spends like an Arab."

"Mona! You're giving me an ulcer!"

"I have an ulcer myself. And I have asthma. I've never been in such terrible condition in my life. Look at what she's doing to me, Ira. She tried to kill me, now she's trying to eliminate Mitch. She comes into the building and talks shit about me. I know she intends to take over as soon as he's gone. I can't have that. You have to talk to her. You can't let this go anymore."

"Mona, she has doctor bills."

"I don't want her around here," Mona said.

"Then make sure she has the money she needs. Don't make me step in here. I'm only the accountant."

"Oh, you're much more than the accountant," Mona said.

"Hey! Don't start with me. You know I don't know the half of what Mitch gets up to. And believe me, I don't want to know. I know what I know, and that's it."

"But I'm all alone with this, Ira. What am I going to do about the money *I* need? Tell me that. I'm stuck here in this big house. I can't carry it. Cassie is a murderer—" She could go on and on.

"Mona, did you know that IRS agents routinely go to banks for canceled checks to prove people are spending money they claimed they'd never earned? If you mess around with Charlie Schwab and he starts looking closely at you and finds out where you live and how you live, he might just think some of your deductions are a little on the high side. He might question your salary, how you're paying for that big house. He might start looking for safe-deposit boxes. Do you have any safe-deposit boxes full of cash that I don't know about?" Ira said furiously.

"No, of course not. I'm shocked to hear you suggest such a thing." Mona tapped her fingers on the desk.

"I don't want to find out down the road you've got cash all over the place."

"I said I don't." Mona checked her nail polish. Why was he acting like such a pig after all the things she'd done for him?

"Then don't start spending it, you hear me? Don't involve me. And don't engage Cassie in your war. I'm telling you, she could do a lot of damage."

"I wouldn't hurt her for the world, Ira. I'll listen to you, Ira. I want you to know I think you're very special. You're all I have. I won't forget it."

Mona hung up and dialed Charlie Schwab's number. She left another message for him when his voice mail answered. She was a woman with a great deal of confidence in her ability to turn any situation around. In spite of their first-date fiasco, and the fact that he hadn't called to thank her for her gifts, she was convinced he liked her.

35

CHARLIE WAS NOT IN HIS OFFICE the many times Mona called him there to apologize for her asthma attack and to thank him for the most wonderful day of her entire life. He was not at home when the baskets of gourmet soft foods were delivered for his father, or the new wardrobe from Polo and Armani and several other expensive stores arrived at the house for him. Since he hadn't acquired any new clothes in the last decade or so, he couldn't resist trying on the suit, four jackets, and coordinated trousers that had been magically altered to fit him—he couldn't imagine how or when.

He opened the door of the closet in his room where his mirror was and turned this way and that to see what Ralph Lauren did for him. He was stunned to see that good clothes made a difference. Very nice; he got the point that he had not been well enough dressed in his own style for even a mob girl like her. He got the point and he was stung. Not only was he the fake Charles Schwab, but he was no snappy dresser. Now he could see that snappy dressing improved his image. He felt like a jerk for not having thought about it before.

He felt like a jerk having to pack up the outrageous sartorial bribes and take them back to the stores from which they were labeled and he thought they had come. He was further bamboozled when no salesperson in the stores where he tried to return the stuff could find a record of any purchases made in Mona's name, or addressed to him. That meant a big investigation would be required to figure out how she'd done it. He took the boxes home and conferred with Gayle on the subject late in the week. After he told her the story, his boss's face flamed with rage.

"If you touched that woman, I'll have your ass, Schwab" was her response. She fell into some kind of instant jealous fit about it.

Charlie stood in front of her desk and swore up and down that he hadn't touched Mona Whitman, and he hadn't even taken a sip of her champagne.

"I don't want a hint of collusion or harassment or anything like that down the road." Her fingers dug into her thick curly dyed black hair, and a light dusting of dandruff drifted down onto her desk.

Charlie pretended not to notice it. "Don't worry about it, Gayle. It's not going to happen. What do you want me to do?"

"Did the stuff come with a card? A letter? Anything we can use against her?"

"Nope. Nothing at all. The woman is very smart. As far as I know, Santa sent it. But I can dig. Who knows, she might have had it sent from out of state. You ready to number this one? The woman knew what side I dress on, for Christ's sake."

Gayle shook her head. "What the hell are you talking about?"

"The inseam."

The face of the woman who, as far as he knew, loved only her cat, froze with understanding. "Jesus, spare me the dirty details, Charlie. And don't number the account yet. Find the juice first, then we'll number and let go of it."

"Okay, if that's the way you want it." Charlie shrugged, thinking of Cassie. "How do you want me to handle it?"

"Your usual will do nicely. Just hurry it up. I don't want to get stuck in this."

"How about the clothes?" he asked innocently.

"If their source can't come back to bite you on the ass, do what you want with them. Toss 'em, wear 'em, bring them into the office and display them. I don't care. As far as I'm concerned, I don't know anything about any clothes. But everybody knows I have a faulty memory," she said, waving him off.

36

CASSIE SPENT HER DAYS VISITING MITCH in the hospital and with lawyers for the hospital, with Mark Cohen, and with Ira Mandel. It turned out at the best of times it wasn't so easy to turn off the respirator of a brain-dead person. No one-two-three procedure at all. Despite the hundreds of thousands of dollars that the insurance company officials quickly informed Cassie it took to keep Mitch ensconced in his glass cocoon day after day, no one at the hospital would give the okay to let him go.

In those meetings, just like in the conspiracy that had gone on for years before the stroke, no principal in the matter mentioned the circumstances of the situation. The girlfriend wanted the vegetable intact because New York State recognized his wife as his heir. The wife wanted the husband dead so she could move on. The IRS matter was now on the back burner. The life-and-death debate centered around the malpractice issue. An army of doctors and lawyers were mobilized to analyze and consult on the potential lethality of Mona Whitman versus the world on the viability-of-Mitchell Sales-as-a-human issue. In other words, was he brain-dead, or not?

In her first meeting with Ira in his office on Fifty-sixth Street in Manhattan, Cassie did not waste her time complaining about Mona's potential lawsuit involving Cassie's alleged harassment and kidnapping.

She now knew such a suit could not even be filed, much less won, without a police report and witnesses.

"All I want is justice," she told Ira, pounding the long mahogany table in his boardroom.

"Cassie, baby, I know just how you feel," he replied, all neutrality. "You look wonderful. I don't know how you do it. Did you lose weight, change your hair?"

Cassie was wearing a simple black linen sheath. She had on big fake gold earrings. New copper-tinged sunglasses dangled from her hand. The old Cassie had disappeared. No one recognized her anymore. Friends failed to recognize her at the supermarket, at the post office, on all her daily rounds. No one recognized her at the bank or Sales Importers, where she went to check things out and get money. Not only that, all the people who hadn't been looking at her for fifteen years were turning their heads when she walked by. The big irony was that the only person who was oblivious to her new face and figure was her husband. The "refreshed" face that was supposed to have rekindled Mitch's love and tolerance for her, have them dancing cheek to cheek on cruise ships and energetically leaping over streams holding hands like the geriatric lovers in Centrum commercials left him absolutely cold. But then, he was in a coma. Cassie smiled.

"I might have lost a few pounds, Ira, over the years. But you haven't seen me in such a long time. How would you know? Your loyalties seem to have shifted in the last few years."

"No way, Cassie. I've always had the greatest respect for you." Ira gave her an oily smile.

Cassie thought it was amazing how men could think women were so stupid. She'd just repeated for the fourteenth time all the things that Mona had done to her, and he was acting as if they were having a walk in the park.

"I want justice. I want those credit card bills paid off and the cards canceled now. This is not a difficult problem."

Ira sat across from her. There was a thin sheen of moisture on his forehead. "Actually, Cassie, this is a difficult problem. I didn't know anything about this debt of yours until you brought it up."

"It's not a debt of *mine*," Cassie said slowly. "It's a debt in my *name*. I want the bills paid and my name cleared."

"I'm not sure how you expect me to do that."

"Somebody has the money to pay those debts. You told me Mitch was very rich. Mona must have money, too."

"Yes, but these things take time. It will have to be done in some kind of settlement, down the road. We have to think of the tax consequences."

"Ira, I don't want it done down the road."

"But you're going to have to wait a little while, stay calm, and be mature about this."

"Mature?" Cassie didn't like the sound of that.

"Well, look at it this way. Your inheritance will cover the debts and then some. I feel certain that if you behave in a dignified manner and don't excite further interest from the IRS, you'll probably be able to keep your house and sustain your lifestyle." He said this looking her right in the eye as if maintaining her modest lifestyle was Cassie's only wish.

"Isn't peace and a reasonable settlement with the greater enemy, without nasty lawsuits, the best justice for us all?" he finished.

Cassie stared at him coldly. "No, Ira, I don't think that's the best justice for us all." She kept her dignity but only just. She was the injured party, the wronged wife. She wasn't accepting the debt. No. Period. End of story. She wasn't accepting it.

Now she could see how people were driven to murder. She could just imagine how the fifty-something Jean Harris had been driven to shoot her lover when she'd found out he'd stolen her diet cookbook and left her for a younger woman.

Mona, the disgusting pig. The girl who'd never been as pretty as she in the first place had been knocking her husband's socks off for years. With just her ass and simpering smile, she'd found a way to steal Cassie's man, her purchasing power, her dignity, her very identity. And then Mona changed herself to fit it. She'd influenced their friends and their doctors, their lawyer, their accountant. Now everyone was telling Cassie to be mature.

She opened her mouth to let him have it, but Ira held up his hand. "Stop, think for a moment, Cassie. Think about the consequences of what you're saying." There it was again. That little think.

"Ira, listen to me carefully. I will not accept the debt. Mona is a thief. I'm not going to let her get away with this."

"Cassie, Cassie, Cassie." Ira shook his head. "Don't get vindictive. You're in a precarious situation here. Think of your future. Don't hurt yourself now."

"I am thinking of my future, Ira."

"Then be reasonable. Be smart. Smile through your tears, honey. How about a cup of coffee? Huh? Make you feel better."

"I'm not smiling through my tears, Ira," Cassie told him angrily. "I don't want coffee." *I want revenge*, she didn't say.

"I understand, you want to play hardball. Then let me be perfectly clear. Any action you take now could sink the boat, you got that? Mitch did a few things I didn't know anything about, and I still don't. We're all in trouble, okay." Ira shook his fist at her. "You girls are driving me crazy."

"What?"

"Forget I said that." He became instantly soothing. "Look, I'm telling you as a friend to trust me on this. Give me the receipts and what- ever else you have. I'll find a way to take care of you, you have my word on it."

You girls are driving me crazy? Give him the receipts?

"Okay. Fine." Once again, Cassie understood the situation perfectly. She could no more trust him than she could trust that snake Parker Hig- gins. She put on one of those new fake smiles of compliance she'd learned recently and said goodbye. She was grateful that she'd already gotten the incriminating files and receipts out of the house and into a safe-deposit box.

37

WHILE THE HOSPITAL ADMINISTRATORS and their lawyers were having yet another meeting that they claimed would be their last and final meeting to decide the fate of Mitchell Sales, Cassie was contemplating her garden from her spot at the kitchen table. Without a power of attorney, she had not a single thing to do but wait for all the people who had control over her life to finish doing what they had to do. She herself was stuck. She couldn't move on. She had nothing to do but weep and brood.

She had been settling in for a good cry when Charlie Schwab walked through the gate into her yard. She saw him through the cracks in her laced fingers that she'd put over her eyes to catch her tears. Right away she saw that he had changed in the ten days since she'd last seen him. She hastily dropped her hands to get a better look. He was wearing a neat navy suit, a French blue shirt bright enough to knock a person's eyes out, and a tomato red tie, the kind of outfit Mitch would wear. His brush-cut hair had grown out some and almost looked as if it had been styled. Somehow he'd passed from the high school stage to a place a lot closer to middle age, where she was. The IRS agent, whose personal interest in her she wasn't supposed to excite, turned out to be a dish.

She hadn't been expecting visitors, though. She herself was wearing only a little makeup, white shorts, and a black T-shirt. Luckily there was nothing wrong with her legs. She opened the back door and called out, "You're back."

"Yep, like the proverbial bad penny. You look very cute. Did you change your hair or something?" He examined her curiously.

"Not really. What's up?"

He strode toward the house. "Oh, I enjoyed our talk. I was thinking about some of the things you said and thought I'd stop in to inquire how your husband is doing."

"Not dead yet," Cassie murmured. But he could have found that out from Ira. "How is the case going?"

"It's . . . unusual, that's for sure." Schwab pinched his lips together and dipped his chin.

"Have you discovered something?" she asked.

"No, no," he said quickly.

"You haven't found the house and car and jewelry and clothes his girlfriend charged to me? Oops." The very cat Cassie wasn't supposed to let out of the bag just jumped out of the bag. What a relief.

"Ah, there's the reason for the gift tax questions you asked." Charlie's newly coiffed head tilted to one side.

"You're very quick."

"It's what I get paid for. Your husband didn't file gift taxes. I checked."

Cassie nodded. Ira told her that if she made an issue of the credit card debt, Mona would certainly claim the items were gifts. The IRS would require the filing of gift tax returns, and that would add another 25, 28 percent to the bills in Cassie's name that had to be paid by some-body no matter what. Over the million point. So much for exciting IRS interest. "I guess it was pretty stupid to tell you," she said.

"Never mind, I guessed anyway." He pointed to the picket fence, the arbor, and pergola over the patio, each covered with several varieties of climbing roses all twined together so that the pinks, blushes, and laven-ders all appeared to be growing on the same bush. He changed the sub-ject. "You're a hell of a gardener. How did you get your roses to do that? I can barely get one color to grow on mine."

"Oh, it's easy. Plant two varieties close together and they twine. You seem unusually interested in flowers. Do you garden yourself?" He hadn't answered this question the last time she'd asked it.

"Oh, I wouldn't call it gardening. But I know a lily border when I see one. My father is the expert. He studies the catalogs."

"Do you think I overdo it on the lilies?" She glanced over at the profusion of dwarf Asiatics in her lawn borders.

"No, they look great. Can I come in?"

"Oh sure. Why not? Maybe you can enlighten me some more. This tax stuff is very complicated." Cassie felt a powerful urge to scratch at the crusty spots in her scalp where the stitches had been. It was an effort to restrain herself from digging her nails in and ripping her mask off.

"Tell me about it," he said.

She smiled, but didn't think she really should. "You want some coffee or a drink?"

"We could start with coffee," he said.

Cassie just happened to have some. They went into the house, where she frothed milk and poured. This time she had too much on her mind to bake anything. She put some grapes on the table. Plump green ones, added a few strawberries. They looked nice together.

Charles Schwab took a seat and sampled his coffee. "Great. Thanks. What would you like to know?"

Cassie took her place opposite him. "All right, here's a big one. What happens if my husband dies? Do you still have to audit?"

"Ah." Charlie put his cup down. "That's a good question. In that case, more departments will become involved. The business audit will progress, but his estate will be affected as well. An estate issue puts you much more in the picture. The liability will be yours. But a different department in the Service would be handling it, if that's what you're asking."

"What department are you?"

"I'm a revenue agent. I just look at the routine audits. When I find something out of the ordinary, the big guns take over."

"I gather you're looking for something out of the ordinary." Cassie played with her spoon.

Charlie nodded. "There have been some possibly illegal conversions made."

Cassie gave in and scratched her head. Illegal conversions. What were they?

"I'm a finder," Schwab said, gazing at her curiously. "What's wrong?"

"I'm a loser," she blurted.

He laughed uneasily. "No, no, far from that. You're a stunning woman." He blew air out of his mouth. "Really. I fell for you the first time I saw you. I'm sure men tell you that all the time."

Cassie had been thinking along a different line. She'd been thinking finders keepers, losers weepers—she'd meant she was a loser and a weeper. She shivered at the compliment.

"Hey, I didn't mean to offend you." All ten of Schwab's fingers tapped restlessly on her kitchen table. He did that thing with his chin. Little tiny thing. His knee was bobbing. He looked like a horse about to bolt.

"Does everybody get nervous around you?" she asked.

"Pretty much," he admitted.

Cassie had a feeling that something momentous was happening, but she didn't know what it was. He had a nervous knee and rapping fingers, but she liked his eyes. She wished he would sit still long enough for her to tell him the story about Mitch and Mona and what they'd done to her. But she didn't think it would help her case.

Ira told her that Mitch had given half of his company away (implying more gift tax on that as well) and had sheltered the other half in another company, a limited liability company, whatever that was, to impact taxes somehow. When she called to ask Parker who owned this new shelter company in Delaware, he implied it wasn't her.

Cassie's cheeks prickled with something that wasn't exactly feeling. Her ears and scalp itched. She was aware of herself as a remade woman with a facade that changed the way people saw her but not yet the way she saw herself. With this attractive man sitting at her kitchen table she felt an old, powerful feeling stir, like a giant teasing at the locked door in her basement. She couldn't help smiling as yearning rose in her body like steam off the heated pool on a chilly day. Her old life was over. She would never be reconciled with Mitch. He would never say he was sorry. She was almost free, a woman who hadn't been kissed in such a long time, she couldn't even remember what it felt like.

She took a deep breath, wishing she had Charlie's ear, his shoulder to lean on. She knew it was his job to disarm her and dipped her own chin, ashamed of herself for falling for it.

"What?" Schwab asked.

"Nothing."

"No, no. You were about to say something."

The moment passed. "Tell me about conversions," she said.

The knee stopped bobbing. He relaxed. "It has to do with money laundering. Do you know what that is?"

"Oh yeah. Mafia stuff." Cassie pressed her lips together.

"The mob doesn't have a lock on it." Charlie laughed. "People who aren't connected do it, too."

"You said you were a finder. I know where some things could be found," she said softly. She could give him Mona's house. That was in Mona's name. Unearned income? And the Jaguar? Unearned, too. She bet Mona was not much of a declarer.

"Here?" Schwab glanced around again.

"No, no. Not here," Cassie said quickly.

"I see." Schwab popped a grape in his mouth. "What about your wine cellar?" he asked.

"How do you know about that?"

"A little bird told me."

"Humph. Is that a conversion, too?"

He popped another grape. "These are good. It may be."

"How?"

"Let's say expensive merchandise is lost or stolen, in transit or from the warehouse. Taxpayer may report the loss and take a deduction. But the merchandise is actually moved to another location, where it becomes a personal, not a business, asset that can be sold privately under the table without capital gains."

Cassie inhaled sharply. "You think the wine downstairs is that?"

"I can check it out."

"Could I say no?"

Charlie shook his head slowly. "Not really."

"How bad will it hurt me?"

"Honestly, I don't know."

"Is there anything I can do to help myself?"

"You could help me."

Now his cute smile made her queasy. It wasn't a big leap to guess where he was going with this. "How would helping you help me?"

"I know how the system works. I could help you with the angles. You think about it." He rose to go. "By the way, I really want to compliment you on the way you're holding up. Believe me, I know how the stress gets to people."

"I'm on Thorazine," Cassie told him, deadpan, disappointed that he was leaving.

"Really?" He stopped short.

"No, that was a smart remark."

"Ha-ha. It was a good one, I'll remember it." He headed for the door. "Thank you."

He was gone as suddenly as he had come, and Cassie sighed at the confusion he'd stirred up. She couldn't tell the good guys from the bad guys anymore. Parker Higgins and Ira Mandel had threatened. Charlie hadn't threatened. It was a nice change. And Cassie had always liked blue eyes. She felt the opposite of the relief she'd had whenever Mitch drove off.

After Charlie was out of the house, an undercurrent of excitement hung around for a while. She'd been getting better about chewing her lip, but now she started gnawing on it again. She wondered if he was married, if his wife was pretty, if she knocked his socks off.

"NO, YOU MAY NOT BRING YOUR GIRLFRIEND," Cassie told Teddy on the phone. She was using her reasonable voice, and it took all her energy to maintain it. It was the Friday of the Fourth of July weekend, and due diligence in Mitch's case was completed. The ethics committee of the hospital had concluded that the brain of Mitchell Sales had died a month ago, and it would no longer serve any useful purpose to sustain his body on life support.

"Teddy, are you there?" she demanded.

"Mommm, why can't Lorraine come? I thought you *liked* Lorraine." Teddy was whining in his office at Ira Mandel's accounting firm, where in addition to his basic job of bookkeeping, he was studying a bunch of difficult courses like calculus and linear programming at night and on the weekend to pass the two-and-a-half-day CPA examination of accounting, auditing, taxation, and other very sophisticated stuff. Ira had told her that only 10 percent of candidates passed, but he believed that Teddy would be one of them. For accountants, apparently, the CPA certificate was everything.

"Liking Lorraine is not the point, Teddy, I want to talk to you and Marsha alone," Cassie told him. She was parked in her place at the kitchen table with an untouched cup of coffee in front of her.

Today was their father's final day on this earth. She wanted her children in the same room with her when she told them.

"Mommm, Marsha's bringing Tom, isn't she? You're making lunch for *him*."

"It's just us, Teddy. And maybe Aunt Edith. I haven't decided."

"Aunt Edith! Why not Lorraine?"

"Aunt Edith is family, Teddy. Lorraine is not."

"Lorraine's my girlfriend. Don't you like my girlfriend?" Teddy demanded.

Cassie didn't want to scream her frustration and rage at Teddy into the phone. Lorraine was a hospital pickup! She was heavy. Cassie had nothing against heavy in general, but heavy like Lorraine on a person so young would mean the thirty-year-old Lorraine would be *massive*. She had no control over what she put in her mouth. In addition, Lorraine didn't have much going on between her ears. Lorraine was not cultured. She had an accent. A terrible accent. Worse than the Bronx, Brooklyn, and Queens all put together. This was the problem with Long Island. Her fingernails and toenails were long and painted blue or green or black. Cassie couldn't imagine how she was able to function in a hospital with nails like those. Plus, she didn't know how to cook. She ordered take-out on a regular basis. What kind of life would that be for someone like Teddy? Cassie didn't simply dislike Lorraine, she loathed her. Call her a snob. Call her shallow. Except for the weight, Mona had been just like her!

"Mommm," Teddy whined.

Cassie took a deep breath. She didn't want to say she hated Lorraine and feared that the fat, callow girl would transform her son the way the ugly, tasteless, fawning, scheming doormat, Mona, had transformed her husband.

"Teddy, I'm on my way out now. I want to see you at the house at noon. Leave now if you have to." Cassie ended the call, stood up, and moved to the sink to dump the coffee down the drain.

An hour and a half later, Cassie told Teddy and Marsha that their father was scheduled to die any minute, and Teddy suddenly stopped agitating for lunch.

"Are you going with me?" she asked. She'd hoped that they would act as a family, but it was up to them. When she dropped the news, they were sitting outside on the patio in a tight little circle around the wrought-iron table they'd always used for picnics. Cassie had asked Teddy to put up the umbrella to shade her face. As soon as he did, a cloud drifted over the sun, and the shade around them deepened to twilight.

For once the contentious children were too stunned to squabble. Teddy and Marsha divided their attention between each other and her. Around them was the fragrant backyard that had been their childhood haven: perfect green grass in the small lawn. Blooming lilies in all the borders. They were thinking the same thing. Mitchell Sales, their daddy, the end. Their mood was gloomy.

It wasn't as if they weren't prepared. Still, death coming on them like this, during a lunch break, was so final, there seemed nothing to say. Teddy studied a worm that had fallen into the pool. The worm must have died yesterday, because already it had faded to tan, bleached by the chlorine. He switched his attention to his shoes. They were the same Italian loafers his boss, Ira Mandel, wore. Suddenly Marsha, who'd taken the day off from her internship in the women's jail on Riker's Island, began weeping quietly.

"Tom didn't tell me Daddy was dying today. Does he know?" She was wearing her jail outfit: black pants, black T-shirt. No makeup. She looked pretty good except for the tears streaking her face.

Cassie felt sorry for her. Until now, Marsha had been detached, almost as if the double catastrophe of her mother's crazy face-lift and her father's crazy stroke both occurring practically at the same time was a kind of parental acting out that would eventually come to a peaceful end as hers always had. Now it wasn't clear whether the loss of her father or the fear of death itself was getting to her.

When Cassie was her age, she'd already been married for several years and had a little girl. She'd thought she was a grown-up, had life all figured out. She watched Teddy's knee bobbing, his foot shaking. It seemed as if his whole body was in motion. These days, twenty-three was infancy, and twenty-five was not much older. Marsha worked with unwed teenage mothers, inmates in prison. What did she know about any of that?

"I don't know, honey. We haven't spoken," she murmured.

"But he's been great, hasn't he?" Marsha sought approval for the skinny young neurologist she never would have liked had her father not been felled by his specialty.

Cassie shook her head.

"Don't you think he's *great*, Mom?" Marsha persisted.

"He's great, Marsha, but what about Daddy?" Cassie asked.

Marsha sneaked another look at Teddy. He glared back at her.

"I don't know about you, but I don't want to watch the bastard croak," Teddy said harshly.

"Teddy, he's your father!" Marsha snarled, her mood shifting from sorrow to barking indignation in an instant.

"Fuck you, Marsha," Teddy tossed off.

"Fuck *me*, Teddy. You're the one he loved. You were Daddy's boy."

"Oh right, Daddy's boy." Teddy snorted.

"The least you could do is stand by him now. . . . You were everything to him." Marsha shifted into that bratty singsong voice that always drove Teddy nuts.

Teddy made the noise of a fart. The two of them balled their fingers into fists, and sibling rivalry erupted into a fight. Cassie was glad she'd isolated herself from them in the last few weeks since she'd found out Teddy was friends with Mona. The hole in her chest opened up. Her own kids had no thought of standing by *her*.

"*Oh? Oh?* Who went with him everywhere?" Marsha taunted.

"Oh Marsha, you had it easy. He left you alone," Teddy parried.

"He wouldn't let me do anything I wanted," she whined.

Teddy made more farting noises. "Like what did you want?"

"I wanted to be a pilot. I wanted to fly," she said plaintively.

"Oh shit, not that again." He kicked a clay pot with a perky red geranium in it. The pot went over, crushing the biggest bloom. Cassie was shocked.

"Daddy said girls can't fly," Marsha sniffed, still smarting over the ancient injury.

"Who'd *want* to fly? Those things go down all the time." Unable to move, Cassie clicked her tongue at the downed geranium. Why had she brought them here? She hated her kids.

"You're all against me," Marsha's voice regressed to age ten.

"No, sweetheart. No, don't think that way. He loved you," Cassie defended by rote, assuring her daughter even now that her father had loved her.

"He said I'd get PMS and crash the plane," Marsha wept.

"I know, honey."

Teddy didn't want to hear any more of this. "I'm telling you, you had it easy. Daddy followed me everywhere, even into the bathroom."

"So what?"

"What's twenty-five times eighty. Quick, Teddy, multiply, don't think. He'd stick his finger in my chest, yell at me to pee and multiply like a man."

"No one cares, Teddy," Marsha said. She was so cold, the tears could have frozen on her cheeks.

"Marsha, that's not true." Cassie jumped to Teddy's defense. She couldn't help defending. It was her nature. "I care," she said.

"I never knew which to do first. If I peed, he'd scream at me for missing. Every single day! In college he was still grilling me at the urinal."

"You flunked all your fucking tests, you dope," Marsha snickered at the direct hit.

"I didn't want to do it, you bitch. Did it ever occur to you he made me do it? He wouldn't let me fail!" Now *Teddy* was in tears, and Cassie was shocked even more. What was the matter with them?

"He took you into the business, didn't he?" Marsha spat out.

"Making me work for fucking *Ira*, you think that's a treat? The shit that goes down there, you wouldn't believe." Teddy kicked another pot. Over it went. This one broke, scattering pot shards and dirt.

"What shit?" Cassie asked, distracted for a moment by business.

Teddy looked away. "Nothing."

"What shit?" Marsha demanded.

"I said, *nothing*."

"You know everything, Teddy. Give," Marsha hissed.

Teddy shook his head.

The opening Cassie had been waiting for had finally come. She licked her lips. "Teddy, you were Daddy's boy. And you were Mona's boy. That's hurt Marsha and me a lot. Did you ever think about that?"

"I didn't mean to." Teddy shook his head. He didn't want to go there.

"Teddy, your loyalty to the family has been tested. We *know* where you stand," Marsha said bitterly.

Ah, now it was coming out.

"She was always very nice to me," he said defensively.

"Oh come on, they were fucking in the bathroom," Marsha retorted angrily.

Cassie reeled. "What?"

"I didn't know that." Teddy looked guiltily at his mother.

"Oh come off it. You had to know it. They couldn't keep their fucking hands off each other. I've known it since I was thirteen. Oops." Marsha glanced at her mother. "Sorry."

"Asshole!" Teddy barked.

"You didn't tell me." Cassie stared at her daughter.

"Oh, you know Daddy. He always denied everything." It was Marsha's turn to look away.

"Marsha!" Cassie grabbed her daughter's arm.

"He gave away my piano, Mom."

"I know, but Marsha!"

"He gave it away. Just like that. I said I knew what he was doing, and that day I came home and it was gone." Marsha shook her head. "He didn't think I'd ever be good."

Cassie nodded sadly. Marsha had cried for weeks. Cassie had been dumb enough to think it was about the piano.

"Every time I complained about Mona, he grounded me. He said I was a big fat pig and he'd never buy me a car. When I was in high school, he told me if I told you any lies about Mona, he'd cut me out of his will."

Teddy held his palms up in denial. "I didn't know about this. I really—"

"Of course you fucking *knew*." Marsha rolled her eyes.

"I thought she was a nice lady. She always defended me when he was a shit." Teddy was breathing heavily now, sweating. The front of his shirt was soaked. He looked at the dead worm at the bottom of the pool, almost white.

The sun came out again, blindingly bright. Cassie blinked. No one suggested they hurry to the hospital. She wondered if her children were afraid the family that bore Mitch's name would terminate when he did. The family's strength and power to protect and keep them safe had disappeared a long time ago, and she felt guilty. She'd always believed she was the only one to suffer in the marriage. It never occurred to her that Mitch had abused his children, too. All this time she'd just stood by. She'd let him.

"That's why I gave you the pajamas that day, why I was so mad at you for getting a face-lift," Marsha was saying.

"What?" Cassie was reeling again.

"I knew it wouldn't make any difference. He was in love with Mona. I thought you'd figure it out. Daddy never gave you anything like that."

Cassie's mouth fell open. "Marsha!"

"I couldn't tell you, Mom. I just couldn't. I'm sorry." Marsha sniffed, then leaned over and put her head on Cassie's shoulder. "I love you so much, Mom, I couldn't."

Cassie gulped. "Marsha, would you like to see your piano now?"

Marsha lifted her head. "My piano?"

"Well, Daddy bought Mona a house—" Cassie began.

"Teddy, do you know about this?" Marsha interrupted.

"What do you think I am?" Teddy asked miserably.

"I think you're a little fuck," Marsha announced.

Teddy opened his mouth and closed it.

"Teddy, you knew about this, didn't you?" Cassie said.

"She paid for the house, Mom," Teddy said in Mona's defense.

"Teddy, she did not pay for the house. I'd like to show you the house." Cassie got to her feet and smoothed her skirt. Mitch was dying, and no one wanted to say goodbye. Fine.

"Now? Isn't that a little crass?"

"Suddenly you have qualms, Marsha?"

"No, I just . . ." Marsha glared at her brother. "Fuck."

"Get in the car, kids. Don't fight anymore. I want to show you the little surprise your father and Mona had planned for me."

The two exchanged uneasy glances. "Do we have to?" Teddy whined.

"Yes."

Groaning, Marsha got up from the table and threw her backpack over her shoulder. Teddy's stomach rumbled loudly because it was way past one and he was used to eating a big lunch. They trudged into the garage.

"Where's the Volvo?" Teddy demanded when he saw only the Porsche and the Mercedes.

"I've upgraded." Cassie got into the Mercedes and slammed the door, thinking about her pathetic old Volvo that used to live outside in the driveway. All she'd gotten for the damn thing was a thousand dollars. How had money become so important? She was positively drowning in thoughts she'd never had before. She'd never cared that much about money, never thought about it. Except she'd always thought she'd be rewarded for sticking with Mitch and someday she'd have a lot of it.

"Do you think Daddy's dead yet?" Teddy whimpered.

Marsha punched him in the arm. "Shut up, Teddy."

Marsha took shotgun in the passenger seat next to her mother. Teddy sat in the back. Neither said anything as they drove out of their pleasant development to Northern Boulevard, then turned east to Glen Cove, and finally across Duck Pond Road.

"She was moving here?" Marsha was surprised.

Cassie slowed the car to a stop in front of the garish giant black and gold painted gates with the Sales logo of grape bunches, wine barrels, fleurs-de-lis, and crossed fucking swords. LE REFUGE was painted in gold on a green estate sign.

"Holy moly." Teddy whistled.

"That's the ugliest fucking thing I have ever seen," Marsha pronounced judgment on the gates.

Now Cassie was sure she was doing the right thing. She wanted her children on her side. She wanted them to feel Mona's evil, to know who their father had been. She pulled into the approach and kept quiet as the luxury car she hadn't been allowed to drive until now cruised up the hill, passing the majestic oaks lining the drive. Her gut tightened just as it had the first and second times she'd come to the place where her husband was planning to live when he left her. The house hadn't been difficult to find. The address was on all those ABC Carpet and Home delivery slips.

"Holy moly," Teddy said again when the castle came into view.

They covered the last thousand feet or so of driveway and stopped in front, right next to the sporty red Jag parked there.

"This is the ugliest house I have ever seen. Look at that turret," Marsha pronounced judgment on the house, craning her neck for a better look.

"Mom, she's here," Teddy said uneasily.

"She won't show herself," Cassie said.

"But what if she does?"

"Go key the car, Teddy. I always hated the bitch," Marsha commanded.

"What's that?" Cassie asked.

"You know, make scratches all over it with a house key," Marsha said.

Teddy giggled nervously. "You really want me to?"

"I'll stand behind you in case she's watching," Marsha promised.

"Go key it yourself," Teddy said.

Cassie killed the engine and got out of the car. "Come on, kids. I want you to see something."

"I don't want to see any more. It's a horrible house, terrible taste. Key the car, Teddy, and let's go." Marsha's lips were tight. "That bastard." About her dad.

"Get out, Teddy," Cassie ordered.

"I don't want to key the car, Mom. What if she calls the cops?"

"Get out, Teddy. You're not keying anything."

Teddy groaned and dragged himself out of the backseat. "Okay, okay."

They all got out and stretched. The stone house had two turrets and huge leaded windows in the living room and dining rooms. French doors beckoned to patios without furniture. In spite of the Jag out front, it had a forlorn and empty look about it. They walked slowly around the house, and Marsha's breath caught at the view down to the pool, the guest house, and tennis court. She was dead silent when she walked back to the French doors and pressed her nose to the glass.

"Jesus." Her Steinway piano, unmistakable with its cherry case, and complete with the matching leather tufted seat, was angled in a corner next to an antique harp. A rococo chair was placed behind the harp to create the illusion that someone actually played it. Maybe a decorator's joke, because it was missing several of its strings.

The furniture that held the place of honor in front of the cavernous fireplace, however, was not Marsha's piano. It was the Napoleon III settee and two armchairs with women's breasts and animals' claws that had been Cassie's mother's. At the time of her death, Cassie had wanted to put the furniture in storage for Marsha, or even herself someday. But Mitch had said no. He'd called the pieces "horrors," and like the piano, they, too, had disappeared. A quarter of a century ago, he claimed to have given them to Planned Parenthood with the rest of Cassie's mother's junk. Compounding the insult, he'd complained that he'd gotten only a small deduction. But he hadn't given it away. He'd stored the pieces in one of his temperature-controlled warehouses and kept the secret just to hurt her. Then they resurfaced, and Mona had them reupholstered.

Teddy put a hand on Cassie's shoulder. "I'm sorry, Mom."

Cassie was moved by her son's sudden compassion. She let her head fall to his shoulder, and he patted it. The three of them closed ranks for a group hug, the first in a long, long time.

"Look on the bright side, maybe she'll move when he dies," he muttered.

"Ira says she won't have the money to keep it up." Cassie blew her nose and pulled herself together. She was ready to go now. Her children had seen the betrayal, and now she had cremation arrangements to make.

"Well, yes, she does have money," Teddy corrected.

"What are you talking about, Teddy? I told you the will is unchanged. We'll have something. And, of course, I'll have the life insurance."

Marsha's face flushed an angry red. "He gave her my piano."

"Mona has the life insurance," Teddy said, deadpan.

"No, Teddy, you're mistaken. I'm the beneficiary on Daddy's life insurance."

Teddy pressed his lips together. "Uh-uh."

"What?" Cassie clutched her heart.

"He changed it years ago. There were new papers. I checked. When he dies, she gets the life insurance. Mom!"

Cassie's knees buckled. Oh, shit. She'd worked so hard to allow him to die just so Mona would get the life insurance and half the company? Mona won? She won?

"Mom!"

Cassie was sitting on the ground. She didn't know how she'd gotten there. Her chest was heaving. Both kids were trying to haul her to her feet. Mona was peering out at them from an upstairs window. Cassie didn't see her. She had only one thought. She had to stop the termination. "Get me to the hospital," she gasped. "Hurry."

39

RUNNING, they were running through the hospital entrance, Cassie in the lead, stumbling along in her black sheath and heels. It was two-thirty in the afternoon. Outpatients, doctors, staff, visitors crowded the lobby. Cassie was panting, weeping. All the betrayals were too much, just too much.

Mark had told her that the Mitch they all knew and loved had gone the day of his stroke. As they had prepared for his end, Mark had assured her, cool as could be, that Mitch's spirit was at peace and no one was home inside of him anymore. But the truth was, Mitch had never had the slack appearance of serenity. With the tubes in his mouth and nose, one eye at half-mast, the grimace on his face, and finger scrabbling desperately at the sheet as if he had something urgent to impart, Mitch had been all along the picture of a tortured man.

Cassie stumbled through the halls to save him. Why should he be released and find peace so easily when she had to live on? Correctly assuming that a catastrophe had occurred, people moved aside as she plowed through. Marsha came next in her prison garb, with a backpack hanging open over one shoulder. Teddy shuffled along after them, looking embarrassed. Cassie had given him quite the tongue-lashing for not having told her about the life insurance before, weeks before.

"It's not my fault," he was talking to himself, getting more agitated the more he said it. They crossed the lobby and entered the glass corridor, passed the contemplation garden with its rocks and pebbles and evergreens that remained exactly the same in every season.

"Mom," Marsha cried, trying to catch Cassie's arm. "Mom, you're going to fall."

"This is crazy," Teddy muttered to himself. "I didn't do anything wrong."

"Teddy, shut *up*," Marsha flung over her shoulder.

Cassie was the first to pass through the arch to the wing that housed the Head Trauma Intensive Care Unit. She charged on, then stopped short, clutching her chest when she saw the curtains drawn over Mitch's picture window.

"Oh God, Marsha. It's over."

Marsha caught her mother's arm, but Cassie's knees gave way. Her body twisted as she fell, and her whole side convulsed with excruciating pain. She was lying on the floor again and didn't know how she'd gotten there. Startled, she saw the ceiling. Then she began to cry.

"Mom!" Marsha dropped to her knees.

Cassie had tried to protect her face when she'd gone down. And now her hands clenched over her eyes to halt the deluge of tears. "Oh God, oh God. It's over."

"Mom, are you all right?"

Cassie's body curled into a fetal position around her pain, and a deeper, keening wail rose from her chest. She heard the sound, a wild animal's cry, and was unaware that her grief had turned into a primal scream. The stress of the last month's revelations and her struggle for balance after a lifetime of denial finally felled her. Her vigil and fight with Mona for control of Mitch's mind and body was finally over, and she collapsed. Mitch was gone, and Cassie was overwhelmed with grief.

She'd shown her children his sins against them, proven all the lies, if not to the lawyers at least to them. In the end, he'd won all the little battles and lost the big one. And now Cassie felt as if she'd been gutted. She was a widow, but not the way she'd hoped. Not a widow with honor—a widow who'd been adored in life and respected in death. She was a middle-aged woman crushed by the loss of love she'd never dared to acknowledge.

Marsha was on her knees, crooning to her softly. "It's okay. I'm here."

Teddy joined her. "I'm sorry, Mom," he said. "I'm really sorry."

Cassie couldn't respond. She wanted to be there on the bed, instead of Mitch, with a sheet over her head. Dead not for a few minutes, but dead for all time. "I don't give a shit anymore," she muttered.

"Oh, come on, Mom, don't say that."

The head nurse rushed out of the monitoring station, calling two orderlies over. The three of them pushed Marsha and Teddy out of the way. Cassie was sobbing again. Down the corridor, sailing in like a massive ship's prow, was Aunt Edith.

"Oh my God, am I too late?" Edith screamed. She was dressed in a black and gold caftan with large jet beads bouncing around the neck. In the crook of her arm she carried a large round black patent leather pocketbook from the fifties that banged against her knees as she hurried along. Up to her elbows were long black cotton evening gloves, also from the postwar period. She was dressed to the nines to watch her hated nephew-in-law meet his maker.

"You okay, Mrs. Sales?" the nurse asked Cassie.

"Oh no." Cassie groaned at the sight of her aunt hurrying toward them.

"Take a minute. It's fine. How about some water?"

Cassie shook her head. No water. She could see Aunt Edith running toward her, sliding on the polished floor. She could see Aunt Edith slipping, going down like an elephant, breaking an arm and shattering a hip. She could see her moving in and needing many fat-filled meals a day brought to her on trays. She could see herself wheeling Edith around in a wheelchair and Edith never leaving the premises for the rest of her life. She could see the two of them having their little treats—a cheap cruise to the Bahamas, a fancy dinner out at Bryant and Cooper. Two old women trying to enjoy themselves on a tiny budget.

"Can you sit up?" The head nurse was talking to her.

Cassie clutched her side, deep in her fantasy of a disastrous future and a terrible death of her own. She couldn't say, "Quick, catch my aunt, she's going to fall." Couldn't say a word.

The nurse and two orderlies had her out of her fetal position and sitting up before she knew it. They quieted her in seconds and got her to her feet in a way that indicated they'd done this kind of thing a thousand times before.

Aunt Edith covered the distance on the slippery floor without mishap. She enveloped Cassie in a massive hug, then gave her the kind of big, smacking wet kisses on the cheek that over the decades had always made Cassie and Mitch and the kids cringe whenever she approached.

"My condolences, sweetheart," she said, wetting Cassie's face some more like some big, overfriendly dog that wouldn't get off one's lap.

Marsha put an arm around her mother's shoulder and handed over a package of tissues.

"No, no, don't—" turn off that machine, Cassie tried to say.

"It's okay, he's not alone. The doctor is with him," the nurse interrupted her.

"Dr. Wellfleet?" Marsha asked hopefully, putting a hand to her hair.

"No, Dr. Cohen."

"Mark?" Cassie was stunned. "Mark is in there?" Mark, who just ordered tests and read results and never did a single thing that was wet or doctorly. Mark was in there, participating in an actual procedure. A termination of life? Inconceivable.

"Yes. They're working on your husband now."

"What! No, no." It was then that Cassie realized it wasn't done. It wasn't too late. They were killing her husband now. They were doing it now. "I have to talk to him. I need to go in!" she cried. "Wait!"

"Just one moment, Mrs. Sales. They're working on him."

"You don't understand. I changed my mind."

"Wait a second, honey, let them get him cleaned up."

"No, no."

"Please, I must insist."

Cassie wouldn't be stopped. She pushed past them and opened the door of the room. Then she couldn't grasp what she was seeing.

"Don't come in, please," Mark said without turning around.

Mark, another doctor in a white coat, and two nurses were standing around Mitch's bed. They were watching him intently. In a room that used to be filled with many sounds, it was now eerily quiet. But they hadn't pulled up the sheet.

Cassie stepped closer and almost fell down again when she realized what had happened. The bed was tilted up. Mitch was in a sitting position. The tubes were out of his nose and throat. There was vomit on his hospital gown. A crooked grin on his face. He was very much alive and breathing on his own. When Cassie entered the circle around him, one of Mitch's eyes made a distinct motion. It was one that she'd begged for that very first day but hadn't seen before. She was horrified to see it now. Mitch winked at her.

ON SATURDAY MORNING, Mitch's condition was downgraded to stable, and he was moved to a private room. Monday was the designated holiday, so Tuesday the hospital arranged for him to be transported to a rehab facility. Since Mitch's insurance wouldn't cover the $5,000-a-day, round-the-clock therapy and care that he needed, the rehab facility wouldn't accept him without an advance payment of $150,000 to cover his first month's stay.

Mark Cohen was elated. He was in a state of absolute ecstasy. He personally had saved one of his best friends. Only twice in his thirty-five years as an internist had he seen a brain-dead patient recover after spending a month on a respirator. He was God, walking on air. Everybody was talking about his miracle, for he had been at Mitch's side when the respirator was turned off. Three clicks to turn the machine off and the room was silent except for one snuffling young nurse who always cried when someone died—didn't matter who it was. Since Mitch's family wasn't there, Mark was the one to hold his hand and whisper into his ear.

"I'm with you, buddy. You take care now."

Mitch's hand had slipped out of Mark's, and Mark had let him go. But when Mitch's death rattle quickly turned into the sound of someone gagging on his own vomit, Mark and the attending physician removed the tubes from the patient's nose and mouth. Mitch's chest heaved. He coughed a few times. They cleared his throat of vomit and mucus. After a few seconds he began breathing on his own, and they all cheered.

Cassie, on the other hand, went into free fall. Mitch had told her time and again throughout their marriage that she would never have to worry about money, and for the last month all she had done was worry about money. Money, money, money. It was enough to make a person crazy. Friday she had even been prepared to kill for it. But since Mitch survived the attempt on his life, the odyssey wasn't over. Money was still the central issue of her life.

There was $3,000 in Mitch's account, and about the same amount in hers. Whatever Cassie said and did, she could not shake his doctor's deep belief that Mitch was a very rich man. Mark's fees for managing the case were in excess of $30,000. She shuddered to think what Mark would charge for raising Mitch from the dead. Not only that, the Sales family insurance covered only 80 percent of the hospital bills, which in Mitch's case were especially excessive because they'd given him the best of everything.

Cassie called Parker Higgins to ask for a power of attorney to access Mitch's assets so she could pay the ridiculous amount the rehab facility demanded before they would take him. Parker suggested she bring Mitch home for a few days while he worked on it. Cassie suspected that Mona was behind his hesitation to give her the power to decide how the case should be handled. What if Mitch recovered only partially, lived for a long time, and Cassie refused to relinquish the control forever? Cassie knew that the spineless Parker was buying time, waiting to see which way the wind blew.

Therefore, on Wednesday, the actual Fourth of July that year, exactly thirty-five days after Mitchell Sales went into intensive care with a massive stroke, he came home. His return was mandated by his diligent lawyer and the vicissitudes of managed care. Many people live their whole lives without having a single wish come true. In less than two months Cassandra Sales had had three wishes come true. First, she became beautiful, noticeable, and desirable again after a sleep as long as Snow White's. Second, her boring life would never be the same. And third, her husband was alive, so his girlfriend could not collect his life insurance. None of it helped her one bit. The only bright spot in the whole story was that Cassie vowed never to pay another of his life insurance premiums again. If he lived only a few months, the policy would lapse. The few hundred thousand of cash surrender values would revert to Mitch's estate. Mona would be left out in the cold. This was the kind of thing Cassie had sunk to wishing for now. She did not have a clue how much the company with her name on it was worth. Not a clue.

IT WAS A VERY DRAMATIC MOMENT when Mitch Sales left North Fork Hospital, for he didn't walk out. Neither was he driven the five miles home in his black Mercedes. His brand-new wheelchair did travel in the trunk of the luxury car, but he himself returned home the way he'd come, in an ambulance.

His condition was exactly the same as it had been when he was on the respirator, except that now all his vital organs were functioning well on their own. He still could not talk. He could not move. It was impossible to know if he understood anything that was said to him, or what was going on around him. He did not react to music, to needle pricks, or to any other physical stimulation. He didn't respond to simple commands or expressions of affection. He could sit up, but only when carefully propped. He could receive food in his mouth and swallow, but only baby food. There was a slight tremor in one of his hands, but he could not use it for holding anything, or for writing. He was wearing adult diapers. His mouth was open, and he drooled.

The day before his return, Cassie, Teddy, and Marsha moved the filing cabinets, the desk, the desk chair, and computer out of his office on the first floor and into the dining room. Marsha vacuumed away all the office dust that had been accumulating since the dawn of time, and Cassie washed the moldings and floor. Her housekeeper had still not returned from Peru. Late Wednesday afternoon, a rented hospital bed, a stool for the shower, and a bunch of other hospital equipment, including sheets and pads, an oxygen tank, blood pressure monitor, and diapers, were delivered and moved in.

"It's only for a few days," Cassie told herself, stunned and unbelieving.

Each breath she took was like inhaling fire. After all this, Mitch was coming home an invalid consigned to her care. And Teddy's girlfriend,

Lorraine Forchette, who was about as French as a flapjack, was coming home with him. At Teddy's urging she'd decided to devote a week of her vacation time to caring for his daddy.

They all arrived at the house at the same time. Cassie and Marsha in the Mercedes. Teddy in the Porsche, which he'd used to collect Lorraine in Rockville Centre, where she lived. Marsha was annoyed that Teddy was showing off with the purloined car, but held her tongue on the matter. Cassie was annoyed by the way Teddy had manipulated Lorraine into their house, but she was holding her tongue, too. They sat in the Mercedes for a moment, watching Teddy help Lorraine out of the car. Then he went back to wrestle her mammoth suitcase out of the trunk.

"Oh my God," Marsha murmured. "Someone needs to talk to her about that."

Lorraine's hair was too orange and too curly. Her hips and bosom and thighs were way too ample for the outfit of pink shorts and halter she was wearing. Not only that, she had on high, wedged sandals with straps wrapped Roman style around her thick ankles and calves. Her toenails were painted orange to match her hair. Her resemblance to a young and chubby Mona was unmistakable.

"I just love your house" was the first thing she called out, oblivious to the sudden presence of neighbors and the ambulance pulling into the driveway. Then, more imperiously, "Teddy, take my luggage inside. I want to get Daddy settled."

Marsha and Cassie exchanged startled glances. Daddy?

"Hi, guys," Lorraine chirped when the ambulance driver emerged and trotted around to open the back doors where, inside, the attendant was caring for the patient.

"How are we doing in there?" she chirped some more.

Cassie didn't hear the exchange that followed. She held her daughter's hand while the two ambulance people took their time moving Mitch out. Teddy came over to the Mercedes to get the wheelchair.

"I'm going to push him. Where do you think he'll want to sit?" Teddy's mood was very up.

"Teddy, he's too sick for that." Cassie jumped out of the car. Mitch wasn't joining the family.

"Oh, come on. Pop the trunk, Mom. I want to push him."

She couldn't believe they were having this discussion. The man had just come out of intensive care. She wasn't going to have him drooling in the living room. She popped the trunk.

"We're going to put Daddy to bed, Teddy."

"Oh, do we have to?" Teddy pulled the wheelchair out, then struggled, trying to figure out how to get it open. "Ah, got it."

"Yes, we have to. He can't visit," Cassie insisted.

"But he needs stimulation, Mom."

"Fine, turn on the TV."

"There's no TV in that room. Hey, this is neat." Teddy experimented with the wheelchair, rolling it this way and that, not so easily on the gravel. "I'm sure Daddy will like this."

"Daddy's a vegetable," Marsha chimed in, taking her mother's side for once.

"No, he's not. He winked at me yesterday."

"Teddy, he's a carrot."

Cassie put her hand to her splitting headache. Her kids were regressing again.

"Look, Mom, I'm an XKE." Teddy tipped the chair all the way back, making the *rmmmm, rmmm* sound of a sports car engine.

Just then Carol Carnahan appeared on the lawn with a casserole.

"Stop it, Teddy," Cassie hissed. She waved at Carol.

Carol hurried over and bestowed a careful kiss on Cassie's cheek. "The girls are organizing casseroles for you, honey. For the next ten days, at least. Then we'll see how it goes. After all you've put up with over the years, you deserve it."

"What?" Cassie's cheeks burned.

"Tonight's tuna noodle. I made it myself, with fresh tuna instead of canned. How's he doing?"

Cassie shook her head. "Carol, that's so nice of you."

"Hi, *Daddy*," Lorraine burbled loudly as the gurney with Mitch strapped on it was lifted out of the ambulance. "Remember me? I'm Lorraine."

An hour later, Mitch was settled in his room. Cassie, Marsha, and Aunt Edith were sitting on the patio, bucking themselves up with unbelievably velvety Château Petrus '45 from the cellar. And Teddy and Lorraine were in the pool, bobbing around in neon inner tubes. Lorraine was in the pink one. Teddy was in the purple one, each chugging beer from a can. Every few minutes, not looking a bit like Venus emerging from her scallop shell, Lorraine got out of the pool in her pink bikini to check on the patient. Fifteen minutes, like clockwork. She was a very responsible girl. Edith was enchanted by her professionalism and weight.

"Isn't it wonderful that Teddy found himself such a lovely, normal kind of girl?" she remarked.

"Wonderful," Cassie said, rather pleased with herself. This was the first time she'd ever taken a single bottle from Mitch's cellar without his express permission. He didn't approve of her drinking, and now she knew why. Wine eased her anxiety, let her be warm and giggly. She didn't think it was so bad to take the rare Pomerol, because even though it was a special Bordeaux, one of the wine auctions' particular darlings because there was so little of it around, Pomerols weren't classed among the great red wines of Bordeaux, like the Château Latour, Château Margaux, Château Haut-Brion, Château Lafite-Rothchild, etc., etc., etc., not in 1855, when quality control was first established in France, or in 1973, like Château Mouton-Rothchild, the only new addition ever made. So the Pomerol was not better than the best, really, by objective standards. Still, it was earthy and deep and almost mystical in the way it made her think about burgeoning cocks, specifically Charlie Schwab's. The first bottle disappeared quickly, and she went down into the cellar for a few more.

After a while a pretty tipsy Marsha got up to dress for her date with Tom Wellfleet. By eight o'clock the two of them had left for dinner at L'Endroit. After Edith and Cassie and Teddy and Lorraine finished Carol Carnahan's tuna noodle casserole, Teddy ordered several take-out pizzas. They ate them in the kitchen while Cassie drove Edith home. When she returned forty minutes later, she noted that the two of them were fooling around outside on one of the deck chairs. Totally sober now, she went into the makeshift hospital room to check on Mitch.

He was raised up slightly in the hospital bed, resting against two down pillows. The lights were on, clearly illuminating his thin hair, very long now and white at the roots. His stubbly cheeks that hadn't been re-lieved of his grizzled beard in many weeks. His open mouth was blowing bubbles. She could see his yellow teeth and wet chin. As in the hospital all month, he didn't register her presence now. But unlike all those other times, tonight she had no interest in getting his attention. She studied him coldly, watching his chest heave as he breathed noisily on his own. Apparently it wasn't so easy staying alive. He was struggling. Stubborn bastard.

She noted that Lorraine had dressed him in a pair of his own expen-sive Sulka pajamas and had made an attempt to neaten his hair. He smelled as if he needed a diaper change, but despite what Edith said, Cassie's contract didn't call for such a service.

"I'm going upstairs now," she told him solemnly. "I'm going to drink a whole bottle of '89 Domaine Romanee-Conti all by myself. I know for *you* it wouldn't be ready. But my sources say the Grands Echezeaux is about perfect now—spicy, firm, with a taste of berries, minerals, and oak. In California, they may cheat and add too much oak—'oaky, oaky,' as you would say—in the Cabernets and Merlots to enhance mediocre grapes. But not in France, right, Mitch?" She paused for a breath, then went on.

"Listen, if you have to stay here for any length of time, I swear to God that I'm going to start dating. I'm going to have sex whenever I want it, wherever I want it. I'm going to drink this cellar down to nothing. I'm going to travel, and I'm going to leave you with a nurse. When I'm here, I'm going to dust you like a piece of furniture. And when I go out, I'm going to leave you in your wheelchair facing the wall. Welcome home, you son of a bitch."

MITCH MAY OR MAY NOT HAVE HEARD HER, may or may not have regis-tered what she said. But the rest of his evening didn't go well. At two in the morning Teddy and Lorraine were necking out by the pool. They'd turned off the lights outside so no one could watch them, but they could easily see the glow from the soft light in the office, where Mitch's hospi-tal bed had been cranked down so he could go to sleep. Lorraine had wanted to turn that light off, too, but Teddy had wanted it on so his dad wouldn't feel disoriented if he woke up in the middle of the night.

"Do you think he knows he's home?" Teddy wondered.

"Of course, honey, don't you worry; he's happy as a clam."

They were lying on a single chaise and it wasn't easy to stay balanced. Teddy was skinny and rested on one hip. Lorraine was tilted toward his chest, her breasts straining to free themselves from the bikini top that barely covered her nipples.

"Kiss my neck, honey," she said.

Teddy leaned forward and touched his lips to Lorraine's floral-scented shoulder. It was soft and round, and damp from the swim they'd taken. He was in terrible pain from all the time she was taking to warm up, and wanted to move along down to the business end of the operation.

"That's nice, a little higher. Okay, that's good, just like that." She threw her head back and received his kisses on her neck where she wanted them. "Like butterflies, that's right."

His arm was draped over her hips and he felt the wonderful curves of her belly, overflowing from the binding band of her tight bikini bottom. All around was the roll he loved to squeeze. But he wanted it all to spill out. He wanted in there, where he knew it was going to be heaven. He pretended some innocent roaming, then began to inch his fingers inside the band.

"No, no."

His hand jumped away at the barking command. She sounded a lot like his sister.

"Not yet, honey. I'm not wet yet."

He lost it for a moment, felt himself deflating.

"There, okay, that's nice. Go ahead."

He struggled with a completely unfamiliar closing on the bikini top, then felt a surge of pure joy when suddenly the two skinny straps parted, the front fell off, and her heavy breasts swung free. "Ohhh," he moaned as he put his face into the glorious orbs and nuzzled away. His little man sprang back to life.

"Hey, take it easy. One at a time, lover. Ohh," Lorraine squeaked. "Oh, that's great. Yes, circle the tongue. That's too hard. Yeah, like that. Now the other."

Teddy was hanging off the edge of the chaise. His shoulder, wedged against the arm of the chair, was what kept him from toppling off. Lorraine was leaning closer.

"Yeah. That's good, lower."

He was panting, in the region of her belly button. He peeled the bottom down just a little, felt the pelt. Oh, God. If only she'd shut up and stop trying to make him her perfect lover . . . hurrah, his hand was in. Ooooo, that was good.

"Ow! Honey, you have a hangnail," Lorraine yelped.

Two fifteen-minute nursing periods passed as Teddy had to go back to square one with his erection killing him. Then it took another fifteen minutes to peel her bottom off, get his condom on just the way she thought it should be, then securely plant himself inside her in exactly the position she liked it. He did not consider it a bad experience when he came almost instantly. In fact, he thought it was a great big plus that he was spared getting any more instruction since he was pretty sure he already knew what to do.

"I always teach my boyfriends how to be my perfect lover," she confided, not seeming to hold a grudge, this time anyway. She reached for a towel and another beer. Then she settled in for a natter and a recap of the plays. He dozed beside her.

Back in the house, Cassie had long since fallen into a deep, drunken slumber. During the poolside frolic, Mitchell Sales heard the mumblings outside and began having trouble breathing.

He made some sounds like "Heel . . ." Too soft to be heard above the gentle drone of the air conditioner in his room. He became further agitated when no one responded to his distress. This was not like the hospital, where the monitor had been on him day and night.

"Heel . . ." He tried to move, but had no control of himself at all. He couldn't sit, and when his body convulsed, he fell over against the bars of his bed. Outside, while Lorraine was lecturing on the proper pressure a tongue should exert on a nipple, Mitch stopped struggling. When she looked in on him nearly an hour later, his body had already begun to cool.

CHAPTER

41

THE GRAY-HAIRED OFFICER FROM THE POLICE DEPARTMENT who came to question Cassie early the next morning was a paunchy man in a uniform that may have fit him five or ten years ago but wasn't looking so good on him now. She kept thinking that if Mitch were alive to see it, he would be disdainful of the man's chest and tummy tugging at his shirt buttons, getting in the way of all his cop paraphernalia so that if he had to pull his gun on her he probably wouldn't be able to reach it. Deputy Sheriff Lou Archer sat on the stiff, Federal-style sofa in Cassie's living room, cradling his belly and smelling of cigarettes, coffee, and Dunkin' Donuts. It was nine in the morning, and he'd been in the house since eight. Cassie tried not to look at his gun and notebook and handcuffs because they made her hands shake.

Outside, the sun had come up on another magnificent summer day. The fifth of July. The pool sparkled. The brilliantly colored lilies and roses perfumed the air. Cassie was all alone in the house, and everything that could be wrong with the world was wrong with the world.

"Tell me once again in your own words what happened last night, Mrs. Sales," the deputy commanded. Then he licked the tip of his pen as if a different answer would be forthcoming on this, his fourth, foray into the subject.

Cassie faced him in the wing chair, hanging on to the arms as if she were on a turbulent flight thirty thousand feet over a bottomless ocean.

She'd been staggering from room to room since around six-thirty A.M., when Teddy and Lorraine woke her from her profound, alcohol-induced sleep to tell her that her husband had died in his sleep.

For the last thirty-six days she had been up and down on a roller coaster of feelings about her husband and herself, about her stolen identity, about sickness and health, children and death. Now her eyes were red-veined and puffy. They just didn't want to stay open for any more reality. Her head throbbed continuously. After all the effort that had been made to save him, Mitch had died in his sleep. She couldn't take it in herself, much less form an appropriate response to a detective's interrogation. She had her first paralyzing hangover in a quarter of a century and could hardly form a coherent sentence.

Three times Cassie had tried to explain that her husband had been released from the hospital late yesterday afternoon after spending a month in intensive care recovering from a stroke. His condition had been so precarious then that he'd returned home in an ambulance and was immediately put to bed by his nurse, Lorraine Forchette. During the night, between one of the regular fifteen-minute checks Miss Forchette made on him, he must have suffered another stroke and died in his sleep. It was a family tragedy, but nothing more sinister than that.

The deputy sheriff, however, didn't see it that way. He wanted to know why she'd brought her husband home in such vulnerable condition. Cassie peered at him blearily. She thought that was a pretty good question, but didn't want to get into the issue of managed care.

Then he wanted to know why a professional nurse hadn't been hired to look after him; and here, Cassie had to take issue.

"Lorraine Forchette is a professional nurse. She works at North Fork Hospital," she protested.

The clincher came on the fourth go-round. Cassie heard it through a fog. Deputy Archer wanted to know why a physician hadn't signed the death certificate before the body was removed to a funeral home instead of afterward. Some legal question or other that Cassie didn't know anything about. She'd had nothing to do with it. Her hands started shaking. For reasons as yet unexplained, when his father died, Teddy had called Mark Cohen and Martini's Funeral Home instead of waking her and calling 911 as he should have. Cassie had no idea why.

Since Mark immediately concluded on the phone that Mitch's was a natural death, the funeral home had sent a hearse to take his remains away. From what Cassie gathered from the sheriff, this was a shady and illegal thing to do.

"Martini's came in the middle of the night?" the detective demanded yet again.

"No, it was morning. You can call and ask Mr. Martini himself."

"Did you arrange this yourself?"

Cassie shook her head. Teddy had done it. She guessed he'd thought the body was spooky and wanted it out of the house. In any case, when Teddy and Lorraine finally got her awake, she couldn't sit up much less understand what they were talking about. So, it turned out that the remains of the man who'd been her husband for twenty-six years were removed before she knew he'd died. The whole thing gave her a terrible feeling. Terrible. She'd been left out of Mitch's life and now she was left out of his death.

Teddy had stood by her bed and informed her that he was the man of the family now, and he'd take care of everything from now on. But all she'd been able to do was hang over the side of the bed and gag. If she hadn't felt so miserable, she might have reacted with the rage she felt now. Who was Teddy to decide he was the man of the family when she'd told him weeks ago that *she* was the man of the family? Cassie wasn't sure yet if Teddy was a fucking incompetent who mismanaged every damn thing he touched, or if something sinister had happened and Mona had somehow *gotten* to him and triumphed over everyone. What if Mitch was actually alive and winking at all of them over on Duck Pond Road? She stared at the detective, wondering what she could do to make him go away so she could lie down.

"I understand you were drinking heavily," he said, referring to his notes.

Cassie squinted at the white specks on the sheriff's broad shoulders and chest and realized it was not doughnut sugar as she'd thought at first. Waves of nausea crashed over her like the tide coming in on a rocky shore. Oceans. Now all her thoughts were of oceans. She wanted to go down to the sea again, and see those waves just one more time before she died.

"I wouldn't say I was drinking heavily. I had a glass of wine," she said slowly. Or two.

"Celebrating?" the sheriff said with a voice that was heavy on the irony.

Cassie blinked raw sandpapery eyes. Her sick feeling of hangover was quickly escalating into hysteria. She didn't want to weep in front of the policeman who was sounding very much as if he suspected that she or Teddy, or Teddy's awful nurse girlfriend, had put a pillow over her husband's head so they could collect his life insurance and live happily ever after in the Cayman Islands with his tax shelter.

Actually, her own disorganized musings had spewed up the same crazy idea, only with Teddy as the perpetrator instead of herself. But why would he do such a terrible thing—to save her from a life of misery? She didn't think he cared enough. To help Mona get rich? She shook her throbbing head. Teddy wouldn't! Even extremely paranoid and terrified, Cassie didn't want to believe he'd murder his own father. She couldn't help it, she started lying.

"I was glad my husband was home. We were together as a family again. Could we finish this some other time?" she asked weakly.

She didn't know what to do. If she called Parker Higgins, Mona would know. If Mona knew, she'd use the sudden death to discredit and threaten, even prosecute, her. She was frightened. The whole thing did look somewhat suspicious, even to her. Cassie held back her tears. And there was no one to corroborate her story or make the detective go away, because this was the moment her idiot son and his dangerous girlfriend had chosen to take off for Martini's to identify Mitch's body so he could be cremated on the spot. Wasn't that . . . strange?

They'd taken the Porsche to the funeral home, and Cassie guessed that after picking out an expensive urn, they would probably stop at the International House of Pancakes for a hearty breakfast on the way home. She was so scared.

Deputy Archer sighed deeply. "We're treating this as a suspicious death," he told her.

She chewed on her bottom lip. "But why? My husband was a very sick man. It's been touch and go for more than a month. His doctor can tell you that. No one expected him to live this long. And it hasn't been a quality month." She shut her mouth. What was she saying?

"Still, we're going to have to investigate. Autopsy the body. The whole nine yards." Archer shrugged apologetically.

Cassie gasped. "Autopsy? Why?"

"To determine if he suffered another stroke, as you allege, or if something else happened to him."

"I'm not alleging anything. Why are you taking it like this?" Cassie looked around wildly. Help, where was help?

The detective shrugged again as though unwilling to put into his own words the kinds of things people did to hurry things along when their relatives were terminally ill and the stakes were high. He closed his notebook and assessed her affect. Was she upset? Was she a grieving widow?

"Are you going to give us lie detector tests?" Cassie asked miserably. How would Teddy and Lorraine do on that?

"Oh, well, we'll have to see about that, won't we?"

Cassie felt as if she were trapped in a sea cave with the tide coming in. Would an autopsy show if someone had put a pillow over Mitch's head, if her own son was a murderer? What would Mark say about this? He'd signed the death certificate. What would Parker say? He was the family lawyer. She tried to remember if she'd told the fat cop that Mitch's remains would be ashes by noon. She wondered if it was against the law to say nothing about that now. She could always pretend later that she didn't know. She couldn't control her terror. The front doorbell rang, and she jumped a foot.

"Someone's at the door," Archer said.

Cassie swallowed a mouthful of saliva. I'm going to heave, she thought. I'm going to barf on the spot. She'd seen all this on TV a hundred times. The bell rang again. She studiously ignored it. She was convinced that outside her door were the cameras, the reporters waiting to tell the story that she was O. J. Simpson, Susan Smith, the Ramseys, Amy Fisher, Jean Harris, right here in quiet Manhasset.

If she opened that door, her bloated, bleary face would appear on every channel. The images would be on the five o'clock news and the six o'clock news. At six-thirty, they'd be on the national news. She knew just how the story would play. Cassie Sales, wife of prominent wine importer, who'd bankrupted the family with her excessive spending, early this morning had boldly murdered her invalid husband to prevent him from leaving her for his mistress—the surgical wonder Mona Whitman, his partner in their thriving business. Just like Jean Harris, she'd be a dead duck.

Mona's final check and mate.

Cassie wanted to vomit. The doorbell rang a third time. Finally Archer got up to see who was out there, then shocked her by opening the door.

"Hey, Schwab, right on schedule. You boys certainly don't let any grass grow under your feet. Come on in while the juice is hot." He lowered his voice, but Cassie had no trouble hearing what he said next.

"As far as I know, only the body's gotten out of here. But the death occurred sometime in the early A.M., and we weren't notified until eight this morning. That gave them a few hours to clean the place out. It's pretty late in the day. Who knows what you'll come up with now—"

"Jeez, the old man is dead? This is news to me." Charles Schwab came into the front hall.

Cassie put a hand to her mouth and bailed out of the wing chair, plunging without a parachute. She staggered into the powder room and dropped to her knees in front of the toilet. "Oh God. Take me now," she moaned. "Just take me into that good night. I'm ready to go."

But God must have been busy with other things. The sound of her vomiting traveled to the living room, where the sheriff and the revenue agent stood talking about sting operations. Seven minutes later, when Cassie staggered out of the bathroom feeling a little better, the living room was empty. She heard some banging around in the kitchen and stumbled into the dining room, where she immediately bumbled into one of the filing cabinets she and Teddy had stuffed in there just yesterday. She gasped. All of Mitch's records, right in plain view with Charlie in the house. Terror clutched at her again.

Various branches of the government were crawling all over the place, and she had no idea what to do or how to stop them. As she tried to scramble out of the maze and get into the kitchen, her hip caught the edge of Mitch's desk.

"Ow." She rubbed the spot and kept moving. When she reached the other side of the dining room, her foot caught on a computer wire. She fell through the swinging door and crashed into the open overhead door of a kitchen cabinet. The flat front of the door hit her in the forehead and stopped her cold.

"Oh God." Her legs turned to rubber and collapsed under her. She hit the floor and closed her eyes.

CASSIE OPENED HER EYES to the smell of coffee. "Oh no," she groaned. She'd hoped she was dead.

"How are you doing?" Charlie Schwab's blue eyes were laughing at her.

She swallowed down a new wave of nausea. "I'm having a bad day," she murmured.

"I heard your husband died last night," Charlie said with some show of concern.

"Uh-huh. That sheriff tell you?" Cassie considered standing up.

Schwab nodded. "I'm sorry for your loss."

"Well, thanks. That cop thinks I killed him. Where is he, searching the garbage for poisoned hypodermic needles?"

Schwab laughed suddenly. "You're a funny girl."

"Oh really?" Cassie snorted. She touched the little bump on her forehead where she'd gone into the door.

"Looks like you tied one on last night."

"I don't know what you're talking about."

"Strong odor of alcohol. You know, you sweat it out of your pores. Unmistakable, believe me, I know."

"Ugh." Humiliated, Cassie dragged herself to her knees, then to her feet. The coffee cup and saucer he'd handed her rattled dangerously in her hand. Charlie grabbed the cup out of her hand.

"Where's that cop?" She peered around, looking for him.

"Oh, he left."

"He left? Really?" Cassie brightened.

"Well, I told him he could go, I'd take over from here."

"You? Take over from here?" The ridiculous feeling of always know-ing less than everybody else overcame Cassie. She stumbled over to a kitchen chair and sat down with her back to the ascending sun. The ra-diance of morning killed. "Oh God, I can't take this."

"You okay there?" Schwab asked.

"No." Cassie put her cheek down on the table and tried breathing slowly enough to make the room stand still.

"Go on, drink up." Schwab put the cup down in front of her.

"There isn't any," she mumbled.

"No, I made some more. How about some aspirin? Where is it?"

"In the drawer there somewhere." She waved her hand vaguely. "One of those drawers."

He found the bottle of Bufferin, tossed out two, and handed them over.

"I'm not drunk," Cassie insisted. "I'm just a little nervous."

"Take them anyway. They'll help."

She picked up her head and swallowed the aspirin. "You're really some sort of cop, aren't you? People who do audits don't come into your house and take over police investigations."

"Well, you know. In the Service we can do pretty much anything we want."

Cassie shook her head. "Which branch of the Service are we talking about now?"

"We bring in whatever branch we need." He appeared serious. He wasn't laughing now.

"You're scaring me."

"That's my job. Would you like to know about some of our powers?"

"Maybe some other time."

"I'll tell you anyway. We can get your bank records without you even knowing it. Anything we ask for is ours. My supervisor has given me carte blanche on this case. I can do anything I want."

Cassie's heart thudded. "You checked my bank account?"

He nodded.

"But there's nothing in it."

He nodded some more. "No juice there."

"Well, you were looking in the wrong place. The juice is in the refrigerator." She really was cross-eyed with all this IRS spy stuff.

"Most people put it in the bank." The twinkle was back.

She didn't know what he was talking about. "They put the juice in the bank?"

"Uh-huh. In safe-deposit boxes. You know what I mean, undeclared income." He repeated it patiently, watching her face closely. "We talked about this before. The IRS looks for undeclared income. I'm a finder, remember."

"I don't have any of that kind of goddamn juice. Could I have a few more of those aspirin?" Now she was in a cold sweat. She knew she must stink unbelievably. Alcohol, vomit. Fear. And she was just a spouse. Imagine the fear real crooks felt.

"No need to get testy." Schwab got the bottle for her and sat down again. "You can also find it in their canceled checks. Purchases. The whole lifestyle. I like to get the big picture before I form an impression."

Cassie swallowed two more aspirin and waited for her brains to tighten up. They felt loose, like unset Jell-O. "My husband died last night. He handled the income and the taxes. I've told you this a million times. I didn't even see his body. Understand?"

"No. Explain me."

"Explain you? Okay. Everybody takes care of things for me. My son took care of my husband's body for me. I never even saw it." She tried to get that across. This was the reason she was in so much trouble. No one let her do anything. She couldn't take control of her own life.

"I met him at the warehouse, seemed like a nice young man," Charlie said about Teddy. Neutral, Cassie liked that. He didn't say her son was an asshole.

"Well, looks can be deceiving," she murmured.

Charlie laughed again. "Maybe he was trying to protect you."

"Well, that's wrong. I don't want other people to mess me up. I can do it just fine by myself." She shook her head again.

"You certainly can." Schwab put his elbows on the table and leaned forward. "You know what else the IRS can do? We can give you summonses to appear anytime we want. We can search your house and seize your property. Your car, your house. Garnish your wages."

"I told you already. No wages. I've always volunteered."

"And speaking of garbage, we can go through your garbage," Charlie added.

"Be my guest." Cassie waved her hand.

"We can take all your records and documents. We can tap your phones. Want to know what else we can do?"

"I'm very afraid already."

He laughed. "You should be. Do you know why we have these powers?"

Cassie heaved a sigh. He wasn't going away. "So you can hurt us?"

"Private taxpayers fund about sixty-one percent of the country's budget." Charlie poured himself more coffee, then liberally added milk. He'd learned to make it, but didn't know how to froth. That gave her some satisfaction.

"Did you know that corporate taxpayers fund only about eleven percent of the budget?" he asked, pointing the spoon at her.

"Uh-uh." Could she take a nap now?

"That's why the wage earner, the small-business taxpayer, is so important to us. You're our all."

"That's interesting." Cassie had always wanted to be somebody's all.

"Paying taxes is completely voluntary, but we have to ensure people don't think it's a joke. We want them to comply. That's the reason we scare you."

She nodded, eager to please. "Believe me, I want those taxpayers to comply. If I had my way we'd all comply a whole lot more."

"You're very funny, did you know that?"

"This is not a funny situation; I'm really scared," she confessed. Voluntary tax payments, who was he kidding?

"But I liked that one about Thorazine. I told it to my supervisor. My dad, too. They both liked it."

"Your dad and your supervisor." Cassie frowned. Where was this going?

"Did you know what we can do to a taxpayer who tries to resist or complain?" Schwab asked.

"Charlie, my husband died today. Could you give me a break?"

"You people! All you want is breaks. Come on, guess. What can we do to taxpayers who resist or complain?" Now Schwab waved his hands. "What?"

Cassie guessed. "Kill us?"

"Ha-ha. That's good. *Another* good one." He slapped his knee.

"I wasn't being funny. Are you going to kill me? Just let me know. I had a bad night. I want to wash my face and brush my teeth before I go."

"No, I'm not going to kill you," he said, a little testy himself now. "It's nothing personal. Personally, I *like* you. I more than like you. I think you're a very lovely lady. In fact, if the situation were different, I'd ask you for a date."

"Look, forget the date," she said quickly. "Just kill me quick."

"Oh come on, you don't mean that." His laugh was a touch strained now.

"Oh, yes. Go ahead, kill me. I bet you have a gun. Shoot me now." Cassie kept at it.

Schwab glanced around the room, then mugged a little for her. "You're a funny girl. You're kidding, right?"

"No, go ahead, kill me. You have all these powers. Why stop at seizing property? Shoot me. No one will complain."

Charlie wagged a finger at her. "I bet you didn't know that a lot of people try to kill *us*. This is a very hazardous line of work."

"Don't turn things around, damn it! I don't give a *shit* about your problems. Just do what you have to do." Cassie put a finger to her head. "Boom."

"Let's not get competitive. I'm not kidding, I do get hate notes every day. People send me things you wouldn't believe. I've had the windshield of my car smashed *three* times. They put water and sugar in my gas tank. I can't keep a decent car. You name it. People do it to me."

Cassie was exasperated. "Well, you must be very good at your job," she said.

He nodded. "I go for quality."

"That's just great. When are you going to shoot me?"

He clicked his tongue, disgusted. "I told you I'm not going to shoot you."

"That's too bad." Cassie wanted a bath. A bubble bath. She needed to sleep for eternity. She didn't want to think about death or taxes. Ever. She wanted to be obliterated. The idea of making calls to tell people that Mitch was gone was terrifying. She didn't want to do it, didn't want to think about it. Schwab startled her out of her thoughts.

"I bet you didn't know that informers make ten percent of the government's take."

Of course she didn't know that. How would she know that? Cassie's eyes glazed over. "I can't take any more of this right now."

"I'm going to level with you. Someone gave us a tip about your husband."

"Oh no." He was going to keep at it.

"An anonymous person," he said, teasing now.

"Really?" That was interesting. Cassie's eyes cleared. The fog in front of her turned into the attractive man with a strong chin and humorous blue eyes. Today he had another really nice outfit on. Cassie had the thought that Mitch would appreciate that. The man who'd come to bury them both was wearing good clothes. Schwab always came early in the morning. What about that? Suddenly she was trying to form an impression. He had a ratty car because people poured things into its gas tank. The big picture. What did he want from her?

"Usually informers just want revenge. They don't collect. The only way they can collect the money is to help gather the necessary information to take to Justice."

Cassie squeezed her eyes shut, trying to follow. Who was they? What was justice? The word reminded her of Mitch again. She opened her eyes and glanced at her watch. Eleven o'clock on the dot. It seemed as if she and her husband were still in some kind of contact. Mitch was scheduled to slide down that chute at Martini's crematorium at eleven o'clock. Teddy and Lorraine were probably there to send him off. Cassie thought about the juice in the wine cellar. She wanted a drink but told herself, no juice until dark.

"So tell me about justice," she said, working hard to hold her head up.

"The Justice Department decides whether to institute criminal proceedings on evasion and fraud cases. Evasion can be hard to prove, since the taxpayer can always claim he was just trying to avoid paying taxes, which is legal. Evading taxes, however, is not legal."

"You just lost me, Charlie."

He smiled. "What's not crystal?"

"Avoidance is legal, evasion is illegal. What's the difference?" Cassie's eyes crossed.

"The Service expects people to pad their business expenses, and shelter their income. It's avoiding taxes on *reported* income. The taxpayer reports income. If we happen to disagree about the deductions on reported income, adjustments are made. The taxpayer pays more. That's it.

"What makes a criminal case is when the taxpayer does not report income and uses illegal means of sheltering it, like taking it out of the country, cooking the books, reporting losses in phony companies, that kind of thing. The Treasury has to prove intent in fraud cases. Are you following me?"

"You have to prove intent in fraud cases," Cassie mumbled.

"About a third of fraud cases are prosecuted and convicted."

"Uh-huh." Cassie propped her head in her hand to keep it from flopping over.

"Convicted felons pay penalties and fines, and they go up the river. Deals can always be made, though, and people can plea down. Got it?"

"I'm not pleading down."

"Now, in evasion cases—that's just hiding income, as I explained— Treasury can be satisfied with penalties, fines, and, of course, full collection of the unpaid revenues. What do you say?"

Cassie hesitated. "I'd really like a bath and a nap."

"I mean about helping us." He gave her a big, friendly grin.

"What?" This caught her by surprise.

"You told me you'd think about it. Haven't you been listening? I might be able to get you immunity."

"From what?" she said numbly.

"Well, I found your box," he said tilting his head engagingly.

Cassie blinked. The safe-deposit box with the receipts of Mona's extravagant lifestyle in it? What did that have to do with anything? Outside, a car horn honked. Sounded like Aunt Edith. But maybe it was Teddy and Lorraine returning from Martini's. They had tasks, telephone calls to make, official mourning to do. She wanted that hospital bed out of the office and Mitch's personal belongings removed from the house — the old magazines, the ancient computers. She wanted some more of that nice juice in the cellar, and she wanted this maniac to go away. The receipts in the box weren't even hers. What crime had she committed? No crime.

"I know this may sound evasive to you, but could you come back tomorrow?" she asked. She needed to do a little research.

Charlie shook his head. "By tomorrow there could be nothing left."

ILOVEDHIMIHATEDHIM. ShouldIhelphimShouldInothelphim? Cassie's brain was whirling again. But now it was whirling around two men instead of one. The dead one whom she wished she could mourn, and the living one who wanted her to inform for the IRS. The breathing one was sexy. Even when he was threatening her she found him pretty devastating. But right now the dead one was going up in smoke and she didn't want confusion. She wanted the whirl to stop, and the world to be simple. There was no chance of that, so she left Charlie doing whatever he did when he was alone with other people's stuff, and went upstairs to bathe and dress.

As she climbed the stairs, she wished for a quiet moment in which to experience some emotion appropriate to the occasion. Whatever happened to basic values? A human being who happened to be a close relative had just passed on. She wanted that to be the primary event. She was still deeply caught in the myth of marriage and didn't want to give it up until the very last moment. Let me love Mitch for just a few moments one last time, so I can feel the loss, so I can mourn, she told herself.

She'd tried to pinpoint her feelings about the marriage a million times since Mitch had become ill, and she'd been hopeful until the day he'd keeled over. What she thought of now was the excitement with which she'd anticipated the arrival in the mail of each of her orchids.

They came from Florida, California, Hawaii, the Philippines, Thailand. So many exotic places. She always ordered them in spike. When they arrived, she watched impatiently for the spikes to bud, and the buds to flower. The day a new plant fully unfurled its first bloom, her personal achievement felt as remarkable as the bloom itself, as if each were her very own creation.

Orchid societies preached the simplicity of orchids, and the growers all promised on the Web that the blooming-age specimens they offered for sale would definitely bloom. But the truth was, orchids were not so very easy. They were like the male member: not particularly attractive when dormant, unpredictable producers or unproducers, all according to whim. Orchids were pretty much Cassie's metaphor for life.

Sometimes she'd be busy outside or involved with some benefit she was planning. She'd look away for a week or two and when she'd look back, a bud would have appeared on a dormant-looking cattleya where none had been due for months. Propelling itself out of its green sheath, much more like an animal with a distinct personality than just a pretty flower, the magnificent botanical creature would burst upon Cassie's little scene silently but with a scent and a splendor that almost stopped her heart with joy. Every time an unexpected gift: happiness.

Other orchids, like her expensive and large cymbidium, would refuse, absolutely refuse, to spike no matter how carefully she treated them, gave them the environment and nourishment she thought they wanted, watched over, and tried to love them. Ugly, barren things, taking up space in the greenhouse and not giving a single pleasure back. Mitch's member, his whole self, had been like that from the day he'd shifted to Mona. And to think that Cassie hadn't wanted to hurt his feelings by complaining.

When Cassie reached the top of the stairs, she realized that even though the remains of her husband were going up in smoke, she still couldn't help thinking orchids. Maybe this was a problem of hers. She could hope, but not love. Inside her room, she noticed the empty bottle of red wine by her bed and threw it in the wastebasket. Didn't want to appear to be a drunk, even to herself.

Old habits die hard. She was a tidy person. She made the bed. As she made the bed, she couldn't help suspecting again that there might be another trick in here somewhere. Maybe Mitch wasn't really (really) dead. Maybe he was hiding and would rise up like Jesus, but not to go to heaven. This frightening thought led her back to Charlie. Surely the government had better things to do than send a cute bully to intrude and torment her with feelings of lust just when she was working so hard to have a noble feeling.

Cassie muttered to herself. Shouldn't she be allowed a tiny respite in this, her time of loss? For a moment, just a moment, please, couldn't she be spared from having to consider betrayal and money. (Lust.) Money and betrayal. Was that all there was to life? Wasn't there a certain lack of sensitivity being exhibited by the government here?

She asked herself, why should she help Charlie? If he had so many branches, shouldn't he be able to get the big picture for himself? And, by the way, who was the snitch who'd informed on Mitch? She peeled off her clothes and eased into the hot bath. She reminded herself that on Charlie's second visit to her she'd only said she'd think about it. She remembered the occasion well. She'd been in the kitchen. He'd been out in the greenhouse. She'd gone out to talk to him. On that occasion he hadn't mentioned juice or informers. He'd talked lilies and conversions. God help her, she'd been attracted to him then. She'd decided then that she would give him Mona's house and the Jaguar. She'd forgotten that the Jaguar was supposed to be hers, so maybe she could claim it now. Take the car back and drive it herself. Maybe she could take back all the things that were supposed to be hers. This was a new and exciting thought.

But now Charlie wasn't talking conversions, he was talking immunity. And still, Cassie thought that even though he had the power to break and send her to prison, he really liked her and wouldn't do that.

The hot water eased her headache and soothed old and new bruises. It was hard to stay focused on the subject. She was feeling better now. Under the water, her body looked pretty good. Hips and thighs could be worse. Her not-bad breasts still looked nice and full, hardly older than Marsha's. They floated alluringly in the bubbles. She kept her feet in the waterfall under the tap. She didn't have bad feet, either. Not that anyone cared about feet. Cassie let her head sink deep into the water, then scrambled rich shampoo into her hair.

"Personally, I think you're a very lovely lady," he'd said with his special little smile. "If the situation were different . . ."

Cassie massaged her scalp cautiously, exploring those terrifying little ridges on which she'd learned only postsurgery that no hair would ever grow back. If anyone with a brain ever played with her hair, he'd know in a second what they were. Did that mean she could never let anyone play with her hair? Her gut churned with anxiety.

And what did "very lovely lady" mean in this context, anyway? Did very lovely lady mean the sort of woman slightly past her prime who did good works like she did? Prayed regularly to God to keep them good, went to yoga at the Y, and did group casseroles for friends whose husbands had strokes. Did very lovely lady imply repressed, but sexy, as when Mark Cohen had called her a very lovely lady? Cassie suspected that Mark would actually get off on performing services of an intimate nature for her while charging her very high fees and thinking he was doing her a favor.

Cassie was not attracted to her married doctor. On the other hand, she was intrigued by her personal IRS stalker. Oh, the irony of the legacy her husband had left her. She rinsed her hair and squeezed on some conditioner and massaged it in. She got out of the tub and massaged everything she could think of with BabySoft, then considered her wardrobe, a depressing collection of marked-down mostly conservative Anne Klein and Liz Claiborne separates dating back to the stone age. Little jackets and skirts (not too short) and slacks (not too tight) and camp shirts, none of which did much for anyone but didn't wear out, and never went out of style. *And were now way too big.* Pink, baby soft, and fragrant, Cassie was thinking Anna Sui. Marsha had left behind her little black vamp dress that was skimpy but not too pushy about it, calf length. And her nice black sandals with a little heel. She put on a robe and snuck down the hall to borrow her daughter's clothes.

WHILE CASSIE WAS DOING HER BATH THING long before the cremation process would be over, Teddy came through the front door calling, "Mom? Mom."

Charlie was sitting in the dining room with two years of Mitch's American Express bills spread out on the dining room table in front of him. The record confirmed what Mona had told him over a drink in a fancy Italian restaurant in Manhattan last week (during which she'd denied having sent him any gifts): that Cassie was a major spender, using company assets to her own advantage à la Leona Helmsley. Charlie discovered the glamorous Mr. and Mrs. Sales trips all over the world and purchases therein. They presented a different picture of Cassie from the one Cassie presented. By then, he'd begun his investigation of the company. He located three Mona Whitman safe-deposit boxes. Unlike Cassie's, which had only receipts, Mona had cash in hers. A lot of cash. That had made him more hopeful about Cassie. Now he saw a not unusual situation. Often an unfaithful husband paid his wife off in booty for accepting the girlfriend, who got the cash. He was disappointed by what he saw. He would rather have had Cassie as thoroughly betrayed as he had been.

"Mom, where are you?" Teddy cried.

Charlie glanced up with no hint of uneasiness. "She's upstairs taking a bath."

Teddy ducked into the room and yelped when he saw who was speaking. "What are you doing here?"

"Hi. Teddy, right?"

Teddy stared. At the open filing cabinet, the piles of statements. He pinched his nose with thumb and index finger as if a dike had started leaking there.

"I'm Charlie," Charlie said.

"I know who you are."

"I'm sorry about your dad."

Teddy frowned. "Where's my mother? Did she let you in?"

"She's waiting for you. The police were here. Where have you been?"

"The police were here? Why?" Teddy sucked air.

"Police sometimes see sudden deaths as suspicious deaths," Charlie said mildly. "They had a few questions."

"Oh, no! Someone asked Mom questions?" Teddy stood frozen in the doorway.

"Yes, someone did."

"What did she say?"

Charlie shrugged. "I wasn't here. You'll have to ask her."

"Is she all right?"

"Oh, she's a little under the weather, but that's not surprising. She just lost her husband."

Teddy shuffled his feet in what Charlie interpreted as a guilty manner. He always knew when people were guilty. The twitching and quivering always took over. Eyes, lips, chin, hands. "What happened last night?" he asked.

Teddy's left eyelid did a little dance. "Poor Mom. I'm really sorry." He shook his head, then honed in on Charlie, the enemy. "What are you doing here, anyway?" he asked, frowning at the files.

"You know what I'm doing here."

"Me?" Now Teddy's eyebrow jumped up in alarm.

"You seem like a nice, honest kind of guy," Charlie said. "Very likable. The kind of guy the government can trust."

"No." Teddy turned and walked out of the room, muttering, "I don't want to hear this." Then he came back into the doorway a second later. "Let's get one thing straight. I don't know anything about this." He fanned his hands out at the piles on the table. "Nothing."

"It's just amazing how no one in this family knows anything," Charlie remarked. "Except the someone who knows everything. I'm guessing that would be you."

"No."

"Yes, Teddy, you know it all."

Teddy squirmed. "Look, I want my mom protected. That's all I want. I may be guilty, but she hasn't done anything wrong. Can you protect her?" Teddy said.

"Aw," Charlie said, tapping his chin.

"I don't care what happens to me." Teddy's tongue rolled around in his head. His mouth twitched. He was in way over his head. "Maybe I should call a lawyer or something," he said finally.

"Good idea, sure. I think you should. But let's talk options a little first. You said you want to help your mom."

"Well," Teddy hesitated. He wasn't sure what to do. Charlie was engaging him in some pretty heavy conversation. He was shaking pretty badly by the time the front door slammed.

"Teddddddie! You fucking idiot. What have you done now?" A very pretty girl came into the dining room and charged Teddy, arms flailing.

"Hey. Marsha, stop it." Teddy hardly had the strength to put his hands up to defend himself.

"You fucking killed *Daddy*. Are you crazy?" She tried to knee him in the groin.

"What are you talking about? I didn't kill him. He died, end of story. Stop that!"

"You didn't call me, you creep! You fucking *creep*." The knee went up. She couldn't get to his balls. "God*damn* it."

"Hey! Stop that." Charlie was on his feet. He moved around the table, pulled the girl away from Teddy, and took a punch on the chest for his trouble.

Marsha tried to punch him again, then stopped, confused by the stranger. "Who's this?"

Teddy shook his head. "Marsha, you just punched a Fed."

"Jesus." She was crying, trying to catch her breath. She hiccuped a few times, wouldn't meet Charlie's eye. "What's he doing here?"

"Are you all right? You look like your mom." Charlie was perfectly affable, but made a note to check out her savings account. This girl was trouble.

Marsha ignored him, snuffling back her tears. "Jesus, why didn't you call me, Teddy?"

Teddy shook his head. She'd left them to stay over at her boyfriend's.

"For God's sake, you're no help. Where's Lorraine? I want to know what happened," Marsha raged.

"I took her home." Teddy shuffled his feet.

"Praise the Lord. Is anybody else here?" Clearly she didn't count the Fed.

"Mom is upstairs." Teddy glanced at Charlie. "This is Charlie Schwab. He's with the IRS."

Marsha tossed her head in his direction, gave him a sharp once-over. Then she became aware of the nonedible spread on the table. Her forehead furrowed. "I'm sorry I hit you. I was aiming for my brother."

Very nice, she apologized. Charlie was impressed. Maybe he

wouldn't arrest her for assault. "No offense taken," he murmured. He was acting like a prince.

"What happened, Teddy?" Marsha was back on the attack. "I leave you for five minutes and Daddy dies. What's the matter with you?"

Teddy shuffled his feet. "You took off for dinner and never came back, you and your M.D. boyfriend. Huh, how about that?" Teddy countered.

"You and that nitbrain were in *charge*. You were supposed to take care of him."

"We did. It's not my fault." Teddy looked guilty as hell.

"Come on. Did you leave, or what?"

Teddy's eye and mouth twitched at the same time. "Where were *you* all night, big mouth?" he said miserably.

Then Marsha got it. They'd been too busy to remember what they were there to do. Her eyes widened. "You forgot him. You were fucking, you and that fat nurse," she screamed. "Your fucking killed Daddy. Oh shit."

Charlie got it, too. Now he could see the scene, how it had played. Marsha was out. Cassie had been drinking. With all that grape in the cellar, she was probably a big wino. Big. Teddy and his girlfriend, in charge of the patient, had been fooling around somewhere out of sight. Mitchell Sales had another stroke. Charlie guessed he might have died anyway. But maybe not. No wonder the shuffling feet. The kid must think he killed his father just to get laid. Ouch.

Footsteps sounded on the parquet landing. Cassie the probable wino clacked down the stairs.

"Oh God. Mommy," Marsha cried wildly.

She hurried out of the room to meet her mother at the bottom of the stairs. "Oh God, I just heard about Daddy. I'm so sorry."

Cassie didn't say anything as she brushed past her and came into the dining room. She sent a stunned look in her son's direction, then turned to embrace her daughter. For a minute they rocked together, and she stroked the girl's hair. Then she said, "It's okay, honey. Whatever happens, it's okay."

Charlie was made uneasy by the intimacy of the two women. Their hugging hit him like a charge from a jumper cable. They looked alike. One was dark-haired and one light-haired, but both were slender and graceful, both easy on the eye, though the younger one had quite a mouth on her. Cassie's tenderness to her child knifed the old injury right through him. His little girl would have been a woman now.

"Mommy, I love you." Finally Marsha pulled away. Then she stared at her mother with horror. "You're wearing my dress!" she said.

FIVE MINUTES LATER Cassie closed the door to the dining room and set-tled her children around the kitchen table. "Look, there's something I have to do right now." She didn't look at Teddy, but she knew he had tears in his eyes.

"What's that man doing here?" Marsha said softly.

"Listen to me, Marsha. You and Teddy are going to have to go through my address book and start calling people."

"Mom, talk to me. What's going on?" Marsha kept her voice low, but she wasn't backing down.

"I told you, he's an IRS agent," Teddy said unhappily.

"Marsha, I want you to call Parker Higgins and tell him your father died." Cassie leaned forward. She didn't have a lot of time and wanted them to pay attention.

"I can call him," Teddy protested.

"You call Ira. Divide up the list."

"An IRS agent? Mom, what are you doing?" Marsha asked.

"I'm taking Charlie to see Mona's house," she replied.

"Why?" Marsha was shocked.

"Because it's juice. Now, do what I tell you for once."

"Mom, don't go psycho on us. The IRS is like explosive stuff." Mar-sha gave her mother one of her superior looks, and Cassie exploded.

"I don't want to hear that from you ever again! I've *never* been psycho, not for one second in my whole life. I've been stupid. I've been in denial, but *psycho*, never!" Cassie realized she was getting loud and lowered her voice. Leaned forward, tried to take control of the plane. Up, up, up, get that cockpit up, she coached herself.

"Now, listen to me. The two of you have to rely on me now. Teddy, I understand what happened last night. Marsha took off, and you were doing your own thing." That was a nice way of putting it. Cassie's lips were set hard against her teeth, but she said it without a trace of irony. They'd been doing their own thing, and their father had died on their watch. It was over. Fact of life.

Marsha gripped her mother's arm. "Mom, calm down."

"I'm perfectly calm. He had Daddy's body removed before I was even up, Marsha. Did he call you at Tom's place? No, he did not. Then he took off with that *girl* and left me here to be interrogated by the police. That cop wanted to arrest me for murder. What were you *thinking?*" she hissed at her son.

Teddy looked like a fifteen-year-old caught out doing everything he wasn't supposed to do. "I was just trying to help. I'm really sorry, Mom."

"Sorry!"

"He was already dead when she went to check on him. I swear," Teddy said.

Cassie didn't want to pursue it now. The girl was not in the house. Good, she didn't want to pursue that, either. Suddenly she felt sick again. She turned her attention to the grain running through the wood in the kitchen table. She'd wiped it clean before she'd gone upstairs to change. Tidy was her middle name. "Is there anything else you want to tell me before I go?" she asked softly.

Teddy took a deep breath. "Well . . ."

"What, Teddy?" Marsha demanded. "What *now?*"

"Gently, gently." Cassie pointed at the dining room door. "I swear to God he must think we're nuts."

"Who cares? We *are* nuts," Marsha muttered.

"Shhh. Marsha!" Cassie told herself she was perfectly calm.

"Don't shhh me. Daddy's dead, and nothing changes around here except now you're wearing my clothes."

"Well, they're better than mine," Cassie pointed out.

"I sent the letter," Teddy blurted.

"What letter?" Marsha gave him the idiot look. For once, Teddy ignored it.

"Mom, I'm really sorry. He was going to marry her. She told me a thousand times that everybody underestimates you, that you'd be okay. She promised me a better life." He squirmed in his chair, crumbling like a cookie.

"Mona promised you a better life than what?" Cassie's brain spun back into its whirl. In an instant she lost her perfect calm.

"She promised she'd always take care of me." Teddy pulled on his fingers until his knuckles cracked. "I had to stop it, that's all."

Mona had promised Teddy a better life? Cassie swallowed bile as a terrible thought struck her: Had Mona been sleeping with her son, too? She shivered in the sun-drenched kitchen. This was the stuff of soap operas. Teddy was their informer. He had nailed his own father. She was speechless.

"What are you talking about? What did you do?" Marsha demanded. She didn't have a clue.

Teddy was telling his story and paying no attention to her. "He was always teaching me lessons. It was time to teach him one."

"For God's sake what did he *do*?" Marsha turned to her mother, and still Teddy wouldn't acknowledge her.

"Mom, I gave him the second set of books."

Cassie's life took another unexpected turn. She was spinning, spinning. Dizzy, dizzy. Where would it stop? "What second set of books?" she asked faintly.

"It was how he taught me accounting. Not even Ira knows." For the first time Teddy glanced guiltily at his sister. "He and Mona cooked the books. Daddy showed me how they did it. Easy as pie. The official set was prepared for Ira, the other for them. He told me everybody did it. He was proud of it. He thought only idiots were honest."

Cassie put her hand to her mouth. She pointed to the dining room. "You gave *him* the books?"

"Well, they were disks, really. He was in here. He would have found them, anyway, and I didn't want to be like that kid in *The Sopranos*."

Cassie frowned. Sopranos? Was that an opera?

"He loved that show. Loved it. He thought he was Tony. I was Tony Jr."

"Oh *God!*" Now Marsha got something. "He thought he was Tony *Soprano*, Mom."

No wonder she'd always hated that show. Cassie waved her hand impatiently. She was still on the cooked books. Teddy gave the juice to the finder. "When did you do that, Teddy?" she demanded.

"Just now. He pretty much promised none of us would go to jail. You're not mad, are you?"

"Ha. They rape boys like you in jail," Marsha crowed. "I hope you get buggered, you crook."

"Marsha!" Cassie said, shocked.

"Well, he *is* a crook, isn't he?"

"Mom, do you forgive me?" Suddenly Teddy was begging, a little kid all over again. "I did it for you," he said. "And her." He pointed at his sister. "She may be a total jerk, but Mona wasn't going to give her a nickel. It wasn't fair."

CHAPTER

45

SO THIS WAS WHERE THE PATH of Cassie Sales's little uneventful life had led. She was in the Mercedes with Charlie Schwab, heading toward Mona's Refuge at just past noon on the day after Independence Day, which happened to be her first of single life in twenty-six years. She was very aware of looking like a vamp from a spy novel. She was wearing Marsha's black wrap dress, Marsha's big dark sunglasses, and Marsha's skimpy sandals. Her stomach was heaving, still in rebellion from the wine she'd drunk last night against a backdrop of exploding fireworks that had set the dogs in the neighborhood howling for hours just about the time Mitch had died alone.

All along she'd thought that her teenage daughter had been just your basic malcontent with multiple pierces and pink hair, and her son was a dolt, a puppet of his overbearing father. Now she realized that her children had minds of their own, and there had been a reason behind everything they did to annoy her. It amazed her how devious the mind was. It turned out that her son was actually tempted by prison because his father had deserved to be there, and her daughter wanted to work with women in prison because she and her mother had been in one. That was Cassie's interpretation.

Oddly, she was relieved that they had some depth. The three of them were eccentric, but possibly not certifiably crazy. In any case, like Teddy, she was setting the record straight regardless of the consequences.

What did any of it matter now but the truth? It was only after she'd gotten into the car and taken the wheel that she remembered she hadn't asked Teddy if the cremation had taken place on schedule so no autopsy could be done of the body. Whatever had or hadn't happened to Mitch in the night, she didn't want anyone to know. So much for true truth.

It was too late to find out now. She became distracted on Duck Pond by how many worlds apart it was from Manhasset, where Teddy and Marsha had gone to public schools. Here was real privilege. Here were the horse farms, the Old Brookville Winery, with its greening suburban vineyard. Here was the estate where a rival importer far more wealthy than Mitch lived behind his iron gates. Here was the old money, the turn-of-the-century banking and oil money to which Mitch and Mona had aspired with their designer clothes, their trips, and their ever improving accents. The road that led to Le Refuge was nearly untraveled at noon on a weekday.

Cassie wondered where Mona was, if she knew yet that Mitch was dead. What would she do when she found out what the IRS had in store for her? She was amazed that she felt drained and elated at the same time. The infiltration of the enemy beside her was almost complete. Soon there would be nothing he didn't know. It was thrilling. He knew of the juice in all its forms, but not where it all was. Now she would show him everything she knew. Her body was electrified, almost singing in its new form. In the back of her mind, she had a feeling that even though Teddy had started the ball rolling on the revelations, Mona was probably behind Charlie's intense interest in *her*. He'd kept on her tail, followed her while her husband was sick, was dying, died, all the time as if she were the one doing wrong. And all the time Mona was the real thief.

"How are you doing?" Charlie interrupted her thoughts.

Cassie was hoping Mona would be tortured by her prison guards, raped, brutalized, tattooed. She was disappointed that it turned out that Charlie had only his own self-interest at heart, after all. She realized that for some inexplicable reason she'd actually been counting on his liking her not for the juice but for herself.

"Did you find any other safe-deposit boxes on your quest?" she asked, glancing at him in the passenger seat. He looked quite meek and tame for a person who had the power of immunity to grant or withhold.

"Yes." Charlie nodded solemnly. "I did."

"Full of juice?" Cassie asked. Still, the whole thing was thrilling. She'd never forget it for the rest of her life.

"Yes. Full of juice."

"May I ask whose?" Mona's, she bet. Mitch's was in the Cayman Islands. Maybe Switzerland, too, for all she knew. She almost laughed out loud. He'd find it. He'd find it all.

"Maybe later. What are we going to see, Cassie?"

"A house," she told him, proud to have something to throw in the pot. "A nice one."

"Ah."

"Did you seize the contents of my safe-deposit box? Or did you leave it?" And what did she have? Nothing.

"Seized, so it wouldn't get away," Charlie said with no hint of an apology.

Cassie blew air out of her mouth. "That's legal?"

"Good things don't happen to people who protest IRS actions." He opened his window and, like a dog, put his nose to the wind.

"Huh. Did you look at the contents of my box?" she asked. What did he think?

"Beautiful day, isn't it? I did give them a cursory examination. Why?"

"Did you notice anything unusual about what I had in there?" Cassie passed a car traveling in the opposite direction at much more than the legal speed limit. It was a Range Rover. A blond woman with sunglasses like Cassie's was driving. A small child was strapped in the backseat. Both looked smiling and happy.

"You spend a lot and don't pay for anything." Charlie drew his head back into the car and tilted his head quizzically at her in that way he had. Cassie wondered if she still smelled of throw-up even after her bath.

"Isn't that kind of thing unusual?" she asked, trying not to be unnerved.

"Well"—he exercised his neck, circling his head one way and then the other—"it's not *that* unusual. More people than you'd think live off their credit cards."

"But wouldn't you say this is a lot of debt to carry?"

"I did wonder why you kept the receipts locked away. Surely your husband knew about them." Now he started with the tilting again, as if his head were so heavy with information, he could hardly hold it up. "But maybe not," he concluded. "People live mysterious lives."

Cassie couldn't resist a bitter laugh. "Yes. I saw the file for the first time after my husband had his stroke. I was looking for a living will. Imagine my surprise when I found a whole other me."

"Amazing," Charlie said wonderingly.

"It was so bizarre. I thought it had to be a mistake. I didn't have those cards. Mitch knew I didn't have those cards. I thought maybe the people in the computer had stolen my identity. Or I had a mental disease, one of those multiple personalities that does things you don't know about. Take that Jaguar. I just couldn't remember buying it or where I kept it. Quite a step up from losing your car in a parking lot, wouldn't you say?" Cassie hiccuped on another laugh.

"Uh-huh, very strange," Charlie agreed.

"The Jag wasn't in my garage. Those curtains with the custom fringe from France, not in my house. As you said, amazing. The dishes and jewelry. Never saw 'em. I said to myself, who's this Cassie buying all this stuff, and where is it?"

"Hmmm," Charlie murmured.

"Guess what happened when I tried to cancel the cards and stop this leak."

"How about, denied."

"How'd you know?" Cassie turned to him, surprised.

"You're not the primary cardholder, am I right?"

"Who would have thought I couldn't cancel the cards with my own name on them? Know what else? This morning I called and told customer service the primary cardholder was dead. They told me they'd need a letter to that effect from his lawyer. When I told them the cards had been *stolen*, they promised to send new ones right out, so I gave up. Ah, here we are."

Cassie made a little sound of triumph and turned in at the iron gates with the Sales logo. She drove up the drive to the stone house. Beside her she could feel Charlie tense as soon as he saw the place in its entirety. It was then that she realized she'd been right: He'd never believed a single word she'd said.

"Voilà, the new house of my husband's partner, Mona Whitman, aka Cassandra Sales." From the front, all looked quiet as Cassie slowed to a stop.

"The little devil." Charlie whistled, and before Cassie had time to kill the engine, he was out of the car taking pictures with the camera that five weeks ago she'd thought was a gun.

"Wait a minute, where are you going?" she asked.

"Going inside. Let's do an inventory and see what items come up. This is interesting."

"But there must be an alarm." Cassie opened the door and inched one leg out of the car. This made her nervous. How many things could go wrong in one day? He might be setting her up for some kind of fall. She was immune now, but what if she went in the house? Would she stop being immune on a B and E? She'd seen this on *Law and Order*.

"So it goes off. What's the worst thing that could happen? The cops could come." She was scared, but Charlie laughed. He was excited now and headed toward the back of the house, firing off rounds of photos as he went.

Cassie wanted to see for herself what was inside the house, but the police had already questioned her once today. She didn't want to get in any deeper. She hitched the sunglasses up higher on her nose, as if she could disguise herself. All her life she'd been afraid of going out on that limb. Afraid to look an attractive man in the eye. Afraid to be bold and have an extramarital orgasm. What the hell, she was going inside.

For once, however, Cassie's fears were for nothing. The house was wide open. Where the service road led, there was a brick-walled courtyard. Inside was a station wagon and a medium-sized van with MOVING DEPOT stenciled on the side. The back doors of the van were gaping wide, and furniture and boxes were scattered all over the tarmac, ready for loading. Looked like Mona was moving, but Cassie knew she was only packing up the juice. The glassed-in mudroom door was propped open for easy access, and Cassie followed Charlie in.

Inside, the huge kitchen and pantry were in complete disarray. Silver and dishes were laid out on the counters in preparation of packing. Two movers were smoking, talking, and wrapping Tiffany china in recycled paper. They didn't bother to look up when Cassie came in.

"Is Miss Whitman around?" she asked.

The packer with the black handkerchief tied around his head said, "She'll be back after lunch, who's asking?"

"I'm her sister," Cassie said. She picked up a huge crystal candlestick and wondered how much it had cost her. "Charlie?" she called.

"In here."

Cassie moved into the dining room, where two men were struggling to take down heavy curtains dripping with beaded fringe. Charlie held his cell phone to his mouth. He was talking excitedly, watching the maneuver with one hand on a hip. Cassie moved into the living room, where her mother's Napoleonic settee and side chairs were now covered in gold brocaded velvet. Seeing them there like sentries in front of the fireplace was a kick in the gut. There was Marsha's piano with its leather stool. What warehouse or secret love nest had they been in all these years? The library was through an archway that could be closed with sliding doors. In there, the shelves were filled with leather-bound books, leather furniture, and more velvet curtains.

Cassie stepped into the large entry gallery and eyed the chandelier with all that crystal. She studied the mahogany staircase with its heavy carving of pineapples, the symbol of fertility. This was not the house she would have chosen for herself. She hesitated for a moment, then climbed the stairs and found her rival's bedroom. Here, she stopped. Like everywhere else in this place, nothing was white, nothing simple. This room was red, red, red, like the library and the dining room. Red satin and velvet and taffeta, different textures. Not bad if you liked Victorian bordello. Cassie moved to the closet where the juice was, but the door was locked. She wanted to see that jewelry. "Charlie," she called out.

"Right behind you," he said.

Didn't take him thirty seconds to get the door open. He was good at B and E; must have gone to break-in school as part of his training. The jewelry box was locked, but he didn't have any trouble with that, either.

Inside, nestled among ropes of pearls and gold chains and diamond tennis bracelets were the Cassie credit cards, bundled together with a few new receipts and a rubber band. Bingo. Charlie stepped back and took some photos. Then he pocketed the cards and moved on, taking notes on a PalmPilot.

46

MONA SAT IN PARKER HIGGINS'S RECEPTION ROOM and waited for twenty of the longest minutes of her whole life. During that time she went to the bathroom twice to check on her makeup. Twice she marched down the hall to see his stupid new secretary, whose name she couldn't remember at the moment.

"He's on the phone, Miss Whitman." The girl did not seem impressed by Mona's outfit, her importance to the firm, or her sweetness. She wasn't helpful at all.

Mona was terribly upset and felt her throat closing up. Parker had never kept her waiting before. Now that Mitch was not behind her with his old-boy friendship and special one-two punch, even the $187,500 certified check for her house (which had cost her only $89,250) in her purse and the new $4,300 Chanel summer suit on her body didn't make her feel as powerful as she really was. The suit was a lovely powder blue—signature Chanel—with a tight skirt that stopped way above her knees, elbow-length sleeves, and a prim white collar and cuffs. She'd bought it in Paris a month ago, and this was her first opportunity to wear it.

Still, Mona knew she didn't look her best. She hadn't slept last night, what with the fireworks going off for the second time that week at all three golf clubs that circled her house; the pressure to pack up the contents of the house for storage in New Jersey in the morning; and her terrifying fears for Mitch under his wife's evil care. She was truly shocked by Parker's lack of sensitivity to Mitch's wishes and his allowing Cassie to take him home. In his fragile condition, Cassie could influence him in a dozen different ways, even make him forget his own name.

Mona was so worried about these dangers that she'd taken extra time to dress carefully for the closing on her house. She had not wanted to go to the closing. If all this hadn't happened, she never would have bothered. She would have signed all the documents in advance and let the money be transferred to her savings account. But with that dickbrain functionary Schwab breathing down her neck, she was afraid to put the money in her own account just in case she really needed it. She'd decided to put it in the account she'd taken out in her mother's name in a bank in New Jersey years ago, near the warehouse where she'd arranged to store her furniture. Mona had opened a number of accounts over the years in her mother's name that her mother didn't know anything about because she was so ridiculously poor at this point, the IRS would never in a million years think of auditing her.

Mona had consulted *The Art of War* last night and this morning as well, but there was nothing new in it about terrain or anything else that would really help her now that Cassie had discovered her new house and its contents, and the dickbrain was not responding to her personally the way she wanted him to. All she could do was retreat to higher ground and regroup her army. Shit maneuvers. As Mona waited for her audience with the lawyer, her hands were shaking with anger at Cassie and Parker and Schwab, and at poor Mitch, too, for not having taken care of things the way he'd promised.

"Mr. Higgins can see you now." That damn girl finally came to get her. When she turned around to lead the way, Mona noticed that she had a fat ass even though she was still a very young person, and also that she had a run in the right heel of her panty hose.

Mona took her time checking her lipstick in her pocket mirror, then rose gracefully and walked around the building to Parker's corner office, swinging her hips. "*Warfare is the way of deception,*" she counseled herself.

She was going to feel good and be sweet no matter what. She was going to offer Parker continued Sales business and secrecy about his private disgusting predilections. If he showed any signs of affection for her, any innuendo of desire at all, she would do her usual thing. Lead him on today. Feign shock at his moves on her tomorrow. The day after that she'd send him gifts and tell him to give her time to think about their relationship. In four days time she'd tell him he had always been her true ideal, her one and only love. And it would be true. He was a wealthy lawyer. He was not bad looking, liked having a good time. Unlike Mitch, he was a careful man with a great deal of real estate. Although he wasn't as classy as Mitch, forming an alliance with him wouldn't be moving down the social ladder in any way. Mona always did the unexpected thing.

The Art of War. She was always nice when about to advance herself in a way that hurt someone else. She didn't think of hurting as hurting, only as survival. Her plan was to strike a deal, then give Parker the blow job of his life (a few weeks from now, because right at the moment she'd rather die than have him think she was that kind of girl). She might promise to let him have anal intercourse with her, but she would not do it. She *might* do it to him if she absolutely had to. She'd read about such things in lesbo porn and had it all worked out how she'd play it.

If he showed no sign of affection or loyalty to her, she would call his wife and tell her he fucked hookers in the ass every Thursday at six-fifteen. And Sundays when he played poker with the guys he always got a massage and blow job afterward to cheer himself up for his losses. She would sue him for malpractice and a whole bunch of other things.

"Oh, Mona, have a seat," Parker said as soon as she stepped through the door onto his thick beige carpet. He said it without seeing her. He had swung his chair around to look at the view of Old Country Road, which hadn't been country in either of their lifetimes. The windows of his building were mirrored so that no one could see in; but from the inside looking out, there was no doubt it was another perfect summer day in the Garden City business district.

He hadn't risen and crossed the carpet as he usually did. Or given her the admiring looks and the hug she needed more than food. Mona was taken aback by his slight.

"Parker!" She stood waiting for him to acknowledge her properly before she sat down. She enjoyed being looked at. She dressed to be looked at. She was not prepared to have that looking stop.

"Mona, sit down."

"This is so hard for me, Parker. Aren't you going to give me a hug?" Mona said in her lost-little-girl voice. "You're the only one who can help me, the only one I ever cared about."

Parker did not swing his chair around, but she heard his sigh. "Oh, come now, Mona. Remember who you're talking to."

Her lips tightened. She and Parker had been friends for a long time, but she would bring him down in a second if she had to. Her breath came hard with her intense feelings of loss as she flashed to the men in her life who'd fallen for her instantly. Like her gymnastics coach when she was nine. She'd worked hard to be the very best gymnast and her coach had loved her so much, too. Their affair began when she was twelve, while she was still living with her grandmother. Davey used to pick her up at school, and then he'd do her in the backseat of his station wagon. Those had been wonderful days. As an adorable little girl whose mommy was a hippie traveling far away in cloud-cuckoo-land and whose grandmother was busy playing bridge, Mona had been able to win anybody, get anything she wanted. Coach Davey had taught her so many things she'd never even imagined. He had taken pictures of her in the summer running in a field, trailing a long scarf behind her like a kite. Her grandmother had loved her so much that her aunts had been jealous of her.

But then when she was thirteen her mother came back *again*, and she had to leave paradise for a dump in fucking Albany. It was six years before her grandmother would have her back on Long Island again. Then another disappointment. Jerry, her first husband, would have done anything for her, but he was a mediocrity, a nothing. He was married now and had four kids, lived in a *maison ordinaire* in Scarsdale. And, of course, there was Mitch, for whom she'd waited all these years and who had to have a stroke before they'd had their chance to marry.

Mona tapped her foot, waiting for recognition. Occasionally, however, there were men who, for reasons Mona could not understand, were reserved, almost suspicious of her. She could feel it in their eyes. Schwab, who had seemed so accommodating and nice at first. Parker, who blew hot and cold with the wind. Teddy, who wouldn't even speak to her anymore. She never forgot the slights, never, and would bring them all down, one by one.

"Parker, sweetheart. Come say hello to me. This is a terrible blow."

She stopped tapping and posed, bringing one knee in front of the other to slim her profile even more, but he didn't swing around to see it.

"Sit down, Mona."

Mona gave up and sat down, pouting at his back. "Why didn't you consult me before letting him go home with that fucking bitch?" she murmured in what she was certain was a soft tone.

"Watch that, now." Parker swung around angrily, and Mona could see that his eyes were red. Oh God, he'd been drinking.

She put on a fast, sad smile. "Oh Parker, I thought we understood each other. Mitch trusted only me. He wanted me to be his power, his rock. How could you leave me out of such a decision?"

For Mona, the eyes were everything, the mirror of the soul. Parker's eyes were unfocused and runny. He was a weak man who could be slain. She would slay him. Her eyes smiled like President Bush's frosty executioner's smile.

He sighed, shaking his head. "You don't understand. I am a lawyer. I can only act according to my client's instructions."

"I am your client, too, Parker," she reminded him, making some noise with her breathing. "I care for you, and I want to help you, be your most important client, your most *lucrative* client."

"Don't twist what I'm saying, Mona. We're talking about Mitch now. Mitch did not give you power of attorney, so you did not have any legal right to make decisions concerning his treatment or his end of the business."

"Parker, I want to get a few things straight." Mona still spoke softly, but there was more than ice in her eyes now.

Parker held up his hand. "Me first."

"Parker, don't interrupt me. I am the woman he loves and his business partner and the beneficiary of his will. I think I have the right to determine where he convalesces."

"No, you didn't."

"Parker! My asthma. Don't upset me." She dropped her chin, coughing weakly.

"Someone else had his power of attorney," Parker said sharply.

Her head shot up. "Who?"

"I did."

Mona glared. She'd come to him that day and he'd said nothing about it. "I don't believe it," she retorted.

"Well, believe it."

"You never mentioned it."

"Look, I didn't want to get into a dispute with you." He shrugged.

The man dared to shrug at her. This was a near-death experience for Mona. "Does Cassie know?" she demanded.

"This was confidential. I was trying to avoid a war between you two women. You're impossible, both of you. And now you're going to have to behave yourself, Mona. I really mean it. You're not top dog anymore."

Mona's heart almost failed her. "How could you insult me like this? You know I'm the most unselfish person in the world. I never think of myself. I'd rather walk away than fight with Cassie. I love the woman. Just ask Mitch how—" Mona would have gone on, but Parker interrupted her again.

"I'm sorry for your loss, Mona. I'm sorry for all our loss. We all loved Mitch. We're all going to miss him. . . ."

"What are you talking about?" Mona stared. Was she missing something?

"Mitch died last night in his sleep. I just heard a few minutes ago."

"Oh." Mona was staring so hard, her eyes teared. The room swam. She almost fell over but decided not to take the chance. Mitch died at home with Cassie? At that awful house with Cassie hanging over him? Her eyes flooded and overflowed. Poor Mitch, he would have hated that.

She took a minute to absorb. Her lover, her husband-to-be, was gone. There would be no wedding, no golden dress, no honeymoon. Mona gulped back her grief and wiped her eyes with her index finger. Well. Mitch had been an absolute vegetable. She never could have cared for him herself. Perhaps God had spared her a terrible decade of marriage to a cripple. Maybe her one true love was yet to come. She blotted her face with the lace-edged handkerchief stuck in her sleeve and started thinking revenge. The lawsuit she would file against Cassie. Wrongful death. Criminal negligence. There were a million things she could do. She blew her nose.

She needed to get home and make sure the house was clean, the credit cards were flushed. She had to call the insurance company and get them to pay up. If she went ahead and filed a wrongful-death suit against Cassie, could that jeopardize her collecting? Hmmm. She realized Parker hadn't said a single thing.

"Parker, the will, I'd like to see it," she told him.

He nodded. "I'll get a copy for you, but you're not mentioned in it."

Then the bomb struck, and her jaw dropped, literally, as Parker explained. It was the very last thing she'd expected.

"This was the arrangement Mitch made when he reorganized the company five years ago. Sales Importers, Inc., of which you are a minority stockholder, is owned by a Delaware corporation called Amity Holdings. The stockholders of Amity are Marsha, Teddy, me, and Mark," Parker said, deadpan.

"You own me?" Mona was flabbergasted.

"You are a shareholder of Sales. So is Cassie. But neither of you own the company."

"This can't be true, Parker. Mitch always told me Cassie had nothing," Mona cried.

Parker shrugged again. "Well, that's a small exaggeration. You know Mitch. He tended to think whatever he wanted was already his. In fact, Cassie's father had invested heavily in the company at its inception with the stipulation that Cassie hold twenty-five percent of Sales in her own name. Mitch's condition on that score was that Cassie not be able to hold any power over his head. He felt it would hurt the marriage, and apparently her father had agreed. So the stock certificates and the agreement have always been kept here with me." Parker said this with a smile that Mona had never seen before. He was relishing this. Relishing it. Cassie's father must not have told her before he died. Mitch hadn't told her, and Parker hadn't told her. All these years Cassie hadn't known she could be a player, and Mona had had no idea that the playing field had been rigged against her from the start. Mona finally saw the true truth: The two stinkers, Mitch and Parker, had been in it for themselves. They were homos.

Mona's eyes started to tear again. She couldn't help it. Mitch and Parker had gone to fucking college with each other, and the bottom line was, they were men. They only trusted each other. Mona's spine stiffened with resolve. She was going to sue Parker for malpractice for sure. She might even do a class action with Cassie. They'd take Parker and Ira to the cleaners. They'd make millions. Who knew, maybe even billions. It was not impossible.

"Is there anything else you'd like to know?" Parker said, swiveling from side to side, suddenly the most clearly evil bastard in the whole wide world.

Mona wanted to wipe the supercilious look right off his fat face. Amity Holdings, what kind of joke was that? She yearned to say something truly devastating, to threaten and have a tantrum, trash his place, break those big mirrored windows and throw him out to his death. Even blow up the whole building. She longed to reveal all the things she could do to him. But . . . it wasn't her style. She was a lady. She was a princess, a princess in distress at the moment, but a princess nonetheless. And she would act like one no matter what.

No wonder she'd been nervous and paranoid all these years. No wonder she'd worried every single day of her life. She'd been a doll to him and everybody else, and they were all nothing but pigs in shit, just like her mother, who'd left her so many times, and Davey, who'd exploited her for his own gain, and her grandmother, who'd sent her away and hadn't let her come back for six long years. But by then she was almost dead, too old to help her at all. And then that adviser in her senior class in high school, who left his wife for her but turned out to have no money at all, so she had to come to New York to be with Granny instead. And stupid, stupid Jerry, who wouldn't set his sights high enough.

Mona hated Parker Higgins so much, she smiled at him kindly. She would kill him slowly. His wife would turn off to him. His friends would shun him. He'd lose his business. He wouldn't know what happened. The room blurred, came back in focus. She needed water. Just a sip.

"Mona, are you okay? How about a cup of coffee?"

"No, no. I'll be fine in a minute," she said, not wanting to touch a single thing in this poisonous place or be the slightest bit of a bother.

47

CHARLIE NOTIFIED HIS BRANCH OFFICE, and Special Agent Marshall Dahl and his supervisor Angelo Carini promised to join them at Le Refuge as soon as they had finished lunch. Mel Arrighi was on his way. D.C. was notified. Cassie was in a hurry to get away before any of them got there, but she wasn't leaving without her credit cards.

She followed Charlie as he traveled from room to room, taking photos. "Charlie, give me those cards."

"What cards?"

"I saw you put them in your pocket. They're my cards."

"Nah."

"Charlie, I saw you."

"Well, if I have them, which I'm not saying I do, they're safe with me. Thanks for your help. You can go home now," Charlie told her breezily.

"Thanks for my help. I can go home now! I broke your fucking case." Cassie's voice rose.

"And the Bureau appreciates it. We really do." Charlie turned to her with a big grin and snapped her photo.

She gasped. "What are you doing?"

"You're a very lovely woman. Thank you," he said solemnly.

"Wait a minute. Mona was taking off with all this stuff she'd bought in my name."

"Looks like it," he agreed, a happy man.

"I need some assurances. Some waiver or something," Cassie went on.

He laughed.

"Look, I did a little checking with my not-so-honest lawyer last week about this house. The house is in Mona's name. She paid four million in cash. The other three came from a mortgage. I'd suggest you find out where that cash came from. If it came from Sales Importers, Inc., that would be what kind of income, would you say? If it came from the *air*, you'd probably like to know that, too. Either way, it's not right, not correct. You never believed me about anything. Give me my cards."

"I always believed you," Charlie said. But he was working now, on top of the world. He knew how Mitch's huge AmEx bills he'd been studying this morning had been paid off without the incoming cash, or the expenses, appearing on his personal or company tax returns. Some offshore bank was automatically paying them. As Charlie saw it, Mitch must have been regularly transferring money to banks out of the country through perfectly legal international credit cards. You weren't supposed to *take* more than a few thousand dollars out of the country without reporting it. But traveling executives in big international companies did it all the time. Cash was moved to banks that wouldn't report it, and international credit card companies did not reveal the money going out unless the IRS requested the transactions documenting it. They didn't routinely go through credit card receipts.

Mitch had accessed the money the same way he had moved it. He'd charged trips and luxury items abroad and paid for them with international cards. Once he got cooperation from the card companies, Charlie would have no trouble tracking it. This did not explain why the technique hadn't been used with the items in this house, unless Cassie was right and she'd been targeted by the two of them all along. He loved it. Mona's purchase of the house had put her at risk. Mitch could easily have purchased it quite legally himself. But the motive must have been divorce. He couldn't appear to have any money, of course. This was quite a feat for a man with so much money. Charlie looked at Cassie and wondered what kind of man would leave a beautiful lady like her.

"You didn't believe me. I know you." Cassie was heating up to a good scream. He put his hand on her arm to calm her down.

"Of course. I always believed you. I was attracted to you from the minute you called the cops on me."

"I hate you," she said.

Undisturbed, he removed his hand from her arm and changed rolls of film in his camera. "Fine. But you'd better go home now. I'll get in touch with you later on this."

"I don't want you to get in touch with me later. I want those cards in my possession. They have to be canceled," Cassie insisted.

Charlie regarded her with awe. Her cheating husband was dead. The IRS was descending with its big guns on the $600 million company of which she was most certainly part owner. The entity with all its tentacles would be opened up and examined with exquisite detail, far greater than any techniques used for a body on the autopsy table. No matter how much the Feds took in fines and unreported back taxes, however, Cassie would still be a rich woman someday. But all she cared about was clearing her name of what amounted (in this massive case) to a rather piddling credit card debt. What a woman!

"I want those cards canceled." Cassie stamped her foot.

She had no idea how much money was involved here, and he was enchanted. "I'll cancel them," he promised. With the new roll in the camera, he snapped another photo of her. "You're adorable when you're angry."

"That's a ridiculous thing to say."

"Well, you don't know me," he said.

"Well, you don't know Mona. You don't know what she can do."

"She can't do anything to me."

"She can hurt anybody. She can twist things around. Please. Give me the cards."

He shook his head. "Uh-uh. What are you going to do with them? You can't prove you got them here."

"I'm going to get an *honest* lawyer," Cassie told him.

Charlie snickered. "Surely a contradiction in terms. And right here you have better than a lawyer." He tapped his chest.

"Charlie, you're going to hurt me, I know it," she said sadly.

Something about her tone, like the unselfconscious embrace she'd given her daughter earlier, stabbed him in a place where he'd long thought he'd lost feeling. The emotion stopped him short. He dropped the arm holding his camera and stared at her, wondering at the very idea. Hurt her? How could he?

"Oh come on, not everybody's bad. The IRS are *good* guys."

She shook her head. "What's going to happen to my son?"

"He's a great guy, an honest man is worth his weight in diamonds. We reward people like him."

"Charlie, that's another lie. Give me the cards."

"Nope." He went back to taking pictures. When he turned around again, she was gone.

AT TWO O'CLOCK, Mona and four IRS operatives in two cars showed up at the same time. By then, the curtain hangers in the station wagon were gone, and the Moving Depot packers had unpacked everything and left it out on the counters and tables. All the furniture that had been outside was back inside. And the van was gone, too.

Mona arrived first and opened the front door of her house to find Charlie sitting on the stairs in the gallery. She almost fainted when she saw him.

"Hi," he said.

"What are you doing here?" she said.

"I could ask you the same question. I thought you lived in Roslyn Heights."

"Well, I do. I'm just here checking on this place for Mitch."

"I thought he died today."

"Oh no. I had no idea." She glanced toward the door.

"Looks to me like you're moving."

"Um, I, ah, just stopped by. I don't know anything about this."

"I found those credit cards you were telling me about."

Mona looked at him dumbly. "I don't know what you're taking about."

"The ones that furnished this house, bought your Jaguar, your clothes, etc."

She shook her head. "You're mistaken. Mitch may have given me a few items. Gifts. I had nothing to do with it. I can prove it. I can prove everything." She was pale, shaky on her feet. She coughed, then whimpered. "I've had a shock," she murmured. "I didn't know poor Mitch was dead."

"My condolences."

"Charlie, can you help me clear this up? I have no one. No one, but you," she repeated. "You're an important man. You can help me if you want to."

"I'll help you," Charlie promised.

Mona's face was white. She tried to arrange her body in an attractive way, but her feet weren't behaving themselves. She made a little misstep with one foot and nearly toppled off her stiletto heels. Then she recovered. "You didn't know Mitch. He was a little naive about things. He bought this house. A shelter. Everything. Gifts." She opened her arms to take it all in. The abundance.

"Absolutely, we'll clear it all up," Charlie said.

Mona fixed him with a devastated expression, then moved into the living room, the dining room. Looking for the movers, he thought. Nothing was missing, and no one was around. "What's going on?" she asked finally.

"We're seizing the house," he told her.

BY TEN O'CLOCK, Cassie was standing at the front door saying good night to the last of her condolence callers. Marsha had finished putting the dirty glasses and cups in the dishwasher, the leftover casseroles in the refrigerator, and was now bundling everything made with sugar, flour, and butter in the garbage. The platters of half-eaten quick breads, cookies, pies, and coffee cakes filled nearly a whole garbage bag.

"What are you doing?" Tom cried.

"Mom shouldn't eat any of that," she explained to him. "I know she's depressed, and I don't want her getting fat again."

"Sweetheart, at a time like this, fat is the least of her problems."

"Uh-uh. You don't understand. She needs to be protected from herself."

"Honey, but this is unkind. She should eat if she wants to."

"Oh no. This is tit for tat. You know what she used to do to me? She threw away all my trick-or-treat candy. Every single piece, right in the garbage, year after year. I used to forage for it in the middle of the night. Believe me, I'm only thinking of her best interests."

"Then you should stay here with her tonight." Tom leaned against the counter, looking grave.

"Absolutely. She's lost without me. Look what happened last night. I'll never forgive myself. Sweetheart, why don't you go home. I'll call you in a little while." She turned to give him a hug.

"I'll stay here with you, if you want me to," he murmured, squeezing her bottom. "Don't want you foraging, either."

She laughed. "I don't do that anymore."

"Are you going to be that kind of mother? Hiding the sweets?"

"No, it doesn't work at that age."

"I think I'll stay."

"No, no. You'd hate it. Two gloomy girls. And my bed is so tiny." She nuzzled his neck.

"I'd be happy in a closet with you," he whispered.

Cassie came into the kitchen yawning, and the couple pulled apart quickly. "I'm beat," she said, ignoring the clinch.

"Where's Teddy?" Marsha asked, repairing her hair.

"He took Edith home." Cassie glanced around the kitchen. "You did it all," she said, surprised.

"Of course." Marsha closed the garbage bag quickly and tied the top to hide the goodies inside. "Is he coming back?"

Cassie shook her head. "I told him to go home and get some sleep. Is the coffee gone?"

"No more coffee for you. What about the monster? Honey, would you take this outside?" Marsha handed Tom the garbage bag and pointed the way. He went out the back door with it.

Cassie raised her eyebrows at the obedience. "Which monster?"

"The *Lorraine* monster."

Cassie shook her head. "Let's not go into it now, Marsha. Teddy says she's history. I'd really like a cup of coffee." She opened a pantry door, looking for the bag of beans.

"No, Mom! You need your rest." Marsha closed the door and kept on about Lorraine. "Do you believe him?"

"Who?" Cassie rolled her eyes heavenward on the coffee issue. They were so resistant to letting her make her own choices. Okay, she'd wait until Marsha and Tom were gone, then she'd drink whatever she wanted. Tom came back into the house.

"You *know* I'm talking about Teddy! He's gotten us into all this trouble. Mom, I'm just so —"

"Shhh, Marsha, not now." Cassie indicated Tom with her head.

"Oh, Tom knows everything."

Tom frowned at Marsha and chose this moment to interject. "Mrs. Sales, I know Dr. Cohen and his wife were here earlier. Did he take care of all your needs?"

"I beg your pardon?" Cassie glared at him. It distressed her that Marsha told him everything. Now she had to worry about gold diggers, too. And this particular question of Tom's seemed to imply he knew that Mark was a creepy womanizer who'd exploit anyone. Mark had patted her ass *four* times, each time she'd come his way with the tray of coffee and dessert for the throng of mourners who'd probably come for the fabulous grape and foie gras she *hadn't* served. Almost a billion-dollar company, she'd had no idea.

"Do you need anything, you know, to sleep?" Tom asked, trying to clarify.

Cassie didn't think she'd ever sleep again. The serious young man was holding Marsha's hand in a decidedly possessive way, and she didn't know whether to be happy for her daughter or not. He looked too austere for Marsha. On the other hand, he had put out the garbage when asked, and he certainly seemed remorseful about the way things had turned out. Mark had been pretty miserable, too, even though he'd been game for action. He'd whispered in Cassie's ear the little fact that Mitch had promised the hospital a million dollars a year for the next ten years, and wanted to know if she was going to honor that pledge.

Cassie had almost laughed in his face. Mark had released the patient, and he'd died instantly. Parker Higgins had been so upset about the way the situation had been handled that he'd visited the liquor cabinet enough times to require three people to carry him to his car and his wife to drive him home. He had good reason to be concerned. He'd lied about everything.

"No, I don't need a thing. Good night, I'm fine." Cassie tried to shoo Marsha down the hall to the living room and out the front door.

"No, Mom. I'm staying, really. Tom will stay, too, won't you Tom?"

"Of course," Tom said staunchly.

Cassie didn't *want* Tom to stay. She didn't want either of them. She'd been good all day. No stimulants or tranquilizers. The fortified wines that were so favored by the English and could last virtually forever, along with Mitch's finest liqueurs, were in the bar. Literally hundreds of dollars a bottle. Cassie knew that several bottles of 1908 Cossart Baul Madeira were in there, and two bottles of 1970 Taylor Fladgate Porto, in addition to a lot of other really costly stuff.

The bar had been open to all who knew where to find it and couldn't resist helping themselves. But Cassie hadn't wanted to break out any of the famous cases of wine, mostly the famous reds, the Rhones, Burgundies, Bordeaux from France, the Chianti Classico Riservas from Italy; some famous Spaniards, among them Gran Coronas Black Label and Bodegas Montecillo; the French Champagnes, more than two dozen cases of those, mostly '90 and '93. A fine selection of whites and dessert wines, Rieslings, and Zinfindels Cassie knew next to nothing about. The ancient Portos and Madeiras. And, just for sport, the garagists, the new boutiquers, start-ups from old wine families, children taking a few acres of their own and making overblown wines in the California style in very small quantities in Médoc, in Graves on the right bank of the Garonne River, with names like La Mondotte, La Gomerie, Gracia, Grand Murailles. And other newcomers from France, Italy, Spain, Chile, and Argentina. Mitch always had to have the latest, most prestigious thing, wines too expensive for most people to even think of drinking.

All those beauties were in the cellar, from about $300 a bottle to $500, right up to $6,500 a bottle. She didn't serve them because she wasn't really sure to whom those bottles belonged or what she should do with them. But she also resented the fact that everybody who'd come to mourn Mitch had asked which wines she was going to serve for the occasion. It was something he would have cared about, planned meticulously.

Cassie wouldn't consider breaking them out. There had always been such hope for her in that cellar, the promise of many joyous occasions in those bottles down there. Mitch had purchased the magnums of 1990 pink Cristal Champagne at about $400 a bottle in anticipation of Marsha's wedding. They were worth a lot more now. She knew the very best in the cellar were the two cases of 1945 Chateau Petrus Pomerol, the legendary vintage of Bordeaux that marked the year of Mitch's birth and the first production of wine following World War II. He'd lectured her the day he'd acquired it how the '45 Petrus had been blessed with some formidable tannins that had encouraged a particularly fine evolution of flavors. As advertised, the Bordeaux had aged magnificently, tasted of summer fruit, licorice, smoke, and truffles. She'd had some last night. Cassie also knew that the wine would be drinkable only for the next few years. Those aged Bordeaux had almost a Port-like richness that, properly cellared, could be kept as long as sixty years. Mitch had always claimed he was saving this one for his sixtieth birthday party. Unfortunately for him, his number came up short.

In any case, Cassie had carried off her first day of callers cold turkey. No vino. But now she thought maybe she'd have a little sip of something. She gave her daughter a reassuring hug and a little push to get her going.

"Marsha, you've done so much already. I'm fine, really." She wanted to open another one of those off-the-wall Pomerols, or maybe a good heavy Côtes du Rhône. She loved the reds, the deepest, plummiest, earthiest ones, made with the top-quality grapes, Grenache, Mourvedre, Syrah, Cinsault, to be drunk with foods like the ripest cheese, foie gras, truffle-stuffed chicken or squab, venison with wild mushrooms, beef ribs and rice. Roast quail.

"No, Mom. I left you last night," Marsha said. "I can't leave you again. I can't. It would be—"

"Honey, I'm so tired."

"But what if you feel bad later?" Marsha argued.

Cassie clicked her tongue. "Sweetheart, do you know how many nights I've been alone in the last, say, ten years?" And never had a sip, not a slice of wild boar, very little smoked salmon. It was terrible to think about it.

"I know, but this is *different.*"

"Uh-uh. Tom, honey, you're a doctor. Tell my baby I know what's right for me. Take her home. I think she needs comfort right now more than I do."

"Yes, ma'am." The man Cassie thought was a prig almost saluted, and Cassie was moved to give him a kiss. Maybe he'd be all right, after all.

She got them out the front door with many protestations of love on Marsha's part. She'd had quite a bit to drink, but Cassie appreciated it, anyway. Then suddenly they were gone. She appreciated that even more. She closed and leaned against the door with a sigh. Ha. Now the precious grape. Sex would have been first on her list, but one had to work with what one had. Almost guiltily, she headed around the house to lock all the doors and windows. She felt as if she were going to perform some secret self-abusing sex act. She was going to open the bottles and savor the wine alone. Get dead drunk a second night in a row.

In the kitchen, however, something outside caught her attention. She stopped short and hit the light switch, holding her breath until she saw what it was. From the shadows, she watched the other monster climb out of a deck chair and head for the garbage. The words "unstoppable," "unflagging," "indefatigable" came to mind. She switched on the spotlight that had been rigged to discourage the scavenging raccoons. It exposed Charlie Schwab's hunkered form. He jumped sheepishly to his feet.

"Cassie, you scared me to death."

"Jesus, Charlie, you don't have to eat leftovers. If you're so hungry, why didn't you come in when I was serving?" she asked.

"No, no. This is not what it looks like."

"Yes, it is," she said. Cool, Cassie had gotten very cool in her responses. "What's in there, anyway? Let's see what you're looking for. All the missing millions?"

Cassie crossed the patio to the corner of the garage, where the garbage cans were neatly housed in a wooden cabinet. "Oh my God, baked goods!" Cassie stared at the bag of food, stunned by Marsha's treachery. And wastefulness! Then she opened the other cans one by one to see if anything else had gotten there without her knowledge. Oh yes, two cans full of empty soft drink, single malts, port, oh yes, the Madeira, vodka, and Perrier bottles; one and a half cans containing Mitch's *National Geographic* and *Gourmet* collections going back twenty-five years. Four old computers, broken printers, and other worn-out gadgets that Mitch had intended to save forever.

"Do you have a shredder here?" Charlie asked.

"No. What's with you? Do you always work this hard? Doesn't your wife complain?"

"I'm not married."

"Figures." Wow! Cassie's heart soared. No wife. She was actually truly excited by the news, even as she realized that what interested Charlie in the garbage were Mitch's old computers. It hit her that that's where her husband may have hidden his foreign bank account numbers.

"When does the garbage truck come?"

"Not till Friday."

"Good." Charlie had his briefcase with him.

Cassie wasn't good enough at this spy stuff. She should have thought of this sooner. "What's in the bag?" she asked.

"Price lists."

"Oh, gee." She shook her head. This guy was a maniac. "There's not enough in two hundred cases of wine to make up your missing millions," she said. A few hundred thousand, maybe.

"You never know." Charlie smiled. "You could hide anything in those cases. Cash, diamonds, cocaine." He shrugged.

"Oh please. Now he's a drug dealer. Why are you doing this tonight? Do you really think I'm like Mona, that I'd move anything today?"

He pointed at the computers.

She pointed at the *National Geographics*. "I was just cleaning up. Really."

"Well, you might have thrown out something important. Sorry, Cassie. I really am."

"Oh, go to hell." He was here for the spy stuff. Disgusted, she turned and went into the house, wanting to kick herself for not thinking of those computers first. Numbered accounts. If she'd had a brain, she could have found them herself. Cash in the cases, she'd never thought of that, either.

He followed her in, the suddenly unmarried man. "Was it a rough night?"

"Yes, Charlie, it was a rough night. Everybody loved him. I'm really tired."

"Me too." Charlie sat down at the table in the kitchen.

Cassie pressed her lips together. "*Really* tired, Charlie. I can't do this tonight."

"Me too," he repeated. He got up for a moment and she thought he was going to leave after all. Her first real prospect in thirty years was taking a powder. Suddenly she felt terrified, let down, as if she'd messed up an important date. But he just took off his jacket, hung it on the back of his chair. Loosened his tie, unbuttoned the button-down collar of his shirt, pulled the tie over his head, and stuffed it into his jacket pocket. Charlie was pretty obsessional. Almost as an afterthought, he unbuttoned the first two buttons of his shirt, too, then sat down again.

What was going on? Cassie was barefoot now. She was wearing black silk pants, a little black sleeveless knit top. Nothing too dressy. Her old Sublime perfume. Her plain gold wedding ring. She felt a little sick, wanted that wine, the food Marsha had put in the refrigerator. She didn't want to think about cash or stock or company woes, or anything else. She wanted to go to bed with her spy. The thought struck her suddenly: Sex was her very first choice.

Charlie had something else in mind, though. From his briefcase he pulled out the stack of credit cards he'd taken from Mona's jewelry box. He removed the rubber band and examined the receipts folded around them. Barneys, Bergdorf's, Armani, Sulka. He smiled, then picked up the phone.

"What are you doing now, Charlie?" Cassie's heart was beating in her cheeks again. She had these ideas. They made her stomach ache and her head spin.

"What's Mitch's date of birth?" he asked, producing his PalmPilot.

"Eight, eighteen, forty-five." She was nothing if not obedient. Touch me, she thought.

"Social Security number?"

"034-98-8441."

"Mother's maiden name?"

"Charles." She blushed.

"No kidding?" Charlie laughed. He responded to a few prompts and finally spoke to a human. "Oh yes, hello, Rita, this is Mitchell Sales, account 3458–93–67–0112. Uh-huh. Charles. 8441. Zip code ..." He turned to Cassie. "Darling, what's our zip?"

Cassie gave him the zip code of the warehouse. Her heart was beating, beating. The spy had called her "darling." She liked it. Him. Really liked him. She could smell the starch in his shirt, still there after the long day. She wanted to taste him, to kiss the blue eyes. What was she thinking?

Charlie passed Mitch's privileged information along to Rita at American Express. "Uh-huh. Thank you. I'd like to close down the account . . . no, no. There's no problem, Rita, none at all. I just don't want any more charges to the account until it's paid off. Thank you. I know it's a revolving account. I still want to close it." He put the black American Express Centurion card on the table and picked up the platinum one.

"Yes, Rita, there *is* something else you can do for me. I have another AmEx account. Yes, that's it. I want to close that account, too." A few minutes later he put the platinum card on the table. He went through the exercise with all the major credit cards, speaking to Ronnie, Roberta, James, Alfred, Betty, Sandra, and Tim.

While he was working, Cassie ran downstairs to the cellar for a bottle of wine, which she promptly opened. She took out two balloon glasses. Huge ones. The wine was supposed to breathe for a while, but she couldn't help herself. She poured some into both glasses, swirled hers, stuck her whole face into it, and breathed deep. The passion of her whole long-lost life filled her with its bouquet. Gimme that wine, she thought, just like Bob Marley. She couldn't wait a second longer. She took a sip, rolled it over her tongue and around her mouth, allowing the complex flavors to fill her palate. She swallowed and savored. The plummy earthiness lingered on. Wow. This was a big wine. Next to her was a big man, too. Both were very good vintages. She nodded at his glass and he sampled, nodded.

"Good, huh." She continued sipping and swirling and savoring while Charlie worked. She marveled at the way men could get away with anything. Anything at all. She hadn't even been able to change her own telephone number. Mitch had been the account holder of that, too.

Charlie poured himself his second glass and made a pile of department store cards with customer service departments that were open only between nine and five. "Tomorrow," he promised her. "Feel better now?"

"Very impressive. Thank you. Tomorrow? Really?" Cassie was inflamed, seriously aroused, by the wine, the show of power, and goodwill.

"See, I'm not such a bad guy." He gave her one of his smiles, patted her hand, left his hand over hers, raised an eyebrow. *Was it all right?*

Sure. She turned her hand over so their palms met. *Sure, it was all right.* He had a warm hand, strong, with long, slender fingers. He laced their fingers together, and heat flamed through her. Oh my, where did that huge feeling come from?

"What?" he asked.

Cassie shook her head, wondering if he knew that she hadn't kissed another man since Mick Jagger couldn't get Satisfaction, since the Beatles had left Abbey Road. Oh, God. She wanted to slide down onto the kitchen floor where she'd been with this man in his blue oxford button-down shirt only . . . this morning in quite a different situation. Her face was hot, her eyes wide. "Oh my."

Was it the wine? She'd drunk only one glass. She could see his chest hairs, light brown, curling out of his shirt, the hollow at the bottom of his throat. His shoulders and arms, very . . . attractive. She was like a teenager, burning up. Worse. She was over fifty like a teenager, burning up. A frown appeared on her brand-new forehead.

His blue eyes questioned. "I don't know what it is about you. I really like you."

"I'm old, probably older than you," she wanted to say but held her tongue. Don't go there, she told herself.

"It's always so hard to leave you. Right from the first day we met, I hated to leave. What is it about you?" He sat back and looked at her, trying to figure it out.

Well, that day she'd had a black eye, stitches, had been covered with bruises, and was ugly beyond belief. He was kidding, right? She licked her lips, nervous.

"I don't know what it was," he murmured. Their knees touched and the heat spread upward. Uh-oh.

The sound escaped Cassie's lips. She clamped them inside her teeth to keep silent.

"You're so cute. And *funny*! This is very good wine. I've never tasted anything like it. Have you always been so sexy? It's, I don't know, really getting to me. Maybe I'd better . . ."

Cassie released her lips from their prison, licked them, leaned over, and gave him a kiss. A little one. It caught him by surprise, hit him on the chin. The next one was better centered, soft, but quick.

"Uh-oh," he said, but took the lead on the third one. It was exploratory, went on for a while.

Cassie was stunned. She had no idea kisses could be like that, so full, so deep, and hungry. Wow. She closed her eyes and forgot herself as his hands became soft, fingers and palms grazing her neck, her chest. The backs of his hands skimming her breasts and sides. He touched a little, here and there, just a little, not letting her grab him and hold too tight the way she wanted to. She had to say he was thorough in his exploration of her fully clothed body, sitting at the table spread with the credit cards. They kissed for a long time, tasting of Pomerol. Not saying anything. Feeling each other up. Knees encroaching between knees. Cassie would have moved faster, but Charlie was thorough. Oh, he was thorough.

Then they did slide down, but not on the kitchen floor. Together they got up and moved toward the stairs, but didn't make it up. Cassie didn't know how it happened, where the volcano of feelings came from. They were halfway up the stairs, then sliding down on the stairs, him on top of her while she was wild to unbutton his shirt, to get to that bare chest and the bulge in his pants. This wasn't like her. Her sweater was over her head, her silk pants around her ankles. She was moving under him, fully alive and overcome by burgeoning the likes of which she'd never thought she'd see again.

"Wow." But he was the one to say it first.

And the volcano kept on; they were panting and the lava was flowing. It didn't stop. They slid down to the first floor, scrambling out of their clothes, feeling each other's arms and legs, chest and backs and insides. Old, old feelings returned, but all new. That thing of making two people one.

"Let me try it," Cassie murmured when he rolled over on his back on the carpet, still burgeoning beyond belief in front of the Federal sofa where no love had ever been made before. "You're very big. Did anybody ever tell you?"

"It's a feature," he admitted.

"Nice. Let's see if I can do it." She was enthusiastic, she was curious. She climbed on, panting with excitement.

"Wow. You're so natural, Cassie!" Charlie groaned and gripped her back and bottom. "Oh my God, darling, you can do to me whatever you want."

TWO HOURS LATER, when they were so sore, they could hardly stand, Cassie realized she was starving and went into the kitchen to put their first real meal together. She pulled a few items from the refrigerator and the pantry. She arranged a thick slab of Petrossian's best truffled foie gras on a platter with tiny cornichons and sour cherries. She took a handful of walnuts and toasted them for a few seconds in a hot skillet to bring out the oils and flavor. She brought out the cheeses.

Marsha had bought seven. A Brillat Savarin, Mitch's favorite triple cream, best served with ripe figs and pink champagne. Cassie thought if this was what killed him, just today she, too, would ingest the poison.

Ah, Marsha had bought her own two favorite blues, the rich blue-streaked French Saga and the highly molded English Stilton (best served with a bottle of Chateauneuf-du-Pape). For simplicity, Marsha had chosen Morbier, the semisoft mountain shepherd's cow's milk cheese with its stripe of edible ash running through the center (best served with a Mâcon-Villages). For diversity, the Mimolette, one of the few cheeses of France with color. Only a tiny piece of the orange ball with the nutty flavor was left, not enough, Cassie thought, to merit opening a bottle of Beaujolais to go with it. And last, a Coulommiers, not so easy to find outside of gourmet shops. The Brie-ish, soft-ripening cheese from the Ile-de-France region was yummy. When fully ripened, it had an even larger taste than a Camembert. Best served with ripe South of France peaches or plums. Marsha hadn't bought any of those, but there were grapes. There were slices of pumpernickel with raisins, Carr's water biscuits, and apples.

She set the kitchen table simply, for two, then went down to the cellar for the wine. The cases were stacked on metal shelves in a room about the size of the living room. It was separated from the furnace and water heater by the laundry room. The cellar was temperature controlled and usually locked. But Charlie hadn't been about to resist. He was sitting on an upended empty crate, naked but for his shirt, checking the case names against one of the many price lists he'd collected from the Internet and other sources. It was quite a sight.

"A few of these seem to be missing," he said, pointing to the opened case of Château Petrus Pomerol '45, clearly not familiar enough with wines to recognize the label.

"Yes." Cassie kissed his ear.

"Sold?"

"No, drunk."

"Who would drink a $6,500-a-bottle wine?" he wondered.

She straightened up, ruffling his hair. "You would, honey. Grab a few more. Dinner's ready."

The party was over. The party was just begun.

EPILOGUE

TEDDY SALES PASSED HIS ACCOUNTANCY TESTS on the second try, when he was just twenty-five. He joined the IRS office in Washington, D.C., where his mother, Cassandra Schwab, has become something of a national celebrity, teaching orchid cultivation and flower arranging on her own cable TV show and Web site, and where his stepfather is, well, the Charles Schwab of the Treasury Department.

Edith Edison, otherwise known as Aunt Edith, was the only person able to persuade Ogden Schwab to have his esophagus shortened to end his lifelong difficulty with swallowing. The surgery was a success, and he promptly gained nearly thirty pounds. Edith lost double that amount, and the two have become a popular pair in the Orlando retirement village where they share a bungalow on a golf course.

Marsha Sales married Dr. Thomas Wellfleet in a big wedding at the Plaza Hotel in Manhattan, but did not finish social work school as she'd planned. During the course of the many civil suits that she, her mother, and brother filed against Mona Whitman and Parker Higgins, she discovered she had an uncanny talent for law and strategic planning. Working with her brother and Ira Mandel, she piloted Sales Importers, Inc., through its difficulties with the IRS. Amity Holdings recently sold Sales Importers for an unpublicized amount to a longtime rival with an Italian name in Florida, one of the so-called top ten distributors in the country. Marsha is due to enter law school in the fall.

Under the threat of a five-year prison sentence, Mona Whitman entered the Witness Protection Program and informed on the many restaurant owners with connections to organized crime who were her former customers. Although she made full restitution, including damages, to Cassandra Sales for the credit card fraud, Mona's tax and civil lawsuits have yet to be resolved. She is not expected to see any proceeds from the sale of Le Refuge, her shares of Sales Importers, Inc., or the contents of her safe-deposit boxes for many years to come. Under the name Margie Mitchell, she's living a quiet life in Lubbock, Texas, where she's working on a serious relationship with a widower in the oil business.

ABOUT THE AUTHOR

Leslie Glass was a journalist at *New York* magazine and a short story and feature writer for *Cosmopolitan* and *Woman's Own* in Great Britain. She is a playwright and the author of the critically acclaimed mystery series featuring NYPD Detective Sergeant April Woo. Ms. Glass lives in New York and Sarasota, Florida.